W9-CJL-592

DANIEL DEFOE was born in St. Giles, Cripplegate, London, about 1660. His father, a London butcher, sent him to Charles Morton's academy to study for the ministry, but Defoe entered the business world instead and achieved some initial success as a commission agent. In 1684 he married Mary Tuffley, a prosperous merchant's daughter. The following year, stirred by the spirit of adventure, he took part in Monmouth's rebellion; and in 1688 he joined a volunteer regiment that acted as William III's escort into London. By 1692 Defoe's business affairs had floundered and creditors filed suit against him. He talked his way out of debtors' prison and took up manufacturing, eventually becoming the owner of some tile works at Tilbury. About this time, he started to write. His poem *The True-Born Englishman*, published in 1701, met with resounding success. In 1702 he attacked the Tories in a pamphlet, *The Shortest Way with the Dissenters*. This work enraged the government, and Defoe was imprisoned. Released in November, 1704, he became a secret agent for the government, working in favor of the union. Defoe continued to write pamphlets, and it was not until some years later that he turned to fiction. Between 1718 and 1724 he published *Robinson Crusoe, Moll Flanders, A Journal of the Plague Year*, and *Roxana*. He lived for a time in style, but gradually the creditors crept back. Forced to go into hiding, Defoe died, a lonely and hunted man, in Ropemaker's Alley, Moorfields, on April 26, 1731.

KATHARINE ROGERS, a specialist in eighteenth-century literature, is Professor of English at Brooklyn College and at the Graduate Center of the City University of New York.

C

SIGNET CLASSICS by British Authors

If you wish to order these titles,

please use the coupon in

the back of this book.

ROXANA

The Fortunate Mistress

or, a History of the
Life and Vast Variety of Fortunes of
Mademoiselle de Beleau, afterwards called
the Countess de Wintselsheim
in Germany
Being the Person known by
the Name of the Lady Roxana
in the time of King Charles II

Daniel Defoe

With an Afterword by
Katharine Rogers

A SIGNET CLASSIC
NEW AMERICAN LIBRARY
TIMES MIRROR
NEW YORK AND SCARBOROUGH, ONTARIO
THE NEW ENGLISH LIBRARY LIMITED, LONDON

NAL BOOKS ARE ALSO AVAILABLE AT DISCOUNTS IN BULK
QUANTITY FOR INDUSTRIAL OR SALES-PROMOTIONAL USE.
FOR DETAILS, WRITE TO PREMIUM MARKETING DIVISION,
NEW AMERICAN LIBRARY, INC., 1301 AVENUE OF THE
AMERICAS, NEW YORK, NEW YORK 10019.

Cover painting: detail from Hogarth's THE ORGY, A RAKE'S
PROGRESS, III. SCENE IN A TAVERN, courtesy of the Trustees
of Sir John Soane's Museum, London, England.

SIGNET CLASSIC TRADEMARK REG. U.S. PAT. OFF. AND FOREIGN COUNTRIES
REGISTERED TRADEMARK—MARCA REGISTRADA
HECHO EN CHICAGO, U.S.A.

SIGNET, SIGNET CLASSICS, MENTOR, PLUME AND MERIDIAN BOOKS
are published in the United States by
The New American Library, Inc., 1301 Avenue of the Americas,
New York, New York 10019, in Canada by
The New American Library of Canada Limited,
81 Mack Avenue, Scarborough, Ontario M1L 1M8,
in the United Kingdom by The New English Library Limited,
Barnard's Inn, Holborn, London, EC1N 2JR, England

First Signet Classic Printing, March, 1979

1 2 3 4 5 6 7 8 9

PRINTED IN THE UNITED STATES OF AMERICA

Preface

The history of this beautiful lady is to speak for itself. If it is not as beautiful as the lady herself is reported to be; if it is not as diverting as the reader can desire, and much more than he can reasonably expect; and if all the most diverting parts of it are not adapted to the instruction and improvement of the reader, the relator says it must be from the defect of his performance; dressing up the story in worse clothes than the lady, whose words he speaks, prepared for the world.

He takes the liberty to say that this story differs from most of the modern performances of this kind, though some of them have met with a very good reception in the world. I say, it differs from them in this great and essential article, namely, that the foundation of this is laid in truth of fact; and so the work is not a story, but a history.

The scene is laid so near the place where the main part of it was transacted that it was necessary to conceal names and persons, lest what cannot be yet entirely forgot in that part of the town should be remembered, and the facts traced back too plainly by the many people yet living, who would know the persons by the particulars.

It is not always necessary that the names of persons should be discovered, though the history may be many ways useful; and if we should be always obliged to name the persons, or not to relate the story, the consequence might be only this—that many a pleasant and delightful history would be buried in the dark, and the world be deprived both of the pleasure and the profit of it.

The writer says he was particularly acquainted with this lady's first husband, the brewer, and with his father, and also with his bad circumstances, and knows that first part of the story to be truth.

This may, he hopes, be a pledge for the credit of the rest, though the latter part of her history lay abroad, and could not so well be vouched as the first; yet, as she has told it herself, we have the less reason to question the truth of that part also.

In the manner she has told the story, it is evident she does not insist upon her justification in any one part of it; much less does she recommend her conduct, or, indeed, any part of it, except her repentance, to our imitation. On the contrary, she makes frequent excursions in a just censuring and condemning her own practice. How often does she reproach herself in the most passionate manner and guide us to just reflections in the like cases!

It is true she met with unexpected success in all her wicked courses; but even in the highest elevations of her prosperity, she makes frequent acknowledegments that the pleasure of her wickedness was not worth the repentance, and that all the satisfaction she had, all the joy in the view of her prosperity—no, nor all the wealth she rolled in, the gaiety of her appearance, the equipages and the honours she was attended with, could quiet her mind, abate the reproaches of her conscience, or procure her an hour's sleep when just reflections kept her waking.

The noble inferences that are drawn from this one part are worth all the rest of the story, and abundantly justify, as they are the professed design of, the publication.

If there are any parts in her story which, being obliged to relate a wicked action, seem to describe it too plainly, the writer says all imaginable care has been taken to keep clear of indecencies and immodest expressions; and 'tis hoped you will find nothing to prompt a vicious mind, but everywhere much to discourage and expose it.

Scenes of crime can scarce be represented in such a manner but some may make a criminal use of them. But when vice is painted in its low-prized colours, 'tis not to make people in love with it, but to expose it; and if the reader makes a wrong use of the figures, the wickedness is his own.

In the meantime, the advantages of the present work are so great, and the virtuous reader has room for so much improvement, that we make no question the story, however meanly told, will find a passage to his best hours, and be read both with profit and delight.

I was born, as my friends told me, at the city of Poitiers, in the province or county of Poitou, in France, from whence I was brought to England by my parents, who fled for their religion about the year 1683*, when the Protestants were banished from France by the cruelty of their persecutors.

I, who knew little or nothing of what I was brought over hither for, was well enough pleased with being here. London, a large and gay city, took with me mighty well, who, from my being a child, loved a crowd, and to see a great many fine folks.

I retained nothing of France but the language, my father and mother being people of better fashion than ordinarily the people called refugees at that time were; and having fled early, while it was easy to secure their effects, had, before their coming over, remitted considerable sums of money, or, as I remember, a considerable value in French brandy, paper, and other goods; and these selling very much to advantage here, my father was in very good circumstances at his coming over, so that he was far from applying to the rest of our nation that were here for countenance and relief. On the contrary, he had his door continually thronged with miserable objects of the poor starving creatures who at that time fled hither for shelter on account of conscience, or something else.

I have indeed heard my father say that he was pestered with a great many of those who, for any religion they had, might even have stayed where they were, but who flocked over hither in droves for what they call in English a livelihood; hearing with what open arms the refugees were received in England, and how they fell readily into business, being, by the charitable assistance of the people in London, encouraged to work in their manufactures in Spitalfields,

* "My parents . . . fled for their religion about the year 1683." King Louis XIV of France persecuted the Huguenots, the French Protestants, with increasing severity during the 1680s, although they were not actually banished until he revoked the Edict of Nantes in 1685. Of the French Protestants who fled to England at this time, many were textile workers who settled in Spitalfields (London) or Canterbury.

Canterbury, and other places, and that they had a much better price for their work than in France, and the like.

My father, I say, told me that he was more pestered with the clamours of these people than of those who were truly refugees, and fled in distress merely for conscience.

I was about ten years old when I was brought over hither, where, as I have said, my father lived in very good circumstances, and died in about eleven years more; in which time, as I had accomplished myself for the sociable part of the world, so I had acquainted myself with some of our English neighbours, as is the custom in London; and as, while I was young, I had picked up three or four play-fellows and companions suitable to my years, so, as we grew bigger, we learnt to call one another intimates and friends; and this forwarded very much the finishing me for conversation and the world.

I went to English schools, and being young, I learnt the English tongue perfectly well, with all the customs of the English young women; so that I retained nothing of the French but the speech. Nor did I so much as keep any remains of the French language tagged to my way of speaking as most foreigners do, but spoke what we call natural English as if I had been born here.

Being to give my own character, I must be excused to give it as impartially as possible, and as if I was speaking of another body; and the sequel will lead you to judge whether I flatter myself or no.

I was (speaking of myself as about fourteen years of age) tall, and very well made; sharp as a hawk in matters of common knowledge; quick and smart in discourse; apt to be satirical; full of repartee, and a little too forward in conversation, or, as we call it in English, bold, though perfectly modest in my behaviour. Being French born, I danced, as some say, naturally, loved it extremely, and sung well also, and so well that, as you will hear, it was afterwards some advantage to me. With all these things, I wanted neither wit, beauty, or money. In this manner I set out into the world, having all the advantages that any young woman could desire to recommend me to others and form a prospect of happy living to myself.

At about fifteen years of age, my father gave me, as he called it in French, 25,000 livres—that is to say, two thousand pounds portion—and married me to an eminent brewer in the city. Pardon me if I conceal his name, for though he was the foundation of my ruin, I cannot take so severe a revenge upon him.

With this thing called a husband I lived eight years in good fashion, and for some part of the time kept a coach, that is to say, a kind of mock-coach. For all the week the horses were kept at work in the dray-carts, but on Sunday I had the privilege to go abroad in my chariot, either to church or otherways, as my husband and I could agree about it, which, by the way, was not very often. But of that hereafter.

Before I proceed in the history of the married part of my life, you must allow me to give as impartial an account of my husband as I have done of myself. He was a jolly, handsome fellow as any woman need wish for a companion; tall and well made; rather a little too large, but not so as to be ungenteel; he danced well, which I think was the first thing that brought us together. He had an old father who managed the business carefully, so that he had little of that part laid on him, but now-and-then to appear and show himself; and he took the advantage of it, for he troubled himself very little about it, but went abroad, kept company, hunted much, and loved it exceedingly.

After I have told you that he was a handsome man and a good sportsman, I have indeed said all; and unhappy was I, like other young people of our sex, I chose him for being a handsome, jolly fellow, as I have said. For he was otherwise a weak, empty-headed, untaught creature as any woman could ever desire to be coupled with. And here I must take the liberty, whatever I have to reproach myself with in my after-conduct, to turn to my fellow-creatures, the young ladies of this country, and speak to them by way of precaution. If you have any regard to your future happiness, any view of living comfortably with a husband, any hope of preserving your fortunes, or restoring them after any disaster, never, ladies, marry a fool; any husband rather than a fool. With some other husbands you may be unhappy, but with a fool you will be miserable; with another husband you may, I say, be unhappy, but with a fool you *must*. Nay, if he would, he cannot make you easy; everything he does is so awkward, everything he says is so empty, a woman of any sense cannot but be surfeited and sick of him twenty times a day. What is more shocking than for a woman to bring a handsome, comely fellow of a husband into company, and then be obliged to blush for him every time she hears him speak? to hear other gentlemen talk sense, and he able to say nothing? and so look like a fool, or, which is worse, hear him talk nonsense and be laughed at for a fool.

In the next place, there are so many sorts of fools, such an

infinite variety of fools, and so hard it is to know the worst of the kind, that I am obliged to say, "No fool, ladies, at all, no kind of fool, whether a mad fool or a sober fool, a wise fool or a silly fool; take anything but a fool. Nay, be anything, be even an old maid, the worst of nature's curses, rather than take up with a fool."

But to leave this a-while—for I shall have occasion to speak of it again—my case was particularly hard, for I had a variety of foolish things complicated in this unhappy match.

First, and which I must confess is very unsufferable, he was a conceited fool, *tout opiniâtre;** everything he said was right, was best, and was to the purpose, whoever was in company, and whatever was advanced by others, though with the greatest modesty imaginable. And yet, when he came to defend what he had said by argument and reason, he would do it so weakly, so emptily, and so nothing to the purpose, that it was enough to make anybody that heard him sick and ashamed of him.

Secondly, he was positive and obstinate, and the most positive in the most simple and inconsistent things, such as were intolerable to bear.

These two articles, if there had been no more, qualified him to be a most unbearable creature for a husband; and so it may be supposed at first sight what a kind of life I led with him. However, I did as well as I could, and held my tongue, which was the only victory I gained over him. For when he would talk after his own empty rattling way with me, and I would not answer or enter into discourse with him on the point he was upon, he would rise up in the greatest passion imaginable and go away, which was the cheapest way I had to be delivered.

I could enlarge here much upon the method I took to make my life passable and easy with the most incorrigible temper in the world; but it is too long and the articles too trifling. I shall mention some of them as the circumstances I am to relate shall necessarily bring them in.

After I had been married about four years, my own father

* *"tout opiniâtre."* Stubborn as a mule.

died, my mother having been dead before. He liked my match so ill, and saw so little room to be satisfied with the conduct of my husband, that though he left me five thousand livres, and more, at his death, yet he left it in the hands of my elder brother, who, running on too rashly in his adventures as a merchant, failed, and lost not only what he had, but what he had for me too, as you shall hear presently.

Thus I lost the last gift of my father's bounty by having a husband not fit to be trusted with it; There's one of the benefits of marrying a fool.

Within two years after my own father's death, my husband's father also died, and, as I thought, left him a considerable addition to his estate, the whole trade of the brewhouse, which was a very good one, being now his own.

But this addition to his stock was his ruin, for he had no genius to business, he had no knowledge of his accounts. He bustled a little about it, indeed, at first, and put on a face of business, but he soon grew slack; it was below him to inspect his books, he committed all that to his clerks and bookkeepers. And while he found money in cash to pay the maltman and the excise, and put some in his pocket, he was perfectly easy and indolent, let the main chance go how it would.

I foresaw the consequence of this, and attempted several times to persuade him to apply himself to his business. I put him in mind how his customers complained of the neglect of his servants on one hand, and how abundance broke in his debt,* on the other hand, for want of the clerk's care to secure him, and the like; but he thrust me by, either with hard words, or fraudulently, with representing the cases otherwise than they were.

However, to cut short a dull story, which ought not to be long, he began to find his trade sunk, his stock declined, and that, in short, he could not carry on his business, and once or twice his brewing utensils were extended for the excise;† and the last time he was put to great extremities to clear them.

This alarmed him, and he resolved to lay down his trade; which, indeed, I was not sorry for, foreseeing that if he did not lay it down in time, he would be forced to do it another

---

* "broke in his debt." Went bankrupt when they owed him money, so they could not pay him. Compare page 8, "broke": Went bankrupt.

† "extended for the excise." Seized to pay the excise tax.

way, namely, as a bankrupt. Also I was willing he should draw out while he had something left, lest I should come to be stripped at home, and be turned out of doors with my children; for I had now five children by him, the only work (perhaps) that fools are good for.

I thought myself happy when he got another man to take his brewhouse clear off his hands; for, paying down a large sum of money, my husband found himself a clear man, all his debts paid, and with between two and three thousand pound in his pocket. And being now obliged to remove from the brewhouse, we took a house at—, a village about two miles out of town; and happy I thought myself, all things considered, that I was got off clear, upon so good terms; and had my handsome fellow had but one cap-full of wit, I had been still well enough.

I proposed to him either to buy some place with the money, or with part of it, and offered to join my part to it, which was then in being, and might have been secured; so we might have lived tolerably at least during his life. But as it is the part of a fool to be void of counsel, so he neglected it, lived on as he did before, kept his horses and men, rid every day out to the forest a-hunting, and nothing was done all this while; but the money decreased apace, and I thought I saw my ruin hastening on without any possible way to prevent it.

I was not wanting with all that persuasions and entreaties could perform, but it was all fruitless. Representing to him how fast our money wasted, and what would be our condition when it was gone, made no impression on him; but like one stupid, he went on, not valuing all that tears and lamentations could be supposed to do. Nor did he abate his figure or equipage, his horses or servants, even to the last, till he had not a hundred pound left in the whole world.

It was not above three years that all the ready-money was thus spending off. Yet he spent it, as I may say, foolishly too, for he kept no valuable company neither, but generally with huntsmen and horse-coursers, and men meaner than himself, which is another consequence of a man's being a fool. Such can never take delight in men more wise and capable than themselves, and that makes them converse with scoundrels, drink belch* with porters, and keep company always below themselves.

---

* "belch." Poor-quality beer.

This was my wretched condition, when one morning my husband told me he was sensible he was come to a miserable condition, and he would go and seek his fortune somewhere or other. He had said something to that purpose several times before that, upon my pressing him to consider his circumstances, and the circumstances of his family, before it should be too late; but as I found he had no meaning in anything of that kind, as, indeed, he had not much in anything he ever said, so I thought they were but words of course now. When he said he would be gone, I used to wish secretly, and even say in my thoughts, "I wish you would, for if you go on thus you will starve us all."

He stayed, however, at home all that day, and lay at home that night; early the next morning he gets out of bed, goes to a window which looked out toward the stables, and sounds his French horn, as he called it, which was his usual signal to call his men to go out a-hunting.

It was about the latter end of August, and so was light yet at five o'clock, and it was about that time that I heard him and his two men go out and shut the yard-gates after them. He said nothing to me more than as usual when he used to go out upon his sport; neither did I rise, or say anything to him that was material, but went to sleep again after he was gone, for two hours or thereabouts.

It must be a little surprising to the reader to tell him at once that after this I never saw my husband more. But, to go farther, I not only never saw him more, but I never heard from him, or of him, neither of any or either of his two servants, or of the horses, either what became of them, where or which way they went, or what they did or intended to do, no more than if the ground had opened and swallowed them all up, and nobody had known it, except as hereafter.

I was not, for the first night or two, at all surprised, no, nor very much the first week or two, believing that if anything evil had befallen them, I should soon enough have heard of that; and also knowing, that as he had two servants and three horses with him, it would be the strangest thing in the world that any thing could befall them all but that I must some time or other hear of them.

But you will easily allow that as time run on a week, two weeks, a month, two months, and so on, I was dreadfully frighted at last, and the more when I looked into my own circumstances and considered the condition in which I was left, with five children, and not one farthing subsistence for them, other than about seventy pound in money and what few things of value I had about me, which, though considerable in themselves, were yet nothing to feed a family, and for a length of time too.

What to do I knew not, nor to whom to have recourse: To keep in the house where I was, I could not, the rent being too great; and to leave it without his order, if my husband should return, I could not think of that neither. So that I continued extremely perplexed, melancholy, and discouraged to the last degree.

I remained in this dejected condition near a twelvemonth. My husband had two sisters, who were married and lived very well, and some other near relations that I knew of and I hoped would do something for me; and I frequently sent to these, to know if they could give me any account of my vagrant creature. But they all declared to me in answer that they knew nothing about him; and, after frequent sending, began to think me troublesome, and to let me know they thought so too, by their treating my maid with very slight and unhandsome returns to her inquiries.

This grated hard and added to my afflictions; but I had no recourse but to my tears, for I had not a friend of my own left me in the world. I should have observed that it was about half a year before this elopement of my husband that the disaster I mentioned above befell my brother, who broke,* and that in such bad circumstances that I had the mortification to hear not only that he was in prison, but that there would be litle or nothing to be had by way of composition.

Misfortunes seldom come alone. This was the forerunner of my husband's flight; and as my expectations were cut off on that side, my husband gone, and my family of children on my hands and nothing to subsist them, my condition was the most deplorable that words can express.

I had some plate and some jewels, as might be supposed, my fortune and former circumstances considered; and my husband, who had never stayed to be distressed, had not been put to the necessity of rifling me, as husbands usually do in such cases. But as I had seen an end of all the ready money during the long time I had lived in a state of expectation for

---

* "broke." See above page 5.

my husband, so I began to make away one thing after another, till those few things of value which I had began to lessen apace, and I saw nothing but misery and the utmost distress before me, even to have my children starve before my face. I leave any one that is a mother of children, and has lived in plenty and good fashion, to consider and reflect what must be my condition. As to my husband, I had now no hope or expectation of seeing him any more; and indeed, if I had, he was the man of all the men in the world the least able to help me, or to have turned his hand to the gaining one shilling towards lessening our distress. He neither had the capacity or the inclination; he could have been no clerk, for he scarce wrote a legible hand; he was so far from being able to write sense that he could not make sense of what others wrote; he was so far from understanding good English that he could not spell good English. To be out of all business was his delight, and he would stand leaning against a post for half an hour together, with a pipe in his mouth, with all the tranquillity in the world, smoking, like Dryden's countryman,* that whistled as he went for want of thought; and this even when his family was, as it were, starving, that little he had wasting, and that we were all bleeding to death; he not knowing, and as little considering, where to get another shilling when the last was spent.

This being his temper, and the extent of his capacity, I confess I did not see so much loss in his parting with me as at first I thought I did; though it was hard and cruel to the last degree in him, not giving me the least notice of his design. And, indeed, that which I was most astonished at was, that seeing he must certainly have intended this excursion some few moments at least before he put it in practice, yet he did not come and take what little stock of money we had left, or at least a share of it, to bear his expense for a little while; but he did not; and I am morally certain he had not five guineas with him in the world when he went away. All that I could come to the knowledge of about him was, that he left his hunting-horn, which he called the French horn, in the stable, and his hunting saddle, went away in a handsome furniture, as they call it, which he used sometimes to travel with,

---

* "like Dryden's countryman." Cymon, an apparently hopeless lout, "trud'd along unknowing what he sought,/ And whistled as he went, for want of Thought" ("Cymon and Iphigenia," lines 84–85, in John Dryden's *Fables Ancient and Modern* [1700]).

having an embroidered housing, a case of pistols, and other things belonging to them; and one of his servants had another saddle with pistols, though plain, and the other a long gun; so that they did not go out as sportsmen, but rather as travellers. What part of the world they went to I never heard for many years.

As I have said, I sent to his relations, but they sent me short and surly answers; nor did any one of them offer to come to see me, or to see the children, or so much as to inquire after them, well perceiving that I was in a condition that was likely to be soon troublesome to them. But it was no time now to dally with them or with the world; I left off sending to them and went myself among them, laid my circumstances open to them, told them my whole case, and the condition I was reduced to, begged they would advise me what course to take, laid myself as low as they could desire, and entreated them to consider that I was not in a condition to help myself, and that without some assistance we must all inevitably perish. I told them that if I had had but one child, or two children, I would have done my endeavour to have worked for them with my needle, and should only have come to them to beg them to help me to some work, that I might get our bread by my labour; but to think of one single woman, not bred to work, and at a loss where to get employment, to get the bread of five children, that was not possible—some of my children being young too, and none of them big enough to help one another.

It was all one; I received not one farthing of assistance from anybody, was hardly asked to sit down at the two sisters' houses, nor offered to eat or drink at two more near relations. The fifth, an ancient gentlewoman, aunt-in-law to my husband, a widow, and the least able also of any of the rest, did, indeed, ask me to sit down, gave me a dinner, and refreshed me with a kinder treatment than any of the rest, but added the melancholy part, viz., that she would have helped me, but that, indeed, she was not able, which, however, I was satisfied was very true.

Here I relieved myself with the constant assistant of the afflicted, I mean tears; for, relating to her how I was received by the other of my husband's relations, it made me burst into tears, and I cried vehemently for a great while together, till I made the good old gentlewoman cry too several times.

However, I came home from them all without any relief,

and went on at home till I was reduced to such inexpressible distress that is not to be described. I had been several times after this at the old aunt's, for I prevailed with her to promise me to go and talk with the other relations, at least that, if possible, she could bring some of them to take off the children, or to contribute something towards their maintenance. And, to do her justice, she did use her endeavour with them; but all was to no purpose, they would do nothing, at least that way. I think, with much entreaty, she obtained, by a kind of collection among them all, about eleven or twelve shillings in money, which, though it was a present comfort, was yet not to be named as capable to deliver me from any part of the load that lay upon me.

There was a poor woman that had been a kind of a dependent upon our family, and who I had often, among the rest of the relations, been very kind to; my maid put it into my head one morning to send to this poor woman, and to see whether she might not be able to help in this dreadful case.

I must remember it here, to the praise of this poor girl, my maid, that though I was not able to give her any wages, and had told her so—nay, I was not able to pay her the wages that I was in arrears to her—yet she would not leave me; nay, and as long as she had any money, when I had none, she would help me out of her own, for which, though I acknowledged her kindness and fidelity, yet it was but a bad coin that she was paid in at last, as will appear in its place.

Amy (for that was her name) put it into my thoughts to send for this poor woman to come to me; for I was now in great distress, and I resolved to do so. But just the very morning that I intended it, the old aunt, with the poor woman in her company, came to see me; the good old gentlewoman was, it seems, heartily concerned for me, and had been talking again among those people, to see what she could do for me, but to very little purpose.

You shall judge a little of my present distress by the posture she found me in. I had five little children, the eldest was under ten years old, and I had not one shilling in the house to buy them victuals, but had sent Amy out with a silver spoon, to sell it, and bring home something from the butcher's; and I was in a parlour, sitting on the ground, with a great heap of old rags, linen, and other things about me, looking them over, to see if I had anything among them that would sell or pawn for a little money, and had been crying ready to burst myself, to think what I should do next.

At this juncture they knocked at the door. I thought it had been Amy, so I did not rise up, but one of the children opened the door, and they came directly into the room where I was, and where they found me in that posture, and crying vehemently, as above. I was surprised at their coming, you may be sure, especially seeing the person I had but just before resolved to send for. But when they saw me, how I looked, for my eyes were swelled with crying, and what a condition I was in as to the house, and the heaps of things that were about me, and especially when I told them what I was doing, and on what occasion, they sat down, like Job's three comforters,* and said not one word to me for a great while, but both of them cried as fast and as heartily as I did.

The truth was, there was no need of much discourse in the case, the thing spoke itself; they saw me in rags and dirt, who was but a little before riding in my coach; thin, and looking almost like one starved, who was before fat and beautiful. The house, that was before handsomely furnished with pictures and ornaments, cabinets, pier-glasses, and everything suitable, was now stripped and naked, most of the goods having been seized by the landlord for rent, or sold to buy necessaries. In a word, all was misery and distress, the face of ruin was everywhere to be seen; we had eaten up almost everything, and little remained, unless, like one of the pitiful women of Jerusalem,† I should eat up my very children themselves.

After these two good creatures had sat, as I say, in silence some time, and had then looked about them, my maid Amy came in, and brought with her a small breast of mutton and two great bunches of turnips, which she intended to stew for our dinner. As for me, my heart was so overwhelmed at seeing these two friends—for such they were, though poor—and at their seeing me in such a condition, that I fell into

---

* "Job's three comforters." The three comforters who came to mourn with Job in his affliction actually did not offer any consolation (Job 2:11–13).

† "the pitiful women of Jerusalem." Flavius Josephus tells how, when the emperor Titus was besieging Jerusalem, a starving woman cooked and ate her own infant (*History of the Jewish War*, Book VI, Section 4).

another violent fit of crying, so that, in short, I could not speak to them again for a great while longer.

During my being in such an agony, they went to my maid Amy at another part of the same room and talked with her. Amy told them all my circumstances, and set them forth in such moving terms, and so to the life, that I could not upon any terms have done it like her myself, and, in a word, affected them both with it in such a manner that the old aunt came to me, and though hardly able to speak for tears, "Look ye, cousin," said she, in a few words, "things must not stand thus; some course must be taken, and that forthwith. Pray, where were these children born?"* I told her the parish where we lived before, that four of them were born there, and one in the house where I now was, where the landlord, after having seized my goods for the rent past, not then knowing my circumstances, had now given me leave to live for a whole year more without any rent, being moved with compassion; but that this year was now almost expired.

Upon hearing this account, they came to this resolution, that the children should be all carried by them to the door of one of the relations mentioned above, and be set down there by the maid Amy, and that I, the mother, should remove for some days, shut up the doors, and be gone; that the people should be told that if they did not think fit to take some care of the children, they might send for the church-wardens if they thought that better, for that they were born in that parish, and there they must be provided for. As for the other child, which was born in the parish of ———, that was already taken care of by the parish-officers there, for indeed they were so sensible of the distress of the family that they had at first word done what was their part to do.

This was what these good women proposed, and bade me leave the rest to them. I was at first sadly afflicted at the thoughts of parting with my children, and especially at that terrible thing, their being taken into the parish-keeping. And

---

* "where were these children born?" Under seventeenth- and eighteenth-century law, every parish was responsible for its own poor. It was obligated to maintain children who were born there, but only those. Though destitute infants were provided with parish nurses, they were often mistreated, as Roxana says. Since paupers could receive help only from the parish they were born or had otherwise settled in, they would, if necessary, be sent back there in a cripple cart, by order of a justice of the peace (see page 18).

then a hundred terrible things came into my thoughts, viz., of parish-children being starved at nurse; of their being ruined, let grow crooked, lamed, and the like, for want of being taken care of; and this sunk my very heart within me.

But the misery of my own circumstances hardened my heart against my own flesh and blood; and when I considered they must inevitably be starved, and I too if I continued to keep them about me, I began to be reconciled to parting with them all, any how and any where, that I might be freed from the dreadful necessity of seeing them all perish, and perishing with them myself. So I agreed to go away out of the house, and leave the management of the whole matter to my maid Amy and to them; and accordingly I did so, and the same afternoon they carried them all away to one of their aunts.

Amy, a resolute girl, knocked at the door, with the children all with her, and bade the eldest, as soon as the door was open, run in, and the rest after her. She set them all down at the door before she knocked, and when she knocked she stayed till a maid-servant came to the door. "Sweetheart," said she, "pray go in and tell your mistress here are her little cousins come to see her from ————," naming the town where we lived, at which the maid offered to go back. "Here, child," says Amy, "take one of 'em in your hand, and I'll bring the rest"; so she gives her the least, and the wench goes in mighty innocently, with the little one in her hand, upon which Amy turns the rest in after her, shuts the door softly, and marches off as fast as she could.

Just in the interval of this, and even while the maid and her mistress were quarrelling (for the mistress raved and scolded at her like a mad-woman, and had ordered her to go and stop the maid Amy, and turn all the children out of the doors again; but she had been at the door, and Amy was gone, and the wench was out of her wits, and the mistress too), I say, just at this juncture came the poor old woman, not the aunt, but the other of the two that had been with me, and knocks at the door. The aunt did not go, because she had pretended to advocate for me, and they would have suspected her of some contrivance; but as for the other woman, they did not so much as know that she had kept up any correspondence with me.

Amy and she had concerted this between them, and it was well enough contrived that they did so. When she came into the house, the mistress was fuming, and raging like one distracted, and called the maid all the foolish jades and sluts that she could think of, and that she would take the children and turn them all out into the streets. The good poor woman, seeing her in such a passion, turned about as if she would be gone again, and said, "Madam, I'll come again another time, I see you are engaged." "No, no, Mrs ———," says the mistress, "I am not much engaged, sit down. This senseless creature here has brought in my fool of a brother's whole house of children upon me, and tells me that a wench brought them to the door and thrust them in, and bade her carry them to me; but it shall be no disturbance to me, for I have ordered them to be set in the street without the door, and so let the church-wardens take care of them, or else make this dull jade carry 'em back to ——— again, and let her that brought them into the world look after them if she will. What does she send her brats to me for?"

"The last indeed had been the best of the two," says the poor woman, "if it had been to be done; and that brings me to tell you my errand, and the occasion of my coming, for I come on purpose about this very business, and to have prevented this being put upon you, if I could, but I see I am come too late."

"How do you mean too late?" says the mistress. "What! have you been concerned in this affair, then? What! have you helped bring this family slur upon us?" "I hope you do not think such a thing of me, madam," says the poor woman. "But I went this morning to ———, to see my old mistress and benefactor, for she had been very kind to me, and when I came to the door I found all fast locked and bolted, and the house looking as if nobody was at home.

"I knocked at the door, but nobody came, till at last some of the neighbours' servants called to me and said, "There's nobody lives there, mistress; what do you knock for?' I seemed surprised at that. 'What, nobody lives here!' said I; 'what d'ye mean? Does not Mrs. ——— live there?' The answer was, 'No, she is gone'; at which I parleyed with one of them, and asked her what was the matter. 'Matter!' says she, 'why, 'tis matter enough: The poor gentlewoman has lived there all alone, and without anything to subsist her, a long time, and this morning the landlord turned her out of doors.'

" 'Out of doors!' says I. 'what! With all her children? Poor lambs, what is become of them?' 'Why, truly, nothing worse,' said they, 'can come to them than staying here, for they were almost starved with hunger. So the neighbours, seeing the poor lady in such distress—for she stood crying and wringing her hands over her children like one distracted—sent for the church-wardens to take care of the children; and they, when they came, took the youngest, which was born in this parish, and have got it a very good nurse and taken care of it; but as for the other four, they had sent them away to some of their father's relations, and who were very substantial people, and who, besides that, lived in the parish where they were born.'

"I was not so surprised at this as not presently to foresee that this trouble would be brought upon you or upon Mr. ———; so I came immediately to bring you word of it, that you might be prepared for it, and might not be surprised. But I see they have been too nimble for me, so that I know not what to advise. The poor woman, it seems, is turned out of doors into the street; and another of the neighbours there told me that when they took her children from her she swooned away, and when they recovered her out of that, she ran distracted and is put into a mad-house by the parish, for there is nobody else to take any care of her."

This was all acted to the life by this good, kind, poor creature, for though her design was perfectly good and charitable, yet there was not one word of it true in fact; for I was not turned out of doors by the landlord, nor gone distracted. It was true, indeed, that at parting with my poor children I fainted, and was like one mad when I came to myself and found they were gone; but I remained in the house a good while after that, as you shall hear.

While the poor woman was telling this dismal story, in came the gentlewoman's husband, and though her heart was hardened against all pity, who was really and nearly related to the children, for they were the children of her own brother, yet the good man was quite softened with the dismal relation of the circumstances of the family. And when the poor woman had done, he said to his wife. "This is a dismal case, my dear, indeed, and something must be done." His wife fell a-raving at him. "What," says she, "do you want to have four children to keep? Have we not children of our own? Would you have these brats come and eat up my children's bread? No, no, let 'em go to the parish and let them take care of them; I'll take care of my own."

"Come, come, my dear," says the husband, "charity is a duty to the poor, and he that gives to the poor lends to the

Lord. Let us lend our heavenly Father a little of our children's bread, as you call it; it will be a store well laid up for them, and will be the best security that our children shall never come to want charity, or be turned out of doors, as these poor innocent creatures are."

"Don't tell me of security," says the wife; "'tis a good security for our children to keep what we have together, and provide for them, and then 'tis time enough to help keep other folks' children. Charity begins at home."

"Well, my dear," says he again, "I only talk of putting out a little money to interest. Our Maker is a good borrower; never fear making a bad debt there, child, I'll be bound for it."

"Don't banter me with your charity and your allegories," says the wife angrily. "I tell you they are my relations, not yours, and they shall not roost here; they shall go to the parish."

"All your relations are my relations now," says the good gentleman very calmly, "and I won't see your relations in distress and not pity them, any more than I would my own; indeed, my dear, they shan't go to the parish. I assure you, none of my wife's relations shall come to the parish, if I can help it."

"What! will you take four children to keep?" says the wife.

"No, no, my dear," says he. "There's your sister ———, I'll go and talk with her; and your uncle ———, I'll send for him, and the rest. I'll warrant you, when we are all together, we will find ways and means to keep four poor little creatures from beggary and starving, or else it would be very hard; we are none of us in so bad circumstances but we are able to spare a mite for the fatherless. Don't shut up your bowels of compassion against your own flesh and blood. Could you hear these poor innocent children cry at your door for hunger and give them no bread?"

"Prithee, what need they cry at our door?" says she. "'Tis the business of the parish to provide for them; they shan't cry at our door. If they do, I'll give them nothing." "Won't you?" says he; "but I will. Remember that dreadful Scripture is directly against us, Prov. 21:13, 'Whoso stoppeth his ears at the cry of the poor, he also shall cry himself, but shall not be heard.'"

"Well, well," says she, "you must do what you will, because you pretend to be master; but if I had my will I would send them where they ought to be sent. I would send them from whence they came."

Then the poor woman put in, and said, "But, madam, that is sending them to starve indeed, for the parish has no obligation to take care of 'em, and so they will lie and perish in the street."

"Or be sent back again," says the husband, "to our parish in a cripple-cart, by the justice's warrant, and so expose us and all the relations to the last degree among our neighbours, and among those who know the good old gentleman their grandfather, who lived and flourished in this parish so many years, and was so well beloved among all people, and deserved it so well."

"I don't value that one farthing, not I," says the wife. "I'll keep none of them."

"Well, my dear," says her husband, "but I value it, for I won't have such a blot lie upon the family, and upon your children. He was a worthy, ancient, and good man, and his name is respected among all his neighbours; it will be a reproach to you, that are his daughter, and to our children, that are his grand-children, that we should let your brother's children perish, or come to be a charge to the public, in the very place where your family once flourished. Come, say no more; I'll see what can be done."

Upon this he sends and gathers all the relations together at a tavern hard by, and sent for the four little children, that they might see them; and they all, at first word, agreed to have them taken care of, and, because his wife was so furious that she would not suffer one of them to be kept at home, they agreed to keep them all together for a-while; so they committed them to the poor woman that had managed the affair for them, and entered into obligations to one another to supply the needful sums for their maintenance. And, not to have one separated from the rest, they sent for the youngest from the parish where it was taken in, and had them all brought up together.

It would take up too long a part of this story to give a particular account with what a charitable tenderness this good person, who was but uncle-in-law to them, managed that affair—how careful he was of them; went constantly to see them, and to see that they were well provided for, clothed, put to school, and at last, put out in the world for their advantage—but 'tis enough to say he acted more like a father to them than an uncle-in-law, though all along much against his wife's consent, who was of a disposition not so tender and compassionate as her husband.

You may believe I heard this with the same pleasure which I now feel at the relating it again; for I was terribly affrighted at the apprehensions of my children being brought to misery and distress, as those must be who have no friends, but are left to parish benevolence.

I was now, however, entering on a new scene of life. I had a great house upon my hands, and some furniture left in it, but I was no more able to maintain myself and my maid Amy in it than I was my five children. Nor had I anything to subsist with but what I might get by working, and that was not a town where much work was to be had.

My landlord had been very kind indeed after he came to know my circumstances; though, before he was acquainted with that part, he had gone so far as to seize my goods, and to carry some of them off too.

But I had lived three quarters of a year in his house after that, and had paid him no rent, and, which was worse, I was in no condition to pay him any. However, I observed he came oftener to see me, looked kinder upon me, and spoke more friendly to me, than he used to do, particularly the last two or three times he had been there. He observed, he said, how poorly I lived, how low I was reduced, and the like; told me it grieved him for my sake; and the last time of all he was kinder still, told me he came to dine with me, and that I should give him leave to treat me. So he called my maid Amy and sent her out to buy a joint of meat; he told her what she should buy; but naming two or three things, either of which she might take, the maid, a cunning wench, and faithful to me as the skin to my back, did not buy anything outright, but brought the butcher along with her, with both the things that she had chosen, for him to please himself. The one was a large, very good leg of veal; the other a piece of the fore-ribs of roasting beef. He looked at them, but bade me chaffer with the butcher for him, and I did so, and came back to him and told him what the butcher had demanded for either of them, and what each of them came to. So he pulls out eleven shillings and threepence, which they came to together, and bade me take them both; the rest, he said, would serve another time.

I was surprised, you may be sure, at the bounty of a man

that had but a little while ago been my terror, and had torn the goods out of my house like a fury. But I considered that my distresses had mollified his temper, and that he had afterwards been so compassionate as to give me leave to live rent-free in the house a whole year.

But now he put on the face, not of a man of compassion only, but of a man of friendship and kindness, and this was so unexpected that it was surprising. We chatted together and were, as I may call it, cheerful, which was more than I could say I had been for three years before. He sent for wine, and beer too, for I had none; poor Amy and I had drank nothing but water for many weeks, and indeed I have often wondered at the faithful temper of the poor girl, for which I but ill requited her at last.

When Amy was come with the wine, he made her fill a glass to him, and with the glass in his hands he came to me and kissed me, which I was, I confess, a little surprised at, but more at what followed; for he told me that as the sad condition which I was reduced to had made him pity me, so my conduct in it, and the courage I bore it with, had given him a more than ordinary respect for me and made him very thoughtful for my good; that he was resolved for the present to do something to relieve me, and to employ his thoughts in the meantime to see if he could, for the future, put me into a way to support myself.

While he found me change colour and look surprised at his discourse—for so I did, to be sure—he turns to my maid, Amy, and looking at her, he says to me, "I say all this, madam, before your maid, because both she and you shall know that I have no ill design, and that I have, in mere kindness, resolved to do something for you if I can. And as I have been a witness of the uncommon honesty and fidelity of Mrs. Amy here to you in all your distresses, I know she may be trusted with so honest a design as mine is; for, I assure you, I bear a proportioned regard to your maid too, for her affection to you."

Amy made him a curtsey, and the poor girl looked so confounded with joy that she could not speak, but her colour came and went, and every now and then she blushed as red as scarlet, and the next minute looked as pale as death. Well, having said this, he sat down, made me sit down, and then drank to me, and made me drink two glasses of wine together; "For," says he, "you have need of it"; and so indeed I had. When he had done so, "Come, Amy," says he, "with your mistress's leave, you shall have a glass too." So he made her drink two glasses also. And then rising up, "And now, Amy," says he, "go and get dinner; and you, madam," says he to me, "go up and dress you, and come down and smile and be merry." adding, "I'll make you easy if I can"; and in the meantime, he said, he would walk in the garden.

When he was gone, Amy changed her countenance indeed and looked as merry as ever she did in her life. "Dear madam," says she, "what does this gentleman mean?" "Nay, Amy," said I, "he means to do us good, you see, don't he? I know no other meaning he can have, for he can get nothing by me." "I warrant you, madam," says she, "he'll ask you a favour by and by." "No, no, you are mistaken, Amy, I dare say," said I; "you have heard what he said, didn't you?" "Ay," says Amy, "it's no matter for that, you shall see what he will do after dinner." "Well, well, Amy," says I, "you have hard thoughts of him. I cannot be of your opinion; I don't see anything in him yet that looks like it." "As to that, madam," says Amy, "I don't see anything of it yet neither; but what should move a gentleman to take pity of us as he does?" "Nay," says I, "that's a hard thing too, that we should judge a man to be wicked because he's charitable, and vicious because he's kind." "Oh, madam," says Amy, "there's abundance of charity begins in that vice; and he is not so unacquainted with things as not to know that poverty is the strongest incentive—a temptation against which no virtue is powerful enough to stand out. He knows your condition as well as you do." "Well, and what then?" "Why, then, he knows too that you are young and handsome, and he has the surest bait in the world to take you with."

"Well, Amy," said I, "but he may find himself mistaken too in such a thing as that." "Why, madam," says Amy, "I hope you won't deny him if he should offer it."

"What d'ye mean by that, hussy?" said I. "No, I'd starve first."

"I hope not, madam, I hope you would be wiser. I'm sure if he will set you up, as he talks of, you ought to deny him nothing; and you will starve if you do not consent, that's certain."

"What! consent to lie with him for bread? Amy," said I, "how can you talk so!"

"Nay, madam," says Amy, "I don't think you would for

anything else; it would not be lawful for anything else, but
for bread, madam. Why, nobody can starve; there's no bearing that, I'm sure."

"Ay," says I, "but if he would give me an estate to live on,
he should not lie with me, I assure you."

"Why, look you, madam, if he would but give you enough
to live easy upon, he should lie with me for it with all my
heart."

"That's a token, Amy, of inimitable kindness to me," said
I, "and I know how to value it; but there's more friendship
than honesty in it, Amy."

"Oh, madam," says Amy, "I'd do anything to get you out
of this sad condition; as to honesty, I think honesty is out of
the question when starving is the case. Are not we almost
starved to death?"

"I am indeed," said I, "and thou art for my sake; but to be
a whore, Amy!" And there I stopped.

"Dear madam," says Amy, "if I will starve for your sake, I
will be a whore or anything for your sake; why, I would die
for you if I were put to it."

"Why, that's an excess of affection, Amy," said I, "I never
met with before; I wish I may be ever in condition to make
you some returns suitable. But, however, Amy, you shall not
be a whore to him to oblige him to be kind to me; no, Amy,
nor I won't be a whore to him, if he would give me much
more than he is able to give me or do for me."

"Why, madam" says Amy, "I don't say I will go and ask
him; but I say if he should promise to do so and so for you,
and the condition was such that he would not serve you
unless I would let him lie with me, he should lie with me as
often as he would, rather than you should not have his assistance. But this is but talk, madam; I don't see any need of
such discourse, and you are of opinion that there will be no
need of it."

"Indeed so I am, Amy. But," said I, "if there was, I tell
you again, I'd die before I would consent, or before you
should consent for my sake."

Hitherto I had not only preserved the virtue itself, but the
virtuous inclination and resolution; and had I kept myself
there I had been happy, though I had perished of mere hunger. For, without question, a woman ought rather to die than
to prostitute her virtue and honour, let the temptation be
what it will.

But to return to my story. He walked about the garden, which was, indeed, all in disorder, and over-run with weeds, because I had not been able to hire a gardener to do anything to it—no, not so much as to dig up ground enough to sow a few turnips and carrots for family use. After he had viewed it, he came in and sent Amy to fetch a poor man, a gardener, that used to help our man-servant, and carried him into the garden, and ordered him to do several things in it, to put it into a little order. And this took him up near an hour.

By this time I had dressed me as well as I could; for though I had good linen left still, yet I had but a poor head-dress, and no knots, but old fragments; no necklace, no ear-rings. All those things were gone long ago for mere bread.

However, I was tight and clean, and in better plight than he had seen me in a great while, and he looked extremely pleased to see me so; for, he said, I looked so disconsolate and so afflicted before, that it grieved him to see me. And he bade me pluck up a good heart, for he hoped to put me in a condition to live in the world and be beholden to nobody.

I told him that was impossible, for I must be beholden to him for it, for all the friends I had in the world would not or could not do so much for me as that he spoke of. "Well, widow," says he (so he called me, and so indeed I was in the worst sense that desolate word could be used in), "if you are beholden to me, you shall be beholden to nobody else."

By this time dinner was ready, and Amy came in to lay the cloth, and indeed it was happy there was none to dine but he and I, for I had but six plates left in the house, and but two dishes; however, he knew how things were and bade me make no scruple about bringing out what I had. He hoped to see me in a better plight. He did not come, he said, to be entertained, but to entertain me, and comfort and encourage me. Thus he went on, speaking so cheerfully to me, and such cheerful things, that it was a cordial to my very soul to hear him speak.

Well, we went to dinner. I'm sure I had not eat a good meal hardly in a twelvemonth, at least not of such a joint of meat as the loin of veal was. I ate, indeed, very heartily, and so did he, and he made me drink three or four glasses of wine. So that, in short, my spirits were lifted up to a degree I had not been used to, and I was not only cheerful, but merry; and so he pressed me to be.

I told him I had a great deal of reason to be merry, seeing

he had been so kind to me, and had given me hopes of recovering me from the worst circumstances that ever woman of any sort of fortune was sunk into; that he could not but believe that what he had said to me was like life from the dead; that it was like recovering one sick from the brink of the grave. How I should ever make him a return any way suitable was what I had not yet had time to think of; I could only say that I should never forget it while I had life, and should be always ready to acknowledge it.

He said that was all he desired of me; that his reward would be the satisfaction of having rescued me from misery; that he found he was obliging one that knew what gratitude meant; that he would make it his business to make me completely easy, first or last, if it lay in his power; and in the meantime he bade me consider of anything that I thought he might do for me, for my advantage, and in order to make me perfectly easy.

After we had talked thus, he bade me be cheerful. "Come," says he, "lay aside these melancholy things, and let us be merry." Amy waited at the table, and she smiled and laughed, and was so merry she could hardly contain it, for the girl loved me to an excess hardly to be described; and it was such an unexpected thing to hear any one talk to her mistress that the wench was beside herself almost, and, as soon as dinner was over, Amy went upstairs and put on her best clothes too, and came down dressed like a gentlewoman.

We sat together talking of a thousand things—of what had been, and what was to be—all the rest of the day, and in the evening he took his leave of me, with a thousand expressions of kindness and tenderness and true affection to me, but offered not the least of what my maid Amy had suggested.

At his going away he took me in his arms, protested an honest kindness to me; said a thousand kind things to me, which I cannot now recollect; and, after kissing me twenty times or thereabouts, put a guinea into my hand, which, he said, was for my present supply, and told me that he would see me again before 'twas out. Also he gave Amy half a crown.

When he was gone, "Well, Amy," said I, "are you convinced now that he is an honest as well as a true friend, and that there has been nothing, not the least appearance of anything, of what you imagined in his behaviour?" "Yes," says

Amy, "I am, but I admire at it. He is such a friend as the world, sure, has not abundance of to show."

"I am sure," says I, "he is such a friend as I have long wanted, and as I have as much need of as any creature in the world has or ever had," And, in short, I was so overcome with the comfort of it that I sat down and cried for joy a good while, as I had formerly cried for sorrow. Amy and I went to bed that night (for Amy lay with me) pretty early, but lay chatting almost all night about it, and the girl was so transported that she got up two or three times in the night and danced about the room in her shift. In short, the girl was half distracted with the joy of it; a testimony still of her violent affection for her mistress, in which no servant ever went beyond her.

We heard no more of him for two days, but the third day he came again. Then he told me, with the same kindness, that he had ordered me a supply of household goods for the furnishing the house; that, in particular, he had sent me back all the goods that he had seized for rent, which consisted indeed, of the best of my former furniture. "And now," says he, "I'll tell you what I have had in my head for you for your present supply, and that is," says he, "that the house being well furnished, you shall let it out to lodgings for the summer gentry," says he, "by which you will easily get a good comfortable subsistence, especially seeing you shall pay me no rent for two years, nor after neither, unless you can afford it."

This was the first view I had of living comfortably indeed, and it was a very probable way, I must confess, seeing we had very good conveniences, six rooms on a floor, and three stories high. While he was laying down the scheme of my management, came a cart to the door with a load of goods, and an upholsterer's man to put them up. They were chiefly the furniture of two rooms which he had carried away for his two years' rent, with two fine cabinets, and some pier-glasses out of the parlour, and several other valuable things.

These were all restored to their places, and he told me he gave them me freely, as a satisfaction for the cruelty he had used me with before; and the furniture of one room being finished and set up, he told me he would furnish one chamber for himself, and would come and be one of my lodgers, if I would give him leave.

I told him he ought not to ask me leave, who had so much

right to make himself welcome. So the house began to look in some tolerable figure, and clean; the garden also, in about a fortnight's work, began to look something less like a wilderness than it used to do; and he ordered me to put up a bill for letting rooms, reserving one for himself, to come to as he saw occasion.

When all was done to his mind, as to placing the goods, he seemed very well pleased, and we dined together again of his own providing; and the upholsterer's man gone, after dinner he took me by the hand. "Come now, madam," says he, "you must show me your house" (for he had a mind to see everything over again). "No, sir," said I, "but I'll go show you your house, if you please." So we went up through all the rooms, and in the room which was appointed for himself Amy was doing something. "Well, Amy," says he, "I intend to lie with you to-morrow night." "To-night if you please, sir," says Amy very innocently; "your room is quite ready." "Well, Amy," says he, "I am glad you are so willing." "No," says Amy, "I mean your chamber is ready tonight," and away she run out of the room, ashamed enough; for the girl meant no harm, whatever she had said to me in private.

However, he said no more then. But when Amy was gone he walked about the room and looked at everything, and taking me by the hand he kissed me, and spoke a great many kind, affectionate things to me indeed; as of his measures for my advantage, and what he would do to raise me again in the world; told me that my afflictions, and the conduct I had shown in bearing them to such an extremity, had so engaged him to me that he valued me infinitely above all the women in the world; that though he was under such engagements that he could not marry me (his wife and he had been parted for some reasons, which make too long a story to intermix with mine), yet that he would be everything else that a woman could ask in a husband. And with that he kissed me again, and took me in his arms, but offered not the least uncivil action to me, and told me he hoped I would not deny him all the favours he should ask, because he resolved to ask nothing of me but what it was fit for a woman of virtue and modesty, for such he knew me to be—to yield.

I confess the terrible pressure of my former misery, the memory of which lay heavy upon my mind, and the surprising kindness with which he had delivered me, and, withal, the expectations of what he might still do for me, were powerful things, and made me have scarce the power to deny him any-thing he would ask. However, I told him thus, with an air of tenderness too, that he had done so much for me that I thought I ought to deny him nothing; only I hoped and de-pended upon him that he would not take the advantage of the infinite obligations I was under to him, to desire anything of me the yielding to which would lay me lower in his esteem than I desired to be; that as I took him to be a man of honour, so I knew he could not like me the better for doing anything that was below a woman of honesty and good man-ners to do.

He told me that he had done all this for me without so much as telling me what kindness or real affection he had for me, that I might not be under any necessity of yielding to him in anything for want of bread; and he would no more oppress my gratitude now than he would my neccessity be-fore, nor ask anything, supposing he would stop his favours or withdraw his kindness, if he was denied. It was true, he said, he might tell me more freely his mind now than before, seeing I had let him see that I accepted his assistance, and saw that he was sincere in his design of serving me; that he had gone thus far to show me that he was kind to me, but that now he would tell me that he loved me, and yet would demonstrate that his love was both honourable, and that what he should desire was what he might honestly ask and I might honestly grant.

I answered that, within those two limitations, I was sure I ought to deny him nothing, and I should think myself not un-grateful only, but very unjust, if I should. So he said no more, but I observed he kissed me more, and took me in his arms in a kind of familiar way more than usual, and which once or twice put me in mind of my maid Amy's words; and yet, I must acknowledge, I was so overcome with his goodness to me in those many kind things he had done that I not only was easy at what he did and made no resistance, but was in-clined to do the like, whatever he had offered to do. But he went no farther than what I have said, nor did he offer so much as to sit down on the bedside with me, but took his leave, said he loved me tenderly, and would convince me of it by such demonstrations as should be to my satisfaction. I told him I had a great deal of reason to believe him, that he was full master of the whole house and of me, as far as was within the bounds we had spoken of, which I believed he would not break, and asked him if he would not lodge there that night.

He said he could not well stay that night, business requiring him in London, but added, smiling, that he would come the next day and take a night's lodging with me. I pressed him to stay that night, and told him I should be glad a friend so valuable should be under the same roof with me. And indeed I began at that time not only to be much obliged to him, but to love him too, and that in a manner that I had not been acquainted with myself.

Oh! let no woman slight the temptation that being generously delivered from trouble is to any spirit furnished with gratitude and just principles. This gentleman had freely and voluntarily delivered me from misery, from poverty, and rags; he had made me what I was, and put me into a way to be even more than I ever was, namely, to live happy and pleased, and on his bounty I depended. What could I say to this gentleman when he pressed me to yield to him, and argued the lawfulness of it? But of that in its place.

I pressed him again to stay that night, and told him it was the first completely happy night that I had ever had in the house in my life, and I should be very sorry to have it be without his company, who was the cause and foundation of it all; that we would be innocently merry, but that it could never be without him. And, in short, I courted him so, that he said he could not deny me, but he would take his horse and go to London, do the business he had to do, which, it seems, was to pay a foreign bill that was due that night, and would else be protested, and that he would come back in three hours at farthest, and sup with me; but bade me get nothing there, for since I was resolved to be merry, which was what he desired above all things, he would send me something from London. "And we will make it a wedding supper, my dear," says he, and with that word, took me in his arms and kissed me so vehemently that I made no question but he intended to do everything else that Amy had talked of.

I started a little at the word wedding. "What do ye mean, to call it by such a name?" says I, adding, "We will have a supper, but t'other is impossible, as well on your side as mine." He laughed. "Well," says he, "you shall call it what you will, but it may be the same thing, for I shall satisfy you it is not so impossible as you make it."

"I don't understand you," said I. "Have not I a husband and you a wife?"

"Well, well," says he, "we will talk of that after supper." So he rose up, gave me another kiss, and took his horse for London.

This kind of discourse had fired my blood, I confess, and I knew not what to think of it. It was plain now that he intended to lie with me, but how he would reconcile it to a legal thing, like a marriage, that I could not imagine. We had both of us used Amy with so much intimacy, and trusted her with everything, having such unexampled instances of her fidelity, that he made no scruple to kiss me and say all these things to me before her; nor had he cared one farthing, if I would have let him lie with me, to have had Amy there too all night. When he was gone, "Well, Amy," says I, "what will all this come to now? I am all in a sweat at him." "Come to, madam?" says Amy, "I see what it will come to: I must put you to bed tonight together." "Why, you would not be so impudent, you jade, you," says I, "would you?" "Yes, I would," says she, "with all my heart, and think you both as honest as ever you were in your lives."

"What ails the slut to talk so?" said I. "Honest! How can it be honest?" "Why, I'll tell you, madam," says Amy. "I sounded* it as soon as I heard him speak, and it is very true too. He calls you widow, and such indeed you are; for as my master has left you so many years, he is dead, to be sure; at least he is dead to you; he is no husband. You are, and ought to be, free to marry who you will; and his wife being gone from him, and refusing to lie with him, then he is a single man again as much as ever; and though you cannot bring the laws of the land to join you together, yet, one refusing to do the office of a wife, and the other of a husband, you may certainly take one another fairly."

"Nay, Amy," says I, "if I could take him fairly, you may be sure I'd take him above all the men in the world; it turned the very heart within me when I heard him say he loved me. How could it do otherwise, when you know what a condition I was in before, despised and trampled on by all the world? I could have took him in my arms and kissed him as freely as he did me, if it had not been for shame."

"Ay, and all the rest too," says Amy, "at the first word. I

* "sounded." Understood.

don't see how you can think of denying him anything. Has he
not brought you out of the devil's clutches, brought you out
of the blackest misery that ever poor lady was reduced to?
Can a woman deny such a man anything?"

"Nay, I don't know what to do, Amy," says I. "I hope he
won't desire anything of that kind of me; I hope he won't attempt it. If he does, I know not what to say to him."

"Not ask you!" says Amy. "Depend upon it, he will ask
you, and you will grant it too. I'm sure my mistress is no
fool. Come, pray, madam, let me go air you a clean shift;
don't let him find you in foul linen the wedding-night."

"But that I know you to be a very honest girl, Amy," says
I, "you would make me abhor you. Why, you argue for the
devil, as if you were one of his privy-counsellors."

"It's no matter for that, madam, I say nothing but what I
think. You own you love this gentleman, and he has given
you sufficient testimony of his affection to you. Your conditions are alike unhappy, and he is of opinion that he may
take another woman, his first wife having broke her honour,
and living from him; and that though the laws of the land
will not allow him to marry formally, yet that he may take
another woman into his arms, provided he keeps true to the
other woman as a wife. Nay, he says it is usual to do so, and
allowed by the custom of the place in several countries
abroad. And, I must own, I'm of the same mind; else 'tis in
the power of a whore, after she has jilted and abandoned her
husband, to confine him from the pleasure as well as convenience of a woman all the days of his life, which would be
very unreasonable, and, as times go, not tolerable to all
people; and the like on your side, madam."

Had I now had my senses about me, and had my reason
not been overcome by the powerful attraction of so kind, so
beneficent a friend; had I consulted conscience and virtue, I
should have repelled this Amy, however faithful and honest
to me in other things, as a viper and engine of the devil. I
ought to have remembered that neither he or I, either by the
laws of God or man, could come together upon any other
terms than that of notorious adultery. The ignorant jade's argument, that he had brought me out of the hands of the
devil, by which she meant the devil of poverty and distress,
should have been a powerful motive to me not to plunge myself into the jaws of hell, and into the power of the real devil,
in recompense for that deliverance. I should have looked

upon all the good this man had done for me to have been the particular work of the goodness of Heaven, and that goodness should have moved me to a return of duty and humble obedience. I should have received the mercy thankfully, and applied it soberly, to the praise and honour of my Maker. Whereas, by this wicked course, all the bounty and kindness of this gentleman became a snare to me, was a mere bait to the devil's hook; I received his kindness at the dear expense of body and soul, mortgaging faith, religion, conscience, and modesty for (as I may call it) a morsel of bread; or, if you will, ruined my soul from a principle of gratitude, and gave myself up to the devil to show myself grateful to my benefactor. I must do the gentleman that justice as to say I verily believe that he did nothing but what he thought was lawful; and I must do that justice upon myself as to say I did what my own conscience convinced me, at the very time I did it, was horribly unlawful, scandalous, and abominable.

But poverty was my snare, dreadful poverty! The misery I had been in was great, such as would make the heart tremble at the apprehensions of its return; and I might appeal to any that has had any experience of the world, whether one so entirely destitute as I was of all manner of all helps or friends, either to support me or to assist me to support myself, could withstand the proposal. Not that I plead this as a justification of my conduct, but that it may move the pity even of those that abhor the crime.

Besides this, I was young, handsome, and with all the mortifications I had met with, was vain, and that not a little; and as it was a new thing, so it was a pleasant thing to be courted, caressed, embraced, and high professions of affection made to me, by a man so agreeable and so able to do me good.

Add to this that if I had ventured to disoblige this gentleman, I had no friend in the world to have recourse to; I had no prospect—no, not of a bit of bread; I had nothing before me but to fall back into the same misery that I had been in before.

Amy had but too much rhetoric in this cause. She represented all those things in their proper colours; she argued them all with her utmost skill; and at last the merry jade, when she came to dress me, "Look ye, madam," said she, "if you won't consent, tell him you'll do as Rachel did to Jacob, when she could have no children—put her maid to bed to him; tell him you cannot comply with him, but there's Amy, he may ask her the question; she has promised me she won't deny you."

"And would you have me say so, Amy?" said I.

"No, madam; but I would really have you do so. Besides, you are undone if you do not; and if my doing it would save you from being undone, as I said before, he shall, if he will; if he asks me, I won't deny him, not I; hang me if I do," says Amy.

"Well, I know not what to do," says I to Amy.

"Do!" says Amy. "Your choice is fair and plain. Here you may have a handsome, charming gentleman, be rich, live pleasantly and in plenty, or refuse him, and want a dinner, go in rags, live in tears; in short, beg and starve. You know this is the case, madam," says Amy. "I wonder how you can say you know not what to do."

"Well, Amy," says I, "the case is as you say, and I think verily I must yield to him; but then," said I, moved by conscience, "don't talk any more of your cant of its being lawful that I ought to marry again, and that he ought to marry again, and such stuff as that; 'tis all nonsense," says I, "Amy, there's nothing in it; let me hear no more of that, for if I yield, 'tis in vain to mince the matter, I am a whore, Amy; neither better nor worse, I assure you."

"I don't think so, madam, by no means," says Amy. "I wonder how you can talk so." And then she run on with her argument of the unreasonableness that a woman should be obliged to live single, or a man to live single, in such cases as before. "Well, Amy," said I, "come, let us dispute no more, for the longer I enter into that part, the greater my scruples will be; but if I let it alone, the necessity of my present circumstances is such that I believe I shall yield to him, if he should importune me much about it; but I should be glad he would not do it at all, but leave me as I am."

"As to that, madam, you may depend," says Amy, "he expects to have you for his bedfellow tonight. I saw it plainly in his management all day; and at last he told you so too, as plain, I think, as he could." "Well, well, Amy," said I, "I don't know what to say; if he will he must, I think; I don't know how to resist such a man, that has done so much for me." "I don't know how you should," says Amy.

Thus Amy and I canvassed the business between us. The jade prompted the crime which I had but too much inclination to commit, that is to say, not as a crime, for I had nothing of the vice in my constitution; my spirits were far from being high, my blood had no fire in it to kindle the flame of desire; but the kindness and good humour of the man and the dread of my own circumstances concurred to bring me to the point, and I even resolved, before he asked, to give up my virtue to him whenever he should put it to the question.

In this I was a double offender, whatever he was, for I was resolved to commit the crime, knowing and owning it to be a crime; he, if it was true as he said, was fully persuaded it was lawful, and in that persuasion he took the measures and used all the circumlocutions which I am going to speak of.

About two hours after he was gone, came a Leadenhall basket-woman with a whole load of good things for the mouth (the particulars are not to the purpose), and brought orders to get supper by eight o'clock. However, I did not intend to begin to dress anything till I saw him; and he gave me time enough, for he came before seven, so that Amy, who had gotten one to help her, got everything ready in time.

We sat down to supper about eight, and were indeed very merry. Amy made us some sport, for she was a girl of spirit and wit, and with her talk she made us laugh very often, and yet the jade managed her wit with all the good manners imaginable.

But to shorten the story. After supper he took me up into his chamber, where Amy had made a good fire, and there he pulled out a great many papers and spread them upon a little table, and then took me by the hand, and after kissing me very much, he entered into a discourse of his circumstances and of mine, how they agreed in several things exactly; for example, that I was abandoned of a husband in the prime of my youth and vigour, and he of a wife in his middle-age; how the end of marriage was destroyed by the treatment we had either of us received, and it would be very hard that we should be tied by the formality of the contract where the essence of it was destroyed. I interrupted him and told him there was a vast difference between our circumstances, and that in the most essential part, namely, that he was rich, and I was poor; that he was above the world, and I infinitely below it; that his circumstances were very easy, mine miserable, and this was an inequality the most essential that could be imagined. "As to that, my dear," says he, "I have taken such measures as shall make an equality still." And with that he showed me a contract in writing, wherein he engaged himself to me to cohabit constantly with me, to provide for me in all respects as a wife, and repeating in the preamble a long account of the nature and reason of our living together, and an obligation in the penalty of £7000 never to abandon me; and at last showed me a bond for £500, to be paid to me, or to my assigns, within three months after his death.

He read over all these things to me, and then, in a most moving, affectionate manner, and in words not to be answered, he said, "Now, my dear, is this not sufficient? Can you object anything against it? If not, as I believe you will not, then let us debate this matter no longer." With that, he pulled out a silk purse, which had three-score guineas in it, and threw them into my lap, and concluded all the rest of his discourse with kisses and protestations of his love, of which indeed I had abundant proof.

Pity human frailty, you that read of a woman reduced in her youth and prime to the utmost misery and distress, and raised again, as above, by the unexpected and surprising bounty of a stranger; I say, pity her if she was not able, after all these things, to make any more resistance.

However, I stood out a little longer still. I asked him how he could expect that I could come into a proposal of such consequence the very first time it was moved to me; and that I ought, if I consented to it, to capitulate* with him that he should never upbraid me with easiness and consenting too soon. He said no; but, on the contrary, he would take it as a mark of the greatest kindness I could show him. Then he went on to give reasons why there was no occasion to use the ordinary ceremony of delay, or to wait a reasonable time of courtship, which was only to avoid scandal; but, as this was private, it had nothing of that nature in it; that he had been courting me some time by the best of courtship, viz., doing acts of kindness to me; and that he had given testimonies of his sincere affection to me by deeds, not by flattering trifles and the usual courtship of words, which were often found to have very little meaning; that he took me not as a mistress, but as his wife, and protested it was clear to him he might lawfully do it, and that I was perfectly at liberty, and assured me, by all that it was possible for an honest man to say, that

---

* "capitulate." Stipulate. Compare pages 124, 158, "capitulation": Agreement or bargain.

he would treat me as his wife as long as he lived. In a word, he conquered all the little resistance I intended to make; he protested he loved me above all the world and begged I would for once believe him; that he had never deceived me, and never would, but would make it his study to make my life comfortable and happy, and to make me forget the misery I had gone through. I stood still a-while and said nothing; but seeing him eager for my answer, I smiled and, looking up at him, "And must I, then," says I, "say yes at first asking? Must I depend upon your promise? Why, then," said I, "upon the faith of that promise, and in the sense of that inexpressible kindness you have shown me, you shall be obliged, and I will be wholly yours to the end of my life." And with that I took his hand, which held me by the hand, and gave it a kiss.

And thus, in gratitude for the favours I received from a man, was all sense of religion and duty to God, all regard to virtue and honour, given up at once, and we were to call one another man and wife, who, in the sense of the laws both of God and our country, were no more than two adulterers; in short, a whore and a rogue. Nor, as I have said above, was my conscience silent in it, though it seems his was; for I sinned with open eyes, and thereby had a double guilt upon me. As I always said, his notions were of another kind, and he either was before of the opinion, or argued himself into it now, that we were both free and might lawfully marry.

But I was quite of another side—nay, and my judgment was right, but my circumstances were my temptation; the terrors behind me looked blacker than the terrors before me; and the dreadful argument of wanting bread, and being run into the horrible distresses I was in before, mastered all my resolution, and I gave myself up as above.

The rest of the evening we spent very agreeably to me; he was perfectly good-humoured and was at that time very merry. Then he made Amy dance with him, and I told him I would put Amy to bed to him. Amy said, with all her heart; she never had been a bride in her life. In short, he made the girl so merry that, had he not been to lie with me the same night, I believe he would have played the fool with Amy for half-an-hour, and the girl would no more have refused him than I intended to do. Yet, before, I had always found her a very modest wench as any I ever saw in all my life; but, in short, the mirth of that night, and a few more such afterwards, ruined the girl's modesty for ever, as shall appear by and by, in its place.

So far does fooling and toying sometimes go that I know nothing a young woman has to be more cautious of; so far had this inncent girl gone in jesting between her and I, and in talking that she should let him lie with her, if he would but be kinder to me, that at last she let him lie with her in earnest; and so empty was I now of all principle that I encouraged the doing it almost before my face.

I say but too justly that I was empty of principle, because, as above, I had yielded to him, not as deluded to believe it lawful, but as overcome by his kindness and terrified at the fear of my own misery if he should leave me. So with my eyes open, and with my conscience, as I may say, awake, I sinned, knowing it to be a sin, but having no power to resist. When this had thus made a hole in my heart, and I was come to such a height as to transgress against the light of my own conscience, I was then fit for any wickedness, and conscience left off speaking where it found it could not be heard.

But to return to our story. Having consented, as above, to his proposal, we had not much more to do. He gave me my writings, and the bond for my maintenance during his life, and for five hundred pounds after his death. And so far was he from abating his affection to me afterwards that two years after we were thus, as he called it, married, he made his will, and gave me a thousand pound more, and all my household stuff, plate, &c., which was considerable too.

Amy put us to bed, and my new friend—I cannot call him husband—was so well pleased with Amy for her fidelity and kindness to me that he paid her all the arrear of her wages that I owed her, and gave her five guineas over; and had it gone no farther, Amy had richly deserved what she had, for never was a maid so true to a mistress in such dreadful circumstances as I was in. Nor was what followed more her own fault than mine, who let her almost into it at first, and quite into it at last; and this may be a farther testimony what a hardness of crime I was now arrived to, which was owing to the conviction, that was from the beginning upon me, that I was a whore, not a wife; nor could I ever frame my mouth to call him husband or to say "my husband" when I was speaking of him.

We lived, surely, the most agreeable life, the grand exception only excepted, that ever two lived together. He was the

most obliging, gentlemanly man, and the most tender of me,
that ever woman gave herself up to. Nor was there ever the
least interruption to our mutual kindness, no, not to the last
day of his life. But I must bring Amy's disaster in at once,
that I may have done with her.

Amy was dressing me one morning, for now I had two
maids, and Amy was my chamber-maid. "Dear madam," says
Amy, "what! a'nt you with child yet?" "No, Amy," says I;
"nor any sign of it."

"Law, madam!" says Amy, "what have you been doing?
Why, you have been married a year and a half. I warrant
you, master would have got me with child twice in that
time." "It may be so, Amy," says I. "Let him try, can't you?"
"No," says Amy. "you'll forbid it now. Before, I told you he
should, with all my heart; but I won't now, now he's all your
own." "Oh," says I, "Amy, I'll freely give you my consent. It
will be nothing at all to me. Nay, I'll put you to bed to him
myself one night or other, if you are willing." "No, madam,
no," says Amy, "not now he's yours."

"Why, you fool you," says I, "don't I tell you I'll put you
to bed to him myself?"

"Nay, nay," says Amy, "if you put me to bed to him, that's
another case; I believe I shall not rise again very soon."

"I'll venture that, Amy," says I.

After supper that night, and before we were risen from
table, I said to him, Amy being by, "Hark ye, Mr. ———, do
you know that you are to lie with Amy to-night?" "No, not I,"
says he; but turns to Amy. "Is it so, Amy?" says he. "No,
sir," says she. "Nay, don't say no, you fool. Did not I
promise to put you to bed to him?" But the girl said "no still,
and it passed off.

At night, when we came to go to bed, Amy came into the
chamber to undress me, and her master slipped into bed first.
Then I began, and told him all that Amy had said about my
not being with child, and of her being with child twice in that
time. "Ay, Mrs. Amy," says he, "I believe so too. Come
hither, and we'll try." But Amy did not go. "Go, you fool,"
says I, "can't you? I freely give you both leave." But Amy
would not go. "Nay, you whore," says I, "you said if I would
put you to bed, you would with all your heart." And with
that I sat her down, pulled off her stockings and shoes, and
all her clothes piece by piece, and led her to the bed to him.
"Here," says I, "try what you can do with your maid, Amy."

She pulled back a little, would not let me pull off her clothes at first, but it was hot weather, and she had not many clothes on, and particularly no stays* on; and at last, when she see I was in earnest, she let me do what I would. So I fairly stripped her, and then I threw open the bed and thrust her in.

I need say no more. This is enough to convince anybody that I did not think him my husband, and that I had cast off all principle and all modesty, and had effectually stifled conscience.

Amy, I dare say, began now to repent, and would fain have got out of bed again. But he said to her, "Nay, Amy, you see your mistress has put you to bed; 'tis all her doing; you must blame her." So he held her fast, and the wench being naked in the bed with him, 'twas too late to look back, so she lay still and let him do what he would with her.

Had I looked upon myself as a wife, you cannot suppose I would have been willing to have let my husband lie with my maid, much less before my face, for I stood by all the while; but as I thought myself a whore, I cannot say but that it was something designed in my thoughts that my maid should be a whore too, and should not reproach me with it.

Amy, however, less vicious than I, was grievously out of sorts the next morning, and cried and took on most vehemently, that she was ruined and undone, and there was no pacifying her; she was a whore, a slut, and she was undone! undone! and cried almost all day. I did all I could to pacify her. "A whore!" says I. "Well, and am not I a whore as well as you?" "No, no," says Amy. "no, you are not, for you are married." "Not I, Amy," says I; "I do not pretend to it. He may marry you to-morrow, if he will, for anything I could do to hinder it. I am not married. I do not look upon it as any thing." Well, all did not pacify Amy, but she cried two or three days about it; but it wore off by degrees.

But the case differed between Amy and her master exceedingly. For Amy retained the same kind temper she always had; but, on the contrary, he was quite altered, for he hated her heartily, and could, I believe, have killed her after it, and he told me so, for he thought this a vile action; whereas what he and I had done he was perfectly easy in, thought it just, and esteemed me as much his wife as if we had been married from our youth, and had neither of us known any other; nay,

* "stays." Corset.

he loved me, I believe, as entirely as if I had been the wife of his youth. Nay, he told me it was true, in one sense, that he had two wives, but that I was the wife of his affection, the other the wife of his aversion.

I was extremely concerned at the aversion he had taken to my maid Amy, and used my utmost skill to get it altered. For though he had, indeed, debauched the wench, I knew that I was the principal occasion of it; and as he was the best-humoured man in the world, I never gave him over till I prevailed with him to be easy with her, and as I was now become the devil's agent, to make others as wicked as myself, I brought him to lie with her again several times after that, till at last, as the poor girl said, so it happened, and she was really with child.

She was terribly concerned at it, and so was he too. "Come, my dear," says I, "when Rachel put her handmaid to bed to Jacob, she took the children as her own. Don't be uneasy; I'll take the child as my own. Had not I a hand in the frolic of putting her to bed to you? It was my fault as much as yours." So I called Amy, and encouraged her too, and told her that I would take care of the child and her too, and added the same argument to her. "For," says I, "Amy, it was all my fault. Did not I drag your clothes off your back, and put you to bed to him?" Thus I, that had, indeed, been the cause of all the wickedness between them, encouraged them both, when they had any remorse about it, and rather prompted them to go on with it than to repent of it.

When Amy grew big, she went to a place I had provided for her, and the neighbours knew nothing but that Amy and I was parted. She had a fine child indeed, a daughter, and we had it nursed; and Amy came again in about half a year to live with her old mistress. But neither my gentleman or Amy either cared for playing that game over again; for, as he said, the jade might bring him a house-full of children to keep.

We lived as merrily and as happily after this as could be expected, considering our circumstances; I mean as to the pretended marriage, &c.; and, as to that, my gentleman had not the least concern about him for it. But as much as I was hardened, and that was as much as I believe ever any wicked creature was, yet I could not help it, there was and would be hours of intervals and of dark reflections which came involuntarily in, and thrust in sighs into the middle of all my songs; and there would be sometimes a heaviness of heart, which intermingled itself with all my joy, and which would often fetch a tear from my eye. And let others pretend what they will, I believe it impossible to be otherwise with anybody. There can be no substantial satisfaction in a life of known wickedness; conscience will, and does often, break in upon them at particular times, let them do what they can to prevent it.

But I am not to preach, but to relate; and whatever loose reflections were, and how often soever those dark intervals came on, I did my utmost to conceal them from him; ay, and to suppress and smother them too in myself; and, to outward appearance, we lived as cheerfully and agreeably as it was possible for any couple in the world to live.

After I had thus lived with him something above two years, truly I found myself with child too. My gentleman was mightily pleased at it, and nothing could be kinder than he was in the preparations he made for me, and for my lying-in, which was, however, very private, because I cared for as little company as possible; nor had I kept up my neighbourly acquaintance, so that I had nobody to invite upon such an occasion.

I was brought to bed very well (of a daughter too, as well as Amy), but the child died at about six weeks old, so all that work was to do over again—that is to say, the charge, the expense, the travail, &c.

The next year I made him amends and brought him a son, to his great satisfaction. It was a charming child, and did very well. After this, my husband, as he called himself, came to me one evening and told me he had a very difficult thing happened to him, which he knew not what to do in, or how to resolve about, unless I would make him easy; this was, that his occasions required him to go over to France for about two months.

"Well, my dear," says I, "and how shall I make you easy?"

"Why, by consenting to let me go," says he. "Upon which condition, I'll tell you the occasion of my going, that you may judge of the necessity there is for it on my side." Then, to make me easy in his going, he told me he would make his will before he went, which should be to my full satisfaction.

I told him the last part was so kind that I could not decline the first part, unless he would give me leave to add that, if it was not for putting him to an extraordinary expense, I would go over along with him.

He was so pleased with this offer that he told me he would give me full satisfaction for it, and accept of it too. So he took me to London with him the next day, and there he made his will and showed it to me, and sealed it before proper witnesses, and then gave it to me to keep. In this will he gave a thousand pounds to a person that we both knew very well, in trust, to pay it, with the interest from the time of his decease, to me or my assigns; then he willed the payment of my jointure, as he called it, viz., his bond of five hundred pounds after his death; also, he gave me all my household stuff, plate, &c.

This was a most engaging thing for a man to do to one under my circumstances; and it would have been hard, as I told him, to deny him anything, or to refuse to go with him anywhere. So we settled everything as well as we could, left Amy in charge with the house, and for his other business, which was in jewels, he had two men he entrusted, who he had good security for, and who managed for him, and corresponded with him.

Things being thus concerted, we went away to France, arrived safe at Calais, and by easy journeys came in eight days more to Paris, where we lodged in the house of an English merchant of his acquaintance, and was very courteously entertained.

My gentleman's business was with some persons of the first rank, and to whom he had sold some jewels of very good value, and received a great sum of money in specie; and, as he told me privately, he gained three thousand pistoles by his bargain, but would not suffer the most intimate friend he had there to know what he had received; for it is not so safe a thing in Paris to have a great sum of money in keeping as it might be in London.

We made this journey much longer than we intended, and my gentleman sent for one of his managers in London to come over to us to Paris with some diamonds, and sent him back to London again to fetch more. Then other business fell into his hands so unexpectedly that I began to think we should take up our constant residence there, which I was not very averse to, it being my native country, and I spoke the language perfectly well. So we took a good house in Paris and lived very well there; and I sent for Amy to come over to me, for I lived gallantly, and my gentleman was two or three times going to keep me a coach, but I declined it, especially at Paris; but as they have those conveniences by the day there, at a certain rate, I had an equipage provided for me whenever I pleased, and I lived here in a very good figure, and might have lived higher if I pleased.

But in the middle of all this felicity a dreadful disaster befell me, which entirely unhinged all my affairs, and threw me back into the same state of life that I was in before; with this one happy exception, however, that whereas before I was poor, even to misery, now I was not only provided for, but very rich.

My gentleman had the name in Paris for a very rich man, and indeed he was so, though not so immensely rich as people imagined. But that which was fatal to him was that he generally carried a shagreen case in his pocket—especially when he went to court, or to the houses of any of the princes of the blood—in which he had jewels of very great value.

It happened one day that, being to go to Versailles to wait upon the Prince of ———, he came up into my chamber in the morning and laid out his jewel-case, because he was not going to show any jewels, but to get a foreign bill accepted, which he had received from Amsterdam. So, when he gave me the case, he said, "My dear, I think I need not carry this with me, because it may be I may not come back till night, and it is too much to venture." I returned, "Then, my dear, you shan't go," "Why?" says he. "Because, as they are too much for you, so you are too much for me to venture, and you shall not go, unless you will promise me not to stay so as to come back in the night."

"I hope there's no danger," said he, "seeing I have nothing about me of any value; and therefore, lest I should, take that too," says he, and gives me his gold watch and a rich diamond which he had in a ring and always wore on his finger.

"Well, but, my dear," says I, "you make me more uneasie now than before; for if you apprehend no danger, why do you use this caution? And if you apprehend there is danger, why do you go at all?"

"There is no danger," says he, "if I do not stay late, and I do not design to do so."

"Well, but promise me, then, that you won't," says I, "or else I cannot let you go."

"I won't indeed, my dear," says he, "unless I am obliged to it. I assure you I do not intend it; but if I should, I am not worth robbing now, for I have nothing about me, but about six pistoles in my little purse and that little ring," showing me a small diamond ring, worth about ten or twelve pistoles, which he put upon his finger, in the room of the rich one he usually wore.

I still pressed him not to stay late, and he said he would not. "But if I am kept late," says he, "beyond my expectation, I'll stay all night, and come next morning." This seemed a very good caution; but still my mind was very uneasy about him, and I told him so, and entreated him not to go. I told him I did not know what might be the reason, but that I had a strange terror upon my mind about his going, and that, if he did go, I was persuaded some harm would attend him. He smiled and returned, "Well, my dear, if it should be so, you are now richly provided for; all that I have here I give to you." And with that he takes up the casket or case. "Here," says he, "hold your hand; there is a good estate for you in this case; if anything happens to me, 'tis all your own. I give it you for yourself." And with that, he put the casket, the fine ring, and his gold watch all into my hands, and the key of his scrutore* besides, adding, "And in my scrutore there is some money; 'tis all your own."

I stared at him as if I was frighted, for I thought all his face looked like a death's-head; and then immediately I thought I perceived his head all bloody, and then his clothes looked bloody too, and immediately it all went off, and he looked as he really did. Immediately I fell a-crying, and hung about him. "My dear," said I, "I am frighted to death; you shall not go. Depend upon it, some mischief will befall you." I did not tell him how my vapourish fancy had represented him to me; that, I thought, was not proper. Besides, he would only have laughed at me and would have gone away with a jest about it. But I pressed him seriously not to go that day, or, if he did, to promise me to come home to Paris again by day light. He looked a little graver then than he did before, told me he was not apprehensive of the least danger, but if there was, he would either take care to come in the day or, as he had said before, would stay all night.

But all these promises came to nothing, for he was set upon in the open day and robbed by three men on horseback, masked, as he went; and one of them, who, it seems, rifled him while the rest stood to stop the coach, stabbed him into

---

* "scrutore." Escritoire, writing desk.

the body with a sword, so that he died immediately. He had a
footman behind the coach, who they knocked down with the
stock or butt-end of a carabine.* They were supposed to kill
him because of the disappointment they met with in not getting his case or casket of diamonds, which they knew he carried about him; and this was supposed because, after they
had killed him, they made the coachman drive out of the
road a long way over the heath, till they came to a convenient place, where they pulled him out of the coach and
searched his clothes more narrowly than they could do while
he was alive.

But they found nothing but his little ring, six pistoles, and
the value of about seven livres in small moneys.

This was a dreadful blow to me, though I cannot say I was
so surprised as I should otherwise have been, for all the while
he was gone my mind was oppressed with the weight of my
own thoughts, and I was as sure that I should never see him
any more that I think nothing could be like it. The impression was so strong that I think nothing could make so
deep a wound that was imaginary; and I was so dejected and
disconsolate that, when I received the news of his disaster,
there was no room for any extraordinary alteration in me. I
had cried all that day, eat nothing, and only waited, as I
might say, to receive the dismal news, which I had brought to
me about five o'clock in the afternoon.

I was in a strange country and, though I had a pretty many
acquaintances, had but very few friends that I could consult
on this occasion. All possible inquiry was made after the
rogues that had been thus barbarous, but nothing could be
heard of them; nor was it possible that the footman could
make any discovery of them by his description, for they
knocked him down immediately, so that he knew nothing of
what was done afterwards. The coachman was the only man
that could say anything, and all his account amounted to no
more than this, that one of them had soldier's clothes, but he
could not remember the particulars of his mounting, so as to
know what regiment he belonged to; and as to their faces,
that he could know nothing of, because they had all of them
masks on.

I had him buried as decently as the place would permit a
Protestant stranger to be buried, and made some of the

---

* "carabine." Carbine, a type of gun.

scruples and difficulties on that account easy by the help of money to a certain person, who went impudently to the curate of the parish St. Sulpitius, in Paris, and told him that the gentleman that was killed was a Catholic; that the thieves had taken from him a cross of gold, set with diamonds, worth six thousand livres; that his widow was a Catholic, and had sent by him sixty crowns to the church of ———, for masses to be said for the repose of his soul. Upon all which, though not one word of it was true, he was buried with all the ceremonies of the Roman Church.

I think I almost cried myself to death for him, for I abandoned myself to all the excesses of grief; and indeed I loved him to a degree inexpressible; and considering what kindness he had shown me at first, and how tenderly he had used me to the last, what could I do less?

Then the manner of his death was terrible and frightful to me, and, above all, the strange notices I had of it. I had never pretended to the second-sight, or anything of that kind, but certainly, if any one ever had such a thing, I had it at this time, for I saw him as plainly in all those terrible shapes as above; first, as a skeleton, not dead only, but rotten and wasted; secondly, as killed, and his face bloody; and, thirdly, his clothes bloody; and all within the space of one minute, or indeed of a very few moments.

These things amazed me, and I was a good while as one stupid. However, after some time I began to recover and look into my affairs. I had the satisfaction not to be left in distress, or in danger of poverty. On the contrary, besides what he had put into my hands fairly in his lifetime, which amounted to a very considerable value, I found above seven hundred pistoles in gold in his scrutore, of which he had given me the key; and I found foreign bills accepted for about twelve thousand livres. So that, in a word, I found myself possessed of almost ten thousand pounds sterling in a very few days after the disaster.

The first thing I did upon this occasion was to send a letter to my maid, as I still called her, Amy, wherein I gave her an account of my disaster, how my husband, as she called him (for I never called him so), was murdered; and as I did not know how his relations or his wife's friends might act upon that occasion, I ordered her to convey away all the plate, linen, and other things of value, and to secure them in a person's hands that I directed her to, and then to sell or dispose the furniture of the house, if she could, and so, without acquainting anybody with the reason of her going, withdraw; sending notice to his head-manager at London that the house was quitted by the tenant, and they might come and take possession of it for the executors. Amy was so dexterous, and did her work so nimbly, that she gutted the house, and sent the key to the said manager, almost as soon as he had notice of the misfortune that befell their master.

Upon their receiving the surprising news of his death, the head-manager came over to Paris, and came to the house. I made no scruple of calling myself Madam ———, the widow of Monsieur ———, the English jeweller. And as I spoke French naturally, I did not let him know but that I was his wife, married in France, and that I had not heard that he had any wife in England, but pretended to be surprised, and exclaim against him for so base an action; and that I had good friends in Poitou, where I was born, who would take care to have justice done me in England out of his estate.

I should have observed that, as soon as the news was public of a man being murdered, and that he was a jeweller, fame did me the favour as to publish presently that he was robbed of his casket of jewels, which he always carried about him. I confirmed this, among my daily lamentations for his disaster, and added that he had with him a fine diamond ring, which he was known to wear frequently about him, valued at one hundred pistoles, a gold watch, and a great quantity of diamonds of inestimable value in his casket, which jewels he was carrying to the Prince of ———, to show some of them to him; and the prince owned that he had spoken to him to bring some such jewels, to let him see them. But I sorely repented this part afterward, as you shall hear.

This rumour put an end to all inquiry after his jewels, his ring, or his watch; and as for the seven hundred pistoles, that I secured. For the bills which were in hand, I owned I had them, but that, as I said I brought my husband thirty thousand livres portion, I claimed the said bills, which came to not above twelve thousand livres, for my *amende;** and this, with the plate and the household stuff, was the principal of all his estate which they could come at. As to the foreign bill which he was going to Versailles to get accepted, it was really lost with him; but his manager, who had remitted the bill to

* *"amende."* Compensation.

him, by way of Amsterdam, bringing over the second bill, the money was saved, as they called it, which would otherwise have been also gone; the thieves who robbed and murdered him were, to be sure, afraid to send anybody to get the bill accepted, for that would undoubtedly have discovered them.

By this time my maid Amy was arrived, and she gave me an account of her management, and how she had secured everything, and that she had quitted the house and sent the key to the head-manager of his business, and let me know how much she had made of everything, very punctually and honestly.

I should have observed, in the account of his dwelling with me so long at ———, that he never passed for anything there but a lodger in the house; and though he was landlord, that did not alter the case. So that at his death, Amy coming to quit the house and give them the key, there was no affinity between that and the case of their master who was newly killed.

I got good advice at Paris from an eminent lawyer, a counsellor of the Parliament there, and laying my case before him, he directed me to make a process in dower upon the estate, for making good my new fortune upon matrimony, which accordingly I did. And, upon the whole, the manager went back to England well satisfied that he had gotten the unaccepted bill of exchange, which was for 2500 pounds, with some other things, which together amounted to 17,000 livres; and thus I got rid of him.

I was visited with great civility on this sad occasion of the loss of my husband, as they thought him, by a great many ladies of quality. And the Prince of ———, to whom it was reported he was carrying the jewels, sent his gentleman with a very handsome compliment of condolence to me; and his gentleman, whether with or without order, hinted as if his Highness did intend to have visited me himself, but that some accident, which he made a long story of, had prevented him.

By the concourse of ladies and others that thus came to visit me, I began to be much known; and as I did not forget to set myself out with all possible advantage, considering the dress of a widow, which in those days was a most frightful thing; I say, as I did thus from my own vanity, for I was not ignorant that I was very handsome; I say, on this account I was soon made very public, and was known by the name of *La Belle Veue de Poitou*, or the pretty widow of Poitou. As I was very well pleased to see myself thus handsomely used in my affliction, it soon dried up all my tears; and though I appeared as a widow, yet, as we say in England, it was of a widow comforted. I took care to let the ladies see that I knew how to receive them; that I was not at a loss how to behave to any of them; and, in short, I began to be very popular there. But I had an occasion afterwards which made me decline that kind of management, as you shall hear presently.

About four days after I had received the compliments of condolence from the Prince ————, the same gentleman he had sent before came to tell me that his Highness was coming to give me a visit. I was indeed surprised at that, and perfectly at a loss how to behave. However, as there was no remedy, I prepared to receive him as well as I could. It was not many minutes after but he was at the door, and came in, introduced by his own gentleman, as above, and after by my woman Amy.

He treated me with abundance of civility, and condoled handsomely the loss of my husband, and likewise the manner of it. He told me he understood he was coming to Versailles to himself, to show him some jewels; that it was true that he had discoursed with him about jewels, but could not imagine how any villains should hear of his coming at that time with them; that he had not ordered him to attend with them at Versailles, but told him that he would come to Paris by such a day, so that he was no way accessory to the disaster. I told him gravely I knew very well that all his Highness had said of that part was true; that these villains knew his profession, and knew, no doubt, that he always carried a casket of jewels about him, and that he always wore a diamond ring on his finger worth a hundred pistoles, which report had magnified to five hundred; and that, if he had been going to any other place, it would have been the same thing. After this, his Highness rose up to go, and told me he had resolved, however, to make me some reparation; and with these words put a silk purse into my hand with a hundred pistoles, and told me he would make me a farther compliment of a small pension, which his gentleman would inform me of.

You may be sure I behaved with a due sense of so much goodness, and offered to kneel to kiss his hand; but he took me up and saluted me, and sat down again (though before he made as if he was going away), making me sit down by him.

He then began to talk with me more familiarly; told me he hoped I was not left in bad circumstances; that Mr. ————

was reputed to be very rich, and that he had gained lately great sums by some jewels, and he hoped, he said, that I had still a fortune agreeable to the condition I had lived in before.

I replied, with some tears, which, I confess, were a little forced, that I believed, if Mr. ———— had lived, we should have been out of danger of want, but that it was impossible to estimate the loss which I had sustained, besides that of the life of my husband; that, by the opinion of those that knew something of his affairs, and of what value the jewels were which he intended to have shown to his Highness, he could not have less about him than the value of a hundred thousand livres; that it was a fatal blow to me, and to his whole family, especially that they should be lost in such a manner.

His Highness returned, with an air of concern, that he was very sorry for it; but he hoped, if I settled in Paris, I might find ways to restore my fortune; at the same time he complimented me upon my being very handsome, as he was pleased to call it, and that I could not fail of admirers. I stood up and humbly thanked his Highness, but told him I had no expectations of that kind; that I thought I should be obliged to go over to England, to look after my husband's effects there, which, I was told, were considerable, but that I did not know what justice a poor stranger would get among them; and as for Paris, my fortune being so impaired, I saw nothing before me but to go back to Poitou to my friends, where some of my relations, I hoped, might do something for me, and added that one of my brothers was an abbot at ————, near Poitiers.

He stood up and, taking me by the hand, led me to a large looking-glass, which made up the pier in the front of the parlour. "Look there, madam," said he; "is it fit that face" (pointing to my figure in the glass) "should go back to Poitou? No, madam," says he, "stay and make some gentleman of quality happy, that may, in return, make you forget all your sorrows." And with that he took me in his arms and, kissing me twice, told me he would see me again, but with less ceremony.

Some little time after this, but the same day, his gentleman came to me again and, with great ceremony and respect, delivered me a black box tied with a scarlet riband and sealed with a noble coat of arms, which, I suppose, was the prince's. There was in it a grant from his Highness, or an assignment —I know not which to call it—with a warrant to his banker to pay me two thousand livres a year during my stay in Paris, as the widow of Monsieur ———, the jeweller, mentioning the horrid murder of my late husband as the occasion of it, as above.

I received it with great submission, and expressions of being infinitely obliged to his master, and of my showing myself on all occasions his Highness's most obedient servant; and after giving my most humble duty to his Highness, with the utmost acknowledgments of the obligation, &c., I went to a little cabinet and, taking out some money, which made a little sound in taking it out, offered to give him five pistoles.

He drew back, but with the greatest respect, and told me he humbly thanked me, but that he durst not take a farthing; that his Highness would take it so ill of him, he was sure he would never see his face more; but that he would not fail to acquaint his Highness what respect I had offered; and added, "I assure you, madam, you are more in the good graces of my master, the Prince of ———, than you are aware of; and I believe you will hear more of him."

Now I began to understand him, and resolved, if his Highness did come again, he should see me under no disadvantages, if I could help it. I told him, if his Highness did me the honour to see me again, I hoped he would not let me be so surprised as I was before; that I would be glad to have some little notice of it, and would be obliged to him if he would procure it me. He told me he was very sure that when his Highness intended to visit me, he should be sent before to give me notice of it, and that he would give me as much warning of it as possible.

He came several times after this on the same errand, that is, about the settlement, the grant requiring several things yet to be done for making it payable without going every time to the prince again for a fresh warrant. The particulars of this part I did not understand; but as soon as it was finished, which was above two months, the gentleman came one afternoon and said his Highness designed to visit me in the evening but desired to be admitted without ceremony.

I prepared not my rooms only, but myself; and when he came in there was nobody appeared in the house but his gentleman and my maid Amy; and of her I bid the gentleman acquaint his Highness that she was an Englishwoman, that she did not understand a word of French, and that she was one also that might be trusted.

When he came into my room, I fell down at his feet before he could come to salute me, and with words that I had prepared, full of duty and respect, thanked him for his bounty and goodness to a poor, desolate woman, oppressed under the weight of so terrible a disaster; and refused to rise till he would allow me the honour to kiss his hand.

"*Levez vous donc,*"* says the prince, taking me in his arms. "I design more favours for you than this trifle", and going on, he added, "You shall for the future find a friend where you did not look for it, and I resolve to let you see how kind I can be to one who is to me the most agreeable creature on earth."

I was dressed in a kind of half-mourning,† had turned off my weeds, and my head, though I had yet no ribands or lace, was so dressed as failed not to set me out with advantage enough, for I began to understand his meaning; and the prince professed I was the most beautiful creature on earth. "And where have I lived," says he, "and how ill have I been served, that I should never till now be showed the finest woman in France?"

This was the way in all the world the most likely to break in upon my virtue, if I had been mistress of any; for I was now become the vainest creature upon earth, and particularly of my beauty, which as other people admired, so I became every day more foolishly in love with myself than before.

He said some very kind things to me after this, and sat down with me for an hour or more, when, getting up and calling his gentleman by his name, he threw open the door. "*Au boire,*"†† says he. Upon which his gentleman immediately brought up a little table covered with a fine damask cloth, the table no bigger than he could bring in his two hands, but upon it was set two decanters, one of champagne and the other of water, six silver plates, and a service of fine sweetmeats in fine china dishes, on a set of rings standing up about twenty inches high, one above another. Below was three roasted partridges and a quail. As soon as his gentleman had set it all down, he ordered him to withdraw. "Now," says the prince, "I intend to sup with you."

---

* *Levez vous donc.*" Come, get up.
† "half-mourning." For some time after their husbands' death, widows muffled themselves in heavy black weeds and wore no ornaments. By gradual stages, they resumed normal dress.
†† "*Au boire.*" Some drink.

When he sent away his gentleman, I stood up and offered to wait on his Highness while he eat; but he positively refused, and told me, "No; to-morrow you shall be the widow of Monsieur ————, the jeweller, but to-night you shall be my mistress; therefore sit here," says he, "and eat with me, or I will get up and serve."

I would then have called up my woman, Amy, but I thought that would not be proper neither; so I made my excuse, that since his Highness would not let his own servant wait, I would not presume to let my woman come up; but if he would please to let me wait, it would be my honour to fill his Highness's wine. But as before, he would by no means allow me; so we sat and eat together.

"Now, madam," says the prince, "give me leave to lay aside my character; let us talk together with the freedom of equals. My quality sets me at a distance from you, and makes you ceremonious. Your beauty exalts you to more than an equality. I must, then, treat you as lovers do their mistresses, but I cannot speak the language; 'tis enough to tell you how agreeable you are to me, how I am surprised at your beauty, and resolve to make you happy, and to be happy with you."

I knew not what to say to him a good while, but blushed and, looking up towards him, said I was already made happy in the favour of a person of such rank, and had nothing to ask of his Highness but that he would believe me infinitely obliged.

After he had eaten, he poured the sweet-meats into my lap; and the wine being out, he called his gentleman again to take away the table, who, at first, only took the cloth and the remains of what was to eat away; and, laying another cloth, set the table on one side of the room with a noble service of plate upon it, worth at least two hundred pistoles. Then, having set the two decanters again upon the table, filled as before, he withdrew; for I found the fellow understood his business very well, and his lord's business too.

About half an hour after, the prince told me that I offered to wait a little before, that if I would now take the trouble, he would give me leave to give him some wine. So I went to the table, filled a glass of wine, and brought it to him on a fine salver, which the glasses stood on, and brought the bottle or decanter for water in my other hand, to mix as he thought fit.

He smiled and bid me look on that salver, which I did, and admired it much, for it was a very fine one indeed. "You may see," says he, "I resolve to have more of your company, for my servant shall leave you that plate for my use." I told him I believed his Highness would not take it ill that I was not furnished fit to entertain a person of his rank, and that I would take great care of it, and value myself infinitely upon the honour of his Highness's visit.

It now began to grow late, and he began to take notice of it. "But," says he, "I cannot leave you; have you not a spare lodging for one night?" I told him I had but a homely lodging to entertain such a guest. He said something exceeding kind on that head, but not fit to repeat, adding that my company would make him amends.

About midnight he sent his gentleman of an errand, after telling him aloud that he intended to stay here all night. In a little time his gentleman brought him a night-gown, slippers, two caps, a neckcloth, and shirt, which he gave me to carry into his chamber, and sent his man home; and then, turning to me, said I should do him the honour to be his chamberlain of the household, and his dresser also. I smiled and told him I would do myself the honour to wait on him upon all occasions.

About one in the morning, while his gentleman was yet with him, I begged leave to withdraw, supposing he would go to bed; but he took the hint, and said, "I'm not going to bed yet; pray let me see you again."

I took this time to undress me, and to come in a new dress, which was, in a manner, *une dishabille,** but so fine, and all about me so clean and so agreeable, that he seemed surprised. "I thought," says he, "you could not have dressed to more advantage than you had done before; but now," says he, "you charm me a thousand times more if that be possible."

"It is only a loose habit, my lord," said I, "that I may the better wait on your Highness." He pulls me to him. "You are perfectly obliging," says he; and, sitting on the bedside, says he, "Now you shall be a princess, and know what it is to oblige the gratefullest man alive." And with that he took me in his arms. . . . I can go no farther in the particulars of what passed at that time, but it ended in this, that, in short, I lay with him all night.

I have given you the whole detail of this story to lay it down as a black scheme of the way how unhappy women are

---

* *"dishabille."* Partial dress, such as a nightgown.

ruined by great men; for, though poverty and want is an irresistible temptation to the poor, vanity and great things are as
irresistible to others. To be courted by a prince, and by a
prince who was first a benefactor, then an admirer; to be
called handsome, the finest woman in France, and to be
treated as a woman fit for the bed of a prince—these are
things a woman must have no vanity in her, nay, no corruption in her, that is not overcome by it; and my case was such
that, as before, I had enough of both.

I had now no poverty attending me; on the contrary, I was
mistress of ten thousand pounds before the prince did anything for me. Had I been mistress of my resolution, had I
been less obliging and rejected the first attack, all had been
safe; but my virtue was lost before, and the devil, who had
found the way to break in upon me by one temptation, easily
mastered me now by another; and I gave myself up to a person who, though a man of high dignity, was yet the most
tempting and obliging that ever I met with in my life.

I had the same particular to insist upon here with the
prince that I had with my gentleman before. I hesitated much
at consenting at first asking, but the prince told me princes
did not court like other men; that they brought more powerful arguments; and he very prettily added that they were
sooner repulsed than other men, and ought to be sooner com-
plied with; intimating, though very genteelly, that after a
woman had positively refused him once, he could not, like
other men, wait with importunities and stratagems, and laying
long sieges; but as such men as he stormed warmly, so, if repulsed, they made no second attacks. And, indeed, it was but
reasonable; for as it was below their rank to be long battering
a woman's constancy, so they ran greater hazards in being
exposed in their amours than other men did.

I took this for a satisfactory answer, and told his Highness
that I had the same thoughts in respect to the manner of his
attacks; for that his person and his arguments were irresistible; that a person of his rank and a munificence so un-
bounded could not be withstood; that no virtue was proof
against him, except such as was able, too, to suffer martyr-
dom; that I thought it impossible I could be overcome, but
that now I found it was impossible I should not be overcome;
that so much goodness, joined with so much greatness, would
have conquered a saint; and that I confessed he had the vic-

tory over me, by a merit infinitely superior to the conquest he had made.

He made me a most obliging answer; told me abundance of fine things, which still flattered my vanity, till at last I began to have pride enough to believe him, and fancied myself a fit mistress for a prince.

As I had thus given the prince the last favour, and he had all the freedom with me that it was possible for me to grant, so he gave me leave to use as much freedom with him another way, and that was to have every thing of him I thought fit to command; and yet I did not ask of him with an air of avarice, as if I was greedily making a penny of him, but I managed him with such art that he generally anticipated my demands. He only requested of me that I would not think of taking another house, as I had intimated to his Highness that I intended, not thinking it good enough to receive his visits in; but he said my house was the most convenient that could possibly be found in all Paris for an amour, especially for him, having a way out into three streets, and not overlooked by any neighbours, so that he could pass and repass without observation; for one of the back-ways opened into a narrow dark alley, which alley was a thoroughfare or passage out of one street into another; and any person that went in or out by the door had no more to do but to see that there was nobody following him in the alley before he went in at the door. This request, I knew, was reasonable, and therefore I assured him I would not change my dwelling, seeing his Highness did not think it too mean for me to receive him in.

He also desired me that I would not take any more servants or set up any equipage, at least for the present. For that it would then be immediately concluded I had been left very rich, and then I should be thronged with the impertinence of admirers, who would be attracted by the money, as well as by the beauty of a young widow, and he should be frequently interrupted in his visits; or that the world would conclude I was maintained by somebody, and would be indefatigable to find out the person; so that he should have spies peeping at him every time he went out or in, which it would be impossible to disappoint; and that he should presently have it talked over all the toilets in Paris that the Prince de ——— had got the jeweller's widow for a mistress.

This was too just to oppose, and I made no scruple to tell his Highness that, since he had stooped so low as to make me his own, he ought to have all the satisfaction in the world that I was all his own; that I would take all the measures he should please to direct me to avoid the impertinent attacks of others; and that, if he thought fit, I would be wholly within-doors, and have it given out that I was obliged to go to England to solicit my affairs there, after my husband's misfortune, and that I was not expected there again for at least a year or two. This he liked very well; only he said that he would by no means have me confined; that it would injure my health, and that I should then take a country-house in some village, a good way off of the city, where it should not be known who I was, and that he should be there sometimes to divert me.

I made no scruple of the confinement, and told his Highness no place could be a confinement where I had such a visitor, and so I put off the country-house, which would have been to remove myself farther from him and have less of his company; so I made the house be, as it were, shut up. Amy, indeed, appeared, and when any of the neighbours and servants enquired, she answered, in broken French, that I was gone to England to look after my affairs, which presently went current through the streets about us. For you are to note that the people of Paris, especially the women, are the most busy and impertinent inquirers into the conduct of their neighbours, especially that of a single woman, that are in the world, though there are no greater intriguers in the universe than themselves. And perhaps that may be the reason of it, for it is an old but a sure rule that

When deep intrigues are close and shy,
The guilty are the first that spy.

Thus his Highness had the most easy, and yet the most undiscoverable, access to me imaginable, and he seldom failed to come two or three nights in a week, and sometimes stayed two or three nights together. Once he told me he was resolved I should be weary of his company, and that he would learn to know what it was to be a prisoner. So he gave out among his servants that he was gone to ———, where he often went a-hunting, and that he should not return under a fortnight; and that fortnight he stayed wholly with me and never went out of my doors.

Never woman in such a station lived a fortnight in so complete a fulness of human delight; for to have the entire possession of one of the most accomplished princes in the world, and of the politest, best-bred man; to converse with him all day, and, as he professed, charm him all night, what could be more inexpressibly pleasing, and especially to a woman of a vast deal of pride, as I was?

To finish the felicity of this part, I must not forget that the devil had played a new game with me, and prevailed with me to satisfy myself with this amour, as a lawful thing; that a prince of such grandeur and majesty, so infinitely superior to me, and one who had made such an introduction by an unparalleled bounty, I could not resist; and, therefore, that it was very lawful for me to do it, being at that time perfectly single, and unengaged to any other man, as I was, most certainly, by the unaccountable absence of my first husband, and the murder of my gentleman who went for my second.

It cannot be doubted but that I was the easier to persuade myself of the truth of such a doctrine as this when it was so much for my ease and for the repose of my mind to have it be so.

> In things we wish, 'tis easy to deceive;
> What we would have, we willingly believe.

Besides, I had no casuists to resolve this doubt; the same devil that put this into my head bade me go to any of the Romish clergy and, under the pretence of confession, state the case exactly, and I should see they would either resolve it to be no sin at all or absolve me upon the easiest penance. This I had a strong inclination to try, but I know not what scruple put me off of it, for I could never bring myself to like having to do with those priests. And though it was strange that I, who had thus prostituted my chastity and given up all sense of virtue in two such particular cases, living a life of open adultery, should scruple anything; yet so it was. I argued with myself that I could not be a cheat in anything that was esteemed sacred; that I could not be of one opinion, and then pretend myself to be of another; nor could I go to confession, who knew nothing of the manner of it, and should betray myself to the priest to be a Huguenot, and then might come into trouble; but, in short, though I was a whore, yet I was a Protestant whore, and could not act as if I was popish, upon any account whatsoever.

But, I say, I satisfied myself with the surprising occasion that as it was all irresistible, so it was all lawful; for that Heaven would not suffer us to be punished for that which it was not possible for us to avoid. And with these absurdities I kept conscience from giving me any considerable disturbance in all this matter; and I was perfectly easy as to the lawfulness of it as if I had been married to the prince and had had no other husband; so possible is it for us to roll ourselves up in wickedness, till we grow invulnerable by conscience; and that sentinel, once dozed, sleeps fast, not to be awakened while the tide of pleasure continues to flow, or till something dark and dreadful brings us to ourselves again.

I have, I confess, wondered at the stupidity that my intellectual part was under all that while; what lethargic fumes dozed the soul; and how it was possible that I, who in the case before, where the temptation was many ways more forcible and the arguments stronger and more irresistible, was yet under a continued inquietude on account of the wicked life I led, could now live in the most profound tranquillity and with an uninterrupted peace, nay, even rising up to satisfaction and joy, and yet in a more palpable state of adultery than before; for before, my gentleman, who called me wife, had the pretence of his wife being parted from him, refusing to do the duty of her office as a wife to him. As for me, my circumstances were the same; but as for the prince, as he had a fine and extraordinary lady, or princess, of his own, so he had had two or three mistresses more besides me, and made no scruple of it at all.

However, I say, as to my own part, I enjoyed myself in perfect tranquility; and as the prince was the only deity I worshipped, so I was really his idol; and however it was with his princess, I assure you his other mistresses found a sensible difference, and though they could never find me out, yet I had good intelligence that they guessed very well that their lord had got some new favourite that robbed them of his company, and, perhaps, of some of his usual bounty too. And now I must mention the sacrifices he made to his idol, and they were not a few, I assure you.

As he loved like a prince, so he rewarded like a prince; for though he declined my making a figure, as above, he let me see that he was above doing it for the saving the expense of it, and so he told me, and that he would make it up in other things. First of all, he sent me a toilet,* with all the appurtenances of silver, even so much as the frame of the table; and then for the house, he gave me the table, or sideboard of plate, I mentioned above, with all things belonging to it of massy silver; so that, in short, I could not for my life study to ask him for anything of plate which I had not.

He could, then, accommodate me in nothing more but jewels and clothes, or money for clothes. He sent his gentleman to the mercer's and bought me a suit, or whole piece, of the finest brocaded silk, figured with gold, and another with silver, and another of crimson; so that I had three suits of clothes such as the Queen of France would not have disdained to have worn at that time. Yet I went out nowhere; but as those were for me to put on when I went out of mourning, I dressed myself in them, one after another, always when his Highness came to see me.

I had no less than five several morning dresses besides these, so that I need never be seen twice in the same dress; to these he added several parcels of fine linen and of lace, so much that I had no room to ask for more or indeed, for so much.

I took the liberty once, in our freedoms, to tell him he was too bountiful, and that I was too chargeable to him for a mistress, and that I would be his faithful servant at less expense to him; and that he not only left me no room to ask him for anything, but that he supplied me with such a profusion of good things that I scarce could wear them, or use them, unless I kept a great equipage, which, he knew, was no way convenient for him or for me. He smiled and took me in his arms, and told me he was resolved, while I was his, I should never be able to ask him for anything, but that he would be daily asking new favours of me.

After we were up (for this conference was in bed), he desired I would dress me in the best suit of clothes I had. It was a day or two after the three suits were made and brought home. I told him, if he pleased, I would rather dress me in that suit which I knew he liked best. He asked me how I could know which he would like best before he had seen them. I told him I would presume for once to guess at his fancy by my own; so I went away and dressed me in the second suit, brocaded with silver, and returned in full dress, with

* "toilet." Dressing table.

a suit of lace upon my head, which would have been worth
in England two hundred pounds sterling; and I was every
way set out as well as Amy could dress me, who was a very
genteel dresser too. In this figure I came to him out of my
dressing-room, which opened with folding-doors into his bed-
chamber.

He sat as one astonished, a good while, looking at me,
without speaking a word, till I came quite up to him, kneeled
on one knee to him, and almost, whether he would or no,
kissed his hand. He took me up, and stood up himself, but
was surprised when, taking me in his arms, he perceived tears
to run down my cheeks. "My dear," says he aloud, "what
mean these tears?" "My lord," said I, after some little check,
for I could not speak presently, "I beseech you to believe me,
they are not tears of sorrow, but tears of joy. It is impossible
for me to see myself snatched from the misery I was fallen
into, and at once to be in the arms of a prince of such goodness, such immense bounty, and be treated in such a manner;
'tis not possible, my lord," said I, "to contain the satisfaction
of it; and it will break out in an excess in some measure proportioned to your immense bounty, and to the affection
which your Highness treats me with, who am so infinitely below you."

It would look a little too much like a romance here to repeat all the kind things he said to me on that occasion, but I
can't omit one passage. As he saw the tears drop down my
cheek, he pulls out a fine cambric handkerchief and was going to wipe the tears off, but checked his hand, as if he was
afraid to deface something; I say, he checked his hand and
tossed the handkerchief to me, to do it myself. I took the hint
immediately, and with a kind of pleasant disdain, "How, my
lord," said I, "have you kissed me so often, and don't you
know whether I am painted or not? Pray let your Highness
satisfy yourself that you have no cheats put upon you; for
once let me be vain enough to say I have not deceived you
with false colours." With this I put a handkerchief into his
hand, and, taking his hand into mine, I made him wipe my
face so hard that he was unwilling to do it, for fear of hurting me.

He appeared surprised more than ever, and swore, which
was the first time that I had heard him swear from my first
knowing him, that he could not have believed there was any
such skin without paint in the world. "Well, my lord," said I,

"your Highness shall have a farther demonstration than this, as to that which you are pleased to accept for beauty, that it is the mere work of nature." And with that I stepped to the door and rung a little bell for my woman, Amy, and bade her bring me a cup-full of hot water, which she did. And when it was come, I desired his Highness to feel if it was warm, which he did, and I immediately washed my face all over with it before him. This was, indeed, more than satisfaction, that is to say, than believing, for it was an undeniable demonstration, and he kissed my cheeks and breasts a thousand times, with expressions of the greatest surprise imaginable.

Nor was I a very indifferent figure as to shape; though I had had two children by my gentleman, and six by my true husband, I say I was no despisable shape; and my prince (I must be allowed the vanity to call him so) was taking his view of me as I walked from one end of the room to the other. At last he leads me to the darkest part of the room and, standing behind me, bade me hold up my head, when, putting both his hands round my neck, as if he was spanning my neck to see how small it was, for it was long and small, he held my neck so long and so hard in his hand that I complained he hurt me a little. What he did it for I knew not, nor had I the least suspicion but that he was spanning my neck; but when I said he hurt me, he seemed to let go, and in half a minute more led me to a pier-glass, and behold I saw my neck clasped with a fine necklace of diamonds; whereas I felt no more what he was doing than if he had really done nothing at all, nor did I suspect it in the least. If I had an ounce of blood in me that did not fly up into my face, neck, and breasts, it must be from some interruption in the vessels. I was all on fire with the sight and began to wonder what it was that was coming to me.

However, to let him see that I was not unqualified to receive benefits, I turned about. "My lord," says I, "your Highness is resolved to conquer, by your bounty, the very gratitude of your servants; you will leave no room for anything but thanks, and make those thanks useless too, by their bearing no proportion to the occasion."

"I love, child," says he, "to see everything suitable. A fine gown and petticoat; a fine laced head, a fine face and neck, and no necklace, would not have made the object perfect. But why that blush, my dear?" says the prince. "My lord," said I, "all your gifts call for blushes, but, above all, I blush to receive what I am so ill able to merit, and may become so ill also."

Thus far I am standing mark of the weakness of great men in their vice, that value not squandering away immense wealth upon the most worthless creatures; or, to sum it up in a word, they raise the value of the object which they pretend to pitch upon by their fancy; I say, raise the value of it at their own expense; give vast presents for a ruinous favor, which is so far from being equal to the price that nothing will at last prove more absurd than the cost men are at to purchase their own destruction.

I could not, in the height of all this fine doings—I say, I could not be without some just reflection, though conscience was, as I said, dumb, as to any disturbance it gave me in my wickedness. My vanity was fed up to such a height that I had no room to give way to such reflections.

But I could not but sometimes look back with astonishment at the folly of men of quality, who, immense in their bounty as in their wealth, give to a profusion and without bounds to the most scandalous of our sex, for granting them the liberty of abusing themselves and ruining both.

I, that knew what this carcase of mine had been but a few years before; how overwhelmed with grief, drowned in tears, frighted with the prospect of beggary, and surrounded with rags and fatherless children; that was pawning and selling the rags that covered me for a dinner, and sat on the ground despairing of help and expecting to be starved, till my children were snatched from me to be kept by the parish; I, that was after this a whore for bread, and, abandoning conscience and virtue, lived with another woman's husband; I, that was despised by all my relations, and my husband's too; I, that was left so entirely desolate, friendless, and helpless that I knew not how to get the least help to keep me from starving—that I should be caressed by a prince, for the honour of having the scandalous use of my prostituted body, common before to his inferiors, and perhaps would not have denied one of his footmen but a little while before, if I could have got my bread by it.

I say, I could not but reflect upon the brutality and blindness of mankind; that because nature had given me a good skin and some agreeable features, should suffer that

beauty to be such a bait to appetite as to do such sordid, unaccountable things to obtain the possession of it.

It is for this reason that I have so largely set down the particulars of the caresses I was treated with by the jeweller, and
also by this prince. Not to make the story an incentive to the
vice, which I am now such a sorrowful penitent for being
guilty of (God forbid any should make so vile a use of so
good a design), but to draw the just picture of a man en-
slaved to the rage of his vicious appetite; how he defaces the
image of God in his soul, dethrones his reason, causes conscience to abdicate the possession, and exalts sense into the
vacant throne; how he deposes the man and exalts the brute.

Oh! could we hear now the reproaches this great man afterwards loaded himself with when he grew weary of this admired creature, and became sick of his vice, how profitable
would the report of them be to the reader of this story! But
had he himself also known the dirty history of my actings
upon the stage of life that little time I had been in the world,
how much more severe would those reproaches have been
upon himself. But I shall come to this again.

I lived in this gay sort of retirement almost three years, in
which time no amour of such a kind, sure, was ever carried
up so high. The prince knew no bounds to his munificence;
he could give me nothing, either for my wearing, or using, or
eating, or drinking, more than he had done from the beginning.

His presents were after that in gold, and very frequent and
large; often a hundred pistoles, never less than fifty at a time.
And I must do myself the justice that I seemed rather backward to receive than craving and encroaching. Not that I had
not an avaricious temper, nor was it that I did not foresee
that this was my harvest, in which I was to gather up, and
that it would not last long; but it was that really his bounty
always anticipated my expectations, and even my wishes; and
he gave me money so fast that he rather poured it in upon
me than left me room to ask it; so that before I could spend
fifty pistoles, I had always a hundred to make it up.

After I had been near a year and half in his arms as
above, or thereabouts, I proved with child. I did not take any
notice of it to him till I was satisfied that I was not deceived;
when one morning early, when we were in bed together, I said
to him, "My lord, I doubt your Highness never gives yourself
leave to think what the case should be if I should have the

honour to be with child by you." "Why, my dear," says he, "we are able to keep it if such a thing should happen; I hope you are not concerned about that." "No, my lord," said I, "I should think myself very happy if I could bring your Highness a son; I should hope to see him a lieutenant-general of the king's armies by the interest of his father, and by his own merit."

"Assure yourself, child," says he, "if it should be so, I will not refuse owning him for my son, though it be, as they call it, a natural son; and shall never slight or neglect him, for the sake of his mother." Then he began to importune me to know if it was so, but I positively denied it so long, till at last I was able to give him the satisfaction of knowing it himself by the motion of the child within me.

He professed himself overjoyed at the discovery, but told me that now it was absolutely necessary for me to quit the confinement which, he said, I had suffered for his sake, and to take a house somewhere in the country, in order for health as well as for privacy, against my lying-in. This was quite out of my way; but the prince, who was a man of pleasure, had, it seems, several retreats of this kind, which he had made use of, I suppose, upon like occasions. And so, leaving it, as it were, to his gentleman, he provided a very convenient house, about four miles south of Paris, at the village of ————, where I had very agreeable lodgings, good gardens, and all things very easy to my content. But one thing did not please me at all, viz., that an old woman was provided, and put into the house to furnish everything necessary to my lying-in, and to assist at my travail.

I did not like this old woman at all. She looked so like a spy upon me, or (as sometimes I was frighted to imagine) like one set privately to dispatch me out of the world, as might best suit with the circumstance of my lying-in. And when his Highness came the next time to see me, which was not many days, I expostulated a little on the subject of the old woman; and by the management of my tongue, as well as by the strength of reasoning, I convinced him that it would not be at all convenient; that it would be the greater risk on his side and that first or last it would certainly expose him and me also. I assured him that my servant, being an English-woman, never knew to that hour who his Highness was; that I always called him the Count de Clerac, and that she knew nothing else of him, nor ever should; that if he would give me leave to choose proper persons for my use, it should be so ordered that not one of them should know who he was, or perhaps ever see his face; and that, for the reality of the child that should be born, his Highness, who had alone been at the first of it, should, if he pleased, be present in the room all the time, so that he would need no witnesses on that account.

This discourse fully satisfied him, so that he ordered his gentleman to dismiss the old woman the same day; and without any difficulty I sent my maid Amy to Calais, and thence to Dover, where she got an English midwife and an English nurse to come over on purpose to attend an English lady of quality, as they styled me, for four months certain. The midwife, Amy had agreed to pay a hundred guineas to, and bear her charges to Paris, and back again to Dover. The poor woman that was to be my nurse had twenty pounds, and the same terms for charges as the other.

I was very easy when Amy returned, and the more because she brought with her the midwife a good motherly sort of woman, who was to be her assistant, and would be very helpful on occasion; and bespoke a man-midwife at Paris too, if there should be any necessity for his help. Having thus made provision for every thing, the Count, for so we all called him in public, came as often to see me as I could expect, and continued exceeding kind, as he had always been. One day, conversing together upon the subject of my being with child, I told him how all things were in order, but that I had a strange apprehension that I should die with that child. He smiled. "So all the ladies say, my dear," says he, "when they are with child." "Well, however, my lord," said I, "it is but just that care should be taken that what you have bestowed in your excess of bounty upon me should not be lost." And upon this I pulled a paper out of my bosom, folded up but not sealed, and I read it to him, wherein I had left order that all the plate and jewels and fine furniture which his Highness had given me should be restored to him by my woman, and the keys be immediately delivered to his gentleman, in case of disaster.

Then I recommended my woman, Amy, to his favour for a hundred pistoles, on condition she gave the keys up as above to his gentleman, and his gentleman's receipt for them. When he saw this, "My dear child," said he, and took me in his arms, "what! have you been making your will and disposing your effects? Pray, who do you make your universal heir?" "So far as to do justice to your Highness, in case of mortality, I have, my lord," said I, "and who should I dispose the valuable things to, which I have had from your hand as pledges of your favour and testimonies of your bounty, but to the giver of them? If the child should live, your Highness will, I don't question, act like yourself in that part, and I shall have the utmost satisfaction that it will be well used by your direction."

I could see he took this very well. "I have forsaken all the ladies in Paris," says he, "for you, and I have lived every day since I knew you to see that you know how to merit all that a man of honour can do for you. Be easy, child; I hope you shall not die, and all you have is your own, to do what with it you please."

I was then within about two months of my time, and that soon wore off. When I found my time was come, it fell out very happily that he was in the house, and I entreated he would continue a few hours in the house, which he agreed to. They called his Highness to come into the room, if he pleased, as I had offered and as I desired him; and I sent word I would make as few cries as possible to prevent disturbing him. He came into the room once, and called to me to be of good courage, it would soon be over, and then he withdrew again; and in about half an hour more Amy carried him the news that I was delivered, and had brought him a charming boy. He gave her ten pistoles for her news, stayed till they had adjusted things about me, and then came into the room again, cheered me and spoke kindly to me, and looked on the child, then withdrew, and came again the next day to visit me.

Since this, and when I have looked back upon these things with eyes unpossessed with crime, when the wicked part has appeared in its clearer light and I have seen it in its own natural colours, when no more blinded with the glittering appearances which at that time deluded me, and as in like cases, if I may guess at others by myself, too much possessed the mind; I say, since this I have often wondered with what pleasure or satisfaction the prince could look upon the poor innocent infant, which, though his own, and that he might that way have some attachment in his affections to it, yet must always afterwards be a remembrancer to him of his most early crime and, which was worse, must bear upon itself, un-merited, an eternal mark of infamy, which should be spoken of, upon all occasions, to its reproach, from the folly of its fa-ther and wickedness of its mother.

Great men are indeed delivered from the burthen of their natural children, or bastards, as to their maintenance. This is the main affliction in other cases, where there is not substance suffcient without breaking into the fortunes of the family. In those cases either a man's legitimate children suffer, which is very unnatural, or the unfortunate mother of that illegitimate birth has a dreadful affliction, either of being turned off with her child and be left to starve, &c., or of seeing the poor in-fant packed off with a piece of money to some of those she-butchers who take children off of their hands, as 'tis called, that is to say, starve 'em and, in a word, murder them.

Great men, I say, are delivered from this burthen, because they are always furnished to supply the expense of their out-of-the-way offspring, by making little assignments upon the Bank of Lyons or the town-house of Paris, and settling those sums, to be received for the maintenance of such expense as they see cause.

Thus, in the case of this child of mine, while he ... ' I con-versed, there was no need to make any appointment as an ap-panage or maintenance for the child or its nurse, for he supplied me more than sufficiently for all those things. But afterward, when time, and a particular circumstance, put an end to our conversing together (as such things always meet with a period, and generally break off abruptly), I say, after that, I found he appointed the children a settled allowance, by an assignment of annual rent upon the Bank of Lyons, which was sufficient for bringing them handsomely, though privately, up in the world, and that not in a manner un-worthy of their fathers blood, though I came to be sunk and forgotten in the case; nor did the children ever know any-thing of their mother to this day, other than as you may have an account hereafter.

But to look back to the particular observation I was mak-ing, which I hope may be of use to those who read my story, I say it was something wonderful to me to see this person so exceedingly delighted at the birth of this child, and so pleased with it; for he would sit and look at it, and with an air of seriousness sometimes a great while together, and particu-larly, I observed, he loved to look at it when it was asleep.

It was indeed a lovely, charming child, and had a certain vivacity in its countenance that is far from being common to all children so young; and he would often say to me that he believed there was something extraordinary in the child, and he did not doubt but he would come to be a great man.

I could never hear him say so, but though secretly it pleased me, yet it so closely touched me another way that I could not refrain sighing, and sometimes tears; and one time in particular it so affected me that I could not conceal it from him; but when he saw tears run down my face, there was no concealing the occasion from him; he was too importunate to be denied in a thing of that moment. So I frankly answered, "It sensibly affects me, my lord," said I, "that, whatever the merit of this little creature may be, he must always have a bend on his arms. The disaster of his birth will be always, not a blot only to his honour, but a bar to his fortunes in the world. Our affection will be ever his affliction, and his mother's crime be the son's reproach. The blot can never be wiped out by the most glorious actions; nay, if it lives to raise a family," said I, "the infamy must descend even to its innocent posterity."

He took the thought, and sometimes told me afterwards that it made a deeper impression on him than he discovered to me at that time; but for the present he put it off with telling me these things could not be helped; that they served for a spur to the spirits of brave men, inspired them with the principles of gallantry, and prompted them to brave actions; that though it might be true that the mention of illegitimacy might attend the name, yet that personal virtue placed a man of honour above the reproach of his birth; that, as he had no share in the offence, he would have no concern at the blot; when, having by his own merit placed himself out of the reach of scandal, his fame should drown the memory of his beginning; that as it was usual for men of quality to make such little escapes, so the number of their natural children were so great, and they generally took such good care of their education, that some of the greatest men in the world had a bend in their coats of arms, and that it was of no consequence to them, especially when their fame began to rise upon the basis of their acquired merit. And upon this he began to reckon up to me some of the greatest families in France, and in England also.

This carried off our discourse for a time. But I went farther with him once, removing the discourse from the part attending our children to the reproach which those children would be apt to throw upon us, their originals; and when speaking a little too feelingly on the subject, he began to receive the impression a little deeper than I wished he had done. At last he told me I had almost acted the confessor to him; that I might, perhaps, preach a more dangerous doctrine to him than we should either of us like, or than I was aware of. "For, my dear," says he, "if once we come to talk of repentance, we must talk of parting."

If tears were in my eyes before, they flowed too fast now to be restrained, and I gave him but too much satisfaction by my looks that I had yet no reflections upon my mind strong enough to go that length, and that I could no more think of parting than he could.

He said a great many kind things, which were great, like himself, and, extenuating our crime, intimated to me that he could no more part with me than I could with him; so we both, as I may say, even against our light and against our conviction, concluded to sin on; indeed, his affection to the child was one great tie to him, for he was extremely fond of it.

The child lived to be a considerable man. He was first an officer of the *Garde du Corps* of France, and afterwards colonel of a regiment of dragoons in Italy, and on many extraordinary occasions showed that he was not unworthy such a father, but many ways deserving a legitimate birth and a better mother. Of which hereafter.

I think I may say now that I lived indeed like a queen; or, if you will have me confess that my condition had still the reproach of a whore, I may say I was, sure, the queen of whores; for no woman was ever more valued or more caressed by a person of such quality only in the station of a mistress. I had, indeed, one deficiency which women in such circumstances seldom are chargeable with, namely, I craved nothing of him; I never asked him for anything in my life, nor suffered myself to be made use of, as is too much the custom of mistresses, to ask favours for others. His bounty always prevented me in the first, and my strict concealing myself in the last, which was no less to my convenience than his.

The only favour I ever asked of him was for his gentleman, who he had all along entrusted with the secret of our affair, and who had once so much offended him by some omissions in his duty that he found it very hard to make his peace. He came and laid his case before my woman, Amy, and begged her to speak to me to intercede for him, which I did, and on my account he was received again and pardoned, for which the grateful dog requited me by getting to bed to his benefactress, Amy, at which I was very angry. But Amy generously acknowledged that it was her fault as much as his; that she loved the fellow so much that she believed if he had not asked her, she should have asked him. I say, this pacified me, and I only obtained of her that she should not let him know that I knew it.

I might have interspersed this part of my story with a great many pleasant parts and discourses which happened between my maid Amy and I, but I omit them on account of my own story, which has been so extraordinary. However I must mention something as to Amy and her gentleman. I inquired of Amy upon what terms they came to be so intimate, but Amy seemed backward to explain herself. I did not care to press her upon a question of that nature, knowing that she might have answered my question with a question, and have said, why, how did I and the prince come to be so intimate? So I left off farther inquiring into it, till, after some time, she told it me all freely of her own accord, which, to cut it short, amounted to no more than this, that, like mistress like maid, as they had many leisure hours together below, while they waited respectively when his lord and I were together above; I say, they could hardly avoid the usual question one to another, namely, why might not they do the same thing below that we did above?

On that account, indeed, as I said above, I could not find in my heart to be angry with Amy. I was, indeed, afraid the girl would have been with child too, but that did not happen, and so there was no hurt done; for Amy had been hanselled before, as well as her mistress, and by the same party too, as you have heard.

After I was up again, and my child provided with a good nurse, and withal, winter coming on, it was proper to think of coming to Paris again, which I did; but as I had now a coach and horses, and some servants to attend me, by my lord's allowance, I took the liberty to have them come to

Paris sometimes, and so to take a tour into the garden of the Tuileries and the other pleasant places of the city. It happened one day that my prince (if I may call him so) had a mind to give me some diversion, and to take the air with me. But, that he might do it and not be publicly known, he comes to me in a coach of the Count de ———, a great officer of the court, attended by his liveries also; so that, in a word, it was impossible to guess by the equipage who I was or who I belonged to; also, that I might be the more effectually concealed, he ordered me to be taken up at a mantua-maker's house, where he sometimes came, whether upon other amours or not was no business of mine to inquire. I knew nothing whither he intended to carry me; but when he was in the coach with me, he told me he had ordered his servants to go to court with me, and he would show me some of the *beau monde*. I told him I cared not where I went while I had the honour to have him with me. So he carried me to the fine palace of Meudon, where the Dauphin then was, and where he had some particular intimacy with one of the Dauphin's domestics, who procured a retreat for me in his lodgings while we stayed there, which was three or four days.

While I was there, the king happened to come thither from Versailles, and making but a short stay, visited Madam the Dauphiness, who was then living. The prince was here incognito, only because of his being with me, and therefore, when he heard that the king was in the gardens, he kept close within the lodgings; but the gentleman in whose lodgings we were, with his lady and several others, went out to see the king, and I had the honour to be asked to go with them.

After we had seen the king, who did not stay long in the gardens, we walked up the broad terrace, and crossing the hall towards the great staircase, I had a sight which confounded me at once, as I doubt not it would have done to any woman in the world. The horse-guards, or what they call there the *gens d'armes,* had, upon some occasion, been either upon duty or been reviewed, or something (I did not understand that part) was the matter that occasioned their being there, I know not what; but, walking in the guard-chamber, and with his jack-boots on, and the whole habit of the troop, as it is worn when our horse-guards are upon duty, as they call it, at St. James's Park; I say, there, to my inexpressible confusion, I saw Mr. ———, my first husband, the brewer.

I could not be deceived; I passed so near him that I almost

brushed him with my clothes, and looked him full in the face, but having my fan before my face, so that he could not know me. However, I knew him perfectly well, and I heard him speak, which was a second way of knowing him. Besides being, you may be sure, astonished and surprised at such a sight, I turned about after I had passed him some steps, and, pretending to ask the lady that was with me some questions, I stood as if I had viewed the great hall, the outer guard-chamber, and some things; but I did it to take a full view of his dress, that I might farther inform myself.

While I stood thus amusing the lady that was with me with questions, he walked, talking with another man of the same cloth, back again, just by me; and to my particular satisfaction, or dissatisfaction—take it which way you will—I heard him speak English, the other being, it seems, an Englishman.

I then asked the lady some other questions. "Pray, madam," says I, "what are these troopers here? Are they the king's guards?" "No," says she, "they are the *gens d'armes;* a small detachment of them, I suppose, attended the king to-day, but they are not his Majesty's ordinary guard." Another lady that was with her said, "No, madam, it seems that is not the case, for I heard them saying the *gens d'armes* were here to-day by special order, some of them being to march towards the Rhine, and these attend for orders; but they go back to-morrow to Orleans, where they are expected."

This satisfied me in part, but I found means after this to inquire whose particular troop it was that the gentlemen that were here belonged to; and with that I heard they would all be at Paris the week after.

Two days after this we returned for Paris, when I took occasion to speak to my lord, that I heard the *gens d'armes* were to be in the city the next week, and that I should be charmed with seeing them march if they came in a body. He was so obliging in such things that I need but just name a thing of that kind and it was done; so he ordered his gentleman (I should now call him Amy's gentleman) to get me a place in a certain house, where I might see them march.

As he did not appear with me on this occasion, so I had the liberty of taking my woman, Amy, with me, and stood where we were very well accommodated for the observation which I was to make. I told Amy what I had seen, and she was as forward to make the discovery as I was to have her, and almost as much surprised at the thing itself. In a word, the *gens d'armes* entered the city, as was expected, and made a most glorious show indeed, being new-clothed and armed, and being to have their standards blessed by the Archbishop of Paris. On this occasion they indeed looked very gay; and as they marched very leisurely, I had time to take as critical a view and make as nice a search among them as I pleased. Here, in a particular rank, eminent for one monstrous-sized man on the right; here, I say, I saw my gentleman again, and a very handsome, jolly fellow he was, as any in the troop, though not so monstrous large as the great one I speak of, who, it seems, was, however, a gentleman of a good family in Gascony, and was called the giant of Gascony.

It was a kind of a good fortune to us, among the other circumstances of it, that something caused the troops to halt in their march a little before that particular rank came right against that window which I stood in, so that then we had occasion to take our full view of him at a small distance, and so as not to doubt of his being the same person.

Amy, who thought she might, on many accounts, venture with more safety to be particular than I could, asked her gentleman how a particular man, who she saw there among the *gens d'armes*, might be inquired after and found out; she having seen an Englishman riding there which was supposed to be dead in England for several years before she came out of London, and that his wife had married again. It was a question the gentleman did not well understand how to answer; but another person that stood by told her, if she would tell him the gentleman's name, he would endeavour to find him out for her, and asked jestingly if he was her lover. Amy put that off with a laugh, but still continued her inquiry, and in such a manner as the gentleman easily perceived she was in earnest; so he left bantering and asked her in what part of the troop he rode. She foolishly told him his name, which she should not have done, and pointing to the cornet* that troop carried, which was not then quite out of sight, she let him easily know whereabouts he rode, only she could not name the captain. However, he gave her such directions afterwards that, in short, Amy, who was an indefatigable girl, found him out. It seems he had not changed his name, not supposing any inquiry would be made after him here; but I say, Amy found him out, and went boldly to his quarters, asked for him, and he came out to her immediately.

* "cornet." The standard of a troop of cavalry.

I believe I was not more confounded at my first seeing him at Meudon than he was at seeing Amy. He started and turned pale as death. Amy believed if he had seen her at first, in any convenient place for so villainous a purpose, he would have murdered her.

But he started, as I say above, and asked in English, with an admiration,* "What are you?" "Sir," says she, "don't you know me?" "Yes," says he, "I knew you when you were alive; but what you are now—whether ghost or substance—I know not." "Be not af iid, sir, of that," says Amy. "I am the same Amy that I was in your service, and do not speak to you now for any hurt, but that I saw you accidentally yesterday ride among the soldiers; I thought you might be glad to hear from your friends at London." "Well, Amy," says he then, having a little recovered himself, "how does everybody do? What! is your mistress here?" Thus they begun.

Amy. My mistress, sir, alas! not the mistress you mean; poor gentlewoman, you left her in a sad condition.

Gent. Why, that's true, Amy, but it could not be helped. I was in a sad condition myself.

Amy. I believe so, indeed, sir, or else you had not gone away as you did; for it was a very terrible condition you left them all in, that I must say.

Gent. What did they do after I was gone?

Amy. Do, sir! Very miserably, you may be sure. How could it be otherwise?

Gent. Well, that's true indeed; but you may tell me, Amy, what became of them, if you please. For though I went so away, it was not because I did not love them all very well, but because I could not bear to see the poverty that was coming upon them, and which it was not in my power to help. What could I do?

Amy. Nay, I believe so indeed; and I have heard my mistress say many times she did not doubt but your affliction was as great as hers, almost, wherever you were.

Gent. Why, did she believe I was alive, then?

Amy. Yes sir; she always said she believed you were alive, because she thought she should have heard something of you if you had been dead.

Gent. Ay, ay, my perplexity was very great indeed, or else I had never gone away.

---

* "with an admiration." With an expression of astonishment.

Amy. It was very cruel, though, to the poor lady, sir, my mistress; she almost broke her heart for you at first, for fear of what might befall you, and at last because she could not hear from you.

Gent. Alas, Amy! what could I do? Things were driven to the last extremity before I went. I could have done nothing but help starve them all if I had stayed; and, besides, I could not bear to see it.

Amy. You know, sir, I can say little to what passed before, but I am a melancholy witness to the sad distresses of my poor mistress as long as I stayed with her, and which would grieve your heart to hear them.

(Here she tells my whole story to the time that the parish took off one of my children, and which she perceived very much affected him; and he shook his head and said some things very bitter when he heard of the cruelty of his own relations to me.)

Gent. Well, Amy, I have heard enough so far. What did she do afterwards?

Amy. I can't give you any farther account, sir; my mistress would not let me stay with her any longer. She said she could neither pay me or subsist me. I told her I would serve her without any wages, but I could not live without victuals, you know; so I was forced to leave her, poor lady, sore against my will; and I heard afterwards that the landlord seized her goods, so she was, I suppose, turned out of doors; for as I went by the door, about a month after, I saw the house shut up; and, about a fortnight after that, I found there were workmen at work, fitting it up, as I suppose, for a new tenant. But none of the neighbours could tell me what was become of my poor mistress, only that they said she was so poor that it was next to begging; that some of the neighbouring gentlefolks had relieved her, or that else she must have starved.

Then she went on, and told him that after that they never heard any more of (me) her mistress, but that she had been seen once or twice in the city, very shabby and poor in clothes, and it was thought she worked with her needle for her bread. All this the jade said with so much cunning, and managed and humoured it so well, and wiped her eyes and cried so artificially that he took it all as it was intended he should, and once or twice she saw tears in his eyes too. He told her it was a moving, melancholy story, and it had almost broke his heart at first, but that he was driven to the last extremity, and could do nothing but stay and see 'em all starve, which he could not bear the thoughts of, but should have pistoled himself if any such thing had happened while he was there; that he left (me) his wife all the money he had in the world but £25, which was as little as he could take with him to seek his fortune in the world. He could not doubt but that his relations, seeing they were all rich, would have taken the poor children off, and not let them come to the parish; and that his wife was young and handsome, and, he thought, might marry again, perhaps to her advantage, and for that very reason he never wrote to her or let her know he was alive, that she might in a reasonable term of years marry, and perhaps mend her fortunes; that he resolved never to claim her, because he should rejoice to hear that she had settled to her mind; and that he wished there had been a law made to empower a woman to marry if her husband was not heard of in so long a time, which time, he thought, should not be above four year, which was long enough to send word in to a wife or family from any part of the world.

Amy said she could say nothing to that but this, that she was satisfied her mistress would marry nobody unless she had certain intelligence that he had been dead from somebody that saw him buried. "But, alas!" says Amy, "my mistress was reduced to such dismal circumstances that nobody would be so foolish to think of her, unless it had been somebody to go a-begging with her."

Amy then, seeing him so perfectly deluded, made a long and lamentable outcry how she had been deluded away to marry a poor footman. "For he is no worse or better," says she, "though he calls himself a lord's gentleman. And here," says Amy, "he has dragged me over into a strange country to make a beggar of me." And then she falls a-howling again, and snivelling, which, by the way, was all hypocrisy, but acted so to the life as perfectly deceived him, and he gave entire credit to every word of it.

"Why, Amy," says he, "you are very well dressed; you don't look as if you were in danger of being a beggar." "Ay, hang him!" says Amy, "they love to have fine clothes here, if they have never a smock under them. But I love to have money in cash rather than a chest full of fine clothes. Besides, sir," says she, "most of the clothes I have were given me in the last place I had, when I went away from my mistress."

Upon the whole of the discourse, Amy got out of him what condition he was in and how he lived, upon her promise to him that if she ever came to England and should see her old mistress, she should not let her know that he was alive. "Alas, sir!" says Amy, "I may never come to see England again as long as I live; and if I should, it would be ten thousand to one whether I shall see my old mistress, for how should I know which way to look for her, or what part of England she may be in? Not I," says she. "I don't so much as know how to inquire for her; and if I should," says Amy, "ever be so happy as to see her, I would not do her so much mischief as to tell her where you were, sir, unless she was in a condition to help herself and you too." This farther deluded him, and made him entirely open in his conversing with her. As to his own circumstances, he told her she saw him in the highest preferment he had arrived to, or was ever like to arrive to; for, having no friends or acquaintance in France, and, which was worse, no money, he never expected to rise; that he could have been made a lieutenant to a troop of light-horse but the week before, by the favour of an officer in the *gens d'armes* who was his friend, but that he must have found eight thousand livres to have paid for it to the gentleman who possessed it, and had leave given him to sell. "But where could I get eight thousand livres," says he, "that have never been master of five hundred livres ready-money at a time since I came into France?"

"Oh dear, sir," says Amy, "I am very sorry to hear you say so. I fancy if you once got up to some preferment, you would think of my old mistress again and do something for her. Poor lady," says Amy, "she wants it, to be sure." And then she falls a-crying again. "'Tis a sad thing indeed," says she, "that you should be so hard put to it for money, when you had got a friend to recommend you, and should lose it for want of money." "Ay, so it was, Amy, indeed," says he, "but what can a stranger do that has neither money or friends?" Here Amy puts in again on my account. "Well," says she, "my poor mistress has had the loss, though she knows nothing of it. Oh dear! how happy it would have been! To be sure, sir, you would have helped her all you could." "Ay," says he, "Amy, so I would with all my heart; and even as I am, I would send her some relief, if I thought she wanted it,

only that then letting her know I was alive might do her
some prejudice, in case of her settling, or marrying anybody."

"Alas," says Amy, "marry! Who will marry her in the poor
condition she is in?" And so their discourse ended for that
time.

All this was mere talk on both sides, and words of course;
for on farther inquiry, Amy found that he had no such offer
of a lieutenant's commision, or anything like it; and that he
rambled in his discourse from one thing to another. But of
that in its place.

You may be sure that this discourse, as Amy at first related
it, was moving to the last degree upon me, and I was once
going to have sent him the eight thousand livres to purchase
the commission he had spoken of; but as I knew his character
better than anybody, I was willing to search a little farther
into it, and so I set Amy to inquire of some other of the
troop, to see what character he had, and whether there was
anything in the story of a lieutenant's commission or no.

But Amy soon came to a better understanding of him, for
she presently learnt that he had a most scoundrel character;
that there was nothing of weight in anything he said; but that
he was, in short, a mere sharper, one that would stick at
nothing to get money, and that there was no depending on
anything he said; and that, more especially, about the lieutenant's commission, she understood that there was nothing at
all in it, but they told her how he had often made use of that
sham to borrow money, and move gentlemen to pity him and
lend him money, in hopes to get him preferment; that he had
reported that he had a wife and five children in England,
who he maintained out of his pay, and by these shifts had
run into debt in several places; and upon several complaints
for such things, he had been threatened to be turned out of
the *gens d'armes;* and that, in short, he was not to be believed in anything he said, or trusted on any account.

Upon this information, Amy began to cool in her farther
meddling with him, and told me it was not safe for me to attempt doing him any good, unless I resolved to put him upon
suspicions and inquiries which might be to my ruin, in the
condition I was now in.

I was soon confirmed in this part of his character, for the
next time that Amy came to talk with him, he discovered
himself more effectually; for, while she had put him in hopes
of procuring one to advance the money for the lieutenant's

commission for him upon easy conditions, he by degrees dropped the discourse, then pretended it was too late and that he could not get it, and then descended to ask poor Amy to lend him five hundred pistoles.

Amy pretended poverty, that her circumstances were but mean, and that she could not raise such a sum; and this she did to try him to the utmost. He descended to three hundred, then to one hundred, then to fifty, and then to a pistole, which she lent him, and he, never intending to pay it, played out of her sight as much as he could. And thus being satisfied that he was the same worthless thing he had ever been, I threw off all thoughts of him; whereas, had he been a man of any sense and of any principle of honour, I had it in my thoughts to retire to England again, send for him over, and have lived honestly with him. But as a fool is the worst of husbands to do a woman good, so a fool is the worst husband a woman can do good to. I would willingly have done him good, but he was not qualified to receive it or make the best use of it. Had I sent him ten thousand crowns instead of eight thousand livres, and sent it with express condition that he should immediately have bought himself the commission he talked of with part of the money, and have sent some of it to relieve the necessities of his poor miserable wife at London, and to prevent his children to be kept by the parish, it was evident he would have been still but a private trooper, and his wife and children should still have starved at London, or been kept of mere charity, as, for aught he knew, they then were.

Seeing, therefore, no remedy, I was obliged to withdraw my hand from him, that had been my first destroyer, and reserve the assistance that I intended to have given him for another more desirable opportunity. All that I had now to do was to keep myself out of his sight, which was not very difficult for me to do, considering in what station he lived.

Amy and I had several consultations then upon the main question, namely, how to be sure never to chop upon him again by chance, and to be surprised into a discovery, which would have been a fatal discovery indeed. Amy proposed that we should always take care to know where the *gens d'armes* were quartered, and thereby effectually avoid them; and this was one way.

But this was not so as to be fully to my satisfaction; no ordinary way of inquiring where the *gens d'armes* were quartered was sufficient to me; but I found out a fellow who was completely qualified for the work of a spy (for France has plenty of such people). This man I employed to be a constant and particular attendant upon his person and motions; and he was especially employed and ordered to haunt him as a ghost, that he should scarce let him be ever out of his sight. He performed this to a nicety, and failed not to give me a perfect journal of all his motions from day to day, and, whether for his pleasures or his business, was always at his heels.

This was somewhat expensive, and such a fellow merited to be well paid, but he did his business so exquisitely punctual that this poor man scarce went out of the house without my knowing the way he went, the company he kept, when he went abroad, and when he stayed at home.

By this extraordinary conduct I made myself safe, and so went out in public or stayed at home as I found he was or was not in a possibility of being at Paris, at Versailles, or any place I had occasion to be at. This, though it was very chargeable, yet as I found it absolutely necessary, so I took no thought about the expense of it, for I knew I could not purchase my safety too dear.

By this management I found an opportunity to see what a most insignificant, unthinking life the poor indolent wretch, who, by his unactive temper, had at first been my ruin, now lived; how he only rose in the morning to go to bed at night; that, saving the necessary motion of the troops, which he was obliged to attend, he was a mere motionless animal, of no consequence in the world; that he seemed to be one who, though he was indeed alive, had no manner of business in life but to stay to be called out of it. He neither kept any company, minded any sport, played at any game, or indeed did anything of moment; but, in short, sauntered about like one that it was not two livres value whether he was dead or alive; that when he was gone, would leave no remembrance behind him that ever he was here; that if ever he did anything in the world to be talked of, it was only to get five beggars and starve his wife. The journal of his life, which I had constantly sent me every week, was the least significant of anything of its kind that was ever seen, as it had really nothing of earnest in it, so it would make no jest to relate it. It was not important enough so much as to make the reader merry withal, and for that reason I omit it.

Yet this nothing-doing wretch was I obliged to watch and guard against, as against the only thing that was capable of doing me hurt in the world. I was to shun him as we would shun a spectre, or even the devil, if he was actually in our way; and it cost me after the rate of a hundred and fifty livres a month, and very cheap too, to have this creature constantly kept in view. That is to say, my spy undertook never to let him be out of his sight an hour, but so as that he could give an account of him, which was much the easier for to be done considering his way of living; for he was sure that, for whole weeks together, he would be ten hours of the day half asleep on a bench at the tavern-door where he quartered, or drunk within the house.

Though this wicked life he led sometimes moved me to pity him, and to wonder how so well-bred, gentlemanly a man as he once was could degenerate into such a useless thing as he now appeared, yet at the same time it gave me most contemptible thoughts of him, and made me often say I was a warning for all the ladies of Europe against marrying of fools. A man of sense falls in the world and gets up again, and a woman has some chance for herself. But with a fool! Once fall, and ever undone; once in the ditch, and die in the ditch; once poor, and sure to starve.

But 'tis time to have done with him. Once I had nothing to hope for but to see him again; now my only felicity was, if possible, never to see him, and, above all, to keep him from seeing me, which, as above, I took effectual care of.

I was now returned to Paris. My little son of honour, as I called him, was left at ———, where my last country seat then was, and I came to Paris at the prince's request. Thither he come to me as soon as I arrived, and told me he came to give me joy of my return, and to make his acknowledgments for that I had given him a son. I thought, indeed, he had been going to give me a present, and so he did the next day, but in what he said then he only jested with me. He gave me his company all the evening, supped with me about midnight, and did me the honour, as I then called it, to lodge me in his arms all the night, telling me, in jest, that the best thanks for a son born was giving the pledge for another.

But as I hinted, so it was; the next morning he laid me down on my toilet a purse with three hundred pistoles. I saw him lay it down and understood what he meant, but I took no notice of it till I came to it, as it were, casually; then I gave a great cry out and fell a-scolding in my way, for he gave me all possible freedom of speech on such occasions. I told him he was unkind, that he would never give me an opportunity to ask for anything, and that he forced me to blush by being too much obliged, and the like; all which I knew was very agreeable to him, for as he was bountiful beyond measure, so he was infinitely obliged by my being so backward to ask any favours; and I was even with him, for I never asked him for a farthing in my life.

Upon this rallying him, he told me I had either perfectly studied the art of humour, or else what was the greatest difficulty to others was natural to me, adding that nothing could be more obliging to a man of honour than not to be soliciting and craving.

I told him nothing could be craving upon him, that he left no room for it; that I hoped he did not give merely to avoid the trouble of being importuned. I told him he might depend upon it that I should be reduced very low indeed before I offered to disturb him that way.

He said a man of honour ought always to know what he ought to do; and as he did nothing but what he knew was reasonable, he gave me leave to be free with him if I wanted anything; that he had too much value for me to deny me anything if I asked, but that it was infinitely agreeable to him to hear me say that what he did was to my satisfaction.

We strained compliments thus a great while, and as he had me in his arms most part of the time, so upon all my expressions of his bounty to me, he put a stop to me with his kisses and would admit me to go on no farther.

I should in this place mention that this prince was not a subject of France, though at that time he resided at Paris and was much at court, where, I suppose, he had or expected some considerable employment. But I mention it on this account, that a few days after this he came to me and told me he was come to bring me not the most welcome news that ever I heard from him in his life. I looked at him a little surprised; but he returned, "Do not be uneasy; it is as unpleasant to me as to you, but I come to consult with you about it and see if it cannot be made a little easy to us both."

I seemed still more concerned and surprised. At last he said it was that he believed he should be obliged to go into Italy, which, though otherwise it was very agreeable to him, yet his parting with me made it a very dull thing but to think of.

I sat mute, as one thunderstruck, for a good while; and it presently occurred to me that I was going to lose him, which, indeed, I could but ill bear the thoughts of; and as he told me I turned pale. "What's the matter?" said he hastily. "I have surprised you indeed," and, stepping to the sideboard, fills a dram of cordial-water, which was of his own bringing, and comes to me. "Be not surprised," said he. "I'll go nowhere without you," adding several other things so kind as nothing could exceed it.

I might indeed turn pale, for I was very much surprised at first, believing that this was, as it often happens in such cases, only a project to drop me, and break off an amour which he had now carried on so long; and a thousand thoughts whirled about my head in the few moments while I was kept in suspense, for they were but a few. I say, I was indeed surprised and might, perhaps, look pale, but I was not in any danger of fainting that I knew of.

However, it not a little pleased me to see him so concerned and anxious about me, but I stopped a little when he put the cordial to my mouth, and, taking the glass in my hand, I said, "My lord, your words are infinitely more of a cordial to me than this citron; for as nothing can be a greater affliction than to lose you, so nothing can be a greater satisfaction than the assurance that I shall not have that misfortune."

He made me sit down and sat down by me, and after saying a thousand kind things to me, he turns upon me with a smile. "Why, will you venture yourself to Italy with me?" says he. I stopped a-while, and then answered that I wondered he would ask me that question, for I would go anywhere in the world, or all over the world, wherever he should desire me, and give me the felicity of his company.

Then he entered into a long account of the occasion of his journey, and how the king had engaged him to go, and some other circumstances which are not proper to enter into here, it being by no means proper to say anything that might lead the reader into the least guess at the person.

But to cut short this part of the story, and the history of our journey and stay abroad, which would almost fill up a volume of itself, I say we spent all that evening in cheerful consultations about the manner of our travelling, the equipage and figure he should go in, and in what manner I should go. Several ways were proposed, but none seemed feasible, till at last I told him I thought it would be so troublesome, so expensive, and so public that it would be many ways inconvenient to him; and though it was a kind of death to me to lose him, yet that, rather than so very much perplex his affairs, I would submit to anything.

At the next visit I filled his head with the same difficulties, and then at last came over him with a proposal that I would stay in Paris, or where else he should direct; and when I heard of his safe arrival, would come away by myself, and place myself as near him as I could.

This gave him no satisfaction at all, nor would he hear any more of it; but if I durst venture myself, as he called it, such a journey, he would not lose the satisfaction of my company; and as for the expense, that was not to be named; neither, indeed, was there room to name it, for I found that he travelled at the king's expense, as well for himself as for all his equipage, being upon a piece of secret service of the last importance.

But after several debates between ourselves, he came to this resolution, viz., that he would travel incognito, and so he should avoid all public notice either of himself or of who went with him; and that then he should not only carry me with him, but have a perfect leisure of enjoying my agreeable company (as he was pleased to call it) all the way.

This was so obliging that nothing could be more. So upon this foot he immediately set to work to prepare things for his journey, and, by his directions, so did I too. But now I had a terrible difficulty upon me, and which way to get over it I knew not; and that was, in what manner to take care of what I had to leave behind me. I was rich, as I have said, very rich, and what to do with it I knew not; nor who to leave in trust I knew not. I had nobody but Amy in the world, and to travel without Amy was very uncomfortable, or to leave all I had in the world with her, and, if she miscarried, be ruined at once, was still a frightful thought; for Amy might die, and whose hands things might fall into I knew not. This gave me great uneasiness, and I knew not what to do; for I could not mention it to the prince, lest he should see that I was richer than he thought I was.

But the prince made all this easy to me; for in concerting measures for our journey, he stated the thing himself, and asked me merrily one evening who I would trust with all my wealth in my absence.

"My wealth, my lord," said I, "except what I owe to your goodness, is but small, but yet that little I have, I confess, causes some thoughtfulness, because I have no acquaintance in Paris that I dare trust with it, nor anybody but my woman to leave in the house; and how to do without her upon the road I do not well know."

"As to the road, be not concerned," says the prince. "I'll provide you servants to your mind; and as for your woman, if you can trust her, leave her here, and I'll put you in a way how to secure things as well as if you were at home." I bowed, and told him I could not be put into better hands than his own, and that, therefore, I would govern all my measures by his directions; so we talked no more of it that night.

The next day he sent me in a great iron chest, so large that it was as much as six lusty fellows could get up the steps into the house; and in this I put, indeed, all my wealth; and for my safety he ordered a good, honest, ancient man and his wife to be in the house with her, to keep her company, and a maid-servant and boy; so that there was a good family, and Amy was madam, the mistress of the house.

Things being thus secured, we set out incog., as he called it. But we had two coaches and six horses, two chaises, and about eight men-servants on horseback, all very well armed.

Never was woman better used in this world that went upon no other account than I did. I had three women-servants to wait on me, one whereof was an old Madam ———, who thoroughly understood her business, and managed everything as if she had been major domo; so I had no trouble. They had one coach to themselves, and the prince and I in the other; only that sometimes, where he knew it necessary, I went into their coach, and one particular gentleman of the retinue rode with him.

I shall say no more of the journey than that when we came to those frightful mountains, the Alps, there was no travelling in our coaches, so he ordered a horse-litter, but carried by mules, to be provided for me, and himself went on horseback. The coaches went some other way back to Lyons. Then we had coaches hired at Turin, which met us at Susa; so that we were accommodated again, and went by easy journeys afterwards to Rome, where his business, whatever it was, called him to stay some time, and from thence to Venice.

He was as good as his word, indeed; for I had the pleasure of his company and, in a word, engrossed his conversation almost all the way. He took delight in showing me everything that was to be seen, and particularly in telling me something of the history of everything he showed me.

What valuable pains were here thrown away upon one who he was sure, at last, to abandon with regret! How below himself did a man of quality and of a thousand accomplishments behave in all this! 'Tis one of my reasons for entering into this part, which otherwise would not be worth relating. Had I been a daughter or a wife, of whom it might be said that he had a just concern in their instruction or improvement, it had been an admirable step. But all this to a whore! To one who he carried with him upon no account that could be rationally agreeable, and none but to gratify the meanest of human frailties—this was the wonder of it.

But such is the power of a vicious inclination. Whoring was, in a word, his darling crime, the worst excursion he made, for he was otherwise one of the most excellent persons in the world. No passions, no furious excursions, no ostentatious pride; the most humble, courteous, affable person in the world. Not an oath, not an indecent word, or the least blemish in behaviour was to be seen in all his conversation, except as before expected. And it has given me occasion for many dark reflections since, to look back and think that I should be the snare of such a person's life; that I should influence him to so much wickedness, and that I should be the instrument in the hand of the devil to do him so much prejudice.

We were near two years upon this grand tour, as it may be called, during most of which I resided at Rome or at Venice, having only been twice at Florence and once at Naples. I made some very diverting and useful observations in all these places, and particularly of the conduct of the ladies; for I had opportunity to converse very much among them, by the help of the old witch that travelled with us. She had been at Naples and at Venice, and had lived in the former several years, where, as I found, she had lived but a loose life, as indeed the women of Naples generally do; and, in short, I found she was fully acquainted with all the intriguing arts of that part of the world.

Here my lord bought me a little female Turkish slave, who,

being taken at sea by a Maltese man of war, was brought in there, and of her I learnt the Turkish language, their way of dressing and dancing, and some Turkish, or rather Moorish, songs, of which I made use to my advantage on an extraordinary occasion some years after, as you shall hear in its place. I need not say I learnt Italian too, for I got pretty well mistress of that before I had been there a year; and as I had leisure enough and loved the language, I read all the Italian books I could come at.

I began to be so in love with Italy, especially with Naples and Venice, that I could have been very well satisfied to have sent for Amy and have taken up my residence there for life.

As to Rome, I did not like it at all. The swarms of ecclesiastics of all kinds on one side, and the scoundrel rabbles of the common people on the other, make Rome the unpleasantest place in the world to live in. The innumerable number of valets, lackeys, and other servants is such that they used to say that there are very few of the common people in Rome but what have been footmen, or porters, or grooms to cardinals or foreign ambassadors. In a word, they have an air of sharping and cozening, quarrelling and scolding, upon their general behaviour; and when I was there the footmen made such a broil between two great families in Rome, about which of their coaches (the ladies being in the coaches on either side) should give way to the other, that there was above thirty people wounded on both sides, five or six killed outright, and both the ladies frighted almost to death.

But I have no mind to write the history of my travels on this side of the world, at least not now; it would be too full of variety.

I must not, however, omit that the prince continued in all this journey the most kind, obliging person to me in the world, and so constant that, though we were in a country where 'tis well known all manner of liberties are taken, I am yet well assured he neither took the liberty he knew he might have, or so much as desired it.

I have often thought of this noble person on that account. Had he been but half so true, so faithful and constant, to the best lady in the world—I mean his princess—how glorious a virtue had it been in him! And how free had he been from those just reflections which touched him in her behalf when it was too late.

We had some very agreeable conversations upon this subject, and once he told me, with a kind of more than ordinary concern upon his thoughts, that he was greatly beholden to me for taking this hazardous and difficult journey, for that I had kept him honest. I looked up in his face and coloured as red as fire. "Well, well," says he, "do not let that surprise you; I do say you have kept me honest." "My lord," said I, "'tis not for me to explain your words, but I wish I could turn 'em my own way. I hope," says I, "and believe we are both as honest as we can be in our circumstances." "Ay, ay," says he, "and honester than I doubt I should have been if you had not been with me. I cannot say but if you had not been here, I should have wandered among the gay world here, in Naples, and in Venice too, for 'tis not such a crime here as 'tis in other places. But I protest," says he, "I have not touched a woman in Italy but yourself; and more than that, I have not so much as had any desire to it. So that, I say, you have kept me honest."

I was silent, and was glad that he interrupted me, or kept me from speaking, with kissing me, for really I knew not what to say. I was once going to say that if his lady, the princess, had been with him, she would doubtless have had the same influence upon his virtue, with infinitely more advantage to him; but I considered this might give him offence; and, besides, such things might have been dangerous to the circumstance I stood in, so it passed off. But I must confess I saw that he was quite another man, as to women, than I understood he had always been before, and it was a particular satisfaction to me that I was thereby convinced that what he said was true, and that he was, as I may say, all my own.

I was with child again in this journey, and lay in at Venice, but was not so happy as before. I brought him another son, and a very fine boy it was, but it lived not above two months; nor, after the first touches of affection (which are usual, I believe, to all mothers) were over, was I sorry the child did not live, the necessary difficulties attending it in our travelling being considered.

After these several perambulations, my lord told me his business began to close, and we would think of returning to France, which I was very glad of, but principally on account of my treasure I had there, which, as you have heard, was very considerable. It is true I had letters very frequently from my maid Amy, with accounts that everything was very safe, and that was very much to my satisfaction. However, as the prince's negotiations were at an end, and he was obliged to return, I was very glad to go. So we returned from Venice to Turin, and in the way I saw the famous city of Milan. From Turin we went over the mountains again, as before, and our coaches met us at Point à Voisin, between Chambery and Lyons; and so, by easy journeys, we arrived safely at Paris, having been absent two years, wanting about eleven days, as above.

I found the little family we left just as we left them, and Amy cried for joy when she saw me, and I almost did the same.

The prince took his leave of me the night before, for, as he told me, he knew he should be met upon the road by several persons of quality, and perhaps by the princess herself; so we lay at two different inns that night, lest some should come quite to the place, as indeed it happened.

After this I saw him not for above twenty days, being taken up in his family, and also with business; but he sent me his gentleman to tell me the reason of it, and bid me not be uneasy, and that satisfied me effectually.

In all this affluence of my good fortune I did not forget that I had been rich and poor once already alternately, and that I ought to know that the circumstances I was now in were not to be expected to last always; that I had one child and expected another; and if I bred often, it would something impair me in the great article that supported my interest—I mean, what he called beauty; that as that declined, I might expect the fire would abate, and the warmth with which I was now so caressed would cool, and in time, like the other mistresses of great men, I might be dropped again; and that therefore it was my business to take care that I should fall as softly as I could.

I say, I did not forget, therefore, to make as good provision for myself as if I had had nothing to have subsisted on but what I now gained; whereas I had not less than ten thousand pounds, as I said above, which I had amassed, or secured rather, out of the ruins of my faithful friend the jeweller, and which he, little thinking of what was so near him when he went out, told me, though in a kind of a jest, was all my own, if he was knocked on the head, and which, upon that title, I took care to preserve.

My greatest difficulty now was how to secure my wealth and to keep what I had got. For I had greatly added to this

wealth by the generous bounty of the Prince ————, and the
more by the private, retired mode of living, which he rather
desired for privacy than parsimony; for he supplied me for a
more magnificent way of life than I desired, if it had been
proper.

I shall cut short the history of this prosperous wickedness
with telling you I brought him a third son, within little more
than eleven months after our return from Italy; that now I
lived a little more openly, and went by a particular name
which he gave me abroad, but which I must omit, viz., the
Countess de ————; and had coaches and servants, suitable to
the quality he had given me the appearance of. And, which is
more than usually happens in such cases, this held eight years
from the beginning, during which time, as I had been very
faithful to him, so I must say, as above, that I believe he was
so separated to me that whereas he usually had two or three
women, which he kept privately, he had not in all that time
meddled with any of them, but that I had so perfectly engrossed him that he dropped them all. Not, perhaps, that he
saved much by it, for I was a very chargeable mistress to
him, that I must acknowledge, but it was all owing to his particular affection to me, not to my extravagance, for, as I said,
he never gave me leave to ask him for anything, but poured
in his favours and presents faster than I expected, and so fast
as I could not have the assurance to make the least mention
of desiring more.

Nor do I speak this of my own guess, I mean about his
constancy to me and his quitting all other women; but the old
harridan, as I may call her, whom he made the guide of our
travelling, and who was a strange old creature, told me a
thousand stories of his gallantry, as she called it, and how, as
he had no less than three mistresses at one time, and, as I
found, all of her procuring, he had of a sudden dropped them
all, and that he was entirely lost to both her and them; that
they did believe he had fallen into some new hands, but she
could never hear who, or where, till he sent for her to go this
journey. And then the old hag complimented me upon his
choice; that she did not wonder I had so engrossed him; so
much beauty, &c., and there she stopped.

Upon the whole, I found by her what was, you may be
sure, to my particular satisfaction, viz., that, as above, I had
him all my own.

But the highest tide has its ebb; and in all things of this

kind there is a reflux which sometimes, also, is more impetu-
ously violent than the first aggression. My prince was a man
of a vast fortune, though no sovereign, and therefore there
was no probability that the expense of keeping a mistress
could be injurious to him, as to his estate. He had also
several employments, both out of France as well as in it; for,
as above, I say he was not a subject of France, though he
lived in that court. He had a princess, a wife with whom he
had lived several years, and a woman (so the voice of fame
reported) the most valuable of her sex, of birth equal to him,
if not superior, and of fortune proportionable; but in beauty,
wit, and a thousand good qualitites superior, not to most
women, but even to all her sex; and as to her virtue, the
character which was most justly her due was that of not only
the best of princesses, but even the best of women.

They lived in the utmost harmony, as with such a princess
it was impossible to be otherwise. But yet the princess was
not insensible that her lord had his foibles, that he did make
some excursions, and particularly that he had one favourite
mistress, which sometimes engrossed him more than she (the
princess) could wish, or be easily satisfied with. However, she
was so good, so generous, so truly kind a wife, that she never
gave him any uneasiness on this account; except so much as
must arise from his sense of her bearing the affront of it with
such patience, and such a profound respect for him as was in
itself enough to have reformed him, and did sometimes shock
his generous mind, so as to keep him at home, as I may call
it, a great while together. And it was not long before I not
only perceived it by his absence, but really got a knowledge
of the reason of it, and once or twice he even acknowledged
it to me.

It was a point that lay not in me to manage. I made a kind
of motion once or twice to him to leave me, and keep himself
to her, as he ought by the laws and rites of matrimony to
do, and argued the generosity of the princess to him, to persuade him; but I was a hypocrite, for had I prevailed with
him really to be honest, I had lost him, which I could not
bear the thoughts of; and he might easily see I was not in
earnest. One time in particular, when I took upon me to talk
at this rate, I found, when I argued so much for the virtue
and honour, the birth, and above all, the generous usage he
found in the person of the princess with respect to his private
amours, and how it should prevail upon him, &c., I found it

began to affect him, and he returned, "And do you indeed," says he, "persuade me to leave you? Would you have me think you sincere?" I looked up in his face, smiling. "Not for any other favourite, my lord," said I, "That would break my heart; but for madam the princess!" said I. And then I could say no more. Tears followed, and I sat silent a-while. "Well," said he, "if ever I do leave you, it shall be on the virtuous account; it shall be for the princess; I assure you it shall be for no other woman." "That's enough my lord," said I. "There I ought to submit; and while I am assured it shall be for no other mistress, I promise your Highness I will not repine; or that, if I do, it shall be a silent grief; it shall not interrupt your felicity."

All this while I said I knew not what, and said what I was no more able to do than he was able to leave me; which, at that time, he owned he could not do—no, not for the princess herself.

But another turn of affairs determined this matter, for the princess was taken very ill, and, in the opinion of all her physicians, very dangerously so. In her sickness she desired to speak with her lord, and to take her leave of him. At this grievous parting she said so many passionate, kind things to him, lamented that she had left him no children (she had had three, but they were dead); hinted to him that it was one of the chief things which gave her satisfaction in death, as to this world, that she should leave him room to have heirs to his family by some princess that should supply her place; with all humility, but with a Christian earnestness, recommended to him to do justice to such princess, whoever it should be, from whom, to be sure, he would expect justice; that is to say, to keep to her singly, according to the solemnest part of the marriage-covenant; humbly asked his Highness pardon if she had any way offended him; and appealing to Heaven, before whose tribunal she was to appear, that she had never violated her honour or her duty to him, and praying to Jesus and the blessed Virgin for his Highness; and thus, with the most moving and most passionate expressions of her affection to him, took her last leave of him and died the next day.

This discourse, from a princess so valuable in herself and so dear to him, and the loss of her following so immediately after, made such deep impressions on him that he looked back with detestation upon the former part of his life, grew melancholy and reserved, changed his society and much of the general conduct of his life; resolved on a life regulated most strictly by the rules of virtue and piety, and, in a word, was quite another man.

The first part of his reformation was a storm upon me; for, about ten days after the princess's funeral, he sent a message to me by his gentleman, intimating, though in very civil terms, and with a short preamble or introduction, that he desired I would not take it ill that he was obliged to let me know that he could see me no more. His gentleman told me a long story of the new regulation of life his lord had taken up; and that he had been so afflicted for the loss of his princess that he thought it would either shorten his life or he would retire into some religious house, to end his days in solitude.

I need not direct anybody to suppose how I received this news. I was indeed exceedingly surprised at it, and had much ado to support myself when the first part of it was delivered, though the gentleman delivered his errand with great respect, and with all the regard to me that he was able, and with a great deal of ceremony, also telling me how much he was concerned to bring me such a message.

But when I heard the particulars of the story at large, and especially that of the lady's discourse to the prince a little before her death, I was fully satisfied. I knew very well he had done nothing but what any man must do that had a true sense upon him of the justice of the princess's discourse to him, and of the necessity there was of his altering his course of life, if he intended to be either a Christian or an honest man. I say, when I heard this I was perfectly easy. I confess it was a circumstance that it might be reasonably expected should have wrought something also upon me, I that had so much to reflect upon more than the prince; that had now no more temptation of poverty, or of the powerful motive which Amy used with me—namely, comply and live, deny and starve; I say, I that had no poverty to introduce vice, but was grown not only well supplied, but rich; and not only rich, but was very rich; in a word, richer than I knew how to think of, for the truth of it was, that thinking of it sometimes almost distracted me, for want of knowing how to dispose of it, and for fear of losing it all again by some cheat or trick, not knowing anybody that I could commit the trust of it to.

Besides, I should add, at the close of this affair, that the prince did not, as I may say, turn me off rudely and with dis-

gust, but with all the decency and goodness peculiar to himself, and that could consist with a man reformed and struck
with the sense of his having abused so good a lady as his late
princess had been. Nor did he send me away empty, but did
everything like himself; and, in particular, ordered his gentleman to pay the rent of the house and all the expense of his
two sons, and to tell me how they were taken care of, and
where, and also that I might at all times inspect the usage
they had, and if I disliked anything it should be rectified.
And having thus finished everything, he retired into Lorraine,
or somewhere that way, where he had an estate, and I never
heard of him more—I mean, not as a mistress.

Now I was at liberty to go to any part of the world, and
take care of my money myself. The first thing that I resolved
to do was to go directly to England, for there, I thought,
being among my countryfolks (for I esteemed myself an Englishwoman, though I was born in France) but there, I say, I
thought I could better manage things than in France; at least,
that I would be in less danger of being circumvented and deceived. But how to get away with such a treasure as I had
with me was a difficult point, and what I was greatly at a loss
about.

There was a Dutch merchant in Paris that was a person of
great reputation for a man of substance and of honesty, but I
had no manner of acquaintance with him, nor did I know
how to get acquainted with him, so as to discover my circumstances to him. But at last I employed my maid Amy (such I
must be allowed to call her, notwithstanding what has been
said of her, because she was in the place of a maid-servant);
I say, I employed my maid Amy to go to him and she got a
recommendation to him from somebody else, I knew not
who, so that she got access to him well enough.

But now was my case as bad as before, for when I came to
him, what could I do? I had money and jewels to a vast
value, and I might leave all those with him; that I might
indeed do; and so I might with several other merchants in
Paris, who would give me bills for it, payable at London; but
then I ran a hazard of my money, and I had nobody at London to send the bills to, and so to stay till I had an account
that they were accepted; for I had not one friend in London
that I could have recourse to, so that indeed I knew not what
to do.

In this case I had no remedy but that I must trust somebody, so I sent Amy to this Dutch merchant, as I said above. He was a little surprised when Amy came to him and talked to him of remitting a sum of about twelve thousand pistoles to England, and began to think she came to put some cheat upon him; but when he found that Amy was but a servant, and that I came to him myself, the case was altered presently.

When I came to him myself, I presently saw such a plainness in his dealing and such honesty in his countenance that I made no scruple to tell him my whole story, viz., that I was a widow, that I had some jewels to dispose of, and also some money which I had a mind to send to England, and to follow there myself; but being but a woman, and having no correspondence in London, or anywhere else, I knew not what to do or how to secure my effects.

He dealt very candidly with me, but advised me, when he knew my case so particularly, to take bills upon Amsterdam, and to go that way to England; for that I might lodge my treasure in the bank there, in the most secure manner in the world, and that there he could recommend me to a man who perfectly understood jewels, and would deal faithfully with me in the disposing them.

I thanked him, but scrupled very much the travelling so far in a strange country, and especially with such a treasure about me; that, whether known or concealed, I did not know how to venture with it. Then he told me he would try to dispose of them there, that is, at Paris, and convert them into money, and so get me bills for the whole. And in a few days he brought a Jew to me, who pretended to buy* the jewels.

As soon as the Jew saw the jewels I saw my folly, and it was ten thousand to one but I had been ruined, and perhaps put to death in as cruel a manner as possible; and I was put in such a fright by it that I was once upon the point of flying for my life, and leaving the jewels and money too in the hands of the Dutchman, without any bills or anything else. The case was thus:

As soon as the Jew saw the jewels he falls a-jabbering, in Dutch or Portuguese, to the merchant; and I could presently perceive that they were in some great surprise, both of them. The Jew held up his hands, looked at me with some horror, then talked Dutch again, and put himself into a thousand

---

* "pretended to buy." Seemed interested in buying.

shapes, twisting his body and wringing up his face this way and that way in his discourse, stamping with his feet, and throwing abroad his hands, as if he was not in a rage only, but in a mere fury. Then he would turn and give a look at me like the devil. I thought I never saw anything so frightful in my life.

At length I put in a word. "Sir," says I to the Dutch merchant, "what is all this discourse to my business? What is this gentleman in all these passions about? I wish, if he is to treat with me, he would speak that I may understand him; or if you have business of your own between you that is to be done first, let me withdraw, and I'll come again when you are at leisure."

"No, no, madam," says the Dutchman very kindly, "you must not go; all our discourse is about you and your jewels, and you shall hear it presently; it concerns you very much, I assure you." "Concern me!" says I. "What can it concern me so much as to put this gentleman into such agonies? And what makes him give me such devil's looks as he does? Why, he looks as if he would devour me."

The Jew understood me presently, continuing in a kind of rage, and spoke in French: "Yes, madam, it does concern you much, very much, very much," repeating the words, shaking his head; and then turning to the Dutchman, "Sir," says he, "pray tell her what is the case." "No," says the merchant, "not yet; let us talk a little farther of it by ourselves." Upon which they withdrew into another room, where still they talked very high, but in a language I did not understand. I began to be a little surprised at what the Jew had said, you may be sure, and eager to know what he meant, and was very impatient till the Dutch merchant came back, and that so impatient that I called one of his servants to let him know I desired to speak with him. When he came in I asked his pardon for being so impatient, but told him I could not be easy till he had told me what the meaning of all this was. "Why, madam," says the Dutch merchant, "in short, the meaning is what I am surprised at too. This man is a Jew, and understands jewels perfectly well, and that was the reason I sent for him, to dispose of them to him for you. But as soon as he saw them, he knew the jewels very distinctly, and, flying out in a passion, as you see he did, told me, in short, that they were the very parcel of jewels which the English jeweller had about him who was robbed going to Versailles, about eight years ago, to show them the Prince de ———, and that it was for these very jewels that the poor gentleman was murdered. And he is in all this agony to make me ask you how you came by them; and he says you ought to be charged with the robbery and murder, and put to the question to discover who were the persons that did it, that they might be brought to justice." While he said this, the Jew came impudently back into the room without calling, which a little surprised me again.

The Dutch merchant spoke pretty good English, and he knew that the Jew did not understand English at all, so he told me the latter part, when the Jew came into the room, in English, at which I smiled, which put the Jew into his mad fit again, and, shaking his head and making his devil's faces again, he seemed to threaten me for laughing, saying, in French, this was an affair I should have little reason to laugh at, and the like. At this I laughed again, and flouted him, letting him see that I scorned him, and, turning to the Dutch merchant, "Sir," says I, "that those jewels were belonging to Mr. ———, the English jeweller" (naming his name readily), in that," says I, "this person is right; but that I should be questioned how I came to have them is a token of his ignorance, which, however, he might have managed with a little more good manners, till I told him who I am; and both he and you too will be more easy in that part when I should tell you that I am the unhappy widow of that Mr. ——— who was so barbarously murdered going to Versailles, and that he was not robbed of those jewels, but of others, Mr. ——— having left those behind him with me, lest he should be robbed. Had I, sir, come otherwise by them, I should not have been weak enough to have exposed them to sale here, where the thing was done, but have carried them farther off."

This was an agreeable surprise to the Dutch merchant, who, being an honest man himself, believed everything I said, which, indeed, being all really and literally true, except the deficiency of my marriage, I spoke with such an unconcerned easiness that it might plainly be seen that I had no guilt upon me, as the Jew suggested.

The Jew was confounded when he heard that I was the jeweller's wife. But as I had raised his passion with saying he looked at me with a devil's face, he studied mischief in his heart and answered, that should not serve my turn; so called

the Dutchman out again, when he told him that he resolved
to prosecute this matter farther.

There was one kind chance in this affair, which, indeed,
was my deliverance, and that was that the fool could not restrain his passion, but must let it fly to the Dutch merchant,
to whom, when they withdrew a second time, as above, he
told that he would bring a process against me for the murder,
and that it should cost me dear for using him at that rate;
and away he went, desiring the Dutch merchant to tell him
when I would be there again. Had he suspected that the
Dutchman would have communicated the particulars to me,
he would never have been so foolish as to have mentioned
that part to him.

But the malice of his thoughts anticipated him, and the
Dutch merchant was so good as to give me an account of his
design, which, indeed, was wicked enough in its nature. But
to me it would have been worse than otherwise it would to
another, for, upon examination, I could not have proved myself to be the wife of the jeweller, so the suspicion might have
been carried on with the better face; and then I should also
have brought all his relations in England upon me, who, finding by the proceedings that I was not his wife, but a mistress,
or, in English, a whore, would immediately have laid claim to
the jewels, as I had owned them to be his.

This thought immediately rushed into my head as soon as
the Dutch merchant had told me what wicked things were in
the head of that cursed Jew; and the villain (for so I must
call him) convinced the Dutch merchant that he was in earnest by an expression which showed the rest of his design,
and that was, a plot to get the rest of the jewels into his
hand.

When first he hinted to the Dutchman that the jewels were
such a man's (meaning my husband's), he made wonderful
exclamations on account of their having been concealed so
long. Where must they have lain? and what was the woman
that brought them? And that she (meaning me) ought to be
immediately apprehended and put into the hands of justice.
And this was the time that, as I said, he made such horrid
gestures and looked at me so like a devil.

The merchant, hearing him talk at that rate, and seeing
him in earnest, said to him, "Hold your tongue a little; this is
a thing of consequence. If it be so, let you and I go into the

next room and consider of it there." And so they withdrew and left me.

Here, as before, I was uneasy, and called him out, and, having heard how it was, gave him that answer, that I was his wife, or widow, which the malicious Jew said should not serve my turn. And then it was that the Dutchman called him out again; and in this time of his withdrawing, the merchant, finding, as above, that he was really in earnest, counterfeited a little to be of his mind, and entered into proposals with him for the thing itself.

In this they agreed to go to an advocate, or counsel, for directions how to proceed, and to meet again the next day, against which time the merchant was to appoint me to come again with the jewels, in order to sell them. "No," says the merchant, "I will go farther with her than so; I will desire her to leave the jewels with me, to show to another person, in order to get the better price for them." "That's right," says the Jew, "and I'll engage she shall never be mistress of them again; they shall either be seized by us," says he, "in the king's name, or she shall be glad to give them up to us to prevent her being put to the torture."

The merchant said yes to everything he offered, and they agreed to meet the next morning about it, and I was to be persuaded to leave the jewels with him, and come to them the next day at four o'clock in order to make a good bargain for them; and on these conditions they parted. But the honest Dutchman, filled with indignation at the barbarous design, came directly to me and told me the whole story. "And now, madam," says he, "you are to consider immediately what you have to do."

I told him, if I was sure to have justice, I would not fear all that such a rogue could do to me; but how such things were carried on in France I knew not. I told him the greatest difficulty would be to prove our marriage, for that it was done in England, and in a remote part of England too; and, which was worse, it would be hard to produce authentic vouchers of it, because we were married in private. "But as to the death of your husband, madam, what can be said to that?" said he. "Nay," said I, "what can they say to it? In England," added I, "if they would offer such an injury to any one, they must prove the fact or give just reason for their suspicions. That my husband was murdered, that every one knows; but that he was robbed, or of what, or how much, that none knows—no, not myself; and why was I not questioned for it then? I have lived in Paris ever since, lived publicly, and no man had yet the impudence to suggest such a thing of me."

"I am fully satisfied of that," says the merchant; "but as this is a rogue who will stick at nothing, what can we say? And who knows what he may swear? Suppose he should swear that he knows your husband had those particular jewels with him the morning when he went out, and that he showed them to him to consider their value, and what price he should ask the Prince de ——— for them?"

"Nay, by the same rule," said I, "he may swear that I murdered my husband, if he finds it for his turn." "That's true," said he, "and if he should, I do not see what could save you," but added, "I have found out his more immediate design. His design is to have you carried to the Châtelet, that the suspicion may appear just, and then to get the jewels out of your hands if possible; then, at last, to drop the prosecution on your consenting to quit the jewels to him. And how you will do to avoid this is the question which I would have you consider of."

"My misfortune, sir," said I, "is that I have no time to consider, and I have no person to consider with or advise about it. I find that innocence may be oppressed by such an impudent fellow as this; he that does not value perjury has any man's life at his mercy. But, sir," said I, "is the justice such here that, while I may be in the hands of the public and under prosecution, he may get hold of my effects and get my jewels into his hands?"

"I don't know," says he, "what may be done in that case; but if not he, if the court of justice should get hold of them, I do not know but you may find it as difficult to get them out of their hands again, and, at least, it may cost you half as much as they are worth. So I think it would be a much better way to prevent their coming at them at all."

"But what course can I take to do that," says I, "now they have got notice that I have them? If they get me into their hands, they will oblige me to produce them, or perhaps sentence me to prison till I do."

"Nay," says he, "as this brute says, too, put you to the question—that is, to the torture, on pretence of making you confess who were the murderers of your husband."

"Confess!" said I. "How can I confess what I know nothing of?"

"If they come to have you to the rack," said he, "they will make you confess you did it yourself, whether you did it or no, and then you are cast."*

The very word rack frighted me to death almost, and I had no spirit left in me. "Did it myself!" said I. "That's impossible!"

"No, madam," says he, " 'tis far from impossible. The most innocent people in the world have been forced to confess themselves guilty of what they never heard of, much less had any hand in."

"What, then, must I do?" said I. "What would you advise me to?"

"Why," says he, "I would advise you to be gone. You intended to go away in four or five days, and you may as well go in two days; and if you can do so, I shall manage it so that he shall not suspect your being gone for several days after." Then he told me how the rogue would have me ordered to bring the jewels the next day for sale, and that then he would have me apprehended; how he had made the Jew believe he would join with him in his design, and that he (the merchant) would get the jewels into his hands. "Now," says the merchant, "I shall give you bills for the money you desired, immediately, and such as shall not fail of being paid. Take your jewels with you, and go this very evening to St. Germain-en-Laye. I'll send a man thither with you, and from thence he shall guide you to-morrow to Rouen, where there lies a ship of mine, just ready to sail for Rotterdam; you shall have your passage in that ship on my account, and I will send orders for him to sail as soon as you are on board, and a letter to my friend at Rotterdam to entertain and take care of you."

This was too kind an offer for me, as things stood, not to be accepted, and be thankful for; and as to going away, I had prepared everything for parting, so that I had little to do but to go back, take two or three boxes and bundles, and such things, and my maid Amy, and be gone.

Then the merchant told me the measures he had resolved to take to delude the Jew while I made my escape, which was

* "east." Convicted. On page 119, cast means defeated in an action at law.

very well contrived indeed. "First," said he, "when he comes to-morrow, I shall tell him that I proposed to you to leave the jewels with me, as we agreed, but that you said you would come and bring them in the afternoon, so that we must stay for you till four o'clock. But then, at that time, I will show a letter from you, as if just come in, wherein you shall excuse your not coming, for that some company came to visit you, and prevented you; but that you desire me to take care that the gentleman be ready to buy your jewels, and that you will come to-morrow at the same hour, without fail.

"When to-morrow is come, we shall wait at the time, but you not appearing, I shall seem most dissatisfied, and wonder what can be the reason; and so we shall agree to go the next day to get out a process against you. But the next day, in the morning, I'll send to give him notice that you have been at my house, but he not being there, have made another appointment, and that I desire to speak with him. When he comes, I'll tell him you appear perfectly blind as to your danger, and that you appeared much disappointed that he did not come, though you could not meet the night before; and obliged me to have him here to-morrow at three o'clock. When to-morrow comes," says he, "you shall send word that you are taken so ill that you cannot come out for that day, but that you will not fail the next day; and the next day you shall neither come or send, nor let us ever hear any more of you; for by that time you shall be in Holland, if you please."

I could not but approve all his measures, seeing they were so well contrived, and in so friendly a manner, for my benefit; and as he seemed to be so very sincere, I resolved to put my life in his hands. Immediately I went to my lodgings, and sent away Amy with such bundles as I had prepared for my travelling. I also sent several parcels of my fine furniture to the merchant's house to be laid up for me, and bringing the key of the lodgings with me, I came back to his house. Here we finished our matters of money, and I delivered into his hands seven thousand eight hundred pistoles in bills and money, a copy of an assignment on the town-house of Paris for four thousand pistoles, at 3 per cent. interest, attested, and a procuration for receiving the interest half-yearly; but the original I kept for myself.

I could have trusted all I had with him, for he was perfectly honest and had not the least view of doing me any wrong. Indeed, after it was so apparent that he had, as it

were, saved my life, or at least saved me from being exposed
and ruined—I say, after this, how could I doubt him in anything?

When I came to him, he had everything ready as I wanted,
and as he had proposed. As to my money, he gave me first of
all an accepted bill, payable at Rotterdam, for four thousand
pistoles, and drawn from Genoa upon a merchant at Rotterdam, payable to a merchant at Paris, and endorsed by him to
my merchant; this, he assured me, would be punctually paid;
and so it was, to a day. The rest I had in other bills of exchange, drawn by himself upon other merchants in Holland.
Having secured my jewels too, as well as I could, he sent me
away the same evening in a friend's coach, which he had procured for me, to St. Germain, and the next morning to
Rouen. He also sent a servant of his own on horseback with
me, who provided everything for me, and who carried his orders to the captain of the ship, which lay about three miles
below Rouen, in the river, and by his directions I went immediately on board. The third day after I was on board, the ship
went away, and we were out at sea the next day after that;
and thus I took my leave of France, and got clear of an ugly
business, which, had it gone on, might have ruined me, and
sent me back as naked to England as I was a little before I
left it.

And now Amy and I were at leisure to look upon the mischiefs that we had escaped; and had I had any religion or
any sense of a Supreme Power, managing, directing, and gov-
erning in both causes and events in this world, such a case as
this would have given anybody room to have been very
thankful to the Power who had not only put such a treasure
into my hand, but given me such an escape from the ruin
that threatened me; but I had none of those things about me.
I had, indeed, a grateful sense upon my mind of the generous
friendship of my deliverer, the Dutch merchant, by whom I
was so faithfully served, and by whom, as far as relates to
second causes, I was preserved from destruction.

I say, I had a grateful sense upon my mind of his kindness
and faithfulness to me, and I resolved to show him some testimony of it as soon as I came to the end of my rambles, for
I was yet but in a state of uncertainty, and sometimes that
gave me a little uneasiness too. I had paper indeed for my
money, and he had showed himself very good to me in con-
veying me away, as above; but I had not seen the end of

things yet, for unless the bills were paid, I might still be a great loser by my Dutchman, and he might, perhaps, have contrived all that affair of the Jew to put me into a fright and get me to run away, and that as if it were to save my life; that if the bills should be refused, I was cheated with a witness, and the like. But these were but surmises and, indeed, were perfectly without cause, for the honest man acted as honest men always do, with an upright and disinterested principle, and with a sincerity not often to be found in the world. What gain he made by the exchange was just; and was nothing but what was his due, and was in the way of his business; but otherwise he made no advantage of me at all.

When I passed in the ship between Dover and Calais and saw beloved England once more under my view—England, which I counted my native country, being the place I was bred up in, though not born there—a strange kind of joy possessed my mind, and I had such a longing desire to be there that I would have given the master of the ship twenty pistoles to have stood over and set me on shore in the Downs; and when he told me he could not do it—that is, that he durst not do it if I would have given him a hundred pistoles—I secretly wished that a storm would rise that might drive the ship over to the coast of England, whether they would or not, that I might be set on shore anywhere upon English ground.

This wicked wish had not been out of my thoughts above two or three hours, but the master steering away to the north, as was his course to do, we lost sight of land on that side, and only had the Flemish shore in view on our right hand, or, as the seamen call it, the starboard side; and then, with the loss of the sight, the wish for landing in England abated, and I considered how foolish it was to wish myself out of the way of my business; that if I had been on shore in England, I must go back to Holland on account of my bills, which were so considerable, and I having no correspondence there, that I could not have managed it without going myself. But we had not been out of sight of England many hours before the weather began to change; the winds whistled and made a noise, and the seamen said to one another that it would blow hard at night. It was then about two hours before sunset, and we were passed by Dunkirk, and I think they said we were in sight of Ostend. But then the wind grew high and the sea swelled, and all things looked terrible, especially to us that understood nothing but just what we saw before us. In short, night came on, and very dark it was; the wind freshened and blew harder and harder, and about two hours within night it blew a terrible storm.

I was not quite a stranger to the sea, having come from Rochelle to England when I was a child, and gone from London, by the river Thames, to France afterward, as I have said. But I began to be alarmed a little with the terrible clamour of the men over my head, for I had never been in a storm, and so had never seen the like, or heard it; and once offering to look out at the door of the steerage, as they called it, it struck me with such horror (the darkness, the fierceness of the wind, the dreadful height of the waves, and the hurry the Dutch sailors were in, whose language I did not understand one word of, neither when they cursed or when they prayed); I say, all these things together filled me with terror, and, in short, I began to be very much frighted.

When I was come back into the great cabin, there sat Amy, who was very sea-sick, and I had a little before given her a sup of cordial-waters to help her stomach. When Amy saw me come back and sit down without speaking, for so I did, she looked two or three times up at me; at last she came running to me. "Dear madam," says she, "what is the matter? What makes you look so pale? Why, you an't well; what is the matter?" I said nothing still, but held up my hands two or three times. Amy doubled her importunities; upon that I said no more but, "Step to the steerage-door and look out, as I did." So she went away immediately, and looked too, as I had bidden her; but the poor girl came back again in the greatest amazement and horror that ever I saw any poor creature in, wringing her hands and crying out she was undone! she was undone! she should be drowned! they were all lost! Thus she ran about the cabin like a mad thing, and as perfectly out of her senses as any one in such a case could be supposed to be.

I was frighted myself, but when I saw the girl in such a terrible agony, it brought me a little to myself, and I began to talk to her and put her in a little hope. I told her there was many a ship in a storm that was not cast away, and I hoped we should not be drowned; that it was true the storm was very dreadful, but I did not see that the seamen were so much concerned as we were. And so I talked to her as well as I could, though my heart was full enough of it, as well as Amy's; and death began to stare in my face; ay, and something else too—that is to say, conscience, and my mind was very much disturbed; but I had nobody to comfort me.

But Amy being in so much worse a condition—that is to say, so much more terrified at the storm than I was—I had something to do to comfort her. She was, as I have said, like one distracted, and went raving about the cabin, crying out she was undone! undone! she should be drowned! and the like. And at last, the ship giving a jerk, by the force, I suppose, of some violent wave, it threw poor Amy quite down, for she was weak enough before with being sea-sick, and as it threw her forward, the poor girl struck her head against the bulk-head, as the seamen call it, of the cabin, and laid her as dead as a stone upon the floor or deck; that is to say, she was so to all appearance.

I cried out for help, but it had been all one to have cried out on the top of a mountain where nobody had been within five miles of me, for the seamen were so engaged and made so much noise that nobody heard me or came near me. I opened the great-cabin door, and looked into the steerage to cry for help, but there, to increase my fright, was two seamen on their knees at prayers, and only one man who steered, and he made a groaning noise too, which I took to be saying his prayers, but it seems it was answering to those above, when they called to him to tell him which way to steer.

Here was no help for me, or for poor Amy, and there she lay still so, and in such a condition that I did not know whether she was dead or alive. In this fright I went to her and lifted her a little way up, setting her on the deck, with her back to the boards of the bulk-head; and I got a little bottle out of my pocket, and I held it to her nose, and rubbed her temples, and what else I could do, but still Amy showed no signs of life, till I felt for her pulse, but could hardly distinguish her to be alive. However, after a great while, she began to revive, and in about half an hour she came to herself, but remembered nothing at first of what had happened to her for a good while more.

When she recovered more fully, she asked me where she was. I told her she was in the ship yet, but God knows how long it might be. "Why, madam," says she, "is not the storm over?" "No, no," says I, "Amy." "Why, madam," says she, "it was calm just now" (meaning when she was in the swooning fit occasioned by her fall). "Calm, Amy!" says I. " 'Tis far from calm. It may be it will be calm by-and-by, when we are all drowned and gone to heaven."

"Heaven, madam!" says she. "What makes you talk so? Heaven! I go to heaven! No, no; if I am drowned I am damned! Don't you know what a wicked creature I have been? I have been a whore to two men, and have lived a wretched, abominable life of vice and wickedness for fourteen years. Oh, madam! you know it, and God knows it, and now I am to die—to be drowned! Oh! what will become of me? I am undone for ever!—ay, madam, for ever! to all eternity! Oh! I am lost! I am lost! If I am drowned, I am lost for ever!"

All these, you will easily suppose, must be so many stabs into the very soul of one in my own case. It immediately occurred to me, "Poor Amy! what art thou that I am not? What hast thou been that I have not been? Nay, I am guilty of my own sin and thine too." Then it came to my remembrance that I had not only been the same with Amy, but that I had been the devil's instrument to make her wicked; that I had stripped her, and prostituted her to the very man that I had been naught with myself; that she had but followed me, I had been her wicked example; and I had led her into all; and that, as we had sinned together, now we were likely to sink together.

All this repeated itself to my thoughts at that very moment, and every one of Amy's cries sounded thus in my ears: "I am the wicked cause of it all! I have been thy ruin, Amy! I have brought thee to this, and now thou art to suffer for the sin I have enticed thee to! And if thou art lost for ever, what must I be? what must be my portion?"

It is true this difference was between us, that I said all these things within myself, and sighed and mourned inwardly; but Amy, as her temper was more violent, spoke aloud, and cried, and called out aloud, like one in agony.

I had but small encouragement to give her, and indeed could say but very little, but I got her to compose herself a little, and not let any of the people of the ship understand what she meant or what she said. But even in her greatest composure she continued to express herself with the utmost dread and terror on account of the wicked life she had lived, and crying out she should be damned, and the like, which was very terrible to me, who knew what condition I was in myself.

Upon these serious considerations, I was very penitent too for my former sins, and cried out, though softly, two or three times, "Lord, have mercy upon me!" To this I added abundance of resolutions of what a life I would live if it should please God but to spare my life but this one time; how I would live a single and virtuous life, and spend a great deal of what I had thus wickedly got in acts of charity and doing good.

Under these dreadful apprehensions, I looked back on the life I had led with the utmost contempt and abhorrence. I blushed, and wondered at myself how I could act thus, how I could divest myself of modesty and honour, and prostitute myself for gain; and I thought, if ever it should please God to spare me this one time from death, it would not be possible that I should be the same creature again.

Amy went farther; she prayed, she resolved, she vowed to lead a new life, if God would spare her but this time. It now began to be daylight, for the storm held all night long, and it was some comfort to see the light of another day, which none of us expected; but the sea went mountains high, and the noise of the water was as frightful to us as the sight of the waves; nor was any land to be seen, nor did the seamen know whereabout they were. At last, to our great joy, they made land, which was in England, and on the coast of Suffolk; and the ship being in the utmost distress, they ran for the shore at all hazards, and with great difficulty got into Harwich, where they were safe, as to the danger of death; but the ship was so full of water and so much damaged that if they had not laid her on shore the same day, she would have sunk before night, according to the opinion of the seamen, and of the workmen on shore too who were hired to assist them in stopping their leaks.

Amy was revived as soon as she heard they had espied land, and went out upon the deck; but she soon came in again to me. "Oh, madam!" says she, "there's the land indeed to be seen. It looks like a ridge of clouds, and may be all a cloud for aught I know; but if it be land, 'tis a great way off, and the sea is in such a combustion, we shall all perish before we can reach it. 'Tis the dreadfullest sight to look at the waves that ever was seen. Why, they are as high as mountains; we shall certainly be swallowed up, for all the land is so near."

I had conceived some hope that, if they saw land, we should be delivered; and I told her she did not understand things of that nature; that she might be sure if they saw land they would go directly towards it, and would make into some harbour; but it was, as Amy said, a frightful distance to it. The land looked like clouds, and the sea went as high as mountains, so that no hope appeared in the seeing the land, but we were in fear of foundering before we could reach it. This made Amy so desponding still; but as the wind, which blew from the east, or that way, drove us furiously towards the land, so when, about half an hour after, I stepped to the steerage-door and looked out, I saw the land much nearer than Amy represented it; so I went in and encouraged Amy again, and indeed was encouraged myself.

In about an hour, or something more, we saw, to our infinite satisfaction, the open harbour of Harwich, and the vessel standing directly towards it, and in a few minutes more the ship was in smooth water, to our inexpressible comfort; and thus I had, though against my will and contrary to my true interest, what I wished for, to be driven away to England, though it was by a storm.

Nor did this incident do either Amy or me much service, for, the danger being over, the fears of death vanished with it; ay, and our fear of what was beyond death also. Our sense of the life we had lived went off, and with our return to life, our wicked taste of life returned, and we were both the same as before, if not worse. So certain is it that the repentance which is brought about by the mere apprehensions of death wears off as those apprehensions wear off, and deathbed repentance, or storm repentance, which is much the same, is seldom true.

However, I do not tell you that this was all at once neither; the fright we had at sea lasted a little while afterwards; at least the impression was not quite blown off as soon as the storm; especially poor Amy, as soon as she set her foot on shore, she fell flat upon the ground and kissed it, and gave God thanks for her deliverance from the sea; and turning to me when she got up, "I hope, madam," says she, "you will never go upon the sea again."

I know not what ailed me, not I; but Amy was much more penitent at sea, and much more sensible of her deliverance when she landed and was safe, than I was. I was in kind of stupidity, I know not well what to call it; I had a mind full of horror in the time of the storm, and saw death before me as plainly as Amy, but my thoughts got no vent, as Amy's did. I had a silent, sullen kind of grief, which could not break out either in words or tears, and which was therefore much the worse to bear.

I had a terror upon me for my wicked life past, and firmly believed I was going to the bottom, launching into death, where I was to give an account of all my past actions; and in this state, and on that account, I looked back upon my wickedness with abhorrence, as I have said above, but I had no sense of repentance from the true motive of repentance; I saw nothing of the corruption of nature, the sin of my life, as an offence against God, as a thing odious to the holiness of His being, as abusing His mercy and despising His goodness. In short, I had no thorough effectual repentance, no sight of my sins in their proper shape, no view of a Redeemer, or hope in Him. I had only such repentance as a criminal has at the place of execution, who is sorry, not that he has committed the crime, as it is a crime, but sorry that he is to be hanged for it.

It is true, Amy's repentance wore off too, as well as mine, but not so soon. However, we were both very grave for a time.

As soon as we could get a boat from the town, we went on shore, and immediately went to a public-house in the town of Harwich, where we were to consider seriously what was to be done, and whether we should go up to London or stay till the ship was refitted, which, they said, would be a fortnight, and then go for Holland, as we intended, and as a business required.

Reason directed that I should go to Holland, for there I had all my money to receive, and there I had persons of good reputation and character to apply to, having letters to them from the honest Dutch merchant at Paris, and they might perhaps give me a recommendation again to merchants in London, and so I should get acquaintance with some people of figure, which was what I loved; whereas now I knew not one creature in the whole city of London, or anywhere else, that I could go and make myself known to. Upon these considerations, I resolved to go to Holland, whatever came of it.

But Amy cried and trembled, and was ready to fall into

fits, when I did but mention going upon the sea again, and begged of me not to go, or if I would go, that I would leave her behind, though I was to send her a-begging. The people in the inn laughed at her and jested with her, asked her if she had any sins to confess that she was ashamed should be heard of, and that she was troubled with an evil conscience; told her, if she came to sea, and to be in a storm, if she had lain with her master, she would certainly tell her mistress of it, and that it was a common thing for poor maids to confess all the young men they had lain with; that there was one poor girl that went over with her mistress, whose husband was a ————r, in ————, in the city of London, who confessed, in the terror of a storm, that she had lain with her master, and all the apprentices, so often, and in such and such places, and made the poor mistress, when she returned to London, fly at her husband, and make such a stir as was indeed the ruin of the whole family. Amy could bear all that well enough, for though she had indeed lain with her master, it was with her mistress's knowledge and consent, and, which was worse, was her mistress's own doing. I record it to the reproach of my own vice, and to expose the excesses of such wickedness as they deserve to be exposed.

I thought Amy's fear would have been over by that time the ship would be gotten ready, but I found the girl was rather worse and worse; and when I came to the point that we must go on board or lose the passage, Amy was so terrified that she fell into fits; so the ship went away without us.

But my going being absolutely necessary, as above, I was obliged to go in the packet-boat some time after, and leave Amy behind at Harwich, but with directions to go to London and stay there to receive letters and orders from me what to do. Now I was become, from a lady of pleasure, a woman of business, and of great business too, I assure you.

I got me a servant at Harwich to go over with me, who had been at Rotterdam, knew the place and spoke the language, which was a great help to me, and away I went. I had a very quick passage and pleasant weather, and, coming to Rotterdam, soon found out the merchant to whom I was recommended, who received me with extraordinary respect. And first he acknowledged the accepted bill for four thousand pistoles, which he afterwards paid punctually; other bills that I had also payable at Amsterdam he procured to be received for me; and whereas one of the bills for one thousand two hundred crowns was protested at Amsterdam, he paid it me himself, for the honour of the endorser, as he called it, which was my friend the merchant at Paris.

There I entered into a negotiation by his means for my jewels, and he brought me several jewellers to look on them, and, particularly, one to value them and to tell me what every particular was worth. This was a man who had great skill in jewels, but did not trade at that time, and he was desired by the gentleman that I was with to see that I might not be imposed upon.

All this work took me up near half a year, and, by managing my business thus myself, and having large sums to do with, I became as expert in it as any she-merchant of them all. I had credit in the bank for a large sum of money, and bills and notes for much more.

After I had been here about three months, my maid Amy writes me word that she had received a letter from her friend, as she called him. That, by the way, was the prince's gentleman, that had been Amy's extraordinary friend indeed, for Amy owned to me he had lain with her a hundred times, that is to say, as often as he pleased, and perhaps in the eight years which that affair lasted, it might be a great deal oftener. This was what she called her friend, who she corresponded with upon this particular subject, and, among other things, sent her this particular news, that my extraordinary friend, my real husband, who rode in the *gens d'armes*, was dead, that he was killed in a rencounter, as they call it, or accidental scuffle among the troopers; and so the jade congratulated me upon my being now a real free woman. "And now, madam," says she at the end of her letter, "you have nothing to do but to come hither and set up a coach and a good equipage, and if beauty and a good fortune won't make you a duchess, nothing will." But I had not fixed my measures yet. I had no inclination to be a wife again. I had had such bad luck with my first husband, I hated the thoughts of it. I found that a wife is treated with indifference, a mistress with a strong passion; a wife is looked upon as but an upper-servant, a mistress is a sovereign; a wife must give up all she has, have every reserve she makes for herself be thought hard of, and be upbraided with her very pin-money,* whereas a mistress makes the saying true, that what the man has is hers, and

---

* "pin-money." An allowance settled on a wife for her private expenditure, which would be stipulated in her marriage settlement.

what she has is her own; the wife bears a thousand insults, and is forced to sit still and bear it, or part, and be undone; a mistress, insulted, helps herself immediately and takes another.

These were my wicked arguments for whoring, for I never set against them the difference another way—I may say, every other way; how that, first, a wife appears boldly and honourably with her husband, lives at home, and possesses his house, his servants, his equipages, and has a right to them all, and to call them her own; entertains his friends, owns his children, and has the return of duty and affection from them, as they are here her own, and claims upon his estate, by the custom of England, if he dies and leaves her a widow.

The whore skulks about in lodgings, is visited in the dark, disowned upon all occasions before God and man; is maintained, indeed, for a time, but is certainly condemned to be abandoned at last, and left to the miseries of fate and her own just disaster. If she has any children, her endeavour is to get rid of them, and not maintain them; and if she lives, she is certain to see them all hate her, and be ashamed of her. While the vice rages, and the man is in the devil's hand, she has him; and while she has him, she makes a prey of him; but if he happens to fall sick, if any disaster befalls him, the cause of all lies upon her. He is sure to lay all his misfortunes at her door; and if once he comes to repentance, or makes but one step towards a reformation, he begins with her—leaves her, uses her as she deserves, hates her, abhors her, and sees her no more; and that with this never-failing addition, namely, that the more sincere and unfeigned his repentance is, the more earnestly he looks up, and the more effectually he looks in, the more his aversion to her increases, and he curses her from the bottom of his soul; nay, it must be from a kind of excess of charity if he so much as wishes God may forgive her.

The opposite circumstances of a wife and whore are such and so many, and I have since seen the difference with such eyes, as I could dwell upon the subject a great while; but my business is history. I had a long scene of folly yet to run over. Perhaps the moral of all my story may bring me back again to this part, and if it does, I shall speak of it fully.

While I continued in Holland I received several letters from my friend (so I had good reason to call him) the merchant in Paris, in which he gave me a farther account of the

conduct of that rogue, the Jew, and how he acted after I was
gone; how impatient he was while the said merchant kept
him in suspense, expecting me to come again; and how he
raged when he found I came no more.

It seems, after he found I did not come, he found out by
his unwearied enquiry where I had lived, and that I had been
kept as a mistress by some great person; but he could never
learn by who, except that he learnt the colour of his livery.
In pursuit of this enquiry he guessed at the right person, but
could not make it out or offer any positive proof of it; but
he found out the prince's gentleman, and talked so saucily to
him of it that the gentleman treated him, as the French call
it, *à coup de baton*—that is to say, caned him very severely,
as he deserved; and that not satisfying him, or curing his in-
solence, he was met one night late upon Pont Neuf, in Paris,
by two men, who, muffling him up in a great cloak, carried
him into a more private place and cut off both his ears, telling him it was for talking impudently of his superiors; adding
that he should take care to govern his tongue better and behave with more manners, or the next time they would cut his
tongue out of his head.

This put a check to his sauciness that way; but he comes
back to the merchant and threatened to begin a process
against him for corresponding with me, and being accessory
to the murder of the jeweller, &c.

This merchant found by his discourse that he supposed I
was protected by the said Prince de ———; nay, the rogue
said he was sure I was in his lodgings at Versailles, for he
never had so much as the least intimation of the way I was
really gone; but that I was there he was certain, and certain
that the merchant was privy to it. The merchant bade him de-
fiance. However, he gave him a great deal of trouble and
put him to a great charge, and had like to have brought him
in for a party to my escape; in which case he would have been
obliged to have produced me, and that in the penalty of some
capital sum of money.

But the merchant was too many for him another way, for
he brought an information against him for a cheat; wherein
laying down the whole fact, how he intended falsely to accuse
the widow of the jeweller for the supposed murder of her
husband; that he did it purely to get the jewels from her; and
that he offered to bring him (the merchant) in, to be confed-

erate with him and to share the jewels between them; proving also his design to get the jewels into his hands, and then to have dropped the prosecution upon condition of my quitting the jewels to him. Upon this charge, he got him laid by the heels; so he was sent to the Conciergerie—that is to say, to Bridewell—and the merchant cleared. He got out of jail in a little while, though not without the help of money, and continued teasing the merchant a long while, and at last threatening to assassinate and murder him. So the merchant, who, having buried his wife about two months before, was now a single man, and not knowing what such a villain might do, thought fit to quit Paris and came away to Holland also.

It is most certain that, speaking of originals, I was the source and spring of all that trouble and vexation to this honest gentleman; and as it was afterwards in my power to have made him full satisfaction, and did not, I cannot say but I added ingratitude to all the rest of my follies; but of that I shall give a fuller account presently.

I was surprised one morning, when, being at the merchant's house who he had recommended me to in Rotterdam, and being busy in his counting-house, managing my bills, and preparing to write a letter to him to Paris, I heard a noise of horses at the door, which is not very common in a city where everybody passes by water; but he had, it seems, ferried over the Maas from Willemstadt, and so came to the very door, and I, looking towards the door upon hearing the horses, saw a gentleman alight and come in at the gate. I knew nothing, and expected nothing, to be sure, of the person; but, as I say, was surprised, and indeed more than ordinarily surprised, when, coming nearer to me, I saw it was my merchant of Paris, my benefactor, and indeed my deliverer.

I confess it was an agreeable surprise to me, and I was exceeding glad to see him, who was so honourable and so kind to me, and who indeed had saved my life. As soon as he saw me, he run to me, took me in his arms, and kissed me with a freedom that he never offered to take with me before. "Dear Madam ————," says he, "I am glad to see you safe in this country; if you had stayed two days longer in Paris, you had been undone." I was so glad to see him that I could not speak a good while, and I burst out into tears without speaking a word for a minute. But I recovered that disorder, and said, "The more, sir, is my obligation to you that saved my life," and added, "I am glad to see you here, that I may consider how to balance an account in which I am so much your debtor."

"You and I will adjust that matter easily," says he, "now we are so near together. Pray where do you lodge?" says he.

"In a very honest, good house," said I, "where that gentleman, your friend, recommended me," pointing to the merchant in whose house we then were.

"And where you may lodge too, sir," says the gentleman, "if it suits with your business and your other conveniency."

"With all my heart," says he. "Then, madam," adds he, turning to me, "I shall be near you, and have time to tell you a story which will be very long, and yet many ways very pleasant to you; how troublesome that devilish fellow, the Jew, has been to me on your account, and what a hellish snare he had laid for you, if he could have found you."

"I shall have leisure too, sir," said I, "to tell you all my adventures since that, which have not been a few, I assure you."

In short, he took up his lodgings in the same house where I lodged, and the room he lay in opened, as he was wishing it would, just opposite to my lodging-room, so we could almost call out of bed to one another; and I was not at all shy of him on that score, for I believed him perfectly honest, and so indeed he was; and if he had not, that article was at present no part of my concern.

It was not till two or three days, and after his first hurries of business were over, that we began to enter into the history of our affairs on every side, but when we began, it took up all our conversation for almost a fortnight. First, I gave him a particular account of everything that happened material upon my voyage, and how we were driven into Harwich by a very terrible storm; how I had left my woman behind me, so frighted with the danger she had been in that she durst not venture to set her foot into a ship again any more, and that I had not come myself if the bills I had of him had not been payable in Holland; but that money, he might see, would make a woman go anywhere.

He seemed to laugh at all our womanish fears upon the occasion of the storm, telling me it was nothing but what was very ordinary in those seas, but that they had harbours on every coast so near that they were seldom in danger of being lost indeed. "For," says he, "if they cannot fetch one coast, they can always stand away for another, and run afore it," as he called it, "for one side or other." But when I came to tell him what a crazy ship it was, and how, even when they got into Harwich, and into smooth water, they were fain to run the ship on shore, or she would have sunk in the very harbour; and when I told him that when I looked out at the cabin-door, I saw the Dutchmen, one upon his knees here, and another there, at their prayers, then indeed he acknowledged I had reason to be alarmed. But, smiling, he added, "But you, madam," says he, "are so good a lady, and so pious, you would but have gone to heaven a little the sooner; the difference had not been much to you."

I confess when he said this, it made all the blood turn in my veins, and I thought I should have fainted. "Poor gentleman," thought I, "you know little of me. What would I give to be really what you really think me to be!" He perceived the disorder, but said nothing till I spoke; when, shaking my head, "Oh, sir!" said I, "death in any shape has some terror in it, but in the frightful figure of a storm at sea and a sinking ship, it comes with a double, a treble, and indeed an inexpressible horror; and if I were that saint you think me to be (which God knows I am not), 'tis still very dismal. I desire to die in a calm, if I can." He said a great many good things, and very prettily ordered his discourse between serious reflection and compliment, but I had too much guilt to relish it as it was meant, so I turned it off to something else, and talked of the necessity I had on me to come to Holland, but I wished myself safe on shore in England again.

He told me he was glad I had such an obligation upon me to come over into Holland, however, but hinted that he was so interested in my welfare, and, besides, had such further designs upon me, that if I had not so happily been found in Holland, he was resolved to have gone to England to see me, and that it was one of the principal reasons of his leaving Paris.

I told him I was extremely obliged to him for so far interesting himself in my affairs, but that I had been so far his debtor before that I knew not how anything could increase the debt; for I owed my life to him already, and I could not be in debt for any-thing more valuable than that.

He answered in the most obliging manner possible that he would put it in my power to pay that debt, and all the obligations besides that ever he had, or should be able to lay upon me.

I began to understand him now, and to see plainly that he

resolved to make love to me, but I would by no means seem to take the hint; and, besides, I knew that he had a wife with him in Paris; and I had, just then at least, no gust to any more intriguing. However, he surprised me into a sudden notice of the thing a little while after by saying something in his discourse that he did, as he said, in his wife's days. I started at that word. "What mean you by that, sir?" said I. "Have you not a wife at Paris?" "No, madam, indeed," said he; "my wife died the beginning of September last," which, it seems, was but a little after I came away.

We lived in the same house all this while, and as we lodged not far off of one another, opportunities were not wanting of as near an acquaintance as we might desire; nor have such opportunities the least agency in vicious minds to bring to pass even what they might not intend at first.

However, though he courted so much at a distance, yet his pretensions were very honourable; and as I had before found him a most disinterested friend, and perfectly honest in his dealings, even when I trusted him with all I had, so now I found him strictly virtuous, till I made him otherwise myself, even almost whether he would or no, as you shall hear.

It was not long after our former discourse, when he repeated what he had insinuated before, namely, that he had yet a design to lay before me, which, if I would agree to his proposals, would more than balance all accounts between us. I told him I could not reasonably deny him anything; and except one thing, which I hoped and believed he would not think of, I should think myself very ungrateful if I did not do everything for him that lay in my power.

He told me what he should desire of me would be fully in my power to grant, or else he should be very unfriendly to offer it; and still, all this while, he declined making the proposal, as he called it, and so for that time we ended our discourse, turning it off to other things. So that, in short, I began to think he might have met with some disaster in his business, and might have come away from Paris in some discredit, or had had some blow on his affairs in general; and as really I had kindness enough to have parted with a good sum to have helped him, and was in gratitude bound to have done so, he having so effectually saved to me all I had, so I resolved to make him the offer the first time I had an opportunity, which two or three days after offered itself, very much to my satisfaction.

He had told me at large, though on several occasions, the treatment he had met with from the Jew, and what expense he had put him to; how at length he had cast* him, as above, and had recovered good damage of him, but that the rogue was unable to make him any considerable reparation. He had told me also how the Prince de ———'s gentleman had resented his treatment of his master, and how he had caused him to be used upon the Pont Neuf, &c., as I have mentioned above, which I laughed at most heartily.

"It is pity," said I, "that I should sit here and make that gentleman no amends; if you would direct me, sir," said I, "how to do it, I would make him a handsome present, and acknowledge the justice he had done to me, as well as to the prince, his master." He said he would do what I directed in it; so I told him I would send him five hundred crowns. "That's too much," said he, "for you are but half interested in the usage of the Jew; it was on his master's account he corrected him, not on yours." Well, however, we were obliged to do nothing in it, for neither of us knew how to direct a letter to him, or to direct anybody to him; so I told him I would leave it till I came to England, for that my woman, Amy, corresponded with him, and that he had made love to her.

"Well, but, sir," said I, "as, in requital for his generous concern for me, I am careful to think of him, it is but just that what expense you have been obliged to be at, which was all on my account, should be repaid you; and therefore," said I, "let me see—" And there I paused, and began to reckon up what I had observed, from his own discourse, it had cost him in the several disputes and hearings which he had with that dog of a Jew, and I cast them up at something above 2130 crowns. So I pulled out some bills which I had upon a merchant in Amsterdam, and a particular account in bank, and was looking on them in order to give them to him.

When he, seeing evidently what I was going about, interrupted me with some warmth, and told me he would have nothing of me on that account, and desired I would not pull out my bills and papers on that score; that he had not told me the story on that account or with any such view; that it had been his misfortune first to bring that ugly rogue to me, which, though it was with a good design, yet he would punish himself with the expense he had been at for his being so unlucky to me;

* "cast." See above, page 101.

that I could not think so hard of him as to suppose he would take money of me, a widow, for serving me, and doing acts of kindness to me in a strange country, and in distress too; but he said he would repeat what he had said before, that he kept me for a deeper reckoning, and that, as he had told me, he would put me into a posture to even all that favour, as I called it, at once, so we should talk it over another time and balance all together.

Now I expected it would come out, but still he put it off, as before, from whence I concluded it could not be matter of love, for that those things are not usually delayed in such a manner, and therefore it must be matter of money. Upon which thought, I broke the silence, and told him that as he knew I had, by obligation, more kindness for him than to deny any favour to him that I could grant, and that he seemed backward to mention his case, I begged leave of him to give me leave to ask him whether anything lay upon his mind with respect to his business and effects in the world; that if it did, he knew what I had in the world as well as I did, and that, if he wanted money, I would let him have any sum for his occasion, as far as five or six thousand pistoles, and he should pay me as his own affairs would permit; and that, if he never paid me, I would assure him that I would never give him any trouble for it.

He rose up with ceremony, and gave me thanks in terms that sufficiently told me he had been bred among people more polite and more courteous than is esteemed the ordinary usage of the Dutch; and after his compliment was over, he came nearer to me and told me he was obliged to assure me, though with repeated acknowledgments of my kind offer, that he was not in any want of money; that he had met with no uneasiness in any of his affairs—no, not of any kind whatever, except that of the loss of his wife and one of his children, which indeed had troubled him much; but that this was no part of what he had to offer to me, and by granting which I should balance all obligations; but that, in short, it was that, seeing Providence had (as it were for that purpose) taken his wife from him, I would make up the loss to him; and with that he held me fast in his arms and, kissing me, would not give me leave to say no, and hardly to breathe.

At length, having got room to speak, I told him that, as I had said before, I could deny him but one thing in the world;

I was very sorry he should propose that thing only that I could not grant.

I could not but smile, however, to myself that he should make so many circles and round-about motions to come at a discourse which had no such rarity at the bottom of it, if he had known all. But there was another reason why I resolved not to have him, when, at the same time, if he had courted me in a manner less honest or virtuous, I believe I should not have denied him; but I shall come to that part presently.

He was, as I have said, long a-bringing it out, but when he had brought it out, he pursued it with such importunities as would admit of no denial; at least he intended they should not; but I resisted them obstinately, and yet with expressions of the utmost kindness and respect for him that could be imagined, often telling him there was nothing else in the world that I could deny him, and showing him all the respect, and upon all occasions treating him with intimacy and freedom, as if he had been my brother.

He tried all the ways imaginable to bring his design to pass, but I was inflexible. At last he thought of a way which, he flattered himself, would not fail; nor would he have been mistaken, perhaps, in any other woman in the world but me. This was, to try if he could take me at an advantage and get to bed to me, and then, as was most rational to think, I should willingly enough marry him afterwards.

We were so intimate together that nothing but man and wife could, or at least ought, to be more; but still our freedoms kept within the bounds of modesty and decency. But one evening, above all the rest, we were very merry, and I fancied he pushed the mirth to watch for his advantage, and I resolved that I would at least feign to be as merry as he; and that, in short, if he offered anything, he should have his will easily enough.

About one o'clock in the morning—for so long we sat up together—I said, "Come, 'tis one o'clock; I must go to bed." "Well," says he, "I'll go with you." "No, no," says I; "go to your own chamber." He said he would go to bed with me. "Nay," says I, "if you will, I don't know what to say; if I can't help it, you must." However, I got from him, left him, and went into my chamber, but did not shut the door, and as he could easily see that I was undressing myself, he steps to his own room, which was but on the same floor, and in a few

minutes undresses himself also, and returns to my door in his
gown and slippers.

I thought he had been gone indeed, and so that he had
been in jest; and, by the way, thought either he had no mind
to the thing, or that he never intended it; so I shut my
door—that is, latched it, for I seldom locked or bolted it—
and went to bed. I had not been in bed a minute but he
comes in his gown to the door and opens it a little way, but
not enough to come in or look in, and says softly, "What! are
you really gone to bed?" "Yes, yes," says I; "get you gone."
"No, indeed," says he, "I shall not be gone; you gave me
leave before to come to bed, and you shan't say 'Get you
gone' now." So he comes into my room, and then turns about
and fastens the door, and immediately comes to the bedside
to me. I pretended to scold and struggle, and bid him begone
with more warmth than before; but it was all one; he had not
a rag of clothes on but his gown and slippers and shirt, so
he throws off his gown, and throws open the bed, and came
in at once.

I made a seeming resistance, but it was no more indeed;
for, as above, I resolved from the beginning he should lie
with me if he would, and, for the rest, I left it to come after.

Well, he lay with me that night, and the two next, and very
merry we were all the three days between; but the third night
he began to be a little more grave. "Now, my dear," says he,
"though I have pushed this matter farther than ever I intended, or than I believe you expected from me, who never made
any pretences to you but what were very honest, yet to heal it
all up, and let you see how sincerely I meant at first, and
how honest I will ever be to you, I am ready to marry you
still, and desire you to let it be done to-morrow morning; and
I will give you the same fair conditions of marriage as I
would have done before."

This, it must be owned, was a testimony that he was very
honest, and that he loved me sincerely; but I construed it
quite another way, namely, that he aimed at the money. But
how surprised did he look, and how was he confounded,
when he found me receive his proposal with coldness and indifference, and still tell him that it was the only thing I could
not grant!

He was astonished. "What! not take me now," says he,
"when I have been a-bed with you!" I answered coldly,
though respectfully still, "It is true, to my shame be it spo-

ken," says I, "that you have taken me by surprise, and have had your will of me; but I hope you will not take it ill that I cannot consent to marry, for all that. If I am with child," said I, "care must be taken to manage that as you shall direct; I hope you won't expose me for my having exposed myself to you, but I cannot go any farther." And at that point I stood, and would hear of no matrimony by any means.

Now, because this may seem a little odd, I shall state the matter clearly, as I understood it myself. I knew that, while I was a mistress, it is customary for the person kept to receive from them that keep; but if I should be a wife, all I had then was given up to the husband, and I was thenceforth to be under his authority only; and as I had money enough, and needed not fear being what they call a cast-off mistress, so I had no need to give him twenty thousand pounds to marry me, which had been buying my lodging too dear a great deal.

Thus his project of coming to bed to me was a bite upon himself, while he intended it for a bite upon me; and he was no nearer his aim of marrying me than he was before. All his arguments he could urge upon the subject of matrimony were at an end, for I positively declined marrying him; and as he had refused the thousand pistoles which I had offered him in compensation for his expenses and loss at Paris with the Jew, and had done it upon the hopes he had of marrying me, so when he found his way difficult still, he was amazed, and, I had some reason to believe, repented that he had refused the money.

But thus it is when men run into wicked measures to bring their designs about. I, that was infinitely obliged to him before, began to talk to him as if I had balanced accounts with him now, and that the favour of lying with a whore was equal, not to the thousand pistoles only, but to all the debt I owed him for saving my life and all my effects.

But he drew himself into it, and though it was a dear bargain, yet it was a bargain of his own making; he could not say I had tricked him into it. But as he projected and drew me in to lie with him, depending that it was a sure game in order to a marriage, so I granted him the favour, as he called it, to balance the account of favours received from him, and keep the thousand pistoles with a good grace.

He was extremely disappointed in this article, and knew not how to manage for a great while; and as I dare say, if he

had not expected to have made it an earnest for marrying
me, he would never have attempted me the other way, so, I
believed, if it had not been for the money which he knew I
had, he would never have desired to marry me after he had
lain with me. For where is the man that cares to marry a
whore, though of his own making? And as I knew him to be
no fool, so I did him no wrong when I supposed that, but for
the money, he would not have had any thoughts of me that
way, especially after my yielding as I had done; in which it is
to be remembered that I made no capitulation* for marrying
him when I yielded to him, but let him do just what he
pleased, without any previous bargain.

Well, hitherto we went upon guesses at one another's
designs; but as he continued to importune me to marry,
though he had lain with me, and still did lie with me as often
as he pleased, and I continued to refuse to marry him, though
I let him lie with me whenever he desired it; I say, as these
two circumstances made up our conversation, it could not
continue long thus, but we must come to an explanation.

One morning, in the middle of our unlawful freedoms—
that is to say, when we were i bed together—he sighed, and
told me he desired my leave to ask me one question, and that
I would give him an answer to it with the same ingenuous
freedom and honesty that I had used to treat him with. I told
him I would. Why, then, his question was, why I would not
marry him, seeing I allowed him all the freedom of a husband. "Or," says he, "my dear, since you have been so kind as
to take me to your bed, why will you not make me your own
and take me for good-and-all, that we may enjoy ourselves
without any reproach to one another?"

I told him, that as I confessed it was the only thing I could
not comply with him in, so it was the only thing in all my actions that I could not give him a reason for; that it was true I
had let him come to bed to me, which was supposed to be the
greatest favour a woman could grant; but it was evident, and
he might see it, that, as I was sensible of the obligation I was
under to him for saving me from the worst circumstance it
was possible for me to be brought to, I could deny him nothing; and if I had had any greater favour to yield him, I
should have done it, that of matrimony only excepted, and he
could not but see that I loved him to an extraordinary degree,
in every part of my behaviour to him; but that as to marry-

* "capitulation." see above, page 35.

ing, which was giving up my liberty, it was what once he knew I had done, and he had seen how it had hurried me up and down in the world, and what it had exposed me to; that I had an aversion to it, and desired he would not insist upon it. He might easily see I had no aversion to him; and that, if I was with child by him, he should see a testimony of my kindness to the father, for that I would settle all I had in the world upon the child.

He was mute a good while. At last says he, "Come, my dear, you are the first woman in the world that ever lay with a man and then refused to marry him, and therefore there must be some other reason for your refusal; and I have therefore one other request, and that is, if I guess at the true reason, and remove the objection, will you then yield to me?" I told him if he removed the objection, I must needs comply, for I should certainly do everything that I had no objection against.

"Why then, my dear, it must be that either you are already engaged or married to some other man, or you are not willing to dispose of your money to me, and expect to advance yourself higher with your fortune. Now, if it be the first of these, my mouth will be stopped, and I have no more to say; but if it be the last, I am prepared effectually to remove the objection and answer all you can say on that subject."

I took him up short at the first of these, telling him he must have base thoughts of me indeed, to think that I could yield to him in such a manner as I had done, and continue it with so much freedom as he found I did, if I had a husband or were engaged to any other man; and that he might depend upon it, that was not my case, nor any part of my case.

"Why then," said he, "as to the other, I have an offer to make to you that shall take off all the objection, viz., that I will not touch one pistole of your estate more than shall be with your own voluntary consent, neither now or at any other time, but you shall settle it as you please for your life, and upon who you please after your death"; that I should see he was able to maintain me without it, and that it was not for that that he followed me from Paris.

I was indeed surprised at that part of his offer, and he might easily perceive it; it was not only what I did not expect, but it was what I knew not what answer to make to. He had, indeed, removed my principal objection—nay, all my objections, and it was not possible for me to give any answer; for, if upon so generous an offer I should agree with him, I then did as good as confess that it was upon the account of my money that I refused him; and that though I could give up my virtue and expose myself, yet I would not give up my money, which, though it was true, yet was really too gross for me to acknowledge, and I could not pretend to marry him upon that principle neither. Then as to having him, and make over all my estate out of his hands, so as not to give him the management of what I had, I thought it would be not only a little Gothic and inhuman, but would be always a foundation of unkindness between us, and render us suspected one to another; so that, upon the whole, I was obliged to give a new turn to it, and talk upon a kind of an elevated strain, which really was not in my thoughts, at first, at all; for I own, as above, the divesting myself of my estate and putting my money out of my hand was the sum of the matter that made me refuse to marry; but, I say, I gave it a new turn upon this occasion, as follows:

I told him I had, perhaps, different notions of matrimony from what the received custom had given us of it; that I thought a woman was a free agent as well as a man, and was born free, and, could she manage herself suitably, might enjoy that liberty to as much purpose as the men do; that the laws of matrimony were indeed otherwise, and mankind at this time acted quite upon other principles, and those such that a woman gave herself entirely away from herself, in marriage, and capitulated, only to be, at best, but an upper-servant, and from the time she took the man, she was no better or worse than the servant among the Israelites, who had his ears bored—that is, nailed to the door-post—who by that act gave himself up to be a servant during life; that the very nature of the marriage-contract was, in short, nothing but giving up liberty, estate, authority, and everything to the man, and the woman was indeed a mere woman ever after—that is to say, a slave.

He replied, that though in some respects it was as I had said, yet I ought to consider that, as an equivalent to this, the man had all the care of things devolved upon him; that the weight of business lay upon his shoulders, and as he had the trust, so he had the toil of life upon him; his was the labour, his the anxiety of living; that the woman had nothing to do but to eat the fat and drink the sweet; to sit still and look round her, be waited on and made much of, be served and loved and made easy, especially if the husband acted as became him; and that, in general, the labour of the man was appointed to make the woman live quiet and unconcerned in the world; that they had the name of subjection without the thing; and if in inferior families they had the drudgery of the house and care of the provisions upon them, yet they had indeed much the easier part; for, in general, the women had only the care of managing—that is, spending what their husbands get; and that a woman had the name of subjection, indeed, but that they generally commanded, not the men only, but all they had; managed all for themselves; and where the man did his duty, the woman's life was all ease and tranquillity, and that she had nothing to do but to be easy, and to make all that were about her both easy and merry.

I returned, that while a woman was single, she was a masculine in her politic capacity; that she had then the full command of what she had, and the full direction of what she did; that she was a man in her separated capacity, to all intents and purposes that a man could be so to himself; that she was controlled by none, because accountable to none, and was in subjection to none. So I sung these two lines of Mr. ————'s:

> Oh, 'tis pleasant to be free,
> The sweetest *Miss* is Liberty.

I added, that whoever the woman was that had an estate, and would give it up to be the slave of a great man, that woman was a fool and must be fit for nothing but a beggar; that it was my opinion a woman was fit to govern and enjoy her own estate without a man, as a man was without a woman; and that, if she had a mind to gratify herself as to sexes, she might entertain a man, as a man does a mistress; that while she was thus single, she was her own, and if she gave away that power, she merited to be as miserable as it was possible that any creature could be.

All he could say could not answer the force of this as to argument; only this, that the other way was the ordinary method that the world was guided by; that he had reason to expect I should be content with that which all the world was contented with; that he was of the opinion that a sincere affection between a man and his wife answered all the objections that I had made about the being a slave, a servant, and the like; and where there was a mutual love, there could be no bondage, but that there was but one interest, one aim, one design, and all conspired to make both very happy.

"Ay," said I, "that is the thing I complain of. The pretence of affection takes from a woman everything that can be called herself; she is to have no interest, no aim, no view; but all is the interest, aim, and view of the husband; she is to be the passive creature you spoke of," said I. "She is to lead a life of perfect indolence, and living by faith, not in God, but in her husband, she sinks or swims, as he is either fool or wise man, unhappy or prosperous; and in the middle of what she thinks is her happiness and prosperity, she is engulfed in misery and beggary, which she had not the least notice, knowledge, or suspicion of. How often have I seen a woman living in all the splendour that a plentiful fortune ought to allow her, with her coaches and equipages, her family and rich furniture, her attendants and friends, her visitors and good company, all about her to-day; to-morrow surprised with a disaster, turned out of all by a commission of bankrupt, stripped to the clothes on her back; her jointure, suppose she had it, is sacrificed to the creditors so long as her husband lived, and she turned into the street, and left to live on the charity of her friends, if she has any, or follow the monarch, her husband, into the Mint,* and live there on the wreck of his fortunes, till he is forced to run away from her even there; and then she sees her children starve, herself miserable, breaks her heart, and cries herself to death! This," says I, "is the state of many a lady that has had ten thousand pound to her portion."

He did not know how feelingly I spoke this, and what extremities I had gone through of this kind; how near I was to the very last article above, viz., crying myself to death; and how I really starved for almost two years together.

But he shook his head, and said, where had I lived? and what dreadful families had I lived among, that had frighted me into such terrible apprehensions of things? that these things indeed might happen where men run into hazardous things in trade, and, without prudence or due consideration, launched their fortunes in a degree beyond their strength, grasping at adventures beyond their stocks, and the like; but that, as he was stated in the world, if I would embark with

* "the Mint." An area in which debtors could not be arrested.

him, he had a fortune equal with mine; that together we should have no occasion of engaging in business any more, but that in any part of the world where I had a mind to live—whether England, France, Holland, or where I would—we might settle, and live as happily as the world could make any one live; that if I desired the management of our estate, when put together, if I would not trust him with mine, he would trust me with his; that we would be upon one bottom, and I should steer. "Ay," says I, "you'll allow me to steer—that is, hold the helm—but you'll conn the ship, as they call it; that is, as at sea, a boy serves to stand at the helm, but he that gives him the orders is pilot."

He laughed at my simile. "No," says he, "you shall be pilot then; you shall conn the ship." "Ay," says I, "as long as you please; but you can take the helm out of my hand when you please, and bid me go spin. It is not you," says I, "that I suspect, but the laws of matrimony puts the power into your hands, bids you do it, commands you to command, and binds me, forsooth, to obey. You, that are now upon even terms with me, and I with you," says I, "are the next hour set up upon the throne, and the humble wife placed at your footstool; all the rest, all that you call oneness of interest, mutual affection, and the like, is courtesy and kindness then, and a woman is indeed infinitely obliged where she meets with it, but can't help herself where it fails."

Well, he did not give it over yet, but came to the serious part, and there he thought he should be too many for me. He first hinted that marriage was decreed by Heaven; that it was the fixed state of life, which God had appointed for man's felicity, and for establishing a legal posterity; that there could be no legal claim of estates by inheritance but by children born in wedlock; that all the rest was sunk under scandal and illegitimacy; and very well he talked upon that subject indeed.

But it would not do; I took him short there. "Look you, sir," said I, "you have an advantage of me there indeed, in my particular case, but it would not be generous to make use of it. I readily grant that it were better for me to have married you than to admit you to the liberty I have given you, but as I could not reconcile my judgment to marriage, for the reasons above, and had kindness enough for you, and obligation too much on me to resist you, I suffered your rudeness and gave up my virtue. But I have two things before me to

heal up that breach of honour without that desperate one of
marriage, and those are, repentance for what is past, and putting an end to it for time to come."

He seemed to be concerned to think that I should take him
in that manner. He assured me that I misunderstood him;
that he had more manners as well as more kindness for me,
and more justice than to reproach me with what he had been
the aggressor in, and had surprised me into; that what he
spoke referred to my words above, that the woman, if she
thought fit, might entertain a man, as a man did a mistress;
and that I seemed to mention that way of living as justifiable,
and setting it as a lawful thing, and in the place of matrimony.

Well, we strained some compliments upon those points, not
worth repeating; and I added, I supposed when he got to bed
to me he thought himself sure of me; and, indeed, in the ordinary course of things, after he had lain with me, he ought
to think so, but that, upon the same foot of argument which I
had discoursed with him upon, it was just the contrary; and
when a woman had been weak enough to yield up the last
point before wedlock, it would be adding one weakness to another to take the man afterwards, to pin down the shame of
it upon herself all the days of her life, and bind herself to live
all her time with the only man that could upbraid her with it;
that in yielding at first, she must be a fool, but to take the
man is to be sure to be called fool; that to resist a man is to
act with courage and vigour, and to cast off the reproach,
which, in the course of things, drops out of knowledge and
dies. The man goes one way and the woman another, as fate
and the circumstances of living direct; and if they keep one
another's counsel, the folly is heard no more of. "But to take
the man," says I, "is the most preposterous thing in nature,
and (saving your presence) is to befoul one's-self, and live always in the smell of it. No, no," added I, "after a man has
lain with me as a mistress, he ought never to lie with me as a
wife. That's not only preserving the crime in memory, but it
is recording it in the family. If the woman marries the man
afterwards, she bears the reproach of it to the last hour. If
her husband is not a man of a hundred thousand, he sometime or other upbraids her with it. If he has children, they
fail not one way or other to hear of it. If the children are virtuous, they do their mother the justice to hate her for it; if
they are wicked, they give her the mortification of doing the

like, and giving her for the example. On the other hand, if the man and the woman part, there is an end of the crime and an end of the clamour; time wears out the memory of it, or a woman may remove but a few streets, and she soon outlives it and hears no more of it."

He was confounded at this discourse, and told me he could not say but I was right in the main. That as to that part relating to managing estates, it was arguing *à la cavalier;* *it was in some sense right, if the women were able to carry it on so, but that in general the sex were not capable of it; their heads were not turned for it, and they had better choose a person capable and honest, that knew how to do them justice as women, as well as to love them; and that then the trouble was all taken off their hands.

I told him it was a dear way of purchasing their ease, for very often when the trouble was taken off of their hands, so was their money too; and that I thought it was far safer for the sex not to be afraid of the trouble, but to be really afraid of their money; that if nobody was trusted, nobody would be deceived, and the staff in their own hands was the best security in the world.

He replied that I had started a new thing in the world; that however I might support it by subtle reasoning, yet it was a way of arguing that was contrary to the general practice, and that he confessed he was much disappointed in it; that, had he known I would have made such a use of it, he would never have attempted what he did, which he had no wicked design in, resolving to make me reparation, and that he was very sorry he had been so unhappy; that he was very sure he should never upbraid me with it hereafter, and had so good an opinion of me as to believe I did not suspect him; but seeing I was positive in refusing him, notwithstanding what had passed, he had nothing to do but secure me from reproach by going back again to Paris, that so, according to my own way of arguing, it might die out of memory, and I might never meet with it again to my disadvantage.

I was not pleased with this part at all, for I had no mind to let him go neither, and yet I had no mind to give him such hold of me as he would have had; and thus I was in a kind of suspense, irresolute, and doubtful what course to take.

I was in the house with him, as I have observed, and I saw

---

* "à la cavalier." Cavalierly, arrogantly, and without sufficient consideration.

evidently that he was preparing to go back to Paris; and particularly I found he was remitting money to Paris, which was, as I understood afterwards, to pay for some wines which he had given order to have bought for him at Troyes, in Champagne, and I knew not what course to take; and, besides that, I was very loth to part with him. I found also that I was with child by him, which was what I had not yet told him of, and sometimes I thought not to tell him of it at all; but I was in a strange place, and had no acquaintance, though I had a great deal of substance, which indeed, having no friends there, was the more dangerous to me.

This obliged me to take him one morning when I saw him, as I thought, a little anxious about his going, and irresolute. Says I to him, "I fancy you can hardly find in your heart to leave me now." "The more unkind is it in you," said he, "severely unkind, to refuse a man that knows not how to part with you."

"I am so far from being unkind to you," said I, "that I will go over all the world with you if you desired me, except to Paris, where you know I can't go."

"It is pity so much love," said he, "on both sides should ever separate."

"Why, then," said I, "do you go away from me?"

"Because," said he, "you won't take me."

"But if I won't take you," said I, "you may take me, anywhere, but to Paris."

He was very loth to go anywhere, he said, without me, but he must go to Paris or the East Indies.

I told him I did not use to court, but I durst venture myself to the East Indies with him, if there was a necessity of his going.

He told me, God be thanked he was in no necessity of going anywhere, but that he had a tempting invitation to go to the Indies.

I answered, I would say nothing to that, but that I desired he would go anywhere but to Paris, because there he knew I must not go.

He said he had no remedy but to go where I could not go, for he could not bear to see me if he must not have me.

I told him that was the unkindest thing he could say of me, and that I ought to take it very ill, seeing I knew how very well to oblige him to stay, without yielding to what he knew I could not yield to.

This amazed him, and he told me I was pleased to be mysterious, but that he was sure it was in nobody's power to hinder him going, if he resolved upon it, except me, who had influence enough upon him to make him do anything.

Yes, I told him, I could hinder him, because I knew he could no more do an unkind thing by me than he could do an unjust one; and to put him out of his pain, I told him I was with child.

He came to me and taking me in his arms and kissing me a thousand times almost, said, why would I be so unkind not to tell him that before?

I told him 'twas hard, that to have him stay, I should be forced to do as criminals do to avoid the gallows, plead my belly; and that I thought I had given him testimonies enough of an affection equal to that of a wife, if I had not only lain with him, been with child by him, shown myself unwilling to part with him, but offered to go to the East Indies with him; and except one thing that I could not grant, what could he ask more?

He stood mute a good while, but afterwards told me he had a great deal more to say if I could assure him that I would not take ill whatever freedom he might use with me in his discourse.

I told him he might use any freedom in words with me; for a woman who had given leave to such other freedoms as I had done had left herself no room to take anything ill, let it be what it would.

"Why, then," he said, "I hope you believe, madam, I was born a Christian, and that I have some sense of sacred things upon my mind. When I first broke in upon my own virtue and assaulted yours; when I surprised and, as it were, forced you to that which neither you intended or I designed but a few hours before, it was upon a presumption that you would certainly marry me, if once I could go that length with you, and it was with an honest resolution to make you my wife.

"But I have been surprised with such a denial that no woman in such circumstances ever gave to a man; for certainly it was never known that any woman refused to marry a man that had first lain with her, much less a man that had gotten her with child. But you go upon different notions from all the world, and though you reason upon it so strongly that a man knows hardly what to answer, yet I must own there is something in it shocking to nature, and something very unkind to yourself. But, above all, it is unkind to the child that is yet unborn, who, if we marry, will come into the world with advantage enough, but if not, is ruined before it is born; must bear the eternal reproach of what it is not guilty of; must be branded from its cradle with a mark of infamy, be loaded with the crimes and follies of its parents, and suffer for sins that it never committed. This I take to be very hard and, indeed, cruel to the poor infant not yet born, who you cannot think of with any patience, if you have the common affection of a mother, and not do that for it which should at once place it on a level with the rest of the world, and not leave it to curse its parents for what also we ought to be ashamed of. I cannot, therefore," says he, "but beg and entreat you, as you are a Christian and a mother, not to let the innocent lamb you go with be ruined before it is born, and leave it to curse and reproach us hereafter for what may be so easily avoided.

"Then, dear madam," said he, with a world of tenderness (and I thought I saw tears in his eyes), "allow me to repeat it, that I am a Christian, and consequently I do not allow what I have rashly, and without due consideration, done; I say, I do not approve of it as lawful, and therefore, though I did, with the view I have mentioned, one unjustifiable action, I cannot, therefore," says he, "but beg and entreat you, as practice of what in judgment we must both condemn; and though I love you above all the women in the world, and have done enough to convince you of it by resolving to marry you after what has passed between us, and by offering to quit all pretensions to any part of your estate, so that I should, as it were, take a wife after I had lain with her, and without a farthing portion, which, as my circumstances are, I need not do; I say, notwithstanding my affection to you, which is inexpressible, yet I cannot give up soul as well as body, the interest of this world and the hopes of another; and you cannot call this my disrespect to you."

If ever any man in the world was truly valuable for the strictest honesty of intention, this was the man; and if ever woman in her senses rejected a man of merit on so trivial and frivolous a pretence, I was the woman; but surely it was the most preposterous thing that ever woman did.

He would have taken me as a wife, but would not entertain me as a whore. Was ever woman angry with any gentleman on that head? And was ever woman so stupid to choose to be a whore, where she might have been an honest wife? But infatuations are next to being possessed of the devil. I was inflexible, and pretended to argue upon the point of a woman's liberty as before, but he took me short, and with more warmth than he had yet used with me, though with the utmost respect, replied, "Dear madam, you argue for liberty, at the same time that you restrain yourself from that liberty which God and nature has directed you to take, and, to supply the deficiency, propose a vicious liberty, which is neither honourable or religious. Will you propose liberty at the expense of modesty?"

I returned, that he mistook me; I did not propose it; I only said that those that could not be content without concerning the sexes in that affair might do so indeed; might entertain a man as men do a mistress, if they thought fit, but he did not hear me say I would do so; and though, by what had passed, he might well censure me in that part, yet he should find, for the future, that I should freely converse with him without any inclination that way.

He told me he could not promise that for himself, and thought he ought not to trust himself with the opportunity, for that, as he had failed already, he was loth to lead himself into the temptation of offending again, and that this was the true reason of his resolving to go back to Paris; not that he could willingly leave me, and would be very far from wanting my invitation; but if he could not stay upon terms that became him, either as an honest man or a Christian, what could he do? And he hoped, he said, I could not blame him that he was unwilling anything that was to call him father should upbraid him with leaving him in the world to be called bastard; adding that he was astonished to think how I could satisfy myself to be so cruel to an innocent infant not yet born; professed he could neither bear the thoughts of it, much less bear to see it, and hoped I would not take it ill that he could not stay to see me delivered, for that very reason.

I saw he spoke this with a disturbed mind, and that it was with some difficulty that he restrained his passion, so I declined any farther discourse upon it; only said I hoped he would consider of it. "Oh, madam!" says he, "do not bid me consider; 'tis for you to consider." And with that he went out of the room, in a strange kind of confusion, as was easy to be seen in his countenance.

If I had not been one of the foolishest as well as wickedest creatures upon earth, I could never have acted thus. I had one of the honestest, completest gentlemen upon earth at my hand. He had in one sense saved my life, but he had saved that life from ruin in a most remarkable manner. He loved me even to distraction, and had come from Paris to Rotterdam on purpose to seek me. He had offered me marriage even after I was with child by him, and had offered to quit all his pretensions to my estate, and give it up to my own management, having a plentiful estate of his own. Here I might have settled myself out of the reach even of disaster itself; his estate and mine would have purchased even then above two thousand pounds a year, and I might have lived like a queen—nay, far more happy than a queen; and, which was above all, I had now an opportunity to have quitted a life of crime and debauchery, which I had been given up to for several years, and to have sat down quiet in plenty and honour, and to have set myself apart to the great work which I have since seen so much necessity of and occasion for—I mean that of repentance.

But my measure of wickedness was not yet full. I continued obstinate against matrimony, and yet I could not bear the thoughts of his going away neither. As to the child, I was not very anxious about it. I told him I would promise him that it should never come to him to upbraid him with its being illegitimate; that if it was a boy, I would breed it up like the son of a gentleman, and use it well for his sake; and after a little more such talk as this, and seeing him resolved to go, I retired, but could not help letting him see the tears run down my cheeks. He came to me and kissed me, entreated me, conjured me by the kindness he had shown me in my distress, by the justice he had done me in my bills and money affairs, by the respect which made him refuse a thousand pistoles from me for his expenses with that traitor the Jew, by the pledge of our misfortunes—so he called it—which I carried with me, and by all that the sincerest affection could propose to do, that I would not drive him away.

But it would not do. I was stupid and senseless, deaf to all his importunities, and continued so to the last. So we parted, only desiring me to promise that I would write him word when I was delivered, and how he might give me an answer; and this I engaged my word I would do. And upon his desiring to be informed which way I intended to dispose of myself,

I told him I resolved to go directly to England, and to London, where I proposed to lie-in; but since he resolved to leave me, I told him I supposed it would be of no consequence to him what became of me.

He lay in his lodgings that night, but went away early in the morning, leaving me a letter in which he repeated all he had said, recommended the care of the child, and desired of me that as he had remitted to me the offer of a thousand pistoles which I would have given him for the recompense of his charges and trouble with the Jew, and had given it me back, so he desired I would allow him to oblige me to set apart that thousand pistoles, with its improvement, for the child, and for its education; earnestly pressing me to secure that little portion for the abandoned orphan when I should think fit, as he was sure I would, to throw away the rest upon something as worthless as my sincere friend at Paris. He concluded with moving me to reflect, with the same regret as he did, on our follies we had committed together; asked me forgiveness for being the aggressor in the fact, and forgave me everything, he said, but the cruelty of refusing him, which he owned he could not forgive me so heartily as he should do, because he was satisfied it was an injury to myself, would be an introduction to my ruin, and that I would seriously repent of it. He foretold some fatal things, which, he said, he was well assured I should fall into, and that at last I would be ruined by a bad husband; bid me be the more wary, that I might render him a false prophet; but to remember that, if ever I came into distress, I had a fast friend at Paris, who would not upbraid me with the unkind things past, but would be always ready to return me good for evil.

This letter stunned me. I could not think it possible for anyone that had not dealt with the devil to write such a letter, for he spoke of some particular things which afterwards were to befall me with such an assurance that it frighted me before-hand; and when those things did come to pass, I was persuaded he had some more than human knowledge. In a word, his advices to me to repent were very affectionate, his warnings of evil to happen to me were very kind, and his promises of assistance, if I wanted him, were so generous that I have seldom seen the like; and though I did not at first set much by that part because I looked upon them as what might not happen, and as what was improbable to happen at that time, yet all the rest of his letter was so moving that it left me very melancholy, and I cried four and twenty hours after, almost without ceasing, about it; and yet even all this while, whatever it was that bewitched me, I had not one serious wish that I had taken him. I wished heartily, indeed, that I could have kept him with me, but I had a mortal aversion to marrying him, or indeed anybody else, but formed a thousand wild notions in my head that I was yet gay enough, and young and handsome enough, to please a man of quality, and that I would try my fortune at London, come of it what would.

Thus blinded by my own vanity, I threw away the only opportunity I then had to have effectually settled my fortunes, and secured them for this world; and I am a memorial to all that shall read my story, a standing monument of the madness and distraction which pride and infatuations from hell run us into, how ill our passions guide us, and how dangerously we act when we follow the dictates of an ambitious mind.

I was rich, beautiful, and agreeable, and not yet old. I had known something of the influence I had had upon the fancies of men even of the highest rank. I never forgot that the Prince de ———— had said, with an ecstasy, that I was the finest woman in France. I knew I could make a figure at London, and how well I could grace that figure. I was not at a loss how to behave, and having already been adored by princes, I thought of nothing less than of being mistress to the king himself. But I go back to my immediate circumstances at that time.

I got over the absence of my honest merchant but slowly at first. It was with infinite regret that I let him go at all; and when I read the letter he left, I was quite confounded. As soon as he was out of call and irrecoverable, I would have given half I had in the world for him back again; my notions of things changed in an instant, and I called myself a thousand fools for casting myself upon a life of scandal and hazard, when, after the shipwreck of virtue, honour, and principle, and sailing at the utmost risk in the stormy seas of crime and abominable levity, I had a safe harbour presented, and no heart to cast anchor in it.

His predictions terrified me; his promises of kindness if I came to distress melted me into tears, but frighted me with the apprehensions of ever coming into such distress, and filled my head with a thousand anxieties and thoughts how it should be possible for me, who had now such a fortune, to sink again into misery.

Then the dreadful scene of my life, when I was left with my five children, &c., as I have related, represented itself again to me, and I sat considering what measures I might take to bring myself to such a state of desolation again, and how I should act to avoid it.

But these things wore off gradually. As to my friend the merchant, he was gone, and gone irrecoverably, for I durst not follow him to Paris, for the reasons mentioned above. Again, I was afraid to write to him to return, lest he should have refused, as I verily believed he would; so I sat and cried intolerably for some days—nay, I may say for some weeks; but, I say, it wore off gradually, and as I had a pretty deal of business for managing my effects, the hurry of that particular part served to divert my thoughts, and in part to wear out the impressions which had been made upon my mind.

I had sold my jewels, all but the fine diamond ring which my gentleman the jeweller used to wear, and this, at proper times, I wore myself; as also the diamond necklace which the prince had given me, and a pair of extraordinary ear-rings worth about 600 pistoles; the other, which was a fine casket, he left with me at his going to Versailles, and a small case with some rubies and emeralds, &c. I say I sold them at the Hague for 7600 pistoles. I had received all the bills which the merchant had helped me to at Paris, and with the money I brought with me, they made up 13,900 pistoles more; so that I had in ready-money, and in account in the bank at Amsterdam, above one and twenty thousand pistoles, besides jewels; and how to get this treasure to England was my next care.

The business I had had now with a great many people for receiving such large sums and selling jewels of such considerable value gave me opportunity to know and converse with several of the best merchants of the place, so that I wanted no direction now how to get my money remitted to England. Applying, therefore, to several merchants, that I might neither risk it all on the credit of one merchant, nor suffer any single man to know the quantity of money I had; I say, applying myself to several merchants, I got bills of exchange payable in London for all my money. The first bills I took with me; the second bills I left in trust (in case of any disaster at sea) in the hands of the first merchant, him to whom I was recommended by my friend from Paris.

Having thus spent nine months in Holland, refused the best offer ever woman in my circumstances had, parted unkindly, and indeed barbarously, with the best friend and honestest man in the world, got all my money in my pocket, and a bastard in my be`y, I took shipping at the Brill in the packet-boat, and arrived safe at Harwich, where my woman, Amy, was come by my direction to meet me.

I would willingly have given ten thousand pounds of my money to have been rid of the burthen I had in my belly, as above; but it could not be, so I was obliged to bear with that part, and get rid of it by the ordinary method of patience and a hard travail.

I was above the contemptible usage that women in my circumstances oftentimes meet with. I had considered all that beforehand; and having sent Amy beforehand, and remitted her money to do it, she had taken me a very handsome house in ———— Street, near Charing-Cross; had hired me two maids and a footman, who she had put in a good livery; and having hired a glass-coach and four horses, she came with them and the man-servant to Harwich to meet me, and had been there near a week before I came, so I had nothing to do but to go away to London to my own house, where I arrived in very good health, and where I passed for a French lady, by the title of ————.

My first business was to get all my bills accepted, which, to cut the story short, was all both accepted and currently paid; and I then resolved to take me a country-lodging somewhere near the town, to be incognito, till I was brought to bed; which, appearing in such a figure and having such an equipage, I easily managed without anybody's offering the usual insults of parish inquiries. I did not appear in my new house for some time, and afterwards I thought fit, for particular reasons, to quit that house, and not to come to it at all, but take handsome large apartments in the Pall-Mall, in a house out of which was a private door into the king's garden, by the permission of the chief gardener, who had lived in the house.

I had now all my effects secured; but my money being my great concern at that time, I found it a difficulty how to dispose of it so as to bring me in an annual interest. However, in some time I got a substantial safe mortgage for £14,000 by the assistance of the famous Sir Robert Clayton,* for which I

* Sir Robert Clayton (1629–1707) was a wealthy self-made businessman and Whig politician whom Defoe admired.

had an estate of £1800 a year bound to me, and had £700 per annum interest for it.

This, with some other securities, made me a very handsome estate of above a thousand pounds a year; enough, one would think, to keep any woman in England from being a whore.

I lay-in at ————, about four miles from London, and brought a fine boy into the world, and, according to my promise, sent an account of it to my friend at Paris, the father of it; and in the letter told him how sorry I was for his going away, and did as good as intimate that, if he would come once more to see me, I should use him better than I had done. He gave me a very kind and obliging answer, but took not the least notice of what I had said of his coming over, so I found my interest lost there for ever. He gave me joy of the child, and hinted that he hoped I would make good what he had begged for the poor infant, as I had promised, and I sent him word again that I would fulfil his order to a tittle; and such a fool and so weak I was in this last letter, notwithstanding what I have said of his not taking notice of my invitation, as to ask his pardon almost for the usage I gave him at Rotterdam, and stooped so low as to expostulate with him for not taking notice of my inviting him to come to me again, as I had done; and, which was still more, went so far as to make a second sort of an offer to him, telling him, almost in plain words, that if he would come over now I would have him; but he never gave me the least reply to it at all, which was as absolute a denial to me as he was ever able to give; so I sat down, I cannot say contented, but vexed heartily that I had made the offer at all, for he had, as I may say, his full revenge of me in scorning to answer, and to let me twice ask that of him which he with so much importunity begged of me before.

I was now up again, and soon came to my city lodging in the Pall-Mall, and here I began to make a figure suitable to my estate, which was very great; and I shall give you an account of my equipage in a few words, and of myself too.

I paid £60 a year for my new apartments, for I took them by the year; but then they were handsome lodgings indeed, and very richly furnished. I kept my own servants to clean and look after them, found my own kitchen-ware and firing. My equipage was handsome, but not very great; I had a

coach, a coachman, a footman, my woman Amy, who I now
dressed like a gentlewoman and made her my companion,
and three maids; and thus I lived for a time. I dressed to the
height of every mode, went extremely rich in clothes, and, as
for jewels, I wanted none. I gave a very good livery, laced
with silver, and as rich as anybody below the nobility could
be seen with; and thus I appeared, leaving the world to guess
who or what I was, without offering to put myself forward.

I walked sometimes in the Mall with my woman, Amy, but
I kept no company and made no acquaintances, only made as
gay a show as I was able to, and that upon all occasions. I
found, however, the world was not altogether so unconcerned
about me as I seemed to be about them; and first I understood that the neighbours begun to be mighty inquisitive
about me, as who I was, and what my circumstances were.

Amy was the only person that could answer their curiosity
or give any account of me; and she, a tattling woman and a
true gossip, took care to do that with all the art that she was
mistress of. She let them know that I was the widow of a person of quality in France, that I was very rich, that I came
over hither to look after an estate that fell to me by some of
my relations who died here, that I was worth £40,000 all in
my own hands, and the like.

This was all wrong in Amy, and in me too, though we did
not see it at first, for this recommended me indeed to those
sort of gentlemen they call fortune-hunters, and who always
besieged ladies, as they called it—on purpose to take them
prisoners, as I called it—that is to say, to marry the women
and have the spending of their money. But if I was wrong in
refusing the honourable proposals of the Dutch merchant,
who offered me the disposal of my whole estate, and had as
much of his own to maintain me with, I was right now in refusing those offers which came generally from gentlemen of
good families and good estates, but who, living to the extent
of them, were always needy and necessitous, and wanted a
sum of money to make themselves easy, as they call it—that
is to say, to pay off encumbrances, sisters' portions, and the
like; and then the woman is prisoner for life, and may live as
they please to give her leave. This life I had seen into clearly
enough, and therefore I was not to be catched that way.
However, as I said, the reputation of my money brought
several of those sort of gentry about me, and they found
means, by one stratagem or other, to get access to my la-

dyship; but, in short, I answered them all well enough, that I lived single and was happy; that as I had no occasion to change my condition for an estate, so I did not see that by the best offer that any of them could make me, I could mend my fortune; that I might be honoured with titles indeed, and in time rank on public occasions with the peeresses (I mention that because one that offered at me was the eldest son of a peer), but that I was as well without the title as long as I had the estate, and while I had £2000 a year of my own, I was happier than I could be in being prisoner of state to a nobleman, for I took the ladies of that rank to be little better.

As I have mentioned Sir Robert Clayton, with whom I had the good fortune to become acquainted, on account of the mortgage which he helped me to, it is necessary to take notice that I had much advantage in my ordinary affairs by his advice, and therefore I call it my good fortune; for as he paid me so considerable an annual income as £700 a year, so I am to acknowledge myself much a debtor, not only to the justice of his dealings with me, but to the prudence and conduct which he guided me to, by his advice, for the management of my estate. And as he found I was not inclined to marry, he frequently took occasion to hint how soon I might raise my fortune to a prodigious height if I would but order my family economy so far within my revenue as to lay up every year something to add to the capital.

I was convinced of the truth of what he said, and agreed to the advantages of it. You are to take it as you go that Sir Robert supposed by my own discourse, and especially by my woman Amy, that I had £2000 a year income. He judged, as he said, by my way of living that I could not spend above one thousand, and so, he added, I might prudently lay by £1000 every year to add to the capital; and by adding every year the additional interest or income of the money to the capital, he proved to me that in ten year I should double the £1000 per annum that I laid by. And he drew me out a table, as he called it, of the increase, for me to judge by; and by which, he said, if the gentlemen of England would but act so, every family of them would increase their fortunes to a great degree, just as merchants do by trade; whereas now, says Sir Robert, by the humour of living up to the extent of their fortunes, and rather beyond, the gentlemen, says he, ay, and the nobility too, are almost all of them borrowers, and all in necessitous circumstances.

As Sir Robert frequently visited me, and was (if I may say so from his own mouth) very well pleased with my way of conversing with him, for he knew nothing, nor so much as guessed at what I had been; I say, as he came often to see me, so he always entertained me with this scheme of frugality; and one time he brought another paper, wherein he showed me, much to the same purpose as the former, to what degree I should increase my estate if I would come into his method of contracting my expenses; and by this scheme of his, it appeared that, laying up a thousand pounds a year, and every year adding the interest to it, I should in twelve years' time have in bank one and twenty thousand and fifty-eight pounds, after which I might lay up two thousand pounds a year.

I objected that I was a young woman, that I had been used to live plentifully, and with a good appearance, and that I knew not how to be a miser.

He told me that if I thought I had enough, it was well, but if I desired to have more, this was the way; that in another twelve year I should be too rich, so that I should not know what to do with it.

"Ay, sir," says I, "you are contriving how to make me a rich old woman, but that won't answer my end; I had rather have £20,000 now than £60,000 when I am fifty year old."

"Then, madam," says he, "I suppose your honour has no children?"

"None, Sir Robert," said I, "but what are provided for." So I left him in the dark as much as I found him. However, I considered his scheme very well, though I said no more to him at that time, and I resolved, though I would make a very good figure, I say I resolved to abate a little of my expense, and draw in, live closer, and save something, if not so much as he proposed to me. It was near the end of the year that Sir Robert made this proposal to me, and when the year was up, I went to his house in the City, and there I told him I came to thank him for his scheme of frugality; that I had been studying much upon it, and though I had not been able to mortify myself so much as to lay up a thousand pounds a year, yet, as I had not come to him for my interest half-yearly, as was usual, I was now come to let him know that I had resolved to lay up that seven hundred pound a year, and never use a penny of it, desiring him to help me to put it out to advantage.

Sir Robert, a man thoroughly versed in arts of improving money, but thoroughly honest, said to me, "Madam, I am glad you approve of the method that I proposed to you; but you have begun wrong; you should have come for your interest at the half-year, and then you had had the money to put out. Now you have lost half a year's interest of £350, which is £9; for I had but 5 per cent. on the mortgage."

"Well, well, sir," says I, "can you put this out for me now?"

"Let it lie, madam," says he, "till the next year, and then I'll put out your £1400 together, and in the meantime I'll pay you interest for the £700." So he gave me his bill for the money, which he told me should be no less than £6 per cent. Sir Robert Clayton's bill was what nobody would refuse, so I thanked him and let it lie; and next year I did the same, and the third year Sir Robert got me a good mortgage for £2200 at £6 per cent. interest. So I had £132 a year added to my income, which was a very satisfying article.

But I return to my history. As I have said, I found that my measures were all wrong; the posture I set up in exposed me to innumerable visitors of the kind I have mentioned above. I was cried up for a vast fortune, and one that Sir Robert Clayton managed for; and Sir Robert Clayton was courted for me as much as I was for myself. But I had given Sir Robert his cue. I had told him my opinion of matrimony, in just the same terms as I had done my merchant, and he came into it presently. He owned that my observation was just, and that if I valued my liberty, as I knew my fortune, and that it was in my own hands, I was to blame if I gave it away to any one.

But Sir Robert knew nothing of my design, that I aimed at being a kept mistress, and to have a handsome maintenance; and that I was still for getting money, and laying it up too, as much as he could desire me, only by a worse way.

However, Sir Robert came seriously to me one day, and told me he had an offer of matrimony to make to me that was beyond all that he had heard had offered themselves, and this was a merchant. Sir Robert and I agreed exactly in our notions of a merchant. Sir Robert said, and I found it to be true, that a true-bred merchant is the best gentleman in the nation; that in knowledge, in manners, in judgment of things, the merchant outdid many of the nobility; that having once mastered the world, and being above the demand of business, though no real estate, they were then superior to most gentle-men, even in estate; that a merchant in flush business and a capital stock is able to spend more money than a gentleman of £5000 a year estate; that while a merchant spent, he only spent what he got, and not that, and that he laid up great sums every year; that an estate is a pond, but that a trade was a spring; that if the first is once mortgaged, it seldom gets clear, but embarrassed the person for ever; but the mer-chant had his estate continually flowing; and upon this he named me merchants who lived in more real splendour and spent more money than most of the noblemen in England could singly expend, and that they still grew immensely rich.

He went on to tell me that even the tradesmen in London, speaking of the better sort of trades, could spend more money in their families, and yet give better fortunes to their children, than, generally speaking, the gentry of England from £1000 a year downward could do, and yet grow rich too.

The upshot of all this was to recommend to me rather the bestowing my fortune upon some eminent merchant, who lived already in the first figure of a merchant, and who, not being in want or scarcity of money, but having a flourishing business and a flowing cash, would at the first word settle all my fortune on myself and children, and maintain me like a queen.

This was certainly right, and had I taken his advice, I had been really happy; but my heart was bent upon an indepen-dency of fortune, and I told him I knew no state of matri-mony but what was at best a state of inferiority, if not of bondage; that I had no notion of it; that I lived a life of ab-solute liberty now, was free as I was born, and, having a plentiful fortune, I did not understand what coherence the words "honour and obey" had with the liberty of a free woman; that I knew no reason the men had to engross the whole liberty of the race, and make the woman, notwith-standing any disparity of fortune, be subject to the laws of marriage, of their own making; that it was my misfortune to be a woman, but I was resolved it should not be made worse by the sex; and, seeing liberty seemed to be the men's property, I would be a man-woman, for, as I was born free, I would die so.

Sir Robert smiled, and told me I talked a kind of Amazonian language; that he found few women of my mind, or that, if they were, they wanted resolution to go on with it; that, notwithstanding all my notions, which he could not but say had once some weight in them, yet he understood I had broke in upon them, and had been married. I answered, I had so; but he did not hear me say that I had any encouragement from what was past to make a second venture; that I was got well out of the toil, and if I came in again, I should have nobody to blame but myself.

Sir Robert laughed heartily at me, but gave over offering any more arguments, only told me he had pointed me out for some of the best merchants in London, but since I forbad him, he would give me no disturbance of that kind. He applauded my way of managing my money, and told me I should soon be monstrous rich; but he neither knew or mistrusted that, with all this wealth, I was yet a whore, and was not averse to adding to my estate at the farther expense of my virtue.

But to go on with my story as to my way of living. I found, as above, that my living as I did would not answer; that it only brought the fortune-hunters and bites about me, as I have said before, to make a prey of me and my money; and, in short, I was harassed with lovers, beaux, and fops of quality, in abundance, but it would not do. I aimed at other things, and was possessed with so vain an opinion of my own beauty, that nothing less than the king himself was in my eye. And this vanity was raised by some words let fall by a person I conversed with, who was, perhaps, likely enough to have brought such a thing to pass, had it been sooner; but that game began to be pretty well over at court. However, he having mentioned such a thing, it seems a little too publicly, it brought abundance of people about me, upon a wicked account too.

And now I began to act in a new sphere. The court was exceeding gay and fine, though fuller of men than of women, the queen not affecting to be very much in public. On the other hand, it is no slander upon the courtiers to say, they were as wicked as anybody in reason could desire them. The king had several mistresses, who were prodigious fine, and there was a glorious show on that side indeed. If the sovereign gave himself a loose, it could not be expected the rest of the court should be all saints; so far was it from that, though I would not make it worse than it was, that a woman that had anything agreeable in her appearance could never want followers.

I soon found myself thronged with admirers, and I received visits from some persons of very great figure, who always introduced themselves by the help of an old lady or two who were now become my intimates; and one of them, I understood afterwards, was set to work on purpose to get into my favour, in order to introduce what followed.

The conversation we had was generally courtly, but civil. At length some gentlemen proposed to play, and made what they called a party. This, it seems, was a contrivance of one of my female hangers-on, for, as I said, I had two of them, who thought this was the way to introduce people as often as she pleased; and so indeed it was. They played high and stayed late, but begged my pardon, only asked leave to make an appointment for the next night. I was as gay and as well pleased as any of them, and one night told one of the gentlemen, my Lord ———, that seeing they were doing me the honour of diverting themselves at my apartment, and desired to be there sometimes, I did not keep a gaming-table, but I would give them a little ball the next day if they pleased, which they accepted very willingly.

Accordingly, in the evening the gentlemen began to come, where I let them see that I understood very well what such things meant. I had a large dining-room in my apartments, with five other rooms on the same floor, all which I made drawing-rooms for the occasion, having all the beds taken down for the day. In three of these I had tables placed, covered with wine and sweetmeats, the fourth had a green table for play, and the fifth was my own room, where I sat, and where I received all the company that came to pay their compliments to me. I was dressed, you may be sure, to all the advantage possible, and had all the jewels on that I was mistress of. My Lord ———, to whom I had made the invitation, sent me a set of fine music from the play-house, and the ladies danced, and we began to be very merry, when about eleven o'clock I had notice given me that there were some gentlemen coming in masquerade.

I seemed a little surprised, and began to apprehend some disturbance, when my Lord ——— perceiving it, spoke to me to be easy, for that there was a party of the guards at the door which should be ready to prevent any rudeness; and another gentleman gave me a hint as if the king was among the masks. I coloured as red as blood itself could make a face look, and expressed a great surprise; however, there was no going back, so I kept my station in my drawing-room, but with the folding-doors wide open.

A-while after, the masks came in and began a dance *à la comique*, performing wonderfully indeed. While they were dancing, I withdrew, and left a lady to answer for me that I would return immediately. In less than half an hour I returned, dressed in the habit of a Turkish princess; the habit I got at Leghorn, when my foreign prince bought me a Turkish slave, as I have said. The Maltese man-of-war had, it seems, taken a Turkish vessel going from Constantinople to Alexandria, in which were some ladies bound for Grand Cairo in Eygpt; and as the ladies were made slaves, so their fine clothes were thus exposed; and with this Turkish slave I bought the rich clothes too. The dress was extraordinary fine indeed; I had bought it as a curiosity, having never seen the like. The robe was a fine Persian or India damask, the ground white, and the flowers blue and gold, and the train held five yards. The dress under it was a vest of the same, embroidered with gold, and set with some pearl in the work and some turquoise stones. To the vest was a girdle five or six inches wide, after the Turkish mode; and on both ends where it joined, or hooked, was set with diamonds for eight inches either way, only they were not true diamonds, but nobody knew that but myself.

The turban, or head-dress, had a pinnacle on the top, but not above five inches, with a piece of loose sarcenet hanging from it; and on the front, just over the forehead, was a good jewel which I had added to it.

This habit, as above, cost me about sixty pistoles in Italy, but cost much more in the country from whence it came; and little did I think when I bought it that I should put it to such a use as this, though I had dressed myself in it many times by the help of my little Turk, and afterwards between Amy and I, only to see how I looked in it. I had sent her up before to get it ready, and when I came up, I had nothing to do but slip it on, and was down in my drawing-room in a little more than a quarter of an hour. When I came there, the room was full of company; but I ordered the folding-doors to be shut for a minute or two till I had received the compliments of the ladies that were in the room, and had given them a full view of my dress.

But my Lord ———, who happened to be in the room, slipped out at another door and brought back with him one of the masks, a tall, well-shaped person, but who had no name, being all masked; nor would it have been allowed to ask any person's name on such an occasion. The person spoke in French to me, that it was the finest dress he had ever seen, and asked me if he should have the honour to dance with me. I bowed, as giving my consent, but said, as I had been a Mahometan, I could not dance after the manner of this country; I supposed their music would not play *à la Moresque.* He answered merrily I had a Christian's face, and he'd venture it that I could dance like a Christian, adding that so much beauty could not be Mahometan. Immediately the folding-doors were flung open, and he led me into the room. The company were under the greatest surprise imaginable; the very music stopped a-while to gaze, for the dress was indeed exceedingly surprising, perfectly new, very agreeable, and wonderful rich.

The gentleman, whoever he was, for I never knew, led me only *à courant,* and then asked me if I had a mind to dance an antic—that is to say, whether I would dance the antic as they had danced in masquerade, or anything by myself. I told him any thing else rather, if he pleased; so we danced only two French dances, and he led me to the drawing-room door, when he retired to the rest of the masks. When he left me at the drawing-room door, I did not go in, as he thought I would have done, but turned about and showed myself to the whole room, and calling my woman to me, gave her some directions to the music, by which the company presently understood that I would give them a dance by myself. Immediately all the house rose up and paid me a kind of a compliment by removing back every way to make me room, for the place was exceeding full. The music did not at first hit the tune that I directed, which was a French tune, so I was forced to send my woman to 'em again, standing all this while at my drawing-room door; but as soon as my woman spoke to them again, they played it right, and I, to let them see it was so, stepped forward to the middle of the room. Then they began it again, and I danced by myself a figure which I learnt in France, when the Prince de ——— desired I would dance for his diversion. It was, indeed, a very fine figure, invented by a famous master at Paris for a lady or a gentleman to dance single; but being perfectly new, it pleased the company ex-

ceedingly, and they all thought it had been Turkish; nay, one
gentleman had the folly to expose himself so much as to say,
and I think swore too, that he had seen it danced at Constantinople, which was ridiculous enough.

At the finishing the dance, the company clapped and almost shouted; and one of the gentlemen cried out "Roxana!
Roxana!* by ————," with an oath; upon which foolish accident I had the name of Roxana presently fixed upon me all
over the court end of town as effectually as if I had been
christened Roxana. I had, it seems, the felicity of pleasing
everybody that night to an extreme; and my ball, but especially my dress, was the chat of the town for that week; and so
the name of Roxana was the toast at and about the court; no
other health was to be named with it.

Now things began to work as I would have them, and I began to be very popular, as much as I could desire. The ball
held till (as well as I was pleased with the show) I was sick
of the night; the gentlemen masked went off about three
o'clock in the morning, the other gentlemen sat down to play;
the music held it out, and some of the ladies were dancing at
six in the morning.

But I was mighty eager to know who it was danced with
me. Some of the lords went so far as to tell me I was very
much honoured in my company; one of them spoke so broad
as almost to say it was the king, but I was convinced afterwards it was not; and another replied if he had been his
Majesty, he should have thought it no dishonour to lead up a
Roxana; but to this hour I never knew positively who it was;
and by his behaviour I thought he was too young, his Majesty
being at that time in an age that might be discovered from a
young person, even in his dancing.

Be that as it would, I had five hundred guineas sent me the
next morning, and the messenger was ordered to tell me that
the persons who sent it desired a ball again at my lodgings on
the next Tuesday, but that they would have my leave to give
the entertainment themselves. I was mighty well pleased with
this, to be sure, but very inquisitive to know who the money
came from; but the messenger was silent as death as to that

* "Roxana." The leading woman in Nathaniel Lee's very popular
heroic tragedy *The Rival Queens* (1677), Roxana was a beautiful,
wicked, passionate Oriental queen (from Bactria, in present-day Afghan-
istan).

point and, bowing always at my inquiries, begged me to ask no questions which he could give an obliging answer to.

I forgot to mention, that the gentlemen that played gave a hundred guineas to the box, as they called it, and at the end of their play they asked for my gentlewoman of the bedchamber, as they called her (Mrs. Amy, forsooth), and gave it her, and gave twenty guineas more among the servants.

These magnificent doings equally both pleased and surprised me, and I hardly knew where I was; but especially that notion of the king being the person that danced with me, puffed me up to that degree, that I not only did not know anybody else, but indeed was very far from knowing myself.

I had now, the next Tuesday, to provide for the like company. But, alas! it was all taken out of my hand. Three gentlemen, who yet were, it seems, but servants, came on the Saturday, and bringing sufficient testimonies that they were right, for one was the same who brought the five hundred guineas; I say, three of them came, and brought bottles of all sorts of wines, and hampers of sweetmeats to such a quantity, it appeared they were designed to hold the trade on more than once, and that they would furnish everything to a profusion.

However, as I found a deficiency in two things, I made provision of about twelve dozen of fine damask napkins, with tablecloths of the same, sufficient to cover all the tables, with three tablecloths upon every table, and sideboards in proportion. Also I bought a handsome quantity of plate, necessary to have served all the sideboards; but the gentlemen would not suffer any of it to be used, telling me they had bought fine china dishes and plates for the whole service, and that in such public places they could not be answerable for the plate. So it was set all up in a large glass cupboard in the room I sat in, where it made a very good show indeed.

On Tuesday there came such an appearance of gentlemen and ladies, that my apartments were by no means able to receive them, and those who in particular appeared as principals gave order below to let no more company come up. The street was full of coaches with coronets, and fine glass chairs, and, in short, it was impossible to receive the company. I kept my little room as before, and the dancers filled the great room; all the drawing-rooms also were filled, and three rooms below-stairs, which were not mine.

It was very well that there was a strong party of the guards brought to keep the door, for without that there had been such a promiscuous crowd, and some of them scandalous too, that we should have been all disorder and confusion; but the three head-servants managed all that, and had a word to admit all the company by.

It was uncertain to me, and is to this day, who it was that danced with me the Wednesday before, when the ball was my own; but that the king was at this assembly was out of question with me, by circumstances that, I suppose, I could not be deceived in, and particularly that there were five persons who were not masked; three of them had blue garters, and they appeared not to me till I came out to dance.

This meeting was managed just as the first, though with much more magnificence, because of the company. I placed myself (exceedingly rich in clothes and jewels) in the middle of my little room, as before, and made my compliment to all the company as they passed me, as I did before. But my Lord ———, who had spoken openly to me the first night, came to me and, unmasking, told me the company had ordered him to tell me they hoped they should see me in the dress I had appeared in the first day, which had been so acceptable that it had been the occasion of this new meeting. "And, madam," says he, "there are some in this assembly who it is worth your while to oblige."

I bowed to my Lord ——— and immediately withdrew. While I was above, a-dressing in my new habit, two ladies, perfectly unknown to me, were conveyed into my apartment below, by the order of a noble person, who, with his family, had been in Persia; and here, indeed, I thought I should have been outdone, or perhaps balked.

One of these ladies was dressed most exquisitely fine indeed, in the habit of a virgin lady of quality of Georgia, and the other in the same habit of Armenia, with each of them a woman slave to attend them.

The ladies had their petticoats short, to their ankles, but pleated all round, and before them short aprons, but of the finest point that could be seen. Their gowns were made with long antique sleeves hanging down behind, and a train let down. They had no jewels, but their heads and breasts were dressed up with flowers, and they both came in veiled.

Their slaves were bare-headed, but their long, black hair was braided in locks hanging down behind to their waists, and tied up with ribands. They were dressed exceeding rich

and were as beautiful as their mistresses; for none of them
had any masks on. They waited in my room till I came
down, and all paid their respects to me after the Persian
manner, and sat down on a *safra*—that is to say, almost
cross-legged, on a couch made up of cushions laid on the
ground.

This was admirably fine, and I was indeed startled at it.
They made their compliment to me in French, and I replied
in the same language. When the doors were opened, they
walked into the dancing-room and danced such a dance as
indeed nobody there had ever seen, and to an instrument like
a guitar, with a small low-sounding trumpet, which indeed
was very fine, and which my Lord ——— had provided.

They danced three times all alone, for nobody indeed
could dance with them. The novelty pleased, truly, but yet
there was something wild and *bizarre* in it, because they really acted to the life the barbarous country whence they came;
but as mine had the French behaviour under the Mahometan
dress, it was every way as new, and pleased much better
indeed.

As soon as they had shown their Georgian and Armenian
shapes, and danced, as I have said, three times, they withdrew, paid their compliment to me (for I was queen of the
day), and went off to undress.

Some gentlemen then danced with ladies all in masks; and
when they stopped, nobody rose up to dance, but all called
out, "Roxana, Roxana." In the interval, my Lord ——— had
brought another masked person into my room, who I knew
not, only that I could discern it was not the same person that
led me out before. This noble person (for I afterwards understood it was the Duke of ———), after a short compliment,
led me out into the middle of the room.

I was dressed in the same vest and girdle as before, but the
robe had a mantle over it, which is usual in the Turkish
habit, and it was of crimson and green, the green brocaded
with gold; and my *tyhiaal*, or head-dress, varied a little from
that I had before, as it stood higher, and had some jewels
about the rising part, which made it look like a turban
crowned.

I had no mask, neither did I paint, and yet I had the day
of all the ladies that appeared at the ball, I mean of those
that appeared with faces on. As for those masked, nothing
could be said of them, no doubt there might be many finer

than I was; it must be confessed that the habit was infinitely advantageous to me, and everybody looked at me with a kind of pleasure, which gave me great advantage too.

After I had danced with that noble person, I did not offer to dance by myself, as I had before; but they all called out "Roxana" again; and two of the gentlemen came into the drawing-room to entreat me to give them the Turkish dance, which I yielded to readily, so I came out and danced just as at first.

While I was dancing, I perceived five persons standing all together, and among them only one with his hat on. It was an immediate hint to me who it was, and had at first almost put me into some disorder; but I went on, received the applause of the house, as before, and retired into my own room. When I was there, the five gentlemen came across the room to my side, and, coming in, followed by a throng of great persons, the person with his hat on said, "Madam Roxana, you perform to admiration." I was prepared, and offered to kneel to kiss his hand, but he declined it and saluted me, and so, passing back again through the great room, went away.

I do not say here who this was, but I say I came afterwards to know something more plainly. I would have withdrawn and disrobed, being somewhat too thin in that dress, unlaced and open-breasted, as if I had been in my shift; but it could not be, and I was obliged to dance afterwards with six or eight gentlemen, most, if not all of them, of the first rank; and I was told afterwards that one of them was the D—— of M——.

About two or three o'clock in the morning, the company began to decrease; the number of women especially dropped away home, some and some at a time; and the gentlemen retired downstairs, where they unmasked and went to play.

Amy waited at the room where they played, sat up all night to attend them, and in the morning when they broke up, they swept the box into her lap, when she counted out to me sixty-two guineas and a half; and the other servants got very well too. Amy came to me when they were all gone. "Law, madam," says Amy, with a long gaping cry, "what shall I do with all this money?" And indeed the poor creature was half-mad with joy.

I was now in my element. I was as much talked of as anybody could desire, and I did not doubt but something or other would come of it; but the report of my being so rich

rather was a balk to my view than anything else; for the
gentlemen that would perhaps have been troublesome enough
otherwise, seemed to be kept off, for Roxana was too high for
them.

There is a scene which came in here which I must cover
from human eyes or ears. For three years and about a
month, Roxana lived retired, having been obliged to make an
excursion in a manner, and with a person which duty and
private vows obliges her not to reveal, at least not yet.

At the end of this time I appeared again; but, I must add,
that as I had in this time of retreat made hay, &c., so I did
not come aboard again with the same lustre, or shine with so
much advantage as before. For as some people had got at
least a suspicion of where I had been, and who had had me
all the while, it began to be public that Roxana was, in short,
a mere Roxana, neither better nor worse, and not that
woman of honour and virtue that was at first supposed.

You are now to suppose me about seven years come to
town, and that I had not only suffered the old revenue, which
I hinted was managed by Sir Robert Clayton, to grow, as was
mentioned before, but I had laid up an incredible wealth, the
time considered; and had I yet had the least thought of re-
forming, I had all the opportunity to do it with advantage that
ever woman had. For the common vice of all whores, I mean
money, was out of the question, nay, even avarice itself
seemed to be glutted; for, including what I had saved in reserving the interest of £14,000, which, as above, I had left to
grow, and including some very good presents I had made to
me in mere compliment upon these shining masquerading
meetings, which I held up for about two years, and what I
made of three years of the most glorious retreat, as I call it,
that ever woman had, I had fully doubled my first substance
and had near £5000 in money, which I kept at home, besides
abundance of plate and jewels, which I had either given me
or had bought to set myself out for public days.

In a word, I had now five and thirty thousand pounds estate; and as I found ways to live without wasting either principal or interest, I laid up £2000 every year at least out of
the mere interest, adding it to the principal, and thus I went
on.

After the end of what I call my retreat, and out of which I
brought a great deal of money, I appeared again, but I
seemed like an old piece of plate that had been hoarded up

some years, and comes out tarnished and discoloured; so I came out blown, and looked like a cast-off mistress; nor, indeed, was I any better, though I was not at all impaired in beauty except that I was a little fatter than I was formerly, and always granting that I was four years older.

However, I preserved the youth of my temper, was always bright, pleasant in company, and agreeable to everybody, or else everybody flattered me; and in this condition I came abroad to the world again. And though I was not so popular as before, and indeed did not seek it, because I knew it could not be, yet I was far from being without company, and that of the greatest quality (of subjects I mean), who frequently visited me, and sometimes we had meetings for mirth and play at my apartments, where I failed not to divert them in the most agreeable manner possible.

Nor could any of them make the least particular application to me, from the notion they had of my excessive wealth, which, as they thought, placed me above the meanness of a maintenance, and so left no room to come easily about me.

But at last I was very handsomely attacked by a person of honour, and (which recommended him particularly to me) a person of a very great estate. He made a long introduction to me upon the subject of my wealth. "Ignorant creature!" said I to myself, considering him as a lord, "was there ever woman in the world that could stoop to the baseness of being a whore, and was above taking the reward of her vice! No, no, depend upon it, if your lordship obtains anything of me, you must pay for it; and the notion of my being so rich serves only to make it cost you the dearer, seeing you cannot offer a small matter to a woman of £2000 a year estate."

After he had harangued upon that subject a good while, and had assured me he had no design upon me, that he did not come to make a prize of me, or to pick my pocket, which, by the way, I was in no fear of, for I took too much care of my money to part with any of it that way, he then turned his discourse to the subject of love, a point so ridiculous to me without the main thing, I mean the money, that I had no patience to hear him make so long a story of it.

I received him civilly, and let him see I could bear to hear a wicked proposal without being affronted, and yet I was not to be brought into it too easily. He visited me a long while and, in short, courted me as closely and assiduously as if he had been wooing me to matrimony. He made me several valuable presents, which I suffered myself to be prevailed with to accept, but not without great difficulty.

Gradually I suffered also his other importunities; and when he made a proposal of a compliment or appointment to me for a settlement, he said that though I was rich, yet there was not the less due from him to acknowledge the favours he received; and that if I was to be his, I should not live at my own expense, cost what it would. I told him I was far from being extravagant, and yet did not live at the expense of less than £500 a year out of my own pocket; that, however, I was not covetous of settled allowances, for I looked upon that as a kind of golden chain, something like matrimony; that though I knew how to be true to a man of honour, as I knew his lordship to be, yet I had a kind of aversion to the bonds; and though I was not so rich as the world talked me up to be, yet I was not so poor as to bind myself to hardships for a pension.

He told me he expected to make my life perfectly easy, and intended it so; that he knew of no bondage there could be in a private engagement between us; that the bonds of honour he knew I would be tied by, and think them no burthen; and for other obligations, he scorned to expect anything from me but what he knew as a woman of honour I could grant. Then as to maintenance, he told me he would soon show me that he valued me infinitely above £500 a year, and upon this foot we began.

I seemed kinder to him after this discourse, and as time and private conversation made us very intimate, we began to come nearer to the main article, namely, the £500 a year. He offered that at first word, and to acknowledge it as an infinite favour to have it be accepted of; and I, that thought it was too much by all the money, suffered myself to be mastered, or prevailed with to yield, even on but a bare engagement upon parole.

When he had obtained his end that way, I told him my mind. "Now you see, my lord," said I, "how weakly I have acted, namely, to yield to you without any capitulation,* or anything secured to me but that which you may cease to allow when you please. If I am the less valued for such a confidence, I shall be injured in a manner that I will endeavour not to deserve."

He told me that he would make it evident to me that he

* "capitulation." See above, page 35.

did not seek me by way of bargain, as such things were often done; that as I had treated him with a generous confidence, so I should find I was in the hands of a man of honour, and one that knew how to value the obligation; and upon this he pulled out a goldsmith's bill for £300, which (putting it into my hand), he said, he gave me as a pledge that I should not be a loser by my not having made a bargain with him.

This was engaging indeed, and gave me a good idea of our future correspondence; and, in short, as I could not refrain treating him with more kindness than I had done before, so one thing begetting another, I gave him several testimonies that I was entirely his own by inclination as well as by the common obligation of a mistress, and this pleased him exceedingly.

Soon after this private engagement I began to consider whether it were not more suitable to the manner of life I now led to be a little less public; and, as I told my lord, it would rid me of the importunities of others, and of continual visits from a sort of people who he knew of, and who, by the way, having now got the notion of me which I really deserved, began to talk of the old game, love and gallantry, and to offer at what was rude enough—things as nauseous to me now as if I had been married and as virtuous as other people. The visits of these people began indeed to be uneasy to me, and particularly as they were always very tedious and impertinent; nor could my Lord —— be pleased with them at all if they had gone on. It would be diverting to set down here in what manner I repulsed these sort of people; how in some I resented it as an affront, and told them that I was sorry they should oblige me to vindicate myself from the scandal of such suggestions by telling them that I could see them no more, and by desiring them not to give themselves the trouble of visiting me, who, though I was not willing to be uncivil, yet thought myself obliged never to receive any visit from any gentleman after he had made such proposals as those to me. But these things would be too tedious to bring in here. It was on this account I proposed to his lordship my taking new lodgings for privacy; besides, I considered that as I might live very handsomely, and yet not so publicly, so I needed not spend so much money by a great deal; and if I made £500 a year of this generous person, it was more than I had any occasion to spend by a great deal.

My lord came readily into this proposal, and went further

than I expected, for he found out a lodging for me in a very handsome house, where yet he was not known—I suppose he had employed somebody to find it out for him—and where he had a convenient way to come into the garden by a door that opened into the park, a thing very rarely allowed in those times.

By this key he could come in at what time of night or day he pleased; and as we had also a little door in the lower part of the house which was always left upon a lock, and his was the master-key, so if it was twelve, one, or two o'clock at night, he could come directly into my bed-chamber. *N.B.* I was not afraid I should be found a-bed with anybody else, for, in a word, I conversed with nobody at all.

It happened pleasantly enough one night, his lordship had stayed late, and I, not expecting him that night, had taken Amy to bed with me, and when my lord came into the chamber we were both fast asleep. I think it was near three o'clock when he came in, and a little merry, but not at all fuddled or what they call in drink; and he came at once into the room.

Amy was frighted out of her wits and cried out. I said calmly, "Indeed, my lord, I did not expect you to-night, and we have been a little frighted to-night with fire." "Oh!" says he, "I see you have got a bedfellow with you." I began to make an apology. "No, no," says my lord, "you need no excuse, 'tis not a man-bedfellow, I see." But then, talking merrily enough, he catched his words back. "But, hark ye," says he, "now I think on't, how shall I be satisfied it is not a man-bedfellow?" "Oh," says I, "I dare say your lordship is satisfied 'tis poor Amy." "Yes," says he, " 'tis Mrs. Amy; but how do I know what Amy is? It may be Mr. Amy for aught I know; I hope you'll give me leave to be satisfied." I told him, yes, by all means, I would have his lordship satisfied; but I supposed he knew who she was.

Well, he fell foul of poor Amy, and indeed I thought once he would have carried the jest on before my face, as was once done in a like case; but his lordship was not so hot neither, but he would know whether Amy was Mr. Amy or Mrs. Amy, and so, I suppose, he did; and then being satisfied in that doubtful case, he walked to the farther end of the room, and went into a little closet and sat down.

In the meantime Amy and I got up, and I bid her run and make the bed in another chamber for my lord, and I gave her sheets to put into it; which she did immediately, and I put my lord to bed there, and when I had done, at his desire went to bed to him. I was backward at first to come to bed to him, and made my excuse because I had been in bed with Amy, and had not shifted me; but he was past those niceties at that time; and as long as he was sure it was Mrs. Amy, and not Mr. Amy, he was very well satisfied, and so the jest passed over. But Amy appeared no more all that night, or the next day, and when she did, my lord was so merry with her upon his *éclaircissement*, as he called it, that Amy did not know what to do with herself.

Not that Amy was such a nice lady in the main, if she had been fairly dealt with, as has appeared in the former part of this work; but now she was surprised, and a little hurried, that she scarce knew where she was; and besides, she was, as to his lordship, as nice a lady as any in the world, and for anything he knew of her she appeared as such. The rest was to us only that knew of it.

I held this wicked scene of life out eight years, reckoning from my first coming to England; and though my lord found no fault, yet I found, without much examining, that anyone who looked in my face might see I was above twenty years old; and yet, without flattering myself, I carried my age, which was above fifty, very well too.

I may venture to say that no woman ever lived a life like me, of six and twenty years of wickedness, without the least signals of remorse, without any signs of repentance, or without so much as a wish to put an end to it; I had so long habituated myself to a life of vice, that really it appeared to be no vice to me. I went on smooth and pleasant, I wallowed in wealth, and it flowed in upon me at such a rate, having taken the frugal measures that the good knight directed, so that I had at the end of the eight years two thousand eight hundred pounds coming yearly in, of which I did not spend one penny, being maintained by my allowance from my Lord ————, and more than maintained by above £200 per annum; for though he did not contract for £500 a year, as I made dumb signs to have it be, yet he gave me money so often, and that in such large parcels, that I had seldom so little as seven to eight hundred pounds a year of him, one year with another.

I must go back here, after telling openly the wicked things I did, to mention something which, however, had the face of doing good. I remembered that when I went from England, which was fifteen years before, I had left five little children, turned out as it were to the wide world, and to the charity of their father's relations; the eldest was not six years old, for we had not been married full seven years when their father went away.

After my coming to England, I was greatly desirous to hear how things stood with them, and whether they were all alive or not, and in what manner they had been maintained; and yet I resolved not to discover myself to them in the least, or to let any of the people that had the breeding of them up know that there was such a body left in the world as their mother.

Amy was the only body I could trust with such a commission, and I sent her into Spitalfields, to the old aunt and to the poor woman that were so instrumental in disposing the relations to take some care of the children, but they were both gone, dead and buried some years. The next inquiry she made was at the house where she carried the poor children, and turned them in at the door. When she came there, she found the house inhabited by other people, so that she could make little or nothing of her inquiries, and came back with an answer that indeed was no answer to me, for it gave me no satisfaction at all. I sent her back to inquire in the neighbourhood what was become of the family that lived in that house; and if they were removed, where they lived, and what circumstances they were in; and, withal, if she could, what became of the poor children, and how they lived, and where, how they had been treated; and the like.

She brought me back word upon this second going that she heard, as to the family, that the husband, who, though but uncle-in-law to the children, had yet been kindest to them, was dead; and that the widow was left but in mean circumstances—that is to say, she did not want, but that she was not so well in the world as she was thought to be when her husband was alive.

That, as to the poor children, two of them, it seems, had been kept by her, that is to say, by her husband, while he lived, for that it was against her will, that we all knew; but the honest neighbours pitied the poor children, they said, heartily; for that their aunt used them barbarously, and made them little better than servants in the house to wait upon her and her children, and scarce allowed them clothes fit to wear.

These were, it seems, my eldest and third, which were daughters; the second was a son, the fourth a daughter, and the youngest a son.

To finish the melancholy part of this history of my two unhappy girls, she brought me word that as soon as they were able to go out and get any work, they went from her, and some said she had turned them out of doors; but it seems she had not done so, but she used them so cruelly that they left her, and one of them went to service to a neighbour's, a little way off, who knew her, an honest, substantial weaver's wife, to whom she was chamber-maid, and in a little time she took her sister out of the Bridewell* of her aunt's house, and got her a place too.

This was all melancholy and dull. I sent her then to the weaver's house, where the eldest had lived, but found that, her mistress being dead, she was gone, and nobody knew there whither she went, only that they heard she had lived with a great lady at the other end of town; but they did not know who that lady was.

These inquiries took us up three or four weeks, and I was not one jot better for it, for I could hear nothing to my satisfaction. I sent her next to find out the honest man who, as in the beginning of my story I observed, made them be entertained, and caused the youngest to be fetched from the town where we lived, and where the parish officers had taken care of him. This gentleman was still alive; and there she heard that my youngest daughter and eldest son was dead also; but that my youngest was alive, and was at that time about seventeen years old, and that he was put out apprentice by the kindness and charity of his uncle, but to a mean trade, and at which he was obliged to work very hard.

Amy was so curious in this part that she went immediately to see him, and found him all dirty and hard at work. She had no remembrance at all of the youth, for she had not seen him since he was about two years old; and it was evident he could have no knowledge of her.

However, she talked with him, and found him a good, sensible, mannerly youth; that he knew little of the story of his father or mother, and had no view of anything but to work hard for his living; and she did not think fit to put any great

* "Bridewell." A prison for those who had committed minor offenses.

things into his head, lest it should take him off of his
business, and perhaps make him turn giddy-headed and be
good for nothing; but she went and found out that kind man,
his benefactor, who had put him out, and finding him a plain,
well-meaning, honest, and kind-hearted man, she opened her
tale to him the easier. She made a long story, how she had a
prodigious kindness for the child, because she had the same
for his father and mother; told him that she was the servant-
maid that brought all of them to their aunt's door, and run
away and left them; that their poor mother wanted bread,
and what came of her after she would have been glad to
know. She added that her circumstances had happened to
mend in the world, and that, as she was in condition, so she
was disposed to show some kindness to the children if she
could find them out.

He received her with all the civility that so kind a proposal
demanded, gave her an account of what he had done for the
child, how he had maintained him, fed and clothed him, put
him to school, and at last put him out to a trade. She said he
had indeed been a father to the child. "But, sir," says she,
" 'tis a very laborious, hard-working trade, and he is but a
thin, weak boy." "That's true," says he, "but the boy chose
the trade, and I assure you I gave £20 with him, and am to
find him clothes all his apprenticeship; and as to its being a
hard trade," says he, "that's the fate of his circumstances,
poor boy. I could not well do better for him."

"Well, sir, as you did all for him in charity," says she, "it
was exceeding well; but, as my resolution is to do something
for him, I desire you will, if possible, take him away again
from that place, where he works so hard, for I cannot bear to
see the child work so very hard for his bread, and I will do
something for him that shall make him live without such hard
labour."

He smiled at that. "I can, indeed," says he, "take him
away, but then I must lose my £20 that I gave with him."

"Well, sir," said Amy, "I'll enable you to lose that £20 immediately." And so she put her hand in her pocket and pulls
out her purse.

He begun to be a little amazed at her, and looked her hard
in the face, and that so very much that she took notice of it
and said, "Sir, I fancy by your looking at me you think you
know me, but I am assured you do not, for I never saw your
face before. I think you have done enough for the child, and

that you ought to be acknowledged as a father to him; but you ought not to lose by your kindness to him more than the kindness of bringing him up obliges you to; and therefore there's the £20," added she, "and pray let him be fetched away."

"Well, madam," says he, "I will thank you for the boy, as well as for myself; but will you please to tell me what I must do with him?"

"Sir," says Amy, "as you have been so kind to keep him so many years, I beg you will take him home again one year more, and I'll bring you a hundred pound more, which I will desire you to lay out in schooling and clothes for him, and to pay you for his board. Perhaps I may put him in a condition to return your kindness."

He looked pleased, but surprised very much, and inquired of Amy, but with very great respect, what he should go to school to learn, and what trade she would please to put him out to.

Amy said he should put him to learn a little Latin, and then merchant's accounts, and to write a good hand, for she would have him be put to a Turkey-merchant.*

"Madam," says he, "I am glad for his sake to hear you talk so; but do you know that a Turkey-merchant will not take him under £400 or £500?"

"Yes, sir," says Amy, "I know it very well."

"And," says he, "that it will require as many thousands to set him up?"

"Yes, sir," says Amy, "I know that very well too," and, resolving to talk very big, she added, "I have no children of my own, and I resolve to make him my heir, and if £10,000 be required to set him up, he shall not want it. I was but his mother's servant when he was born, and I mourned heartily for the disaster of the family, and I always said, if ever I was worth anything in the world, I would take the child for my own, and I'll be as good as my word now, though I did not then foresee that it would be with me as it has been since." And so Amy told him a long story how she was troubled for me, and what she would give to hear whether I was dead or alive, and what circumstances I was in; that if she could but

---

* "Turkey merchant." A trader in goods from Turkey. Compare "Italian merchant" on page 175; one who traded in Italian goods. It would be expensive to apprentice a boy to such merchants, because both trades were very profitable.

find me, if I was ever so poor, she would take care of me, and make a gentlewoman of me again.

He told her that, as to the child's mother, she had been reduced to the last extremity and was obliged (as he supposed she knew) to send the children all among her husband's friends; and if it had not been for him, they had all been sent to the parish; but that he obliged the other relations to share the charge among them; that he had taken two, whereof he had lost the eldest, who died of the small-pox, but that he had been as careful of this as of his own, and had made very little difference in their breeding up, only that when he came to put him out, he thought it was best for the boy to put him to a trade which he might set up in without a stock, for otherwise his time would be lost; and that as to his mother, he had never been able to hear one word of her, no, not though he had made the utmost inquiry after her; that there went a report that she had drowned herself, but that he could never meet with anybody that could give him a certain account of it.

Amy counterfeited a cry for her poor mistress; told him she would give anything in the world to see her, if she was alive; and a great deal more such-like talk they had about that; then they returned to speak of the boy.

He inquired of her why she did not seek after the child before, that he might have been brought up from a younger age suitable to what she designed to do for him.

She told him she had been out of England and was but newly returned from the East Indies. That she had been out of England, and was but newly returned, was true, but the latter was false, and was put in to blind him and provide against farther inquiries; for it was not a strange thing for young women to go away poor to the East Indies and come home vastly rich. So she went on with directions about him, and both agreed in this, that the boy should by no means be told what was intended for him, but only that he should be taken home again to his uncle's, that his uncle thought the trade too hard for him, and the like.

About three days after this Amy goes again, and carried him the hundred pound she promised him, but then Amy made quite another figure than she did before; for she went in my coach, with two footmen after her, and dressed very fine also, with jewels and a gold watch; and there was indeed no great difficulty to make Amy look like a lady, for she was a very handsome, well-shaped woman, and genteel enough. The coachman and servants were particularly ordered to show her the same respect as they would to me, and to call her Madam Collins, if they were asked any questions about her.

When the gentleman saw what a figure she made, it added to the former surprise, and he entertained her in the most respectful manner possible, congratulated her advancement in fortune, and particularly rejoiced that it should fall to the poor child's lot to be so provided for, contrary to all expectation.

Well, Amy talked big, but very free and familiar, told them she had no pride in her good fortune (and that was true enough, for, to give Amy her due, she was far from it, and was as good-humoured a creature as ever lived); that she was the same as ever; and that she always loved this boy, and was resolved to do something extraordinary for him.

Then she pulled out her money and paid him down a hundred and twenty pounds, which, she said, she paid him that he might be sure he should be no loser by taking him home again, and that she would come and see him again, and talk farther about things with him, that so all might be settled for him in such a manner as the accidents, such as mortality, or anything else, should make no alteration to the child's prejudice.

At this meeting the uncle brought his wife out, a good, motherly, comely, grave woman, who spoke very tenderly of the youth and, as it appeared, had been very good to him, though she had several children of her own. After a long discourse, she put in a word of her own. "Madam," says she, "I am heartily glad of the good intentions you have for this poor orphan, and I rejoice sincerely in it for his sake; but, madam, you know, I suppose, that there are two sisters alive too; may we not speak a word for them? Poor girls," says she, "they have not been so kindly used as he has, and are turned out to the wide world."

"Where are they, madam?" says Amy.

"Poor creatures," says the gentlewoman, "they are out at service, nobody knows where but themselves; their case is very hard."

"Well, madam," says Amy, "though if I could find them I would assist them, yet my concern is for my boy, as I call him, and I will put him into a condition to take care of his sisters."

"But, madam," says the good, compassionate creature, "he may not be so charitable perhaps by his own inclination, for brothers are not fathers, and they have been cruelly used already, poor girls; we have often relieved them, both with victuals and clothes too, even while they were pretended to be kept by their barbarous aunt."

"Well, madam," says Amy, "what can I do for them? They are gone, it seems, and cannot be heard of. When I see them, 'tis time enough."

She pressed Amy then to oblige their brother, out of the plentiful fortune he was like to have, to do something for his sisters when he should be able.

Amy spoke coldly of that still, but said she would consider of it; and so they parted for that time. They had several meetings after this, for Amy went to see her adopted son, and ordered his schooling, clothes, and other things, but enjoined them not to tell the young man anything, but that they thought the trade he was at too hard for him, and they would keep him at home a little longer, and give him some schooling to fit him for better business; and Amy appeared to him, as she did before, only as one that had known his mother and had some kindness for him.

Thus this matter passed on for near a twelve-month, when it happened that one of my maid-servants having asked Amy leave (for Amy was mistress of the servants, and took and put out such as she pleased)—I say, having asked leave to go into the city to see her friends, came home crying bitterly, and in a most grievous agony she was, and continued so several days till Amy, perceiving the excess, and that the maid would certainly cry herself sick, she took an opportunity with her and examined her about it.

The maid told her a long story, that she had been to see her brother, the only brother she had in the world, and that she knew he was put out apprentice to a ———; but there had come a lady in a coach to his uncle ———, who had brought him up, and made him take him home again; and so the wench run on with the whole story just as 'tis told above, till she came to that part that belonged to herself. "And there," says she, "I had not let them know where I lived, and the lady would have taken me, and, they say, would have provided for me too, as she has done for my brother; but nobody could tell where to find me, and so I have lost it all, and all the hopes of being anything but a poor servant all my days." And then the girl fell a-crying again.

Amy said, "What's all this story? Who could this lady be? It must be some trick, sure." "No," she said, "it was not a trick, for she had made them take her brother home from apprentice, and bought him new clothes, and put him to have more learning; and the gentlewoman said she would make him her heir."

"Her heir!" says Amy. "What does that amount to? It may be she had nothing to leave him; she might make anybody her heir."

"No, no," says the girl, "she came in a fine coach and horses, and I don't know how many footmen to attend her, and brought a great bag of gold and gave it to my uncle ——, he that brought up my brother, to buy him clothes and to pay for his schooling and board."

"He that brought up your brother?" says Amy. "Why, did not he bring you up too as well as your brother? Pray who brought you up, then?"

Here the poor girl told a melancholy story, how an aunt had brought up her and her sister, and how barbarously she had used them, as we have heard.

By this time Amy had her head full enough, and her heart too, and did not know how to hold it, or what to do, for she was satisfied that this was no more than my own daughter, for she told her all the history of her father and mother, and how she was carried by their maid to her aunt's door, just as is related in the beginning of my story.

Amy did not tell me this story for a great while, nor did she well know what course to take in it; but as she had authority to manage everything in the family, she took occasion some time after, without letting me know anything of it, to find some fault with the maid and turn her away.

Her reasons were good, though at first I was not pleased when I heard of it, but I was convinced afterwards that she was in the right, for if she had told me of it, I should have been in great perplexity between the difficulty of concealing myself from my own child and the inconvenience of having my way of living be known among my first husband's relations, and even to my husband himself; for as to his being dead at Paris, Amy, seeing me resolved against marrying any-more, had told me that she had formed that story only to make me easy when I was in Holland, if anything should offer to my liking.

However, I was too tender a mother still, notwithstanding what I had done, to let this poor girl go about the world drudging, as it were, for bread, and slaving at the fire and in the kitchen as a cook-maid; besides, it came into my head that she might perhaps marry some poor devil of a footman, or a coachman, or some such thing, and be undone that way, or, which was worse, be drawn in to lie with some of that coarse, cursed kind, and be with child, and be utterly ruined that way; and in the midst of all my prosperity this gave me great uneasiness.

As to sending Amy to her, there was no doing that now, for, as she had been servant in the house, she knew Amy as well as Amy knew me; and no doubt, though I was much out of her sight, yet she might have had the curiosity to have peeped at me, and seen me enough to know me again if I had discovered myself to her; so that, in short, there was nothing to be done that way.

However, Amy, a diligent indefatigable creature, found out another woman, and gave her her errand, and sent her to the honest man's house in Spitalfields, whither she supposed the girl would go after she was out of her place; and bade her talk with her, and tell her at a distance that as something had been done for her brother, so something would be done for her too; and, that she should not be discouraged, she carried her £20 to buy her clothes, and bid her not go to service any-more, but think of other things; that she should take a lodging in some good family, and that she should soon hear farther.

The girl was overjoyed with this news, you may be sure, and at first a little too much elevated with it, and dressed herself very handsomely indeed, and as soon as she had done so came and paid a visit to Madam Amy, to let her see how fine she was. Amy congratulated her, and wished it might be all as she expected, but admonished her not to be elevated with it too much; told her humility was the best ornament of a gentlewoman, and a great deal of good advice she gave her, but discovered* nothing.

All this was acted in the first years of my setting up my new figure here in town, and while the masks and balls were

---

* "discovered." Disclosed.

In agitation; and Amy carried on the affair of setting out my son into the world, which we were assisted in by the sage advice of my faithful counsellor, Sir Robert Clayton, who procured us a master for him, by whom he was afterwards sent abroad to Italy, as you shall hear in its place; and Amy managed my daughter too very well, though by a third hand.

My armour with my Lord —— began now to draw to an end, and indeed, notwithstanding his money, it had lasted so long that I was much more sick of his lordship than he could be of me. He grew old and fretful, and captious, and I must add, which made the vice itself begin to grow surfeiting and nauseous to me, he grew worse and wickeder the older he grew, and that to such a degree as is not fit to write of, and made me so weary of him that upon one of his capricious humours, which he often took occasion to trouble me with, I took occasion to be much less complaisant to him than I used to be; and as I knew him to be hasty, I first took care to put him into a little passion, and then to resent it, and this brought us to words, in which I told him I thought he grew sick of me; and he answered in a heat that truly so he was. I answered that I found his lordship was endeavouring to make me sick too; that I had met with several such rubs from him of late, and that he did not use me as he used to do, and I begged his lordship he would make himself easy. This I spoke with an air of coldness and indifference such as I knew he could not bear; but I did not downright quarrel with him and tell him I was sick of him too, and desire him to quit me, for I knew that would come of itself; besides, I had received a great deal of handsome usage from him, and I was loth to have the breach be on my side, that he might not be able to say I was ungrateful.

But he put the occasion into my hands, for he came no more to me for two months; indeed I expected a fit of absence, for such I had several times before, but not for above a fortnight or three weeks at most. But after I had stayed a month, which was longer than ever he kept away yet, I took a new method with him, for I was resolved now it should be in my power to continue or not, as I thought fit. At the end of a month, therefore, I removed, and took lodgings at Kensington Gravel Pits, at that part next to the road to Acton, and left nobody in my lodgings but Amy and a footman, with proper instructions how to behave when his lordship, being come to himself, should think fit to come again, which I knew he would.

About the end of two months, he came in the dusk of the evening as usual. The footman answered him, and told him his lady was not at home, but there was Mrs. Amy above; so he did not order her to be called down, but went upstairs into the dining-room, and Mrs. Amy came to him. He asked where I was. "My lord," said she, "my mistress has been removed a good while from hence and lives at Kensington." "Ah, Mrs. Amy! how come you to be here, then?" "My lord," said she, "we are here till the quarter-day, because the goods are not removed, and to give answers if any comes to ask for my lady." "Well, and what answer are you to give me?" "Indeed, my lord," says Amy, "I have no particular answer to your lordship, but to tell you and everybody else where my lady lives, that they may not think she's run away." "No, Mrs. Amy," says he, "I don't think she's run away; but, indeed, I can't go after her so far as that." Amy said nothing to that, but made a curtsey, and said she believed I would be there again for a week or two in a little time. "How little time, Mrs. Amy?" says my lord. "She comes next Tuesday," says Amy. "Very well," says my lord, "I'll come and see her then." And so he went away.

Accordingly, I came on the Tuesday and stayed a fortnight, but he came not; so I went back to Kensington, and after that I had very few of his lordship's visits, which I was very glad of, and in a little time after was more glad of it than I was at first, and upon a far better account, too.

For now I began not to be sick of his lordship only, but really I began to be sick of the vice; and as I had good leisure now to divert and enjoy myself in the world as much as it was possible for any woman to do that ever lived in it, so I found that my judgment began to prevail upon me to fix my delight upon nobler objects than I had formerly done, and the very beginning of this brought some just reflections upon me relating to things past, and to the former manner of my living; and though there was not the least hint in all this from what may be called religion or conscience, and far from anything of repentance, or anything that was a-kin to it, especially at first, yet the sense of things, and the knowledge I had of the world, and the vast variety of scenes that I had acted my part in, began to work upon my senses, and it came so very strong upon my mind one morning when I had been lying awake some time in my bed, as if somebody had asked me the question, What was I a whore for now? It occurred naturally upon this inquiry that at first I yielded to the importunity of my circumstances, the misery of which the devil dismally aggravated, to draw me to comply; for I confess I had strong natural aversions to the crime at first, partly owing to a virtuous education, and partly to a sense of religion; but the devil, and that greater devil of poverty, prevailed; and the person who laid siege to me did it in such an obliging, and I may almost say irresistible manner, all still managed by the evil spirit; for I must be allowed to believe that he has a share in all such things, if not the whole management of them. But, I say, it was carried on by that person in such an irresistible manner that, as I said when I related the fact, there was no withstanding it. These circumstances, I say, the devil managed not only to bring me to comply, but he continued them as arguments to fortify my mind against all reflection, and to keep me in that horrid course I had engaged in, as if it were honest and lawful.

But not to dwell upon that now; this was a pretence, and here was something to be said, though I acknowledge it ought not to have been sufficient to me at all; but, I say, to leave that, all this was out of doors; the devil himself could not form one argument, or put one reason into my head now, that could serve for an answer—no, not so much as a pretended answer to this question, why I should be a whore now.

It had for a-while been a little kind of excuse to me that I was engaged with this wicked old lord, and that I could not in honour forsake him; but how foolish and absurd did it look, to repeat the word "honour" on so vile an occasion! As if a woman should prostitute her honour in point of honour—horrid inconsistency! Honour called upon me to detest the crime and the man too, and to have resisted all the attacks which, from the beginning, had been made upon my virtue; and honour, had it been consulted, would have preserved me honest from the beginning:

For "honesty" and "honour" are the same.

This, however, shows us with what faint excuses and with what trifles we pretend to satisfy ourselves, and suppress the attempts of conscience, in the pursuit of agreeable crime, and in the possessing those pleasures which we are loth to part with.

But this objection would now serve no longer, for my lord had in some sort broke his engagements (I won't call it honour again) with me, and had so far slighted me as fairly to justify my entire quitting of him now; and so, as the objection was fully answered, the question remained still unanswered, Why am I a whore now? Nor indeed had I anything to say for myself, even to myself. I could not without blushing, as wicked as I was, answer that I loved it for the sake of the vice, and that I delighted in being a whore, as such; I say, I could not say this, even to myself, and all alone, nor indeed would it have been true. I was never able, in justice and with truth, to say I was so wicked as that; but as necessity first debauched me, and poverty made me a whore at the beginning, so excess of avarice for getting money and excess of vanity continued me in the crime, not being able to resist the flatteries of great persons; being called the finest woman in France; being caressed by a prince; and afterwards, I had pride enough to expect and folly enough to believe, though indeed without ground, by a great monarch. These were my baits, these the chains by which the devil held me bound, and by which I was indeed too fast held for any reasoning that I was then mistress of to deliver me from.

But this was all over now; avarice could have no pretence. I was out of the reach of all that fate could be supposed to do to reduce me; now I was so far from poor, or the danger of it, that I had £50,000 in my pocket at least; nay, I had the income of £50,000, for I had £2500 a year coming in upon very good land security, besides three or four thousand pounds in money, which I kept by me for ordinary occasions, and, besides, jewels, and plate, and goods, which were worth near £5000 more; these put together, when I ruminated on it all in my thoughts, as you may be sure I did often, added weight still to the question, as above, and it sounded continually in my head, "What next? What am I a whore for now?"

It is true this was, as I say, seldom out of my thoughts, but yet it made no impressions upon me of that kind which might be expected from a reflection of so important a nature, and which had so much of substance and seriousness in it.

But, however, it was not without some little consequences, even at this time, and which gave a little turn to my way of living at first, as you shall hear in its place.

But one particular thing intervened besides this which gave me some uneasiness at this time, and made way for other things that followed. I have mentioned in several little digressions the concern I had upon me for my children, and in what manner I had directed that affair; I must go on a little with that part, in order to bring the subsequent parts of my story together.

My boy, the only son I had left that I had a legal right to call "son," was, as I have said, rescued from the unhappy circumstances of being apprentice to a mechanic,* and was brought up upon a new foot; but though this was infinitely to his advantage, yet it put him back near three years in his coming into this world; for he had been near a year at the drudgery he was first put to, and it took up two year more to form him for what he had hopes given him he should hereafter be, so that he was full nineteen years old, or rather twenty years, before he came to be put out as I intended; at the end of which time I put him to a very flourishing Italian merchant,† and he again sent him to Messina, in the island of Sicily; and a little before the juncture I am now speaking of I had letters from him—that is to say, Mrs. Amy had letters from him, intimating that he was out of his time, and that he had an opportunity to be taken into an English house there, on very good terms, if his support from hence might answer what he was bid to hope for; and so begged that what would be done for him might be so ordered that he might have it for his present advancement, referring for the particulars to his master, the merchant in London, who he had been put apprentice to here; who, to cut the story short, gave such a satisfactory account of it, and of my young man, to my steady and faithful counsellor, Sir Robert Clayton, that I made no scruple to pay £4000, which was £1000 more than he demanded, or rather proposed, that he might have encouragement to enter into the world better than he expected.

His master remitted the money very faithfully to him; and finding, by Sir Robert Clayton, that the young gentleman—for so he called him—was well supported, wrote such letters on his account as gave him a credit at Messina equal in value to the money itself.

I could not digest it very well that I should all this while conceal myself thus from my own child, and make all this fa-

---

* "mechanic." Manual laborer.
† "Italian merchant." See above, page 165.

vour due, in his opinion, to a stranger; and yet I could not find in my heart to let my son know what a mother he had, and what a life she lived; when, at the same time that he must think himself infinitely obliged to me, he must be obliged, if he was a man of virtue, to hate his mother, and abhor the way of living by which all the bounty he enjoyed was raised.

This is the reason of mentioning this part of my son's story, which is otherwise no ways concerned in my history, but as it put me upon thinking how to put an end to that wicked course I was in, that my own child, when he should afterwards come to England in a good figure, and with the appearance of a merchant, should not be ashamed to own me.

But there was another difficulty, which lay heavier upon me a great deal, and that was my daughter, who, as before, I had relieved by the hands of another instrument, which Amy had procured. The girl, as I have mentioned, was directed to put herself into a good garb, take lodgings, and entertain a maid to wait upon her, and to give herself some breeding— that is to say, to learn to dance, and fit herself to appear as a gentlewoman; being made to hope that she should, sometime or other, find that she should be put into a condition to support her character, and to make herself amends for all her former troubles. She was only charged not to be drawn into matrimony till she was secured of a fortune that might assist to dispose of herself suitable not to what she then was, but what she was to be.

The girl was too sensible of her circumstances not to give all possible satisfaction of that kind, and indeed she was mistress of too much understanding not to see how much she should be obliged to that part for her own interest.

It was not long after this, but being well equipped, and in everything well set out, as she directed, she came, as I have related above, and paid a visit to Mrs. Amy, and to tell her of her good fortune. Amy pretended to be much surprised at the alteration, and overjoyed for her sake, and began to treat her very well, entertained her handsomely, and when she would have gone away, pretended to ask my leave and sent my coach home with her; and, in short, learning from her where she lodged, which was in the city, Amy promised to return her visit, and did so; and, in a word, Amy and Susan (for she was my own name) began an intimate acquaintance together.

There was an inexpressible difficulty in the poor girl's way, or else I should not have been able to have forborne discovering myself to her, and this was, her having been a servant in my particular family; and I could by no means think of ever letting the children know what a kind of creature they owed their being to, or giving them an occasion to upbraid their mother with her scandalous life, much less to justify the like practice from my example.

Thus it was with me; and thus, no doubt, considering parents always find it that their own children are a restraint to them in their worst courses, when the sense of a superior power has not the same influence. But of that hereafter.

There happened, however, one good circumstance in the case of this poor girl, which brought about a discovery sooner than otherwise it would have been, and it was thus. After she and Amy had been intimate for some time, and had exchanged several visits, the girl, now grown a woman, talking to Amy of the gay things that used to fall out when she was servant in my family, spoke of it with a kind of concern that she could not see (me) her lady. And at last she adds, " 'Twas very strange, madam," says she to Amy, "but though I lived near two years in the house, I never saw my mistress in my life, except it was that public night when she danced in the fine Turkish habit, and then she was so disguised that I knew nothing of her afterwards."

Amy was glad to hear this, but as she was a cunning girl from the beginning, she was not to be bit,* and so she laid no stress upon that at first, but gave me an account of it; and I must confess it gave me a secret joy to think that I was not known to her, and that, by virtue of that only accident, I might, when other circumstances made room for it, discover myself to her, and let her know she had a mother in a condition fit to be owned.

It was a dreadful restraint to me before, and this gave me some very sad reflections, and made way for the great question I have mentioned above; and by how much the circumstance was bitter to me, by so much the more agreeable it was to understand that the girl had never seen me, and consequently did not know me again if she was to be told who I was.

* "bit." Overreached, taken in.

However, the next time she came to visit Amy, I was resolved to put it to a trial, and to come into the room and let her see me, and to see by that whether she knew me or no; but Amy put me by, lest indeed, as there was reason enough to question, I should not be able to contain or forbear discovering myself to her. So it went off for that time.

But both these circumstances, and that is the reason of mentioning them, brought me to consider of the life I lived, and to resolve to put myself into some figure of life in which I might not be scandalous to my own family, and be afraid to make myself known to my own children, who were my own flesh and blood.

There was another daughter I had, which, with all our inquiries, we could not hear of, high nor low, for several years after the first. But I return to my own story.

Being now in part removed from my old station, I seemed to be in a fair way of retiring from my old acquaintances, and consequently from the vile, abominable trade I had driven so long; so that the door seemed to be, as it were, particularly opened to my reformation, if I had any mind to it in earnest. But, for all that, some of my old friends, as I had used to call them, inquired me out and came to visit me at Kensington, and that more frequently than I wished they would do; but it being once known where I was, there was no avoiding it, unless I would have downright refused and affronted them; and I was not yet in earnest enough with my resolutions to go that length.

The best of it was, my old lewd favourite, who I now heartily hated, entirely dropped me. He came once to visit me, but I caused Amy to deny me, and say I was gone out. She did it so oddly, too, that when his lordship went away, he said coldly to her, "Well, well, Mrs. Amy, I find your mistress does not desire to be seen; tell her I won't trouble her any-more," repeating the words "any-more" two or three times over, just at his going away.

I reflected a little on it at first as unkind to him, having had so many considerable presents from him, but, as I have said, I was sick of him, and that on some accounts which, if I could suffer myself to publish them, would fully justify my conduct. But that part of the story will not bear telling, so I must leave it and proceed.

I had begun a little, as I have said above, to reflect upon my manner of living and to think of putting a new face upon it, and nothing moved me to it more than the consideration of my having three children, who were now grown up; and yet that while I was in that station of life I could not converse with them or make myself known to them; and this gave me a great deal of uneasiness. At last I entered into talk on this part of it with my woman Amy.

We lived at Kensington, as I have said, and though I had done with my old wicked L———, as above, yet I was frequently visited, as I said, by some others; so that, in a word, I began to be known in the town, not by name only, but by my character too, which was worse.

It was one morning when Amy was in bed with me, and I had some of my dullest thoughts about me, that Amy, hearing me sigh pretty often, asked me if I was not well. "Yes, Amy, I am well enough," says I, "but my mind is oppressed with heavy thoughts, and has been so a good while." And then I told her how it grieved me that I could not make myself known to my own children or form any acquaintances in the world. "Why so?" says Amy. "Why, prithee, Amy," says I, "what will my children say to themselves, and to one another, when they find their mother, however rich she may be, is at best but a whore, a common whore? And as for acquaintance, prithee, Amy, what sober lady or what family of any character will visit or be acquainted with a whore?"

"Why, all that's true, madam," says Amy, "but how can it be remedied now?" " 'Tis true, Amy," said I, "the thing cannot be remedied now, but the scandal of it, I fancy, may be thrown off."

"Truly," says Amy, "I do not see how, unless you will go abroad again, and live in some other nation where nobody has known us or seen us, so that they cannot say they ever saw us before."

That very thought of Amy put what follows into my head, and I returned, "Why, Amy," says I, "is it not possible for me to shift my being from this part of the town and go and live in another part of the city, or another part of the country, and be as entirely concealed as if I had never been known?"

"Yes," says Amy, "I believe it might; but then you must put off all your equipages and servants, coaches and horses, change your liveries—nay, your own clothes, and, if it was possible, your very face."

"Well," says I, "and that's the way, Amy, and that'll do,

and that forthwith; for I am not able to live in this manner any longer." Amy came into this with a kind of pleasure particular to herself—that is to say, with an eagerness not to be resisted; for Amy was apt to be precipitant in her motions and was for doing it immediately. "Well," says I, "Amy, as soon as you will, but what course must we take to do it? We cannot put off servants, and coach and horses, and everything, leave off house-keeping, and transform ourselves into a new shape all in a moment. Servants must have warning, and the goods must be sold off, and a thousand things." And this began to perplex us, and in particular took us up two or three days' consideration.

At last Amy, who was a clever manager in such cases, came to me with a scheme, as she called it. "I have found it out, madam," says she. "I have found a scheme how you shall, if you have a mind to it, begin and finish a perfect entire change of your figure and circumstances in one day, and you shall be as much unknown, madam, in twenty-four hours as you would be in so many years."

"Come, Amy," says I, "let us hear of it, for you please me mightily with the thoughts of it." "Why, then," says Amy, "let me go into the city this afternoon, and I'll inquire out some honest, plain sober family, where I will take lodgings for you, as for a country gentlewoman that desires to be in London for about half a year, and to board yourself and a kinswoman—that is, half a servant, half a companion, meaning myself; and so agree with them by the month.

"To this lodging (if I hit upon one to your mind) you may go to-morrow morning in a hackney-coach, with nobody but me, and leave such clothes and linen as you think fit, but, to be sure, the plainest you have; and then you are removed at once; you need never so much as set your foot in this house again" (meaning where we then were), "or see anybody belonging to it. In the meantime I'll let the servants know that you are going over to Holland upon extraordinary business, and will leave off your equipages, and so I'll give them warning, or, if they will accept of it, give them a month's wages. Then I'll sell off your furniture as well as I can. As to your coach, it is but having it new painted and the lining changed, and getting new harness and hammer-cloths, and you may keep it still or dispose of it, as you think fit. And only take care to let this lodging be in some remote part of the town, and you may be as perfectly unknown as if you had never been in England in your life."

This was Amy's scheme, and it pleased me so well that I resolved not only to let her go, but was resolved to go with her myself. But Amy put me off of that, because, she said, she should have occasion to hurry up and down so long that if I was with her, it would rather hinder than farther her, so I waived it.

In a word, Amy went and was gone five long hours; but when she came back I could see by her countenance that her success had been suitable to her pains, for she came laughing and gaping. "O madam!" says she, "I have pleased you to the life;" and with that she tells me how she had fixed upon a house in a court in the Minories; that she was directed to it merely by accident; that it was a female family, the master of the house being gone to New England, and that the woman had four children, kept two maids, and lived very handsomely, but wanted company to divert her; and that on that very account she had agreed to take boarders.

Amy agreed for a good, handsome price, because she was resolved I should be used well; so she bargained to give her £35 for the half-year, and £50 if we took a maid, leaving that to my choice; and that we might be satisfied we should meet with nothing very gay, the people were Quakers, and I liked them the better.

I was so pleased that I resolved to go with Amy the next day to see the lodgings, and to see the woman of the house, and see how I liked them; but if I was pleased with the general, I was much more pleased with the particulars, for the gentlewoman—I must call her so, though she was a Quaker—was a most courteous, obliging, mannerly person, perfectly well-bred and perfectly well-humoured, and, in short, the most agreeable conversation that ever I met with; and, which was worth all, so grave, and yet so pleasant and so merry, that 'tis scarce possible for me to express how I was pleased and delighted with her company; and particularly, I was so pleased that I would go away no more; so I e'en took up my lodging there the very first night.

In the meantime, though it took up Amy almost a month so entirely to put off all the appearances of house-keeping, as above, it need take me up no time to relate it; 'tis enough to say that Amy quitted all that part of the world and came pack and package to me, and here we took up our abode.

I was now in a perfect retreat indeed, remote from the
eyes of all that ever had seen me, and as much out of the
way of being ever seen or heard of by any of the gang that
used to follow me as if I had been among the mountains in
Lancashire; for when did a blue garter or a coach-and-six
come into a little narrow passage in the Minories or Goodman's Fields? And as there was no fear of them, so really I
had no desire to see them, or so much as to hear from them
any-more as long as I lived.

I seemed in a little hurry while Amy came and went so ev-
ery-day at first, but when that was over, I lived here perfectly
retired, and with a most pleasant and agreeable lady; I must
call her so, for, though a Quaker, she had a full share of
good breeding, sufficient to her if she had been a duchess; in
a word, she was the most agreeable creature in her conversation, as I said before, that ever I met with.

I pretended, after I had been there some time, to be extremely in love with the dress of the Quakers, and this
pleased her so much that she would needs dress me up one
day in a suit of her own clothes; but my real design was to
see whether it would pass upon me for a disguise.

Amy was struck with the novelty, though I had not mentioned my design to her, and when the Quaker was gone out
of the room, says Amy, "I guess your meaning; it is a perfect
disguise to you. Why, you look quite another body; I should
not have known you myself. Nay," says Amy, "more than
that, it makes you look ten years younger than you did."

Nothing could please me better than that, and when Amy
repeated it, I was so fond of it that I asked my Quaker (I
won't call her landlady; 'tis indeed too coarse a word for her,
and she deserved a much better)—I say, I asked her if she
would sell it. I told her I was so fond of it that I would give
her enough to buy her a better suit. She declined it at first,
but I soon perceived that it was chiefly in good manners, because I should not dishonour myself, as she called it, to put
on her old clothes; but if I pleased to accept of them, she
would give me them for my dressing-clothes, and go with me
and buy a suit for me that might be better worth my wearing.

But as I conversed in a very frank, open manner with her,
I bid her do the like with me; that I made no scruples of such
things, but that if she would let me have them, I would satisfy her. So she let me know what they cost, and to make her
amends, I gave her three guineas more than they cost her.

This good (though unhappy) Quaker had the misfortune to have had a bad husband, and he was gone beyond sea. She had a good house, and well furnished, and had some jointure of her own estate which supported her and her children, so that she did not want; but she was not at all above such a help as my being there was to her; so she was as glad of me as I was of her.

However, as I knew there was no way to fix this new acquaintance like making myself a friend to her, I began with making her some handsome presents and the like to her children. And first, opening my bundles one day in my chamber, I heard her in another room, and called her in with a kind of familiar way. There I showed her some of my fine clothes, and having among the rest of my things a piece of very fine new holland, which I had bought a little before, worth about 9s. an ell, I pulled it out. "Here, my friend," says I, "I will make you a present, if you will accept of it." And with that I laid the piece of holland in her lap.

I could see she was surprised, and that she could hardly speak. "What dost thou mean?" says she. "Indeed I cannot have the face to accept so fine a present as this", adding, " 'Tis fit for thy own use, but 'tis above my wear, indeed." I thought she had meant she must not wear it so fine because she was a Quaker. So I returned, "Why, do not you Quakers wear fine linen neither?" "Yes," says she, "we wear fine linen when we can afford it, but this is too good for me." However, I made her take it, and she was very thankful too. But my end was answered another way, for by this I engaged her so, that as I found her a woman of understanding, and of honesty too, I might, upon any occasion, have a confidence in her, which was, indeed, what I very much wanted.

By accustoming myself to converse with her, I had not only learned to dress like a Quaker, but so used myself to "thee" and "thou" that I talked like a Quaker too, as readily and naturally as if I had been born among them; and, in a word, I passed for a Quaker among all people that did not know me. I went but little abroad, but I had been so used to a coach that I knew not how well to go without one; besides, I thought it would be a farther disguise to me, so I told my Quaker friend one day that I thought I lived too close, that I wanted air. She proposed taking a hackney-coach sometimes, or a boat; but I told her I had always had a coach of my own till now, and I could find in my heart to have one again.

She seemed to think it strange at first, considering how close I lived, but had nothing to say when she found I did not value the expense; so, in short, I resolved I would have a coach. When we came to talk of equipages, she extolled the having all things plain. I said so too; so I left it to her direction, and a coach-maker was sent for, and he provided me a plain coach, no gilding or painting, lined with a light-grey cloth, and my coachman had a coat of the same, and no lace on his hat.

When all was ready, I dressed myself in the dress I bought of her and said, "Come, I'll be a Quaker to-day, and you and I'll go abroad." Which we did, and there was not a Quaker in the town looked less like a counterfeit than I did. But all this was my particular plot, to be the more completely concealed, and that I might depend upon being not known, and yet need not be confined like a prisoner and be always in fear; so that all the rest was grimace.

We lived here very easy and quiet, and yet I cannot say I was so in my mind; I was like a fish out of water. I was as gay and as young in my disposition as I was at five and twenty; and as I had always been courted, flattered, and used to love it, so I missed it in my conversation; and this put me many times upon looking back upon things past.

I had very few moments in my life which, in their reflection, afforded me anything but regret; but of all the foolish actions I had to look back upon in my life, none looked so preposterous and so like distraction, nor left so much melancholy on my mind, as my parting with my friend, the merchant of Paris, and the refusing him upon such honourable and just conditions as he had offered; and though on his just (which I called unkind) rejecting my invitation to come to him again, I had looked on him with some disgust, yet now my mind run upon him continually, and the ridiculous conduct of my refusing him, and I could never be satisfied about him. I flattered myself that if I could but see him I could yet master him, and that he would presently forget all that had passed that might be thought unkind; but as there was no room to imagine anything like that to be possible, I threw those thoughts off again as much as I could.

However, they continually returned, and I had no rest night or day for thinking of him, who I had forgot above eleven years. I told Amy of it, and we talked it over sometimes in bed, almost whole nights together. At last Amy started a thing of her own head, which put it in a way of management, though a wild one too. "You are so uneasy, madam," says she, "about this Mr. ———, the merchant at Paris. Come," says she, "if you'll give me leave, I'll go over and see what's become of him."

"Not for ten thousand pounds," said I; "no, nor if you met him in the street, not to offer to speak to him on my account." "No," says Amy, "I would not speak to him at all; or if I did, I warrant you it shall not look to be upon your account. I'll only inquire after him, and if he is in being, you shall hear of him; if not, you shall hear of him still, and that may be enough."

"Why," says I, "if you will promise me not to enter into anything relating to me with him, nor to begin any discourse at all unless he begins it with you, I could almost be persuaded to let you go and try."

Amy promised me all that I desired; and, in a word, to cut the story short, I let her go, but tied her up to so many particulars that it was almost impossible her going could signify anything; and had she intended to observe them, she might as well have stayed at home as have gone, for I charged her, if she came to see him, she should not so much as take notice that she knew him again; and if he spoke to her, she should tell him she was come away from me a great many years ago and knew nothing what was become of me; that she had been come over to France six years ago, and was married there, and lived at Calais; or to that purpose.

Amy promised me nothing, indeed; for, as she said, it was impossible for her to resolve what would be fit to do, or not to do, till she was there upon the spot and had found out the gentleman, or heard of him; but that then, if I would trust her, as I had always done, she would answer for it that she would do nothing but what should be for my interest, and what she would hope I should be very well pleased with.

With this general commission, Amy, notwithstanding she had been so frighted at the sea, ventured her carcass once more by water, and away she goes to France. She had four articles of confidence in charge to inquire after for me, and, as I found by her, she had one for herself—I say, four for me, because, though her first and principal errand was to inform herself of my Dutch merchant, yet I gave her in charge to inquire, second, after my husband, who I left a trooper in the *gens d'armes;* third, after that rogue of a Jew, whose very name I hated, and of whose face I had such a frightful idea that Satan himself could not counterfeit a worse; and, lastly, after my foreign prince. And she discharged herself very well of them all, though not so successful as I wished.

Amy had a very good passage over the sea, and I had a letter from her, from Calais, in three days after she went from London. When she came to Paris she wrote me an account, that as to her first and most important inquiry, which was after the Dutch merchant, her account was, that he had returned to Paris, lived three years there, and quitting that city, went to live at Rouen; so away goes Amy for Rouen.

But as she was going to bespeak a place in the coach to Rouen, she meets very accidentally in the street with her gentleman, as I called him—that is to say, the Prince de ————'s gentleman, who had been her favourite, as above.

You may be sure there were several other kind things happened between Amy and him, as you shall hear afterwards; but the two main things were, first, that Amy inquired about his lord, and had a full account of him, of which presently; and, in the next place, telling him whither she was going and for what, he bade her not go yet, for that he would have a particular account of it the next day from a merchant that knew him; and, accordingly, he brought her word the next day that he had been for six years before that gone for Holland, and that he lived there still.

This, I say, was the first news from Amy for some time—I mean about my merchant. In the meantime, Amy, as I have said, inquired about the other persons she had in her instructions. As for the prince, the gentleman told her he was gone into Germany, where his estate lay, and that he lived there; that he had made great inquiry after me; that he (his gentleman) had made all the search he had been able for me, but that he could not hear of me; that he believed, if his lord had known I had been in England, he would have gone over to me; but that, after long inquiry, he was obliged to give it over; but that he verily believed, if he could have found me, he would have married me; and that he was extremely concerned that he could hear nothing of me.

I was not at all satisfied with Amy's account, but ordered her to go to Rouen herself, which she did, and there with much difficulty (the person she was directed to being dead)—I say, with much difficulty she came to be informed that my merchant had lived there two years, or something more, but that, having met with a very great misfortune, he had gone back to Holland, as the French merchant said, where he had stayed two years; but with this addition, viz., that he came back again to Rouen, and lived in good reputation there another year; and afterwards he was gone to England, and that he lived in London. But Amy could by no means learn how to write to him there, till, by great accident, an old Dutch skipper, who had formerly served him, coming to Rouen, Amy was told of it; and he told her that he lodged in St. Lawrence Pountney's Lane, in London, but was to be seen every day upon the Exchange, in the French walk.

This, Amy thought, it was time enough to tell me of when she came over; and, besides, she did not find this Dutch skipper till she had spent four or five months and been again at Paris, and then come back to Rouen for farther information. But in the meantime she wrote to me from Paris that he was not to be found by any means; that he had been gone from Paris seven or eight years; that she was told he had lived at Rouen, and she was a-going thither to inquire, but that she had heard afterward that he was gone also from thence to Holland, so she did not go.

This, I say, was Amy's first account; and I, not satisfied with it, had sent her an order to go to Rouen to inquire there also, as above.

While this was negotiating, and I received these accounts from Amy several times, a strange adventure happened to me which I must mention just here. I had been abroad to take the air as usual with my Quaker, as far as Epping Forest, and we were driving back towards London, when, on the road between Bow and Mile-End, two gentlemen on horseback came riding by, having over-taken the coach and passed it, and went forwards towards London.

They did not ride apace though they passed the coach, for we went very softly; nor did they look into the coach at all, but rode side by side, earnestly talking to one another and inclining their faces sideways a little towards one another, he that went nearest the coach with his face from it, and he that was farthest from the coach with his face towards it, and passing in the very next tract to the coach, I could hear them talk Dutch very distinctly. But it is impossible to describe the confusion I was in when I plainly saw that the farthest of the two, him whose face looked towards the coach, was my friend the Dutch merchant of Paris.

If it had been possible to conceal my disorder from my friend the Quaker, I would have done it, but I found she was too well acquainted with such things not to take the hint. "Dost thou understand Dutch?" said she. "Why?" said I. "Why," says she, " 'tis easy to suppose that thou art a little concerned at somewhat those men say; I suppose they are talking of thee." "Indeed, my good friend," said I, "thou art mistaken this time, for I know very well what they are talking of, but 'tis all about ships and trading affairs." "Well," says she, "then one of them is a man-friend of thine, or somewhat is the case; for though thy tongue will not confess it, thy face does."

I was going to have told a bold lie and said I knew nothing of them, but I found it was impossible to conceal it, so I said, "Indeed, I think I know the farthest of them; but I have neither spoken to him or so much as seen him for above eleven years." "Well, then," says she, "thou hast seen him with more than common eyes when thou didst see him, or else seeing him now would not be such a surprise to thee." "Indeed," said I, " 'tis true I am a little surprised at seeing him just now, for I thought he had been in quite another part of the world; and I can assure you I never saw him in England in my life." "Well, then, 'tis the more likely he is come over now on purpose to seek thee." "No, no," said I, "knight-errantry is over. Women are not so hard to come at that men should not be able to please themselves without running from one kingdom to another." "Well, well," says she, "I would have him see thee for all that, as plainly as thou hast seen him." "No, but he shan't," says I, "for I am sure he don't know me in this dress, and I'll take care he shan't see my face, if I can help it." So I held up my fan before my face, and she saw me resolute in that, so she pressed me no farther.

We had several discourses upon the subject, but still I let her know I was resolved he should not know me; but at last I confessed so much, that though I would not let him know who I was or where I lived, I did not care if I knew where he lived and how I might inquire about him. She took the hint immediately, and her servant being behind the coach, she called him to the coach-side and bade him keep his eye upon that gentleman, and as soon as the coach came to the end of Whitechapel, he should get down and follow him closely, so as to see where he put up his horse, and then go into the inn and inquire, if he could, who he was and where he lived.

The fellow followed diligently to the gate of an inn in Bishopgate Street, and seeing him go in, made no doubt but he had him fast; but was confounded when, upon inquiry, he found the inn was a thoroughfare into another street, and that the two gentlemen had only rode through the inn, as the way to the street where they were going; and so, in short, came back no wiser than he went.

My kind Quaker was more vexed at the disappointment, at least apparently so, than I was; and asking the fellow if he was sure he knew the gentleman again if he saw him, the fellow said he had followed him so close and took so much notice of him, in order to do his errand as it ought to be done, that he was very sure he should know him again; and that, besides, he was sure he should know his horse.

This part was, indeed, likely enough; and the kind Quaker, without telling me anything of the matter, caused her man to place himself just at the corner of Whitechapel Church wall every Saturday in the afternoon, that being the day when the citizens chiefly ride abroad to take the air, and there to watch all the afternoon and look for him.

It was not till the fifth Saturday that her man came, with a great deal of joy, and gave her an account that he had found out the gentleman; that he was a Dutchman, but a French merchant; that he came from Rouen, and his name was ————, and that he lodged at Mr. ————'s, on Lawrence Pountney's Hill. I was surprised, you may be sure, when she came and told me one evening all the particulars, except that of having set her man to watch. "I have found out thy Dutch friend," says she, "and can tell thee how to find him too." I coloured again as red as fire. "Then thou hast dealt with the evil one, friend," said I gravely. "No, no," says she, "I have no familiar; but I tell thee I have found him for thee, and his name is So-and-so, and he lives as above recited."

I was surprised again at this, not being able to imagine how she should come to know all this. However, to put me out of pain, she told me what she had done. "Well," said I, "thou art very kind, but this is not worth thy pains; for now I know it, 'tis only to satisfy my curiosity; for I shall not send to him upon any account." "Be that as thou wilt," says she. "Besides," added she, "thou art in the right to say so to me, for why should I be trusted with it? Though, if I were, I assure thee I should not betray thee." "That's very kind," said

I, "and I believe thee; and assure thyself, if I do send to him, thou shalt know it, and be trusted with it too."

During this interval of five weeks I suffered a hundred thousand perplexities of mind. I was thoroughly convinced I was right as to the person, that it was the man. I knew him so well, and saw him so plain, I could not be deceived. I drove out again in the coach (on pretence of air) almost every day in hopes of seeing him again, but was never so lucky as to see him; and now I had made the discovery, I was as far to seek what measures to take as I was before.

To send to him, or speak to him first, I should see him, so as to be known to him, that I resolved not to do if I died for it. To watch him about his lodging, that was as much below my spirit as the other. So that, in a word, I was at a perfect loss how to act or what to do.

At length came Amy's letter, with the last account which she had at Rouen from the Dutch skipper, which, confirming the other, left me out of doubt that this was my man; but still, no human invention could bring me to the speech of him in such a manner as would suit with my resolutions. For, after all, how did I know what his circumstances were? whether married or single? And if he had a wife, I knew he was so honest a man he would not so much as converse with me, or so much as know me if he met me in the street.

In the next place, as he entirely neglected me, which, in short, is the worst way of slighting a woman, and had given no answer to my letters, I did not know but he might be the same man still; so I resolved that I could do nothing in it unless some fairer opportunity presented, which might make my way clearer to me; for I was determined he should have no room to put any more slights upon me.

In these thoughts I passed away near three months; till at last, being impatient, I resolved to send for Amy to come over, and tell her how things stood, and that I would do nothing till she came. Amy, in answer, sent me word she would come away with all speed, but begged of me that I would enter into no engagement with him, or anybody, till she arrived; but still keeping me in the dark as to the thing itself which she had to say; at which I was heartily vexed, for many reasons.

But while all these things were transacting, and letters and answers passed between Amy and I a little slower than usual, at which I was not so well pleased as I used to be with Amy's dispatch—I say, in this time the following scene opened.

It was one afternoon, about four o'clock, my friendly Quaker and I sitting in her chamber upstairs, and very cheerful, chatting together (for she was the best company in the world), when somebody ringing hastily at the door, and no servant just then in the way, she ran down herself to the door, when a gentleman appears, with a footman attending, and making some apologies, which she did not thoroughly understand, he speaking but broken English, he asked to speak with me, by the very same name that I went by in her house, which, by the way, was not the name that he had known me by.

She, with very civil language, in her way, brought him into a very handsome parlour below-stairs and said she would go and see whether the person who lodged in her house owned that name, and he should hear farther.

I was a little surprised, even before I knew anything of who it was, my mind foreboding the thing as it happened (whence that arises, let the naturalists explain to us); but I was frighted and ready to die when my Quaker came up all gay and crowing. "There," says she, "is the Dutch French merchant come to see thee." I could not speak one word to her nor stir off of my chair, but sat as motionless as a statue. She talked a thousand pleasant things to me, but they made no impression on me. At last she pulled me and teased me. "Come, come," says she, "be thyself and rouse up. I must go down again to him; what shall I say to him?" "Say," said I, "that you have no such body in the house." "That I cannot do," says she, "because it is not the truth. Besides, I have owned thou art above. Come, come, go down with me." "Not for a thousand guineas," said I. "Well," says she, "I'll go and tell him thou wilt come quickly." So, without giving me time to answer her, away she goes.

A million of thoughts circled in my head while she was gone, and what to do I could not tell; I saw no remedy but I must speak with him, but would have given £500 to have shunned it; yet had I shunned it, perhaps then I would have given £500 again that I had seen him. Thus fluctuating and unconcluding were my thoughts, what I so earnestly desired I declined when it offered itself; and what now I pretended to decline was nothing but what I had been at the expense of £40 or £50 to send Amy to France for, and even without any

view, or, indeed, any rational expectation of bringing it to
pass; and what for half a year before I was so uneasy about
that I could not be quiet night or day till Amy proposed to
go over to inquire after him. In short, my thoughts were all
confused and in the utmost disorder. I had once refused and
rejected him, and I repented it heartily; then I had taken ill
his silence, and in my mind rejected him again, but had repented that too. Now I had stooped so low as to send after
him into France, which if he had known, perhaps, he had
never come after me; and should I reject him a third time!
On the other hand, he had repented too, in his turn, perhaps,
and not knowing how I had acted, either in stooping to send
in search after him or in the wickeder part of my life, was
come over hither to seek me again; and I might take him,
perhaps with the same advantages as I might have done before, and would I now be backward to see him! Well, while I
was in this hurry my friend the Quaker comes up again, and
perceiving the confusion I was in, she runs to her closet and
fetched me a little pleasant cordial; but I would not taste it.
"Oh," says she, "I understand thee. Be not uneasy; I'll give
thee something shall take off all the smell of it; if he kisses
thee a thousand times, he shall be no wiser." I thought with
myself, "Thou art perfectly acquainted with affairs of this
nature; I think you must govern me now." So I began to incline to go down with her. Upon that, I took the cordial, and
she gave me a kind of spicy preserve after it, whose flavour
was so strong, and yet so deliciously pleasant, that it would
cheat the nicest smelling, and it left not the least taint of the
cordial on the breath.

Well, after this, though with some hesitation still, I went
down a pair of back-stairs with her, and into a dining-room,
next to the parlour in which he was; but there I halted, and
desired she would let me consider of it a little. "Well, do so,"
says she, and left me with more readiness than she did before. "Do, consider, and I'll come to thee again."

Though I hung back with an awkwardness that was really
unfeigned, yet when she so readily left me, I thought it was
not so kind, and I began to think she should have pressed me
still on to it; so foolishly backward are we to the thing which,
of all the world, we most desire; mocking ourselves with a
feigned reluctance, when the negative would be death to us.
But she was too cunning for me; for while I, as it were,
blamed her in my mind for not carrying me to him, though,

at the same time, I appeared backward to see him, on a sudden she unlocks the folding-doors, which looked into the next parlour, and throwing them open, "There," says she (ushering him in), "is the person who, I suppose, thou inquirest for." And the same moment, with a kind decency, she retired, and that so swift that she would not give us leave hardly to know which way she went.

I stood up, but was confounded with a sudden inquiry in my thoughts how I should receive him, and with a resolution as swift as lightning, in answer to it, said to myself, "It shall be coldly." So on a sudden I put on an air of stiffness and ceremony and held it for about two minutes; but it was with great difficulty.

He restrained himself too, on the other hand, came towards me gravely and saluted me in form; but it was, it seems, upon his supposing the Quaker was behind him, whereas she, as I said, understood things too well, and had retired as if she had vanished, that we might have full freedom; for, as she said afterwards, she supposed we had seen one another before, though it might have been a great while ago.

Whatever stiffness I had put on my behaviour to him, I was surprised in my mind, and angry at his, and began to wonder what kind of a ceremonious meeting it was to be. However, after he perceived the woman was gone, he made a kind of a hesitation, looking a little round him. "Indeed," said he, "I thought the gentlewoman was not withdrawn." And with that he took me in his arms and kissed me three or four times; but I, that was prejudiced to the last degree with the coldness of his first salutes, when I did not know the cause of it, could not be thoroughly cleared of the prejudice though I did know the cause, and thought that even his return, and taking me in his arms, did not seem to have the same ardour with which he used to receive me, and this made me behave to him awkwardly, and I know not how for a good while; but this by the way.

He began with a kind of an ecstasy upon the subject of his finding me out; how it was possible that he should have been four years in England, and had used all the ways imaginable, and could never so much as have the least intimation of me, or of any one like me; and that it was now above two years that he had despaired of it, and had given over all inquiry;

and that now he should chop upon me, as it were, unlooked and unsought for.

I could easily have accounted for his not finding me if I had but set down the detail of my real retirement; but I gave it a new, and indeed a truly hypocritical turn. I told him that anyone that knew the manner of life I led might account for his not finding me; that the retreat I had taken up would have rendered it a hundred thousand to one odds that he ever found me at all; that, as I had abandoned all conversation, taken up another name, lived remote from London, and had not preserved one acquaintance in it, it was no wonder he had not met with me; that even my dress would let him see that I did not desire to be known by anybody.

Then he asked if I had not received some letters from him. I told him no, he had not thought fit to give me the civility of an answer to the last I wrote to him, and he could not suppose I should expect a return after a silence in a case where I had laid myself so low and exposed myself in a manner I had never been used to; that indeed I had never sent for any letters after that to the place where I had ordered his to be directed; and that, being so justly, as I thought, punished for my weakness, I had nothing to do but to repent of being a fool, after I had strictly adhered to a just principle before; that, however, as what I did was rather from motions of gratitude than from real weakness, however it might be construed by him, I had the satisfaction in myself of having fully discharged the debt. I added, that I had not wanted occasions of all the seeming advancements which the pretended felicity of a marriage life was usually set off with, and might have been what I desired not to name; but that, however low I had stooped to him, I had maintained the dignity of female liberty against all the attacks either of pride or avarice; and that I had been infinitely obliged to him for giving me an opportunity to discharge the only obligation that endangered me, without subjecting me to the consequence; and that I hoped he was satisfied I had paid the debt by offering myself to be chained, but was infinitely debtor to him another way, for letting me remain free.

He was so confounded at this discourse that he knew not what to say, and for a good while he stood mute indeed; but recovering himself a little, he said I run out into a discourse he hoped was over and forgotten, and he did not intend to revive it; that he knew I had not had his letters, for that, when

he first came to England, he had been at the place to which
they were directed and found them all lying there but one,
and that the people had not known how to deliver them; that
he thought to have had a direction there how to find me, but
had the mortification to be told that they did not so much as
know who I was; that he was under a great disappointment;
and that I ought to know, in answer to all my resentments,
that he had done a long and, he hoped, a sufficient penance
for the slight that I had supposed he had put upon me; that it
was true (and I could not suppose any other) that upon the
repulse I had given him in a case so circumstanced as his
was, and after such earnest entreaties and such offers as he
had made me, he went away with a mind heartily grieved
and full of resentment; that he had looked back on the crime
he had committed with some regret, but on the cruelty of
my treatment of the poor infant I went with at that time with
the utmost detestation, and that this made him unable to send
an agreeable answer to me; for which reason he had sent
none at all for some time; but that in about six or seven
months, those resentments wearing off by the return of his affection to me and his concern in the poor child—There he
stopped, and indeed tears stood in his eyes; while in a paren-
thesis he only added, and to this minute he did not know
whether it was dead or alive. He then went on: Those resentments wearing off, he sent me several letters—I think he said
seven or eight—but received no answer; that then his business
obliging him to go to Holland, he came to England, as in his
way, but found, as above, that his letters had not been called
for, but that he left them at the house after paying the
postage of them; and going then back to France, he was yet
uneasy, and could not refrain the knight-errantry of coming
to England again to seek me, though he knew neither where
or of who to inquire for me, being disappointed in all his inquiries before; that he had yet taken up his residence here,
firmly believing that one time or other he should meet me, or
hear of me, and that some kind chance would at last throw
him in my way; that he had lived thus above four years, and
though his hopes were vanished, yet he had not any thoughts
of removing any more in the world, unless it should be at
last, as it is with other old men, he might have some inclination to go home to die in his own country, but that he had
not thought of it yet; that if I would consider all these steps, I
would find some reasons to forget his first resentments, and to

think that penance, as he called it, which he had undergone
in search of me, an *amende honorable*, in reparation of the
affront given to the kindness of my letter of invitation; and
that we might at last make ourselves some satisfaction on
both sides for the mortifications past.

I confess I could not hear all this without being moved
very much, and yet I continued a little stiff and formal too a
good while. I told him that before I could give him any reply
to the rest of his discourse, I ought to give him the satisfaction of telling him that his son was alive, and that indeed,
since I saw him so concerned about it, and mention it with
such affection, I was sorry that I had not found out some
way or other to let him know it sooner; but that I thought,
after his slighting the mother, as above, he had summed up
his affection to the child in the letter he had wrote to me
about providing for it; and that he had, as other fathers often
do, looked upon it as a birth which, being out of the way,
was to be forgotten, as its beginning was to be repented of;
that in providing sufficiently for it, he had done more than all
such fathers used to do, and might be well satisfied with it.

He answered me that he should have been very glad if I
had been so good but to have given him the satisfaction of
knowing the poor unfortunate creature was yet alive, and he
would have taken some care of it upon himself, and particularly by owning it for a legitimate child, which, where nobody had known to the contrary, would have taken off the
infamy which would otherwise cleave to it, and so the child
should not itself have known anything of its own disaster; but
that he feared it was now too late.

He added that I might see by all his conduct since that,
what unhappy mistake drew him into the thing at first, and
that he would have been very far from doing the injury to
me, or being instrumental to add *une miserable* (that was his
word) to the world, if he had not been drawn into it by the
hopes he had of making me his own; but that, if it was possible to rescue the child from the consequences of its unhappy birth, he hoped I would give him leave to do it, and he
would let me see that he had both means and affection still to
do it; and that, notwithstanding all the misfortunes that had
befallen him, nothing that belonged to him, especially by a
mother he had such a concern for as he had for me, should
ever want what he was in a condition to do for it.

I could not hear this without being sensibly touched with

it. I was ashamed that he should show that he had more real affection for the child, though he had never seen it in his life, than I that bore it, for indeed I did not love the child, nor love to see it; and though I had provided for it, yet I did it by Amy's hand, and had not seen it above twice in four years, being privately resolved that when it grew up, it should not be able to call me mother.

However, I told him the child was taken care of, and that he need not be anxious about it, unless he suspected that I had less affection for it than he that had never seen it in his life; that he knew what I had promised him to do for it, namely, to give it the thousand pistoles which I had offered him, and which he had declined; that I assured him I had made my will, and that I had left it £5000, and the interest of it till he should come of age, if I died before that time; that I would still be as good as that to it; but if he had a mind to take it from me into his government, I would not be against it; and to satisfy him that I would perform what I said, I would cause the child to be delivered to him, and the £5000 also for its support, depending upon it that he would show himself a father to it by what I saw of his affection to it now.

I had observed that he had hinted two or three times in his discourse, his having had misfortunes in the world, and I was a little surprised at the expression, especially at the repeating it so often; but I took no notice of that part yet.

He thanked me for my kindness to the child with a tenderness which showed the sincerity of all he had said before, and which increased the regret with which, as I said, I looked back on the little affection I had showed to the poor child. He told me he did not desire to take him from me, but so as to introduce him into the world as his own, which he could still do, having lived absent from his other children (for he had two sons and a daughter which were brought up at Nimeguen, in Holland, with a sister of his) so long that he might very well send another son of ten years old to be bred up with them, and suppose his mother to be dead or alive, as he found occasion; and that, as I had resolved to do so handsomely for the child, he would add to it something considerable, though, having had some great disappointments (repeating the words), he could not do for it as he would otherwise have done.

I then thought myself obliged to take notice of his having

so often mentioned his having met with disappointments. I told him I was very sorry to hear he had met with anything afflicting to him in the world; that I would not have anything belonging to me add to his loss, or weaken him in what he might do for his other children; and that I would not agree to his having the child away, though the proposal was infinitely to the child's advantage, unless he would promise me that the whole expense should be mine, and that, if he did not think £5000 enough for the child, I would give it more.

We had so much discourse upon this and the old affairs that it took up all our time at his first visit. I was a little importunate with him to tell me how he came to find me out, but he put it off for that time, and only obtaining my leave to visit me again, he went away; and indeed my heart was so full with what he had said already that I was glad when he went away. Sometimes I was full of tenderness and affection for him, and especially when he expressed himself so earnestly and passionately about the child; other times I was crowded with doubts about his circumstances. Sometimes I was terrified with apprehensions lest, if I should come into a close correspondence with him, he should any way come to hear what kind of life I had led at Pall-Mall and in other places, and it might make me miserable afterwards; from which last thought I concluded that I had better repulse him again than receive him. All these thoughts, and many more, crowded in so fast, I say, upon me that I wanted to give vent to them and get rid of him, and was very glad when he was gone away.

We had several meetings after this, in which still we had so many preliminaries to go through that we scarce ever bordered upon the main subject. Once, indeed, he said something of it, and I put it off with a kind of a jest. "Alas!" says I, "those things are out of the question now; 'tis almost two ages since those things were talked between us," says I. "You see I am grown an old woman since that." Another time he gave a little push at it again, and I laughed again. "Why, what dost thou talk of?" said I in a formal way. "Dost thou not see I am turned Quaker? I cannot speak of those things now." "Why," says he, "the Quakers marry as well as other people, and love one another as well. Besides," says he, "the Quakers' dress does not ill become you," and so jested with me again, and so it went off for a third time. However, I began to be kind to him in process of time, as they call it, and

we grew very intimate; and if the following accident had not
unluckily intervened, I had certainly married him, or consented to marry him, the very next time he had asked me.

I had long waited for a letter from Amy, who, it seems,
was just at that time gone to Rouen the second time, to make
her inquiries about him; and I received a letter from her at
this unhappy juncture, which gave me the following account
of my business:—

I. That for my gentleman, who I had now, as I may say,
in my arms, she said he had been gone from Paris, as I have
hinted, having met with some great losses and misfortunes;
that he had been in Holland on that very account, whither he
had also carried his children; that he was after that settled for
some time at Rouen; that she had been at Rouen, and found
there (by a mere accident), from a Dutch skipper, that he
was at London, had been there above three years; that he was
to be found upon the Exchange, on the French walk; and
that he lodged at St. Lawrence Pountney's Lane, and the like;
so Amy said she supposed I might soon find him out, but that
she doubted he was poor, and not worth looking after. This
she did because of the next clause, which the jade had most
mind to, on many accounts.

II. That as to the Prince————; that, as above, he was gone
into Germany, where his estate lay; that he had quitted the
French service and lived retired; that she had seen his gentleman, who remained at Paris to solicit his arrears, &c.; that he
had given her an account how his lord had employed him to
inquire for me and find me out, as above, and told her what
pains he had taken to find me; that he had understood that I
was gone to England; that he once had orders to go to England to find me; that his lord had resolved, if he could have
found me, to have called me a countess, and so have married
me, and have carried me into Germany with him; and that
his commission was still to assure me that the prince would
marry me if I would come to him, and that he would send
him an account that he had found me, and did not doubt but
he would have orders to come over to England to attend me
in a figure suitable to my quality.

Amy, an ambitious jade who knew my weakest part—
namely, that I loved great things, and that I loved to be flattered and courted—said abundance of kind things upon this
occasion, which she knew were suitable to me and would
prompt my vanity; and talked big of the prince's gentleman

having orders to come over to me with a procuration to marry me by proxy (as princes usually do in like cases), and to furnish me with an equipage, and I know not how many fine things; but told me, withal, that she had not yet let him know that she belonged to me still, or that she knew where to find me or to write to me; because she was willing to see the bottom of it, and whether it was a reality or a gasconade.* She had indeed told him that, if he had any such commission, she would endeavour to find me out, but no more.

III. For the Jew, she assured me that she had not been able to come at a certainty what was become of him, or in what part of the world he was; but that thus much she had learned from good hands, that he had committed a crime, in being concerned in a design to rob a rich banker at Paris; and that he was fled and had not been heard of there for above six years.

IV. For that of my husband, the brewer, she learned that, being commanded into the field upon an occasion of some action in Flanders, he was wounded at the battle of Mons, and died of his wounds in the Hospital of the Invalids; so there was an end of my four inquiries, which I sent her over to make.

This account of the prince, and the return of his affection to me, with all the flattering great things which seemed to come along with it; and especially as they came gilded and set out by my maid Amy—I say this account of the prince came to me in a very unlucky hour, and in the very crisis of my affair.

The merchant and I had entered into close conferences upon the grand affair. I had left off talking my platonics, and of my independency and being a free woman, as before; and he having cleared up my doubts too, as to his circumstances and the misfortunes he had spoken of, I had gone so far that we had begun to consider where we should live, and in what figure, what equipage, what house, and the like.

I had made some harangues upon the delightful retirement of a country life, and how we might enjoy ourselves so effectually without the encumbrances of business and the world; but all this was grimace, and purely because I was afraid to make any public appearance in the world, for fear some impertinent person of quality should chop upon me again and

* "gasconade." An empty boast.

cry out, "Roxana, Roxana, by ———!" with an oath, as had been done before.

My merchant, bred to business and used to converse among men of business, could hardly tell how to live without it; at least, it appeared he should be like a fish out of water, uneasy and dying. But, however, he joined with me; only argued that we might live as near London as we could, that he might sometimes come to 'Change* and hear how the world should go abroad, and how it fared with his friends and his children.

I answered that if he chose still to embarrass himself with business, I supposed it would be more to his satisfaction to be in his own country, and where his family was so well known, and where his children also were.

He smiled at the thoughts of that, and let me know that he should be very willing to embrace such an offer; but that he could not expect it of me, to whom England was, to be sure, so naturalized now as that it would be carrying me out of my native country, which he would not desire by any means, however agreeable it might be to him.

I told him he was mistaken in me; that as I had told him so much of a married state being a captivity, and the family being a house of bondage, that when I married I expected to be but an upper servant; so, if I did notwithstanding submit to it, I hoped he should see I knew how to act the servant's part and do everything to oblige my master; that if I did not resolve to go with him wherever he desired to go, he might depend I would never have him. "And did I not," said I, "offer myself to go with you to the East Indies?"

All this while this was indeed but a copy of my countenance; for, as my circumstances would not admit of my stay in London, at least not so as to appear publicly, I resolved, if I took him, to live remote in the country or go out of England with him.

But in an evil hour, just now came Amy's letter, in the very middle of all these discourses; and the fine things she had said about the prince began to make strange work with me. The notion of being a princess, and going over to live where all that had happened here would have been quite sunk out of knowledge as well as out of memory (conscience excepted), was mighty taking. The thoughts of being sur-

---

* " 'Change." A place where merchants met to transact business.

rounded with domestics, honoured with titles, be called her Highness, and live in all the splendour of a court, and, which was still more, in the arms of a man of such rank, and who I knew loved and valued me—all this, in a word, dazzled my eyes, turned my head, and I was as truly crazed and distracted for about a fortnight as most of the people in Bedlam,* though perhaps not quite so far gone.

When my gentleman came to me the next time, I had no notion of him; I wished I had never received him at all. In short, I resolved to have no more to say to him, so I feigned myself indisposed; and though I did come down to him and speak to him a little, yet I let him see that I was so ill that I was (as we say) no company, and that it would be kind in him to give me leave to quit him for that time.

The next morning he sent a footman to inquire how I did, and I let him know I had a violent cold and was very ill with it. Two days after he came again, and I let him see me again, but feigned myself so hoarse that I could not speak to be heard, and that it was painful to me but to whisper; and, in a word, I held him in this suspense near three weeks.

During this time I had a strange elevation upon my mind; and the prince, or the spirit of him, had such a possession of me that I spent most of this time in the realising all the great things of a life with the prince, to my mind, pleasing my fancy with the grandeur I was supposing myself to enjoy, and withal wickedly studying in what manner to put off this gentleman and be rid of him forever.

I cannot but say that sometimes the baseness of the action stuck hard with me; the honour and sincerity with which he had always treated me, and, above all, the fidelity he had showed me at Paris, and that I owed my life to him— I say, all these stared in my face, and I frequently argued with myself upon the obligation I was under to him, and how base would it be now too, after so many obligations and engagements, to cast him off.

But the title of highness, and of a princess, and all those fine things, as they came in, weighed down all this; and the sense of gratitude vanished as if it had been a shadow.

At other times I considered the wealth I was mistress of; that I was able to live like a princess, though not a princess; and that my merchant (for he had told me all the affair of

* "Bedlam." The lunatic asylum in London. Compare "a bedlam" on page 232: a crazy person.

his misfortunes) was far from being poor, or even mean; that together we were able to make up an estate of between three and four thousand pounds a year, which was in itself equal to some princes abroad. But though this was true, yet the name of princess, and the flutter of it—in a word, the pride—weighed 'em down; and all these arguings generally ended to the disadvantage of my merchant; so that, in short, I resolved to drop him and give him a final answer at his next coming; namely, that something had happened in my affairs which had caused me to alter my measures unexpectedly, and, in a word, to desire him to trouble himself no farther.

I think, verily, this rude treatment of him was for some time the effect of a violent fermentation in my blood; for the very motion which the steady contemplation of my fancied greatness had put my spirits into, had thrown me into a kind of fever, and I scarce knew what I did.

I have wondered since that it did not make me mad; nor do I now think it strange to hear of those who have been quite lunatic with their pride, that fancied themselves queens and empresses, and have made their attendants serve them upon the knee, given visitors their hand to kiss, and the like; for certainly, if pride will not turn the brain, nothing can.

However, the next time my gentleman came, I had not courage enough, or not ill nature enough, to treat him in the rude manner I had resolved to do, and it was very well I did not; for soon after, I had another letter from Amy, in which was the mortifying news, and indeed surprising to me, that my prince (as I, with a secret pleasure, had called him) was very much hurt by a bruise he had received in hunting and engaging with a wild boar, a cruel and desperate sport which the noblemen of Germany, it seems, much delight in.

This alarmed me indeed, and the more because Amy wrote me word that his gentleman was gone away express to him, not without apprehensions that he should find his master was dead before his coming home; but that he (the gentleman) had promised her that as soon as he arrived, he would send back the same courier to her with an account of his master's health, and of the main affair; and that he had obliged Amy to stay at Paris fourteen days for his return; she having promised him before to make it her business to go to England and to find me out for his lord if he sent her such orders; and he was to send her a bill for fifty pistoles for her journey. So Amy told me she waited for the answer.

This was a blow to me several ways; for, first, I was in a state of uncertainty as to his person, whether he was alive or dead; and I was not unconcerned in that part, I assure you; for I had an inexpressible affection remaining for his person, besides the degree to which it was revived by the view of a firmer interest in him. But this was not all, for in losing him I forever lost the prospect of all the gaiety and glory that had made such an impression upon my imagination.

In this state of uncertainty, I say, by Amy's letter, I was like still to remain another fortnight; and had I now continued the resolution of using my merchant in the rude manner I once intended, I had made perhaps a sorry piece of work of it indeed, and it was very well my heart failed me as it did.

However, I treated him with a great many shuffles and feigned stories to keep him off from any closer conferences than we had already had, that I might act afterwards as occasion might offer, one way or other. But that which mortified me most was that Amy did not write, though the fourteen days were expired. At last, to my great surprise, when I was, with the utmost impatience, looking out at the window, expecting the postman that usually brought the foreign letters— I say I was agreeably surprised to see a coach come to the yard-gate where we lived, and my woman, Amy, alight out of it and come towards the door, having the coachman bringing several bundles after her.

I flew like lightning downstairs to speak to her, but was soon damped with her news. "Is the prince alive or dead, Amy?" says I. She spoke coldly and slightly. "He is alive, madam," said she, "but it is not much matter. I had as lief he had been dead." So we went upstairs again to my chamber, and there we began a serious discourse of the whole matter.

First, she told me a long story of his being hurt by a wild boar, and of the condition he was reduced to, so that everyone expected he should die, the anguish of the wound having thrown him into a fever, with abundance of circumstances too long to relate here; how he recovered of that extreme danger, but continued very weak; how the gentleman had been *homme de parole*,* and had sent back the courier as punctually as if it had been to the king; that he had given a long account of his lord, and of his illness and recovery; but the sum of the matter, as to me, was, that as to the lady, his

---

* *"homme de parole."* A man of his word.

lord was turned penitent, was under some vows for his recovery, and could not think any-more on that affair; and especially, the lady being gone, and that it had not been offered to her, so there was no breach of honour; but that his lord was sensible of the good offices of Mrs. Amy, and had sent her the fifty pistoles for her trouble, as if she had really gone the journey.

I was, I confess, hardly able to bear the first surprise of this disappointment. Amy saw it and gapes out (as was her way), "Lawd, madam! never be concerned at it; you see he is gotten among the priests, and I suppose they have saucily imposed some penance upon him, and, it may be, sent him of an errand barefoot to some Madonna or Nôtredame, or other; and he is off of his amours for the present. I'll warrant you he'll be as wicked again as ever he was when he is got thorough well, and gets but out of their hands again. I hate this out-o'-season repentance. What occasion had he, in his repentance, to be off of taking a good wife? I should have been glad to see you have been a princess, and all that; but if it can't be, never afflict yourself; you are rich enough to be a princess to yourself; you don't want him, that's the best of it."

Well, I cried for all that, and was heartily vexed, and that a great while; but as Amy was always at my elbow, and always jogging it out of my head with her mirth and her wit, it wore off again.

Then I told Amy all the story of my merchant, and how he had found me out when I was in such a concern to find him; how it was true that he lodged in St. Lawrence Pountney's Lane; and how I had had all the story of his misfortune, which she had heard of, in which he had lost above £8000 sterling; and that he had told me frankly of it before she had sent me any account of it, or at least before I had taken any notice that I had heard of it.

Amy was very joyful at that part. "Well, madam, then," says Amy, "what need you value the story of the prince, and going I know not whither into Germany to lay your bones in another world, and learn the devil's language, called High Dutch? You are better here by half," says Amy. "Lawd, madam!" says she, "why, are you not as rich as Crassus?"*

* "Crassus." Amy's slip for Croesus, a proverbially rich king of Lydia, in ancient Asia Minor.

Well, it was a great while still before I could bring myself off of this fancied sovereignty; and I, that was so willing once to be mistress to a king, was now ten thousand times more fond of being wife to a prince.

So fast a hold has pride and ambition upon our minds that when once it gets admission, nothing is so chimerical but, under this possession, we can form ideas of in our fancy and realise to our imagination. Nothing can be so ridiculous as the simple steps we take in such cases; a man or a woman becomes a mere *malade imaginaire,*† and, I believe, may as easily die with grief or run mad with joy (as the affair in his fancy appears right or wrong) as if all was real, and actually under the management of the person.

I had indeed two assistants to deliver me from this snare, and these were, first, Amy, who knew my disease, but was able to do nothing as to the remedy; the second, the merchant, who really brought the remedy, but knew nothing of the distemper.

I remember, when all these disorders were upon my thoughts, in one of the visits my friend the merchant made me, he took notice that he perceived I was under some unusual disorder; he believed, he said, that my distemper, whatever it was, lay much in my head, and it being summer weather and very hot, proposed to me to go a little way into the air.

I started at his expression. "What!" says I, "do you think, then, that I am crazed? You should, then, propose a madhouse for my cure." "No, no," says he, "I do not mean anything like that; I hope the head may be distempered and not the brain." Well, I was too sensible that he was right, for I knew I had acted a strange, wild kind of part with him; but he insisted upon it and pressed me to go into the country. I took him short again. "What need you," says I, "send me out of your way? It is in your power to be less troubled with me, and with less inconvenience to us both."

He took that ill and told me I used to have a better opinion of his sincerity, and desired to know what he had done to forfeit my charity. I mention this only to let you see how far I had gone in my measures of quitting him—that is to say, how near I was of showing him how base, ungrateful, and

---

† *"malade imaginaire."* Imaginary invalid, or hypochondriac, probably taken from the title character of Molière's play (1673).

how vilely I could act. But I found I had carried the jest far enough, and that a little matter might have made him sick of me again, as he was before; so I began by little and little to change my way of talking to him, and to come to discourse to the purpose again as we had done before.

A while after this, when we were very merry and talking familiarly together, he called me, with an air of particular satisfaction, his princess. I coloured at the word, for it indeed touched me to the quick; but he knew nothing of the reason of my being touched with it. "What d'ye mean by that?" said I. "Nay," says he, "I mean nothing but that you are a princess to me." "Well," says I, "as to that I am content, and yet I could tell you, I might have been a princess if I would have quitted you, and believe I could be so still." "It is not in my power to make you a princess," says he, "but I can easily make you a lady here in England, and a countess too if you will go out of it."

I heard both with a great deal of satisfaction, for my pride remained, though it had been balked, and I thought with myself that this proposal would make me some amends for the loss of the title that had so tickled my imagination another way, and I was impatient to understand what he meant, but I would not ask him by any means; so it passed off for that time.

When he was gone, I told Amy what he had said, and Amy was as impatient to know the manner how it could be as I was; but the next time (perfectly unexpected to me) he told me that he had accidentally mentioned a thing to me last time he was with me, having not the least thought of the thing itself; but not knowing but such a thing might be of some weight to me, and that it might bring me respect among people where I might appear, he had thought since of it, and was resolved to ask me about it.

I made light of it and told him that, as he knew I had chosen a retired life, it was of no value to me to be called lady, or countess either; but that if he intended to drag me, as I might call it, into the world again, perhaps it might be agreeable to him; but, besides that, I could not judge of the thing, because I did not understand how either of them was to be done.

He told me that money purchased titles of honour in almost all parts of the world, though money could not give principles of honour, they must come by birth and blood;

that, however, titles sometimes assist to elevate the soul and to infuse generous principles into the mind, and especially where there was a good foundation laid in the persons; that he hoped we should neither of us misbehave, if we came to it; and that as we knew how to wear a title without undue elevations, so it might sit as well upon us as on another; that as to England, he had nothing to do but to get an act of naturalization in his favour, and he knew where to purchase a patent for baronet—that is to say, to have the honour and title transferred to him; but if I intended to go abroad with him, he had a nephew, the son of his elder brother, who had the title of count, with the estate annexed, which was but small, and that he had frequently offered to make it over to him for a thousand pistoles, which was not a great deal of money, and considering it was in the family already, he would, upon my being willing, purchase it immediately.

I told him I liked the last best, but then I would not let him buy it unless he would let me pay the thousand pistoles. "No, no," says he, "I refused a thousand pistoles that I had more right to have accepted than that, and you shall not be at so much expense now." "Yes," says I, "you did refuse it, and perhaps repented it afterwards." "I never complained," says he. "But I did," says I, "and often repented it for you." "I do not understand you," says he. "Why," says I, "I repented that I suffered you to refuse it." "Well, well," said he, "we may talk of that hereafter, when you shall resolve which part of the world you will make your settled residence in." Here he talked very handsomely to me, and for a good while together; how it had been his lot to live all his days out of his native country, and to be often shifting and changing the situation of his affairs; and that I myself had not always had a fixed abode, but that now, as neither of us was very young, he fancied I would be for taking up our abode where, if possible, we might remove no more; that, as to his part, he was of that opinion entirely, only with this exception, that the choice of the place should be mine, for that all places in the world were alike to him, only with this single addition, namely, that I was with him.

I heard him with a great deal of pleasure, as well for his being willing to give me the choice as for that I resolved to live abroad, for the reason I have mentioned already, namely, lest I should at any time be known in England, and all that story of Roxana and the balls should come out; as also I was not a little tickled with the satisfaction of being still a countess, though I could not be a princess.

I told Amy all this story, for she was still my privy-counsellor; but when I asked her opinion, she made me laugh heartily. "Now, which of the two shall I take, Amy?" said I. "Shall I be a lady—that is, a baronet's lady in England, or a countess in Holland?" The ready-witted jade, that knew the pride of my temper too, almost as well as I did myself, answered (without the least hesitation), "Both, madam. Which of them?" says she (repeating the words). "Why not both of them? And then you will be really a princess; for, sure, to be a lady in English and a countess in Dutch may make a princess in High Dutch." Upon the whole, though Amy was in jest, she put the thought into my head, and I resolved that, in short, I would be both of them, which I managed as you shall hear.

First, I seemed to resolve that I would live and settle in England, only with this condition, namely, that I would not live in London. I pretended that it would choke me up; that I wanted breath when I was in London, but that anywhere else I would be satisfied; and then I asked him whether any seaport town in England would not suit him; because I knew, though he seemed to leave off, he would always love to be among business, and conversing with men of business; and I named several places, either nearest for business with France or with Holland; as Dover or Southampton, for the first; and Ipswich, or Yarmouth, or Hull for the last; but I took care that we would resolve upon nothing; only by this it seemed to be certain that we should live in England.

It was time now to bring things to a conclusion, and so in about six weeks' time more, we settled all our preliminaries; and, among the rest, he let me know that he should have the bill for his naturalization passed time enough, so that he would be (as he called it) an Englishman before we married. That was soon perfected, the Parliament being then sitting, and several other foreigners joining in the said bill to save the expense.

It was not above three or four days after, but that, without giving me the least notice that he had so much as been about the patent for baronet, he brought it me in a fine embroidered bag and, saluting me by the name of my Lady ———— (joining his own surname to it), presented it to me with his picture set with diamonds, and at the same time gave me a breast-jewel worth a thousand pistoles, and the next morning we were married. Thus I put an end to all the intriguing part of my life—a life full of prosperous wickedness; the reflections upon which were so much the more afflicting as the time had been spent in the grossest crimes, which, the more I looked back upon, the more black and horrid they appeared, effectually drinking up all the comfort and satisfaction which I might otherwise have taken in that part of life which was still before me.

The first satisfaction, however, that I took in the new condition I was in was in reflecting that at length the life of crime was over, and that I was like a passenger coming back from the Indies, who, having, after many years' fatigues and hurry in business, gotten a good estate, with innumerable difficulties and hazards, is arrived safe at London with all his effects, and has the pleasure of saying he shall never venture upon the seas any-more.

When we were married, we came back immediately to my lodgings (for the church was but just by), and we were so privately married that none but Amy and my friend the Quaker was acquainted with it. As soon as we came into the house, he took me in his arms and, kissing me, "Now you are my own," says he. "Oh that you had been so good to have done this eleven years ago!" "Then," said I, "you, perhaps, would have been tired of me long ago; 'tis much better now, for now all our happy days are to come. Besides," said I, "I should not have been half so rich." But that I said to myself, for there was no letting him into the reason of it. "Oh!" says he, "I should not have been tired of you; but, besides having the satisfaction of your company, it had saved me that unlucky blow at Paris, which was a dead loss to me of above eight thousand pistoles, and all the fatigues of so many years' hurry and business." And then he added, "But I'll make you pay for it all, now I have you." I started a little at the words. "Ay," said I, "do you threaten already? Pray what d'ye mean by that?" and began to look a little grave.

"I'll tell you," says he, "very plainly what I mean," and still he held me fast in his arms. "I intend from this time never to trouble myself with any-more business, so I shall never get one shilling for you more than I have already; all that you will lose one way. Next, I intend not to trouble myself with any of the care or trouble of managing what either you have for me or what I have to add to it; but you shall even take it all upon yourself, as the wives do in Holland; so you will pay for it that way too, for all the drudgery shall be yours. Thirdly, I intend to condemn you to the constant bondage of my impertinent company, for I shall tie you like a pedlar's pack at my back. I shall scarce ever be from you; for I am sure I can take delight in nothing else in this world." "Very well," says I, "but I am pretty heavy. I hope you'll set me down sometimes when you are a-weary." "As for that," says he, "tire me if you can."

This was all jest and allegory; but it was all true, in the moral of the fable, as you shall hear in its place. We were very merry the rest of the day, but without any noise or clutter; for he brought not one of his acquaintance or friends, either English or foreigner. The honest Quaker provided us a very noble dinner indeed, considering how few we were to eat it; and every day that week she did the like, and would at last have it be all at her own charge, which I was utterly averse to: first, because I knew her circumstances not to be very great, though not very low; and next, because she had been so true a friend, and so cheerful a comforter to me, ay, and counsellor too, in all this affair, that I had resolved to make her a present that should be some help to her when all was over.

But to return to the circumstances of our wedding. After being very merry, as I have told you, Amy and the Quaker put us to bed, the honest Quaker little thinking we had been a-bed together eleven years before. Nay, that was a secret which, as it happened, Amy herself did not know. Amy grinned and made faces, as if she had been pleased; but it came out in so many words, when he was not by, the sum of her mumbling and muttering was that this should have been done ten or a dozen years before; that it would signify little now; that was to say, in short, that her mistress was pretty near fifty, and too old to have any children. I chid her; the Quaker laughed, complimented me upon my not being so old as Amy pretended, that I could not be above forty, and might have a house-full of children yet. But Amy and I too knew better than she how it was, for, in short, I was old enough to have done breeding, however I looked; but I made her hold her tongue.

In the morning my Quaker landlady came and visited us before we were up, and made us eat cakes and drink chocolate in bed; and then left us again and bid us take a nap upon it, which I believe we did. In short, she treated us so handsomely, and with such an agreeable cheerfulness, as well as plenty, as made it appear to me that Quakers may, and that this Quaker did, understand good manners as well as any other people.

I resisted her offer, however, of treating us for the whole week; and I opposed it so long that I saw evidently that she took it ill, and would have thought herself slighted if we had not accepted it. So I said no more, but let her go on, only told her I would be even with her; and so I was. However, for that week she treated us as she said she would, and did it so very fine, and with such a profusion of all sorts of good things, that the greatest burthen to her was how to dispose of things that were left; for she never let anything, how dainty or however large, be so much as seen twice among us.

I had some servants indeed, which helped her off a little; that is to say, two maids, for Amy was now a woman of business, not a servant, and ate always with us. I had also a coachman and a boy. My Quaker had a man-servant too, but had but one maid; but she borrowed two more of some of her friends for the occasion, and had a man-cook for dressing the victuals.

She was only at a loss for plate, which she gave me a whisper of; and I made Amy fetch a large strong-box, which I had lodged in a safe hand, in which was all the fine plate which I had provided on a worse occasion, as is mentioned before; and I put it into the Quaker's hand, obliging her not to use it as mine, but as her own, for a reason I shall mention presently.

I was now my Lady ———, and I must own I was exceedingly pleased with it; 'twas so big and so great to hear myself called "her ladyship," and "your ladyship," and the like, that I was like the Indian king at Virginia, who, having a house built for him by the English, and a lock put upon the door, would sit whole days together with the key in his hand, locking and unlocking, and double-locking, the door, with an unaccountable pleasure at the novelty. So I could have sat a whole day together to hear Amy talk to me, and call me "your ladyship" at every word; but after a-while the novelty wore off and the pride of it abated, till at last, truly, I wanted the other title as much as I did that of ladyship before.

We lived this week in all the innocent mirth imaginable, and our good-humoured Quaker was so pleasant in her way that it was particularly entertaining to us. We had no music at all, or dancing; only I now and then sung a French song to divert my spouse, who desired it, and the privacy of our mirth greatly added to the pleasure of it. I did not make many clothes for my wedding, having always a great many rich clothes by me, which, with a little altering for the fashion, were perfectly new. The next day he pressed me to dress, though we had no company. At last, jesting with him, I told him I believed I was able to dress me so, in one kind of dress that I had by me, that he would not know his wife when he saw her, especially if anybody else was by. No, he said, that was impossible, and he longed to see that dress. I told him I would dress me in it, if he would promise me never to desire me to appear in it before company. He promised he would not, but wanted to know why too; as husbands, you know, are inquisitive creatures, and love to inquire after anything they think is kept from them; but I had an answer ready for him. "Because," said I, "it is not a decent dress in this country and would not look modest." Neither, indeed, would it, for it was but one degree off from appearing in one's shift, but was the usual wear in the country where they were used. He was satisfied with my answer, and gave me his promise never to ask me to be seen in it before company. I then withdrew, taking only Amy and the Quaker with me; and Amy dressed me in my old Turkish habit which I danced in formerly, &c., as before. The Quaker was charmed with the dress, and merrily said that if such a dress should come to be worn here, she should not know what to do; she should be tempted not to dress in the Quaker's way any-more.

When all the dress was put on, I loaded it with jewels, and in particular I placed the large breast-jewel which he had given me of a thousand pistoles upon the front of the *tyhaia*, or head-dress, where it made a most glorious show indeed. I had my own diamond necklace on, and my hair was *tout brilliant*, all glittering with jewels.

His picture set with diamonds I had placed stitched to my vest, just, as might be supposed, upon my heart (which is the compliment in such cases among the Eastern people); and all being open at the breast, there was no room for anything of a jewel there. In this figure, Amy holding the train of my robe, I came down to him. He was surprised, and perfectly astonished. He knew me, to be sure, because I had prepared him, and because there was nobody else there but the Quaker and

Amy; but he by no means knew Amy, for she had dressed herself in the habit of a Turkish slave, being the garb of my little Turk which I had at Naples, as I have said; she had her neck and arms bare, was bare-headed, and her hair braided in a long tassel hanging down her back; but the jade could neither hold her countenance or her chattering tongue so as to be concealed long.

Well, he was so charmed with this dress that he would have me sit and dine in it; but it was so thin, and so open before, and the weather being also sharp, that I was afraid of taking cold; however, the fire being enlarged and the doors kept shut, I sat to oblige him, and he professed he never saw so fine a dress in his life. I afterwards told him that my husband (so he called the jeweller that was killed) bought it for me at Leghorn, with a young Turkish slave which I parted with at Paris; and that it was by the help of that slave that I learned how to dress in it, and how everything was to be worn, and many of the Turkish customs also, with some of their language. This story agreeing with the fact, only changing the person, was very natural, and so it went off with him; but there was good reason why I should not receive any company in this dress—that is to say, not in England. I need not repeat it; you will hear more of it.

But when I came abroad, I frequently put it on, and upon two or three occasions danced in it, but always at his request.

We continued at the Quaker's lodgings for above a year; for now, making as though it was difficult to determine where to settle in England to his satisfaction, unless in London, which was not to mine, I pretended to make him an offer, that, to oblige him, I began to incline to go and live abroad with him; that I knew nothing could be more agreeable to him, and that, as to me, every place was alike; that, as I had lived abroad without a husband so many years, it could be no burthen to me to live abroad again, especially with him. Then we fell to straining our courtesies upon one another. He told me he was perfectly easy at living in England and had squared all his affairs accordingly; for that, as he had told me he intended to give over all business in the world, as well the care of managing it as the concern about it, seeing we were both in condition neither to want it or to have it be worth our while, so I might see it was his intention, by his getting himself naturalized, and getting the patent of baronet, &c. Well, for all that, I told him I accepted his compliment, but I could not but know that his native country, where his children were breeding up, must be most agreeable to him, and that, if I was of such value to him, I would be there then, to enhance the rate of his satisfaction; that wherever he was would be a home to me, and any place in the world would be England to me if he was with me; and thus, in short, I brought him to give me leave to oblige him with going to live abroad, when, in truth, I could not have been perfectly easy at living in England, unless I had kept constantly within doors, lest some time or other the dissolute life I had lived here should have come to be known, and all those wicked things have been known too, which I now began to be very much ashamed of.

When we closed up our wedding week, in which our Quaker had been so very handsome to us, I told him how much I thought we were obliged to her for her generous carriage to us; how she had acted the kindest part through the whole, and how faithful a friend she had been to me upon all occasions; and then, letting him know a little of her family unhappiness, I proposed that I thought I not only ought to be grateful to her, but really to do something extraordinary for her, towards making her easy in her affairs. And I added that I had no hangers-on that should trouble him; that there was nobody belonged to me but what was thoroughly provided for; and that if I did something for this honest woman that was considerable, it should be the last gift I would give to anybody in the world but Amy; and as for her, we was not a-going to turn her adrift, but whenever anything offered for her, we would do as we saw cause; that, in the meantime, Amy was not poor, that she had saved together between seven and eight hundred pounds. By the way, I did not tell him how, and by what wicked ways she got it, but that she had it; and that was enough to let him know she would never be in want of us.

My spouse was exceedingly pleased with my discourse about the Quaker, made a kind of a speech to me upon the subject of gratitude, told me it was one of the brightest parts of a gentlewoman, that it was so twisted with honesty, nay, and even with religion too, that he questioned whether either of them could be found where gratitude was not to be found; that in this act there was not only gratitude, but charity; and that to make the charity still more Christian-like, the object too had real merit to attract it. He therefore agreed to the thing with all his heart, only would have had me let him pay it out of his effects.

I told him, as for that, I did not design, whatever I had said formerly, that we should have two pockets; and that though I had talked to him of being a free woman, and an independent, and the like, and he had offered and promised that I should keep all my own estate in my own hands; yet, that since I had taken him, I would even do as other honest wives did—where I thought fit to give myself, I should give what I had too; that if I reserved anything, it should be only in case of mortality, and that I might give it to his children afterwards, as my own gift; and that, in short, if he thought fit to join stocks, we would see to-morrow morning what strength we could both make up in the world, and bringing it all together, consider, before we resolved upon the place of removing, how we should dispose of what we had, as well as of ourselves. This discourse was too obliging, and he too much a man of sense not to receive it as it was meant. He only answered, we would do in that as we should both agree; but the thing under our present care was to show not gratitude only, but charity and affection too, to our kind friend the Quaker; and the first word he spoke of was to settle a thousand pounds upon her for her life—that is to say, sixty pounds a year—but in such a manner as not to be in the power of any person to reach but herself. This was a great thing, and indeed showed the generous principles of my husband, and for that reason I mention it; but I thought that a little too much too, and particularly because I had another thing in view for her, about the plate; so I told him I thought, if he gave her a purse with a hundred guineas as a present first, and then made her a compliment of £40 per annum for her life, secured any such way as she should desire, it would be very handsome.

He agreed to that; and the same day, in the evening, when we were just going to bed, he took my Quaker by the hand and, with a kiss, told her that we had been very kindly treated by her from the beginning of this affair, and his wife before, as she (meaning me) had informed him; and that he thought himself bound to let her see that she had obliged friends who knew how to be grateful; that for his part of the obligation he desired she would accept of that, for an acknowledgment in part only (putting the gold into her hand), and that his wife would talk with her about what farther he

had to say to her; and upon that, not giving her time hardly
to say "Thank ye," away he went upstairs into our bed-chamber,
leaving her confused and not knowing what to say.

When he was gone, she began to make very handsome and
obliging representations of her good-will to us both, but that
it was without expectation of reward; that I had given her
several valuable presents before—and so, indeed, I had; for,
besides the piece of linen which I had given her at first, I had
given her a suit of damask table-linen, of the linen I bought
for my balls, viz., three table-cloths and three dozen of napkins;
and at another time I gave her a little necklace of gold
beads, and the like; but that is by the way. But she mentioned
them, I say, and how she was obliged by me on many other
occasions; that she was not in condition to show her gratitude
any other way, not being able to make a suitable return; and
that now we took from her all opportunity to balance my
former friendship, and left her more in debt than she was before.
She spoke this in a very good kind of a manner, in her
own way, but which was very agreeable indeed, and had as
much apparent sincerity, and I verily believe as real as was
possible to be expressed; but I put a stop to it and bid her say
no more, but accept of what my spouse had given her, which
was but in part, as she had heard him say. "And put it up,"
says I, "and come and sit down here, and give me leave to
say something else to you on the same head, which my
spouse and I have settled between ourselves in your behalf."
"What dost thee mean?" says she, and blushed, and looked
surprised, but did not stir. She was going to speak again, but
I interrupted her, and told her she should make no more apologies
of any kind whatever, for I had better things than all
this to talk to her of; so I went on, and told her, that as she
had been so friendly and kind to us on every occasion, and
that her house was the lucky place where we came together,
and that she knew I was from her own mouth acquainted in
part with her circumstances, we were resolved she should be
the better for us as long as she lived. Then I told her what we
had resolved to do for her, and that she had nothing more to
do but to consult with me how it should be effectually secured
for her, distinct from any of the effects which were her
husband's; and that if her husband did so supply her that she
could live comfortably, and not want it for bread or other
necessaries, she should not make use of it, but lay up the income
of it, and add it every year to the principal, so to in-

crease the annual payment, which in time, and perhaps
before she might come to want it, might double itself; that we
were very willing whatever she should so lay up should be to
herself, and whoever she thought fit after her; but that the
forty pound a year must return to our family after her life,
which we both wished might be long and happy.

Let no reader wonder at my extraordinary concern for this
poor woman, or at my giving my bounty to her a place in
this account. It is not, I assure you, to make a pageantry of
my charity, or to value myself upon the greatness of my soul,
that should give in so profuse a manner as this, which was
above my figure, if my wealth had been twice as much as it
was; but there was another spring from whence all flowed,
and 'tis on that account I speak of it. Was it possible I could
think of a poor desolate woman with four children, and her
husband gone from her, and perhaps good for little if he had
stayed—I say, was I, that had tasted so deep of the sorrows
of such a kind of widowhood, able to look on her, and think
of her circumstances, and not be touched in an uncommon
manner? No, no; I never looked on her and her family,
though she was not left so helpless and friendless as I had
been, without remembering my own condition, when Amy
was sent out to pawn or sell my pair of stays to buy a breast
of mutton and a bunch of turnips. Nor could I look on her
poor children, though not poor and perishing, like mine, without tears, reflecting on the dreadful condition that mine were
reduced to, when poor Amy sent them all into their aunt's in
Spitalfields, and run away from them. These were the original
springs, or fountain-head, from whence my affectionate
thoughts were moved to assist this poor woman.

When a poor debtor, having lain long in the Compter, or
Ludgate, or the King's Bench* for debt, afterwards gets out,
rises again in the world, and grows rich, such an one is a certain benefactor to the prisoners there, and perhaps to every
prison he passes by as long as he lives, for he remembers the
dark days of his own sorrow; and even those who never had
the experience of such sorrows to stir up their minds to acts
of charity would have the same charitable, good disposition,
did they as sensibly remember what it is that distinguishes

---

* "the Compter, or Ludgate, or the King's Bench." Prisons where
debtors were confined. Defoe himself, who went bankrupt twice, feared
being imprisoned for debt.

them from others by a more favourable and merciful Providence.

This, I say, was, however, the spring of my concern for this honest, friendly, and grateful Quaker; and as I had so plentiful a fortune in the world, I resolved she should taste the fruit of her kind usage to me in a manner that she could not expect.

All the while I talked to her I saw the disorder of her mind; the sudden joy was too much for her, and she coloured, trembled, changed, and at last grew pale, and was indeed near fainting, when she hastily rung a little bell for her maid, who coming in immediately, she beckoned to her—for speak she could not—to fill her a glass of wine; but she had no breath to take it in, and was almost choked with that which she took in her mouth. I saw she was ill and assisted her what I could, and with spirits and things to smell too just kept her from fainting, when she beckoned to her maid to withdraw, and immediately burst out in crying, and that relieved her. When she recovered herself a little, she flew to me, and, throwing her arms about my neck, "Oh!" says she, "thou hast almost killed me." And there she hung, laying her head in my neck for half a quarter of an hour, not able to speak, but sobbing like a child that had been whipped.

I was very sorry that I did not stop a little in the middle of my discourse and make her drink a glass of wine before it had put her spirits into such a violent motion; but it was too late, and it was ten to one odds but that it had killed her.

But she came to herself at last, and began to say some very good things in return for my kindness. I would not let her go on, but told her I had more to say to her still than all this, but that I would let it alone till another time. My meaning was about the box of plate, a good part of which I gave her, and some I gave to Amy; for I had so much plate, and some so large, that I thought if I let my husband see it, he might be apt to wonder what occasion I could ever have for so much, and for plate of such a kind too; as particularly a great cistern for bottles, which cost a hundred and twenty pound, and some large candlesticks, too big for any ordinary use. These I caused Amy to sell. In short, Amy sold above three hundred pounds' worth of plate; what I gave the Quaker was worth above sixty pounds, and I gave Amy above thirty pounds' worth, and yet I had a great deal left for my husband.

Nor did our kindness to the Quaker end with the forty pound a year, for we were always, while we stayed with her, which was above ten months, giving her one good thing or another; and, in a word, instead of lodging with her, she boarded with us, for I kept the house, and she and all her family eat and drank with us, and yet we paid her the rent of the house too. In short, I remembered my widowhood, and I made this widow's heart glad many a day the more upon that account.

And now my spouse and I began to think of going over to Holland, where I had proposed to him to live, and in order to settle all the preliminaries of our future manner of living, I began to draw in my effects, so as to have them all at command upon whatever occasion we thought fit; after which, one morning I called my spouse up to me: "Hark ye, sir," said I to him, "I have two very weighty questions to ask of you. I don't know what answer you will give to the first, but I doubt you will be able to give but a sorry answer to the other, and yet, I assure you, it is of the last importance to yourself, and towards the future part of your life, wherever it is to be."

He did not seem to be much alarmed, because he could see I was speaking in a kind of merry way. "Let's hear your questions, my dear," says he, "and I'll give the best answer I can to them." "Why, first," says I:

"1. You have married a wife here, made her a lady, and put her in expectation of being something else still when she comes abroad. Pray have you examined whether you are able to supply all her extravagant demands when she comes abroad, and maintain an expensive Englishwoman in all her pride and vanity? In short, have you inquired whether you are able to keep her?

"2. You have married a wife here, and given her a great many fine things, and you maintain her like a princess, and sometimes call her so. Pray what portion have you had with her, what fortune has she been to you, and where does her estate lie, that you keep her so fine? I am afraid you keep her in a figure a great deal above her estate, at least above all that you have seen of it yet. Are you sure you han't got a bite, and that you have not made a beggar a lady?"

"Well," says he, "have you any more questions to ask? Let's have them all together; perhaps they may be all answered in a few words, as well as these two." "No," says I,

"these are the two grand questions—at least for the present."
"Why, then," says he, "I'll answer you in a few words; that I
am fully master of my own circumstances, and, without farther inquiry, can let my wife you speak of know, that as I
have made her a lady, I can maintain her as a lady, wherever
she goes with me; and this whether I have one pistole of her
portion, or whether she has any portion or no; and as I have
not inquired whether she has any portion or not, so she shall
not have the less respect showed her from me, or be obliged
to live meaner, or be any-ways straitened on that account. On
the contrary, if she goes abroad to live with me in my own
country, I will make her more than a lady, and support the
expense of it too, without meddling with anything she has;
and this, I suppose," says he, "contains an answer to both
your questions together."

He spoke this with a great deal more earnestness in his
countenance than I had when I proposed my questions, and
said a great many kind things upon it, as the consequence of
former discourses, so that I was obliged to be in earnest too.
"My dear," says I, "I was but in jest in my questions; but
they were proposed to introduce what I am going to say to
you in earnest; namely, that if I am to go abroad, 'tis time I
should let you know how things stand, and what I have to
bring you with your wife; how it is to be disposed and secured, and the like. And therefore come," says I, "sit down,
and let me show you your bargain here; I hope you will find
that you have not got a wife without a fortune."

He told me then, that since he found I was in earnest, he
desired that I would adjourn it till to-morrow, and then we
would do as the poor people do after they marry, feel in their
pockets, and see how much money they can bring together in
the world. "Well," says I, "with all my heart." And so we
ended our talk for that time.

As this was in the morning, my spouse went out after dinner to his goldsmith's, as he said, and about three hours after
returns with a porter and two large boxes with him; and his
servant brought another box, which I observed was almost as
heavy as the two that the porter brought, and made the poor
fellow sweat heartily. He dismissed the porter, and in a little
while after went out again with his man, and returning at
night, brought another porter with more boxes and bundles,
and all was carried up, and put into a chamber, next to our

bed-chamber; and in the morning he called for a pretty large round table and began to unpack.

When the boxes were opened, I found they were chiefly full of books, and papers, and parchments, I mean books of accounts, and writings, and such things as were in themselves of no moment to me, because I understood them not; but I perceived he took them all out, and spread them about him upon the table and chairs, and began to be very busy with them; so I withdrew and left him. And he was indeed so busy among them that he never missed me till I had been gone a good while; but when he had gone through all his papers and come to open a little box, he called for me again. "Now," says he, and called me his countess, "I am ready to answer your first question: If you will sit down till I have opened this box, we will see how it stands."

So we opened the box. There was in it indeed what I did not expect, for I thought he had sunk his estate rather than raised it; but he produced me in goldsmiths' bills, and stock in the English East India Company, about sixteen thousand pounds sterling; then he gave into my hands nine assignments upon the Bank of Lyons in France, and two upon the rents of the town-house in Paris, amounting in the whole to 5800 crowns per annum, or annual rent, as 'tis called there; and lastly, the sum of 30,000 rixdollars in the Bank of Amsterdam; besides some jewels and gold in the box to the value of about £1500 or £1600, among which was a very good necklace of pearl of about £200 value; and that he pulled out and tied about my neck, telling me that should not be reckoned into the account.

I was equally pleased and surprised, and it was with an inexpressible joy that I saw him so rich.

"You might well tell me," said I, "that you were able to make me countess, and maintain me as such." In short, he was immensely rich; for besides all this, he showed me, which was the reason of his being so busy among the books, I say, he showed me several adventures he had abroad in the business of his merchandise; as particularly an eighth share in an East India ship then abroad; an account-courant with a merchant at Cadiz in Spain; about £3000 lent upon bottomry, upon ships gone to the Indies; and a large cargo of goods in a merchant's hands, for sale at Lisbon in Portugal; so that in his books there was about £12,000 more; all which put together, made about £27,000 sterling, and £1320 a year.

I stood amazed at this account, as well I might, and said nothing to him for a good while, and the rather because I saw him still busy looking over his books. After a-while, as I was going to express my wonder, "Hold, my dear," says he, "this is not all neither." Then he pulled me out some old seals, and small parchment rolls, which I did not understand; but he told me they were a right of reversion which he had to a paternal estate in his family, and a mortgage of 14,000 rixdollars, which he had upon it, in the hands of the present possessor; so that was about £3000 more.

"But now hold again," says he, "for I must pay my debts out of all this, and they are very great, I assure you." And the first, he said, was a black article of 8000 pistoles, which he had a law-suit about at Paris, but had it awarded against him, which was the loss he had told me of, and which made him leave Paris in disgust; that in other accounts he owed about £5300 sterling; but after all this, upon the whole, he had still £17,000 clear stock in money, and £1320 a year in rent.

After some pause, it came to my turn to speak. "Well," says I, "'tis very hard a gentleman with such a fortune as this should come over to England and marry a wife with nothing; it shall never," says I, "be said, but what I have, I'll bring into the public stock." So I began to produce.

First, I pulled out the mortgage which good Sir Robert had procured for me, the annual rent £700 per annum; the principal money £14,000.

Secondly, I pulled out another mortgage upon land, procured by the same faithful friend, which at three times had advanced £12,000.

Thirdly, I pulled him out a parcel of little securities, procured by several hands, by fee-farm rents, and such petty mortgages as those times afforded, amounting to £10,800 principal money, and paying £636 a year. So that in the whole there was £2056 a year ready-money constantly coming in.

When I had shown him all these, I laid them upon the table and bade him take them, that he might be able to give me an answer to the second question, What fortune he had with his wife; and laughed a little at it.

He looked at them a-while and then handed them all back again to me. "I will not touch them," says he, "nor one of them, till they are all settled in trustees' hands for your own use, and the management wholly your own."

I cannot omit what happened to me while all this was acting; though it was cheerful work in the main, yet I trembled every joint of me, worse for aught I know than ever Belshazzar* did at the handwriting on the wall, and the occasion was every way as just. "Unhappy wretch," said I to myself, "shall my ill-got wealth, the product of prosperous lust, and of a vile and vicious life of whoredom and adultery, be intermingled with the honest well-gotten estate of this innocent gentleman, to be a moth and a caterpillar among it, and bring the judgments of heaven upon him, and upon what he has, for my sake? Shall my wickedness blast his comforts? Shall I be fire in his flax, and be a means to provoke heaven to curse his blessings? God forbid! I'll keep them asunder if it be possible."

This is the true reason why I have been so particular in the account of my vast acquired stock; and how his estate, which was perhaps the product of many years' fortunate industry, and which was equal if not superior to mine at best, was, at my request, kept apart from mine, as is mentioned above.

I have told you how he gave back all my writings into my own hands again. "Well," says I, "seeing you will have it be kept apart, it shall be so, upon one condition, which I have to propose, and no other." "And what is the condition?" says he. "Why," says I, "all the pretence I can have for the making over my own estate to me is, that in case of your mortality, I may have it reserved for me, if I outlive you." " Well," says he, "that is true." "But then," said I, "the annual income is always received by the husband, during his life, as 'tis supposed, for the mutual subsistence of the family; now," says I, "here is £2000 a year, which I believe is as much as we shall spend, and I desire none of it may be saved; and all the income of your own estate, the interest of the £17,000 and the £1320 a year, may be constantly laid by for the increase of your estate. And so," added I, "by joining the interest every year to the capital, you will perhaps grow as rich as you would do if you were to trade with it all, if you were obliged to keep house out of it too."

* "Belshazzar." When Belshazzar, King of Babylon, defied the God of Israel, a supernatural hand wrote a message of doom upon the wall of his banquet hall. That very night the King was slain (Daniel 5).

He liked the proposal very well and said it should be so; and this way I, in some measure, satisfied myself that I should not bring my husband under the blast of a just Providence for mingling my cursed ill-gotten wealth with his honest estate. This was occasioned by the reflections which, at some certain intervals of time, came into my thoughts of the justice of heaven, which I had reason to expect would some time or other still fall upon me or my effects, for the dreadful life I had lived.

And let nobody conclude from the strange success I met with in all my wicked doings, and the vast estate which I had raised by it, that therefore I either was happy or easy. No, no, there was a dart struck into the liver; there was a secret hell within, even all the while, when our joy was at the highest; but more especially now, after it was all over, and when, according to all appearance, I was one of the happiest women upon earth; all this while, I say, I had such a constant terror upon my mind, as gave me every now and then very terrible shocks, and which made me expect something very frightful upon every accident of life.

In a word, it never lightened or thundered, but I expected the next flash would penetrate my vitals, and melt the sword (soul) in this scabbard of flesh. It never blew a storm of wind, but I expected the fall of some stack of chimneys, or some part of the house, would bury me in its ruins; and so of other things.

But I shall perhaps have occasion to speak of all these things again by-and-by; the case before us was in a manner settled; we had full four thousand pounds per annum for our future subsistence, besides a vast sum in jewels and plate; and besides this, I had about eight thousand pounds reserved in money which I kept back from him, to provide for my two daughters, of whom I have yet much to say.

With this estate, settled as you have heard, and with the best husband in the world, I left England again. I had not only, in human prudence, and by the nature of the thing, being now married and settled in so glorious a manner—I say, I had not only abandoned all the gay and wicked course which I had gone through before, but I began to look back upon it with that horror and that detestation which is the certain companion, if not the forerunner, of repentance.

Sometimes the wonders of my present circumstances would work upon me, and I should have some raptures upon my soul, upon the subject of my coming so smoothly out of the arms of hell, that I was not ingulfed in ruin, as most who lead such lives are, first or last. But this was a flight too high for me; I was not come to that repentance that is raised from a sense of Heaven's goodness; I repented of the crime, but it was of another and lower kind of repentance, and rather moved by my fears of vengeance than from a sense of being spared from being punished and landed safe after a storm.

The first thing which happened after our coming to the Hague (where we lodged for a-while) was that my spouse saluted me one morning with the title of countess, as he said he intended to do, by having the inheritance to which the honour was annexed made over to him. It is true, it was a reversion, but it soon fell, and in the meantime, as all the brothers of a count are called counts, so I had the title by courtesy, about three years before I had it in reality.

I was agreeably surprised at this coming so soon, and would have had my spouse have taken the money which it cost him out of my stock, but he laughed at me and went on.

I was now in the height of my glory and prosperity, and I was called the Countess de ———; for I had obtained that unlooked for which I secretly aimed at, and was really the main reason of my coming abroad. I took now more servants, lived in a kind of magnificence that I had not been acquainted with, was called "your honour" at every word, and had a coronet behind my coach; though at the same time I knew little or nothing of my new pedigree.

The first thing that my spouse took upon him to manage was to declare ourselves married eleven years before our arriving in Holland; and consequently to acknowledge our little son, who was yet in England, to be legitimate; order him to be brought over, and added to his family, and acknowledge him to be our own.

This was done by giving notice to his people at Nimeguen, where his children (which were two sons and a daughter) were brought up, that he was come over from England, and that he was arrived at the Hague with his wife, and should reside there some time, and that he would have his two sons brought down to see him; which accordingly was done, and where I entertained them with all the kindness and tenderness that they could expect from their mother-in-law;* and who

---

* "mother-in-law." Stepmother.

pretended to be so ever since they were two or three years old.

This supposing us to have been so long married was not difficult at all in a country where we had been seen together about that time, viz., eleven years and a half before, and where we had never been seen afterwards till we now returned together. This being seen together was so openly owned and acknowledged, of course, by our friend the merchant at Rotterdam, and also by the people in the house where we both lodged in the same city, and where our first intimacies began, and who, as it happened, were all alive; and therefore, to make it the more public, we made a tour to Rotterdam again, lodged in the same house, and was visited there by our friend the merchant, and afterwards invited frequently to his house, where he treated us very handsomely.

This conduct of my spouse, and which he managed very cleverly, was indeed a testimony of a wonderful degree of honesty and affection to our little son; for it was done purely for the sake of the child.

I call it an honest affection, because it was from a principle of honesty that he so earnestly concerned himself to prevent the scandal which would otherwise have fallen upon the child, who was itself innocent; and as it was from this principle of justice that he so earnestly solicited me, and conjured me by the natural affections of a mother, to marry him when it was yet young within me and unborn, that the child might not suffer for the sin of its father and mother; so, though at the same time he really loved me very well, yet I had reason to believe that it was from this principle of justice to the child that he came to England again to seek me, with design to marry me and, as he called it, save the innocent lamb from an infamy worse than death.

It was with a just reproach to myself that I must repeat it again, that I had not the same concern for it, though it was the child of my own body; nor had I ever the hearty affectionate love to the child that he had. What the reason of it was I cannot tell; and, indeed, I had shown a general neglect of the child through all the gay years of my London revels, except that I sent Amy to look upon it now and then, and to pay for its nursing; as for me, I scarce saw it four times in the first four years of its life, and often wished it would go quietly out of the world. Whereas a son which I had by the jeweller I took a different care of, and showed a differing concern for, though I did not let him know me; for I provided very well for him, had him put out very well to school, and when he came to years fit for it, let him go over with a person of honesty and good business to the Indies; and after he had lived there some time, and began to act for himself, sent him over the value of £2000, at several times, with which he traded and grew rich; and, as 'tis to be hoped, may at last come over again with forty or fifty thousand pounds in his pocket, as many do who have not such encouragement at their beginning.

I also sent him over a wife, a beautiful young lady, well-bred, an exceeding good-natured pleasant creature; but the nice young fellow did not like her, and had the impudence to write to me, that is, to the person I employed to correspond with him, to send him another, and promised that he would marry her I had sent him to a friend of his, who liked her better than he did; but I took it so ill that I would not send him another, and withal, stopped another article of £1000 which I had appointed to send him. He considered of it afterwards and offered to take her; but then truly she took so ill the first affront he put upon her that she would not have him, and I sent him word I thought she was very much in the right. However, after courting her two years, and some friends interposing, she took him and made him an excellent wife, as I knew she would, but I never sent him the thousand pound cargo, so that he lost that money for misusing me, and took the lady at last without it.

My new spouse and I lived a very regular, contemplative life; and, in itself, certainly a life filled with all human felicity. But if I looked upon my present situation with satisfaction, as I certainly did, so, in proportion, I on all occasions looked back on former things with detestation, and with the utmost affliction; and now, indeed, and not till now, those reflections began to prey upon my comforts, and lessen the sweets of my other enjoyments. They might be said to have gnawed a hole in my heart before, but now they made a hole quite through it. Now they ate into all my pleasant things, made bitter every sweet, and mixed my sighs with every smile.

Not all the affluence of a plentiful fortune; not a hundred thousand pounds' estate (for, between us, we had little less); not honour and titles, attendants and equipages; in a word, not all the things we call pleasure, could give me any relish, or sweeten the taste of things to me; at least, not so much but I grew sad, heavy, pensive, and melancholy; slept little, and eat little; dreamed continually of the most frightful and terrible things imaginable; nothing but apparitions of devils and monsters, falling into gulfs, and off from steep and high precipices, and the like; so that in the morning, when I should rise and be refreshed with the blessing of rest, I was hag-ridden with frights and terrible things formed merely in the imagination, and was either tired and wanted sleep, or over-run with vapours, and not fit for conversing with my family or anyone else.

My husband, the tenderest creature in the world, and particularly so to me, was in great concern for me and did everything that lay in his power to comfort and restore me; strove to reason me out of it; then tried all the ways possible to divert me. But it was all to no purpose, or to but very little.

My only relief was sometimes to unbosom myself to poor Amy, when she and I was alone; and she did all she could to comfort me. But all was to little effect there; for, though Amy was the better penitent before, when we had been in the storm, Amy was just where she used to be now, a wild, gay, loose wretch, and not much the graver for her age; for Amy was between forty and fifty by this time too.

But to go on with my own story. As I had no comforter, so I had no counsellor; it was well, as I often thought, that I was not a Roman Catholic; for what a piece of work should I have made, to have gone to a priest with such a history as I had to tell him? And what penance would any father confessor have obliged me to perform, especially if he had been honest, and true to his office!

However, as I had none of the recourse, so I had none of the absolution, by which the criminal confessing goes away comforted; but I went about with a heart loaded with crime, and altogether in the dark as to what I was to do; and in this condition I languished near two years. I may well call it languishing, for if Providence had not relieved me, I should have died in little time. But of that hereafter.

I must now go back to another scene and join it to this end of my story, which will complete all my concern with England, at least all that I shall bring into this account.

I have hinted at large what I had done for my two sons, one at Messina, and the other in the Indies; but I have not gone through the story of my two daughters. I was so in danger of being known by one of them that I durst not see her, so as to let her know who I was; and for the other, I could not well know how to see her, and own her, and let her see me, because she must then know that I would not let her sister know me, which would look strange; so that, upon the whole, I resolved to see neither of them at all. But Amy managed all that for me; and when she had made gentlewomen of them both, by giving them a good, though late education, she had like to have blown up the whole case, and herself and me too, by an unhappy discovery of herself to the last of them, that is, to her who was our cook-maid, and who, as I said before, Amy had been obliged to turn away, for fear of the very discovery which now happened. I have observed already in what manner Amy managed her by a third person; and how the girl, when she was set up for a lady, as above, came and visited Amy at my lodgings; after which, Amy going, as was her custom, to see the girl's brother (my son) at the honest man's house in Spitalfields, both the girls were there, merely by accident, at the same time; and the other girl unawares discovered the secret, namely, that this was the lady that had done all this for them.

Amy was greatly surprised at it; but as she saw there was no remedy, she made a jest of it, and so after that conversed openly, being still satisfied that neither of them could make much of it, as long as they knew nothing of me. So she took them together one time and told them the history, as she called it, of their mother, beginning at the miserable carrying them to their aunt's; she owned she was not their mother herself, but described her to them. However, when she said she was not their mother, one of them expressed herself very much surprised, for the girl had taken up a strong fancy that Amy was really her mother, and that she had, for some particular reasons, concealed it from her; and therefore, when she told her frankly that she was not her mother, the girl fell a-crying, and Amy had much ado to keep life in her. This was the girl who was at first my cook-maid in the Pall-Mall. When Amy had brought her to again a little, and she had recovered her first disorder, Amy asked what ailed her. The poor girl hung about her, and kissed her, and was in such a passion still, though she was a great wench of nineteen or twenty years old, that she could not be brought to speak a great while. At last, having recovered her speech, she said still, "But oh! do not say you a'n't my mother! I'm sure you are my mother." And then the girl cried again like to kill herself. Amy could not tell what to do with her a good while; she was loth to say again she was not her mother, because she would not throw her into a fit of crying again, but she went round about a little with her. "Why, child," says she, "why would you have me be your mother? If it be because I am so kind to you, be easy, my dear," says Amy. "I'll be as kind to you still, as if I was your mother."

"Ay, but," says the girl, "I am sure you are my mother too; and what have I done that you won't own me, and that you will not be called my mother? Though I am poor, you have made me a gentlewoman," says she, "and I won't do anything to disgrace you. Besides," added she, "I can keep a secret, too, especially for my own mother, sure." Then she calls Amy her dear mother and hung about her neck again, crying still vehemently.

This last part of the girl's words alarmed Amy, and, as she told me, frightened her terribly; nay, she was so confounded with it that she was not able to govern herself or to conceal her disorder from the girl herself, as you shall hear. Amy was at a full stop and confused to the last degree; and the girl, a sharp jade, turned it upon her. "My dear mother," says she, "do not be uneasy about it; I know it all; but do not be uneasy, I won't let my sister know a word of it, or my brother either, without you give me leave; but don't disown me now you have found me; don't hide yourself from me any longer. I can't bear that," says she, "it will break my heart."

"I think the girl's mad," says Amy. "Why, child, I tell thee, if I was thy mother, I would not disown thee; don't you see I am as kind to you as if I was your mother?" Amy might as well have sung a song to a kettle-drum as talk to her. "Yes," says the girl, "you are very good to me indeed." And that was enough to make anybody believe she was her mother too; but, however, that was not the case, she had other reasons to believe, and to know, that she was her mother; and it was a sad thing she would not let her call her mother, who was her own child.

Amy was so heart-full with the disturbance of it that she did not enter farther with her into the inquiry as she would otherwise have done—I mean, as to what made the girl so positive—but comes away and tells me the whole story.

I was thunder-struck with the story at first, and much more

afterwards, as you shall hear; but, I say, I was thunder-struck
at first, and amazed, and said to Amy, "There must be something or other in it more than we know of." But, having examined farther into it, I found the girl had no notion of
anybody but of Amy; and glad I was that I was not concerned in the pretence, and that the girl had no notion of me
in it. But even this easiness did not continue long; for the
next time Amy went to see her, she was the same thing, and
rather more violent with Amy than she was before. Amy endeavoured to pacify her by all the ways imaginable. First, she
told her she took it ill that she would not believe her; and
told her, if she would not give over such a foolish whimsey,
she would leave her to the wide world as she found her.

This put the girl into fits, and she cried ready to kill herself, and hung about Amy again like a child. "Why," says
Amy, "why can you not be easy with me, then, and compose
yourself, and let me go on to do you good, and show you
kindness, as I would do, and as I intend to do? Can you think
that if I was your mother, I would not tell you so? What
whimsey is this that possesses your mind?" says Amy. Well,
the girl told her in a few words (but those few such as
frighted Amy out of her wits, and me too) that she knew well
enough how it was. "I know," says she, "when you left
————," naming the village, "where I lived when my father
went away from us all, that you went over to France; I know
that too, and who you went with," says the girl. "Did not
my Lady Roxana come back again with you? I know it all
well enough; though I was but a child, I have heard it all."
And thus she run on with such discourse as put Amy out of
all temper again; and she raved at her like a bedlam,* and
told her she would never come near her any more; she might
go a-begging again if she would; she'd have nothing to do
with her. The girl, a passionate wench, told her she knew the
worst of it, she could go to service again, and if she would
not own her own child, she must do as she pleased; then she
fell into a passion of crying again, as if she would kill herself.

In short, this girl's conduct terrified Amy to the last degree,
and me too; and was it not that we knew the girl was quite
wrong in some things, she was yet so right in some others that
it gave me a great deal of perplexity; but that which put Amy
the most to it was that the girl (my daughter) told her that

* "a bedlam." See above, page 202.

she (meaning me, her mother) had gone away with the jeweller, and into France too; she did not call him the jeweller, but with the landlord of the house; who, after her mother fell into distress, and that Amy had taken all the children from her, made much of her and afterwards married her.

In short, it was plain the girl had but a broken account of things, but yet that she had received some accounts that had a reality in the bottom of them, so that, it seems, our first measures, and the amour with the jeweller, were not so concealed as I thought they had been; and, it seems, came in a broken manner to my sister-in-law, who Amy carried the children to, and she made some bustle, it seems, about it. But, as good luck was, it was too late, and I was removed and gone, none knew whither, or else she would have sent all the children home to me again, to be sure.

This we picked out of the girl's discourse, that is to say, Amy did, at several times; but it all consisted of broken fragments of stories, such as the girl herself had heard so long ago that she herself could make very little of it; only that in the main, that her mother had played the whore; had gone away with the gentleman that was landlord of the house; that he married her; that she went into France. And, as she had learned in my family, where she was a servant, that Mrs. Amy and her Lady Roxana had been in France together, so she put all these things together, and joining them with the great kindness that Amy now showed her, possessed the creature that Amy was really her mother, nor was it possible for Amy to conquer it for a long time.

But this, after I had searched into it, as far as by Amy's relation I could get an account of it, did not disquiet me half so much as that the young slut had got the name of Roxana by the end, and that she knew who her Lady Roxana was, and the like; though this, neither, did not hang together, for then she would not have fixed upon Amy for her mother. But some time after, when Amy had almost persuaded her out of it, and that the girl began to be so confounded in her discourses of it that they made neither head nor tail, at last the passionate creature flew out in a kind of rage, and said to Amy, that if she was not her mother, Madam Roxana was her mother then, for one of them, she was sure, was her mother; and then all this that Amy had done for her was by Madam Roxana's order. "And I am sure," says she, "it was my Lady Roxana's coach that brought the gentlewoman, whoever it was, to my uncle's in Spitalfields, for the coachman told me so." Amy fell a-laughing at her aloud, as was her usual way. But, as Amy told me, it was but on one side of her mouth, for she was so confounded at her discourse that she was ready to sink into the ground; and so was I too when she told it me.

However, Amy brazened her out of it all; told her, "Well, since you think you are so high-born as to be my Lady Roxana's daughter, you may go to her and claim your kindred, can't you? I suppose," says Amy, "you know where to find her?" She said she did not question to find her, for she knew where she was gone to live privately; but, though, she might be removed again, "For I know how it is," says she, with a kind of a smile or a grin. "I know how it all is, well enough."

Amy was so provoked that she told me, in short, she began to think it would be absolutely necessary to murder her. That expression filled me with horror, all my blood ran chill in my veins, and a fit of trembling seized me, that I could not speak a good while. At last, "What, is the devil in you, Amy?" said I. "Nay, nay," says she, "let it be the devil or not the devil, if I thought she knew one tittle of your history, I would dispatch her if she were my own daughter a thousand times." "And I," says I in a rage, "as well as I love you, would be the first that should put the halter about your neck, and see you hanged with more satisfaction than ever I saw you in my life. Nay," says I, "you would not live to be hanged, I believe I should cut your throat with my own hand; I am almost ready to do it," said I, "as 'tis, for your but naming the thing." With that, I called her cursed devil and bade her get out of the room.

I think it was the first time that ever I was angry with Amy in all my life; and when all was done, though she was a devilish jade in having such a thought, yet it was all of it the effect of her excess of affection and fidelity to me.

But this thing gave me a terrible shock, for it happened just after I was married and served to hasten my going over to Holland; for I would not have been seen, so as to be known by the name of Roxana, no, not for ten thousand pounds; it would have been enough to have ruined me to all intents and purposes with my husband, and everybody else too; I might as well have been the "German princess."

Well, I set Amy to work; and give Amy her due, she set all

her wits to work to find out which way this girl had her knowledge, but, more particularly, how much knowledge she had—that is to say, what she really knew, and what she did not know, for this was the main thing with me; how she could say she knew who Madam Roxana was, and what notions she had of that affair, was very mysterious to me, for 'twas certain she could not have a right notion of me, because she would have it be that Amy was her mother.

I scolded heartily at Amy for letting the girl ever know her, that is to say, know her in this affair; for that she knew her could not be hid, because she, as I might say, served Amy, or rather under Amy, in my family, as is said before; but she (Amy) talked with her at first by another person, and not by herself; and that secret came out by an accident, as I have said above.

Amy was concerned at it as well as I, but could not help it; and though it gave us great uneasiness, yet, as there was no remedy, we were bound to make as little noise of it as we could, that it might go no farther. I bade Amy punish the girl for it, and she did so, for she parted with her in a huff, and told her she should see she was not her mother, for that she could leave her just where she found her; and seeing she could not be content to be served by the kindness of a friend, but that she would needs make a mother of her, she would, for the future, be neither mother or friend, and so bid her go to service again and be a drudge as she was before.

The poor girl cried most lamentably, but would not be beaten out of it still; but that which dumbfounded Amy more than all the rest was that when she had rated the poor girl a long time, and could not beat her out of it, and had, as I have observed, threatened to leave her, the girl kept to what she said before, and put this turn to it again, that she was sure, if Amy wa'n't, my Lady Roxana was her mother, and that she would go find her out; adding, that she made no doubt but she could do it, for she knew where to inquire the name of her new husband.

Amy came home with this piece of news in her mouth to me. I could easily perceive when she came in that she was mad in her mind, and in a rage at something or other, and was in great pain to get it out; for when she came first in, my husband was in the room. However, Amy going up to undress her, I soon made an excuse to follow her, and coming into the room, "What the d ———— l is the matter, Amy?"

says I. "I am sure you have some bad news." "News," says Amy aloud; "ay, so I have; I think the d ———— l is in that young wench. She'll ruin us all and herself too; there's no quieting her." So she went on and told me all the particulars; but sure nothing was so astonished as I was when she told me that the girl knew I was married, that she knew my husband's name, and would endeavour to find me out. I thought I should have sunk down at the very words. In the middle of all my amazement, Amy starts up and runs about the room like a distracted body. "I'll put an end to it, that I will; I can't bear it—I must murder her, I'll kill the b———;" and swears by her Maker, in the most serious tone in the world, and then repeated it over three or four times, walking to and again in the room. "I will, in short, I will kill her, if there was not another wench in the world."

"Prithee hold thy tongue, Amy," says I. "Why, thou art mad." "Ay, so I am," says she, "stark mad; but I'll be the death of her for all that, and then I shall be sober again." "But you shan't," says I, "You shan't hurt a hair of her head; why, you ought to be hanged for what you have done already, for having resolved on it is doing it; as to the guilt of the fact you are a murderer already, as much as if you had done it already."

"I know that," says Amy, "and it can be no worse; I'll put you out of your pain, and her too; she shall never challenge you for her mother in this world, whatever she may in the next." "Well, well," says I, "be quiet, and do not talk thus, I can't bear it." So she grew a little soberer after a-while.

I must acknowledge, the notion of being discovered carried with it so many frightful ideas, and hurried my thoughts so much, that I was scarce myself any more than Amy, so dreadful a thing is a load of guilt upon the mind.

And yet when Amy began the second time to talk thus abominably of killing the poor child, or murdering her, and swore by her Maker that she would, so that I began to see that she was in earnest, I was farther terrified a great deal, and it helped to bring me to myself again in other cases.

We laid our heads together then to see if it was possible to discover by what means she had learned to talk so, and how she (I mean my girl) came to know that her mother had married a husband; but it would not do, the girl would acknowledge nothing, and gave but a very imperfect account of things still, being disgusted to the last degree with Amy's leaving her so abruptly as she did.

Well, Amy went to the house where the boy was; but it was all one, there they had only heard a confused story of the lady somebody, they knew not who, which this same wench had told them, but they gave no heed to it at all. Amy told them how foolishly the girl had acted, and how she had carried on the whimsey so far, in spite of all they could say to her; that she had taken it so ill, she would see her no more, and so she might even go to service again if she would, for she (Amy) would have nothing to do with her unless she humbled herself and changed her note, and that quickly too.

The good old gentleman, who had been the benefactor to them all, was greatly concerned at it, and the good woman his wife was grieved beyond all expressing, and begged her ladyship (meaning Amy), not to resent it; they promised, too, they would talk with her about it, and the old gentlewoman added, with some astonishment, "Sure she cannot be such a fool but she will be prevailed with to hold her tongue, when she has it from your own mouth that you are not her mother, and sees that it disobliges your ladyship to have her insist upon it." And so Amy came away with some expectation that it would be stopped here.

But the girl was such a fool for all that, and persisted in it obstinately, notwithstanding all they could say to her; nay, her sister begged and entreated her not to play the fool, for that it would ruin her too, and that the lady (meaning Amy) would abandon them both.

Well, notwithstanding this, she insisted, I say, upon it, and which was worse, the longer it lasted the more she began to drop Amy's ladyship, and would have it that the Lady Roxana was her mother, and that she had made some inquiries about it, and did not doubt but she should find her out.

When it was come to this, and we found there was nothing to be done with the girl, but that she was so obstinately bent upon the search after me that she ventured to forfeit all she had in view; I say, when I found it was come to this, I began to be more serious in my preparations of my going beyond sea, and, particularly, it gave me some reason to fear that there was something in it. But the following accident put me beside all my measures, and struck me into the greatest confusion that ever I was in in my life.

I was so near going abroad that my spouse and I had taken measures for our going off; and because I would be sure not to go too public, but so as to take away all possibility of being seen, I had made some exception to my spouse against going in the ordinary public passage-boats. My pretence to him was the promiscuous crowds in those vessels, want of convenience, and the like. So he took the hint and found me out an English merchant-ship, which was bound for Rotterdam, and getting soon acquainted with the master, he hired his whole ship, that is to say, his great cabin, for I do not mean his ship for freight, that so we had all the conveniences possible for our passage; and all things being near ready, he brought home the captain one day to dinner with him, that I might see him, and be acquainted a little with him. So we came after dinner to talk of the ship and the conveniences on-board, and the captain pressed me earnestly to come on-board and see the ship, intimating that he would treat us as well as he could; and in discourse I happened to say I hoped he had no other passengers. He said no, he had not; but, he said, his wife had courted him a good while to let her go over to Holland with him, for he always used that trade, but he never could think of venturing all he had in one bottom; but if I went with him, he thought to take her and her kinswoman along with him this voyage, that they might both wait upon me; and so added, that if we would do him the honour to dine on-board the next day, he would bring his wife on-board, the better to make us welcome.

Who now could have believed the devil had any snare at the bottom of all this? Or that I was in any danger on such an occasion, so remote and out of the way as this was? But the event was the oddest that could be thought of. As it happened, Amy was not at home when we accepted this invitation, and so she was left out of the company; but instead of Amy, we took our honest, good-humoured, never-to-be-omitted friend the Quaker, one of the best creatures that ever lived, sure; and who, besides a thousand good qualities unmixed with one bad one, was particularly excellent for being the best company in the world; though I think I had carried Amy too, if she had not been engaged in this unhappy girl's affair. For on a sudden the girl was lost, and no news was to be heard of her; and Amy had hunted her to every place she could think of, that it was likely to find her in; but all the news she could hear of her was that she was gone to an old comrade's house of hers, which she called sister, and who was married to a master of a ship, who lived at Redriff; and even this the jade never told me. It seems, when this girl was directed by Amy to get her some breeding, go to the boarding-school, and the like, she was recommended to a boarding-school at Camberwell, and there she contracted an acquaintance with a young lady (so they are all called), her bedfellow, that they called sisters, and promised never to break off their acquaintance.

But judge you what an unaccountable surprise I must be in when I came on-board the ship and was brought into the captain's cabin, or what they call it, the great cabin of the ship, to see his lady or wife, and another young person with her, who, when I came to see her near-hand, was my old cook-maid in the Pall-Mall, and, as appeared by the sequel of the story, was neither more or less than my own daughter. That I knew her was out of doubt; for though she had not had opportunity to see me very often, yet I had often seen her, as I must needs, being in my own family so long.

If ever I had need of courage, and a full presence of mind, it was now; it was the only valuable secret in the world to me, all depended upon this occasion; if the girl knew me, I was undone; and to discover any surprise or disorder had been to make her know me, or guess it, and discover herself.

I was once going to feign a swooning and faint away, and so, falling on the ground, or floor, put them all into a hurry and fright, and by that means get an opportunity to be continually holding something to my nose to smell to, and so hold my hand or my handkerchief, or both, before my mouth; then pretend I could not bear the smell of the ship, or the closeness of the cabin. But that would have been only to remove into a clearer air upon the quarter-deck, where we should, with it, have had a clearer light too; and if I had pretended the smell of the ship, it would have served only to have carried us all on-shore to the captain's house, which was hard by; for the ship lay so close to the shore that we only walked over a plank to go on-board, and over another ship which lay within her; so this not appearing feasible, and the thought not being two minutes old, there was no time, for the two ladies rose up, and we saluted, so that I was bound to come so near my girl as to kiss her, which I would not have done had it been possible to have avoided it, but there was no room to escape.

I cannot but take notice here that notwithstanding there was a secret horror upon my mind, and I was ready to sink when I came close to her to salute her, yet it was a secret inconceivable pleasure to me when I kissed her, to know that I kissed my own child, my own flesh and blood, born of my body, and who I had never kissed since I took the fatal farewell of them all, with a million of tears, and a heart almost dead with grief, when Amy and the good woman took them all away, and went with them to Spitalfields. No pen can describe, no words can express, I say, the strange impression which this thing made upon my spirits. I felt something shoot through my blood, my heart fluttered, my head flashed, and was dizzy, and all within me, as I thought, turned about, and much ado I had not to abandon myself to an excess of passion at the first sight of her, much more when my lips touched her face. I thought I must have taken her in my arms and kissed her again a thousand times, whether I would or no.

But I roused up my judgment, and shook it off, and with infinite uneasiness in my mind, I sat down. You will not wonder if upon this surprise I was not conversable for some minutes, and that the disorder had almost discovered itself. I had a complication of severe things upon me, I could not conceal my disorder without the utmost difficulty, and yet upon my concealing it depended the whole of my prosperity; so I used all manner of violence with myself to prevent the mischief which was at the door.

Well, I saluted her, but as I went first forward to the captain's lady, who was at the farther end of the cabin, towards the light, I had the occasion offered to stand with my back to the light, when I turned about to her, who stood more on my left hand, so that she had not a fair sight of me, though I was so near her. I trembled, and knew neither what I did or said; I was in the utmost extremity, between so many particular circumstances as lay upon me, for I was to conceal my disorder from everybody at the utmost peril, and at the same time expected everybody would discern it. I was to expect she would discover that she knew me, and yet was, by all means possible, to prevent it. I was to conceal myself, if possible, and yet had not the least room to do anything towards it. In short, there was no retreat, no shifting anything off, no avoiding or preventing her having a full sight of me, nor was there any counterfeiting my voice, for then my husband would have perceived it. In short, there was not the least circumstance that offered me any assistance, or any favourable thing to help me in this exigence.

After I had been upon the rack for near half an hour, during which I appeared stiff and reserved, and a little too formal, my spouse and the captain fell into discourses about the ship and the sea, and business remote from us women; and by-and-by the captain carried him out upon the quarter-deck and left us all by ourselves in the great cabin. Then we began to be a little freer one with another, and I began to be a little revived by a sudden fancy of my own—namely, I thought I perceived that the girl did not know me, and the chief reason of my having such a notion was because I did not perceive the least disorder in her countenance, or the least change in her carriage, no confusion, no hesitation in her discourse; nor, which I had my eye particularly upon, did I observe that she fixed her eyes much upon me, that is to say, not singling me out to look steadily at me, as I thought would have been the case, but that she rather singled out my friend the Quaker and chatted with her on several things; but I observed, too, that it was all about indifferent matters.

This greatly encouraged me, and I began to be a little cheerful; but I was knocked down again as with a thunder-clap, when turning to the captain's wife, and discoursing of me, she said to her, "Sister, I cannot but think my lady to be very much like such a person." Then she named the person, and the captain's wife said she thought so too. The girl replied again she was sure she had seen me before, but she could not recollect where; I answered (though her speech was not directed to me) that I fancied she had not seen me before in England, but asked if she had lived in Holland. She said, No, no, she had never been out of England, and I added that she could not then have known me in England, unless it was very lately, for I had lived at Rotterdam a great while. This carried me out of that part of the broil pretty well, and to make it go off the better, when a little Dutch boy came into the cabin, who belonged to the captain, and who I easily perceived to be Dutch, I jested and talked Dutch to him, and was merry about the boy, that is to say, as merry as the consternation I was still in would let me be.

However, I began to be thoroughly convinced by this time that the girl did not know me, which was an infinite satisfaction to me, or, at least, that though she had some notion of me, yet that she did not think anything about my being who I was, and which, perhaps, she would have been as glad to have known as I would have been surprised if she had; indeed, it was evident that, had she suspected anything of the truth, she would not have been able to have concealed it.

Thus this meeting went off, and, you may be sure, I was resolved, if once I got off of it, she should never see me again to revive her fancy; but I was mistaken there too, as you shall hear. After we had been on-board, the captain's lady carried us home to her house, which was but just on-shore, and treated us there again very handsomely, and made us promise that we would come again and see her before we went to concert our affairs for the voyage and the like, for she assured us that both she and her sister went the voyage at that time for our company, and I thought to myself, "Then you'll never go the voyage at all." For I saw from that moment that it would be no way convenient for my ladyship to go with them, for that frequent conversation might bring me to her mind, and she would certainly claim her kindred to me in a few days, as indeed would have been the case.

It is hardly possible for me to conceive what would have been our part in this affair had my woman Amy gone with me on-board this ship; it had certainly blown up the whole affair, and I must forever after have been this girl's vassal, that is to say, have let her into the secret, and trusted to her keeping it too, or have been exposed and undone. The very thought filled me with horror.

But I was not so unhappy neither, as it fell out, for Amy was not with us, and that was my deliverance indeed; yet we had another chance to get over still. As I resolved to put off the voyage, so I resolved to put off the visit, you may be sure, going upon this principle, namely, that I was fixed in it that the girl had seen her last of me, and should never see me more.

However, to bring myself well off, and, withal, to see, if I could, a little farther into the matter, I sent my friend the Quaker to the captain's lady to make the visit promised, and to make my excuse that I could not possibly wait on her, for that I was very much out of order; and in the end of the discourse I bade her insinuate to them that she was afraid I should not be able to get ready to go the voyage so soon as the captain would be obliged to go, and that perhaps we might put it off to his next voyage. I did not let the Quaker into any other reason for it than that I was indisposed; and not knowing what other face to put upon that part, I made her believe that I thought I was a-breeding.

It was easy to put that into her head, and she of course hinted to the captain's lady that she found me so very ill that she was afraid I would miscarry, and then, to be sure, I could not think of going.

She went, and she managed that part very dexterously, as I knew she would, though she knew not a word of the grand reason of my indisposition; but I was all sunk and dead-hearted again when she told me she could not understand the meaning of one thing in her visit, namely, that the young woman, as she called her, that was with the captain's lady, and who she called sister, was most impertinently inquisitive into things; as who I was? how long I had been in England, where I had lived, and the like; and that, above all the rest, she inquired if I did not live once at the other end of the town.

"I thought her inquiries so out of the way," says the honest Quaker, "that I gave her not the least satisfaction; but as I saw by thy answers on-board the ship, when she talked of thee, that thou didst not incline to let her be acquainted with thee, so I was resolved that she should not be much the wiser for me; and when she asked me if thou ever lived'st here or there, I always said no, but that thou wast a Dutch lady, and was going home again to thy family, and lived abroad."

I thanked her very heartily for that part, and indeed she served me in it more than I let her know she did: in a word, she thwarted the girl so cleverly that if she had known the whole affair, she could not have done it better.

But, I must acknowledge, all this put me upon the rack again, and I was quite discouraged, not at all doubting but that the jade had a right scent of things, and that she knew and remembered my face, but had artfully concealed her knowledge of me till she might perhaps do it more to my disadvantage. I told all this to Amy, for she was all the relief I had. The poor soul (Amy) was ready to hang herself, that, as she said, she had been the occasion of it all; and that if I was ruined (which was the word I always used to her), she had ruined me; and she tormented herself about it so much that I was sometimes fain to comfort her and myself too.

What Amy vexed herself at was, chiefly, that she should be surprised so by the girl, as she called her; I mean surprised into a discovery of herself to the girl; which indeed was a false step of Amy's, and so I had often told her. But 'twas to no purpose to talk of that now; the business was, how to get clear of the girl's suspicions, and of the girl too, for it looked more threatening every day than other; and if I was uneasy at what Amy had told me of her rambling and rattling to her (Amy), I had a thousand times as much reason to be uneasy now, when she had chopped upon me so unhappily as this; and not only had seen my face, but knew too where I lived, what name I went by, and the like.

And I am not come to the worst of it yet neither, for a few days after my friend the Quaker had made her visit, and excused me on the account of indisposition, as if they had done it in over and above kindness, because they had been told I was not well, they come both directly to my lodgings to visit me: the captain's wife and my daughter (who she called sister), and the captain, to show them the place. The captain only brought them to the door, put them in, and went away upon some business.

Had not the kind Quaker, in a lucky moment, come running in before them, they had not only clapped in upon me, in the parlour, as it had been a surprise, but, which would have been a thousand times worse, had seen Amy with me; I think if that had happened, I had had no remedy but to take the girl by herself, and have made myself known to her, which would have been all distraction.

But the Quaker, a lucky creature to me, happened to see them come to the door, before they rung the bell, and instead of going to let them in, came running in, with some confusion in her countenance, and told me who was a-coming; at which Amy run first and I after her, and bid the Quaker come up as soon as she had let them in.

I was going to bid her deny me, but it came into my thoughts, that having been represented so much out of order, it would have looked very odd; besides, I knew the honest Quaker, though she would do anything else for me, would not lie for me, and it would have been hard to have desired it of her.

After she had let them in and brought them into the parlour, she came up to Amy and I, who were hardly out of the fright, and yet were congratulating one another that Amy was not surprised again.

They paid their visit in form, and I received them as formally, but took occasion two or three times to hint that I was so ill that I was afraid I should not be able to go to Holland, at least not so soon as the captain must go off; and made my compliment how sorry I was to be disappointed of the advantage of their company and assistance in the voyage; and sometimes I talked as if I thought I might stay till the captain returned, and would be ready to go again; then the Quaker put in that then I might be too far gone, meaning with child, that I should not venture at all; and then (as if she should be pleased with it) added, she hoped I would stay and lie in at her house; so as this carried its own face with it, 'twas well enough.

But it was now high time to talk of this to my husband, which, however, was not the greatest difficulty before me; for after this and other chat had taken up some time, the young fool began her tattle again; and two or three times she brought it in that I was so like a lady that she had the honour to know at the other end of the town that she could not put that lady out of her mind when I was by, and once or twice I fancied the girl was ready to cry; by-and-by she was at it again, and at last I plainly saw tears in her eyes; upon which I asked her if the lady was dead, because she seemed to be in some concern for her. She made me much easier by her answer than ever she did before. She said she did not really know, but she believed she was dead.

This, I say, a little relieved my thoughts, but I was soon down again; for, after some time, the jade began to grow talkative; and as it was plain that she had told all that her head could retain of Roxana, and the days of joy which I spent at that part of the town, another accident had like to have blown us all up again.

I was in a kind of dishabille when they came, having on a loose robe, like a morning-gown, but much after the Italian way; and I had not altered it when I went up, only dressed my head a little; and as I had been represented as having been lately very ill, so the dress was becoming enough for a chamber.

This morning vest, or robe, call it as you please, was more shaped to the body than we wear them since, showing the body in its true shape, and perhaps a little too plainly if it had been to be worn where any men were to come; but among ourselves it was well enough, especially for hot weather; the colour was green, figured, and the stuff a French damask, very rich.

This gown or vest put the girl's tongue a-running again, and her sister, as she called her, prompted it; for as they both admired my vest, and were taken up much about the beauty of the dress, the charming damask, the noble trimming, and the like, my girl puts in a word to the sister (captain's wife), "This is just such a thing as I told you," says she, "the lady danced in." "What," says the captain's wife, "the Lady Roxana that you told me of? Oh! that's a charming story," says she. "Tell it my lady." I could not avoid saying so too, though from my soul I wished her in heaven for but naming it; nay, I won't say but if she had been carried t'other way, it had been much as one to me, if I could but have been rid of her, and her story too, for when she came to describe the Turkish dress, it was impossible but the Quaker, who was a sharp, penetrating creature, should receive the impression in a more dangerous manner than the girl, only that indeed she was not so dangerous a person; for if she had known it all, I could more freely have trusted her than I could the girl, by a great deal—nay, I should have been perfectly easy in her.

However, as I have said, her talk made me dreadfully uneasy, and the more when the captain's wife mentioned but the name of Roxana. What my face might do towards betraying me I knew not, because I could not see myself, but my heart beat as if it would have jumped out at my mouth, and my passion was so great that, for want of vent, I thought I should have burst. In a word, I was in a kind of a silent rage, for the force I was under of restraining my passion was such as I never felt the like of. I had no vent, nobody to open myself to, or to make a complaint to, for my relief; I durst not leave the room by any means, for then she would have told all the story in my absence, and I should have been perpetually uneasy to know what she had said or had not said; so that, in a word, I was obliged to sit and hear her tell all the story of Roxana, that is to say, of myself, and not know at the same time whether she was in earnest or in jest, whether she knew me or no; or, in short, whether I was to be exposed or not exposed.

She began only in general with telling where she lived, what a place she had of it, how gallant a company her lady had always had in the house; how they used to sit up all night in the house gaming and dancing; what a fine lady her mistress was, and what a vast deal of money the upper servants got; as for her, she said, her whole business was in the next house, so that she got but little, except one night that there was twenty guineas given to be divided among the servants, when, she said, she got two guineas and a half for her share.

She went on and told them how many servants there was, and how they were ordered; but, she said, there was one Mrs. Amy, who was over them all; and that she, being the lady's favourite, got a great deal. She did not know, she said, whether Amy was her Christian name or her surname, but she supposed it was her surname; that they were told she got threescore pieces of gold at one time, being the same night that the rest of the servants had the twenty guineas divided among them.

I put in at that word and said 'twas a vast deal to give away. "Why," says I, " 'twas a portion for a servant." "O madam!" says she, "it was nothing to what she got afterwards; we that were servants hated her heartily for it; that is to say, we wished it had been our lot in her stead." Then I said again, "Why, it was enough to get her a good husband, and settle her for the world, if she had sense to manage it." "So it might, to be sure, madam," says she, "for we were told she laid up above £500; but, I suppose, Mrs. Amy was too sensible that her character would require a good portion to put her off."

"Oh," said I, "if that was the case 'twas another thing."

"Nay," says she, "I don't know, but they talked very much of a young lord that was very great with her."

"And pray what came of her at last?" said I, for I was willing to hear a little (seeing she would talk of it) what she had to say, as well of Amy as of myself.

"I don't know, madam," said she, "I never heard of her for several years, till t'other day I happened to see her."

"Did you indeed?" says I (and made mighty strange of it); "what! and in rags, it may be," said I. "That's often the end of such creatures."

"Just the contrary, madam," says she. "She came to visit an acquaintance of mine, little thinking, I suppose, to see me, and, I assure you, she came in her coach."

"In her coach!" said I. "Upon my word, she had made her market then; I suppose she made hay while the sun shone. Was she married, pray?"

"I believe she had been married, madam," says she, "but it seems she had been at the East Indies; and if she was married, it was there, to be sure. I think she said she had good luck in the Indies."

"That is, I suppose," said I, "had buried her husband there."

"I understood it so, madam," says she, "and that she had got his estate."

"Was that her good luck?" said I. "It might be good to her, as to the money indeed, but it was but the part of a jade to call it good luck."

Thus far our discourse of Mrs. Amy went, and no farther, for she knew no more of her; but then the Quaker unhappily, though undesignedly, put in a question, which the honest good-humoured creature would have been far from doing if she had known that I had carried on the discourse of Amy on purpose to drop Roxana out of the conversation.

But I was not to be made easy too soon. The Quaker put in, "But I think thou saidst something was behind of thy mistress; what didst thou call her? Roxana, was it not? Pray, what became of her?"

"Ay, ay, Roxana," says the captain's wife. "Pray, sister, let's hear the story of Roxana; it will divert my lady, I'm sure."

"That's a damned lie," said I to myself. "If you knew how little 'twould divert me, you would have too much advantage over me." Well, I saw no remedy, but the story must come on, so I prepared to hear the worst of it.

"Roxana!" says she, "I know not what to say of her; she was so much above us, and so seldom seen, that we could know little of her but by report; but we did sometimes see her too; she was a charming woman indeed, and the footmen used to say that she was to be sent for to court."

"To court!" said I. "Why, she was at court, wasn't she? The Pall-Mall is not far from Whitehall."

"Yes, madam," says she, "but I mean another way."

"I understand thee," says the Quaker. "Thou meanest, I suppose, to be mistress to the king."

"Yes, madam," says she.

I cannot help confessing what a reserve of pride still was left in me; and though I dreaded the sequel of the story, yet when she talked how handsome and how fine a lady this Roxana was, I could not help being pleased and tickled with it, and put in questions two or three times of how handsome she was; and was she really so fine a woman as they talked of; and the like, on purpose to hear her repeat what the people's opinion of me was, and how I had behaved.

"Indeed," says she, at last, "she was a most beautiful creature as ever I saw in my life." "But then," said I, "you never had the opportunity to see her but when she was set out to the best advantage."

"Yes, yes, madam," says she, "I have seen her several times in her dishabille, and, I can assure you, she was a very fine woman; and that which was more still, everybody said she did not paint."

This was still agreeable to me one way; but there was a devilish sting in the tail of it all, and this last article was one; wherein she said she had seen me several times in my dishabille. This put me in mind that then she must certainly know me, and it would come out at last; which was death to me but to think of.

"Well, but, sister," says the captain's wife, "tell my lady about the ball; that's the best of all the story; and of Roxana's dancing in a fine outlandish dress."

"That's one of the brightest parts of her story indeed," says the girl. "The case was this: We had balls and meetings in her ladyship's apartments every week almost; but one time my lady invited all the nobles to come such a time, and she would give them a ball; and there was a vast crowd indeed," says she.

"I think you said the king was there, sister, didn't you?"

"No, madam," says she, "that was the second time, when they said the king had heard how finely the Turkish lady danced, and that he was there to see her; but the king, if his Majesty was there, came disguised."

"That is, what they call incog.," says my friend the Quaker. "Thou canst not think the king would disguise himself." "Yes," says the girl, "it was so; he did not come in public with his guards, but we all knew which was the king well enough, that is to say, which they said was the king."

"Well," says the captain's wife, "about the Turkish dress; pray let us hear that." "Why," says she, "my lady sat in a fine little drawing-room, which opened into the great room, and where she received the compliments of the company; and when the dancing began, a great lord," says she, "I forget who they called him (but he was a very great lord or duke, I don't know which), took her out and danced with her; but after a-while, my lady on a sudden shut the drawing-room and ran upstairs with her woman, Mrs. Amy; and though she did not stay long (for I suppose she had contrived it all before-hand), she came down dressed in the strangest figure that ever I saw in my life; but it was exceeding fine."

Here she went on to describe the dress, as I have done already; but did it so exactly that I was surprised at the manner of her telling it; there was not a circumstance of it left out.

I was now under a new perplexity, for this young slut gave so complete an account of everything in the dress that my friend the Quaker coloured at it, and looked two or three times at me, to see if I did not do so too; for (as she told me afterwards) she immediately perceived it was the same dress that she had seen me have on, as I have said before. However, as she saw I took no notice of it, she kept her thoughts private to herself; and I did so too, as well as I could.

I put in two or three times, that she had a good memory, that could be so particular in every part of such a thing.

"Oh, madam!" says she, "we that were servants stood by ourselves in a corner, but so as we could see more than some strangers. Besides," says she, "it was all our conversation for several days in the family, and what one did not observe, another did." "Why," says I to her, "this was no Persian dress; only, I suppose your lady was some French comedian, that is to say, a stage Amazon, that put on a counterfeit dress to please the company, such as they used in the play of *Tamerlane* at Paris, or some such."

"No, indeed, madam," says she, "I assure you my lady was no actress; she was a fine modest lady, fit to be a princess; everybody said if she was a mistress, she was fit to be a mistress to none but the king; and they talked her up for the king as if it had really been so. Besides, madam," says she, "my lady danced a Turkish dance; all the lords and gentry said it was so; and one of them swore he had seen it danced in Turkey himself, so that it could not come from the theatre at Paris; and then the name Roxana," says she, "was a Turkish name."

"Well," said I, "but that was not your lady's name, I suppose?"

"No, no, madam," said she, "I know that. I know my lady's name and family very well; Roxana was not her name, that's true, indeed."

Here she run me a-ground again, for I durst not ask her what was Roxana's real name, lest she had really dealt with the devil and had boldly given my own name in for answer; so that I was still more and more afraid that the girl had really gotten the secret somewhere or other; though I could not imagine neither how that could be.

In a word, I was sick of the discourse and endeavoured many ways to put an end to it, but it was impossible; for the captain's wife, who called her sister, prompted her and pressed her to tell it, most ignorantly thinking that it would be a pleasant tale to all of us.

Two or three times the Quaker put in that this Lady Roxana had a good stock of assurance; and that 'twas likely, if she had been in Turkey, she had lived with, or been kept by, some great bashaw there. But still she would break in upon all such discourse and fly out into the most extravagant praises of her mistress, the famed Roxana. I run her down as some scandalous woman; that it was not possible to be otherwise; but she would not hear of it; her lady was a person of such and such qualifications that nothing but an angel was like her, to be sure; and yet, after all she could say, her own account brought her down to this, that, in short, her lady kept little less than a gaming ordinary; or, as it would be called in the times since that, an assembly for gallantry and play.

All this while I was very uneasy, as I said before, and yet the whole story went off again without any discovery, only that I seemed a little concerned that she should liken me to this gay lady, whose character I pretended to run down very much, even upon the foot of her own relation.

But I was not at the end of my mortifications yet, neither, for now my innocent Quaker threw out an unhappy expression, which put me upon the tenters again. Says she to me, "This lady's habit, I fancy, is just such a one as thine, by the description of it." And then turning to the captain's wife, says she, "I fancy my friend has a finer Turkish or Persian dress, a great deal." "Oh," says the girl, " 'tis impossible to be finer; my lady's," says she, "was all covered with gold and diamonds; her hair and head-dress, I forgot the name they gave it," said she, "shone like the stars, there was so many jewels in it."

I never wished my good friend the Quaker out of my company before now; but, indeed, I would have given some guineas to have been rid of her just now; for beginning to be curious in the comparing the two dresses, she innocently began a description of mine; and nothing terrified me so much as the apprehension lest she should importune me to show it, which I was resolved I would never agree to.

But before it came to this, she pressed my girl to describe the *tyhaia,* or head-dress, which she did so cleverly that the Quaker could not help saying mine was just such a one; and after several other similitudes, all very vexatious to me, out comes the kind motion to me to let the ladies see my dress; and they joined their eager desires of it, even to importunity.

I desired to be excused, though I had little to say at first why I declined it; but at last it came into my head to say it was packed up with my other clothes that I had least occasion for, in order to be sent on board the captain's ship; but that if we lived to come to Holland together (which, by the way, I resolved should never happen), then, I told them, at unpacking my clothes, they should see me dressed in it; but they must not expect I should dance in it, like the Lady Roxana in all her fine things.

This carried it off pretty well; and getting over this, got over most of the rest, and I began to be easy again; and, in a word, that I may dismiss the story too, as soon as may be, I got rid at last of my visitors, who I had wished gone two hours sooner than they intended it.

As soon as they were gone, I run up to Amy, and gave vent to my passions by telling her the whole story, and letting her see what mischiefs one false step of hers had like, unluckily, to have involved us all in; more, perhaps, than we could ever have lived to get through. Amy was sensible of it enough, and was just giving her wrath a vent another way, viz., by calling the poor girl all the damned jades and fools (and sometimes worse names) that she could think of, in the middle of which up comes my honest, good Quaker and put an end to our discourse. The Quaker came in smiling (for she was always soberly cheerful). "Well," says she, "thou art delivered at last; I come to joy thee of it; I perceived thou wert tired grievously of thy visitors."

"Indeed," says I, "so I was. That foolish young girl held us all in a Canterbury story;* I thought she would never have done with it." "Why, truly, I thought she was very careful to let thee know she was but a cook-maid." "Ay," says I, "and at a gaming-house, or gaming-ordinary, and at t'other end of

---

* "Canterbury story." A long, improbable tale.

the town too; all which (by the way) she might know would add very little to her good name among us citizens."

"I can't think," says the Quaker, "but she had some other drift in that long discourse; there's something else in her head," says she, "I am satisfied of that." Thought I, "Are you satisfied of it? I am sure I am the less satisfied for that; at least 'tis but small satisfaction to me to hear you say so. "What can this be?" says I. "And when will my uneasiness have an end?" But this was silent, and to myself, you may be sure. But in answer to my friend the Quaker, I returned by asking her a question or two about it; as what she thought was in it, and why she thought there was anything in it. "For," says I, "she can have nothing in it relating to me."

"Nay," says the kind Quaker, "if she had any view towards thee, that's no business of mine; and I should be far from desiring thee to inform me."

This alarmed me again; not that I feared trusting the good-humoured creature with it, if there had been anything of just suspicion in her; but this affair was a secret I cared not to communicate to anybody. However, I say, this alarmed me a little; for as I had concealed everything from her, I was willing to do so still; but as she could not but gather up abundance of things from the girl's discourse, which looked towards me, so she was too penetrating to be put off with such answers as might stop another's mouth. Only there was this double felicity in it, first, that she was not inquisitive to know or find anything out, and not dangerous if she had known the whole story. But, as I say, she could not but gather up several circumstances from the girl's discourse, as particularly the name of Amy, and the several descriptions of the Turkish dress, which my friend the Quaker had seen and taken so much notice of, as I have said above.

As for that, I might have turned it off by jesting with Amy, and asking her who she lived with before she came to live with me. But that would not do, for we had unhappily anticipated that way of talking by having often talked how long Amy had lived with me; and, which was still worse, by having owned formerly that I had had lodgings in the Pall-Mall; so that all those things corresponded too well. There was only one thing that helped me out with the Quaker, and that was the girl's having reported how rich Mrs. Amy was grown, and that she kept her coach. Now, as there might be many more Mrs. Amys besides mine, so it was not likely to be my Amy, because she was far from such a figure as keeping her coach; and this carried it off from the suspicions which the good, friendly Quaker might have in her head.

But as to what she imagined the girl had in her head, there lay more real difficulty in that part a great deal, and I was alarmed at it very much, for my friend the Quaker told me she observed the girl was in a great passion when she talked of the habit, and more when I had been importuned to show her mine, but declined it. She said she several times perceived her to be in disorder, and to restrain herself with great difficulty; and once or twice she muttered to herself that she had found it out, or that she would find it out, she could not tell whether; and that she often saw tears in her eyes; that when I said my suit of Turkish clothes was put up, but that she should see it when we arrived in Holland, she heard her say softly she would go over on purpose then.

After she had ended her observations, I added: "I observed, too, that the girl talked and looked oddly, and that she was mighty inquisitive, but I could not imagine what it was she aimed at." "Aimed at," says the Quaker; "'tis plain to me what she aims at. She believes thou art the same Lady Roxana that danced in the Turkish vest, but she is not certain." "Does she believe so?" says I. "If I had thought that, I would have put her out of her pain." "Believe so!" says the Quaker. "Yes, and I began to think so too, and should have believed so still, if thou had'st not satisfied me to the contrary by thy taking no notice of it, and by what thou hast said since." "Should you have believed so?" said I warmly. "I am very sorry for that. Why, would you have taken me for an actress, or a French stage-player?" "No," says the good, kind creature, "thou carriest it too far; as soon as thou madest thy reflections upon her, I knew it could not be; but who could think any other when she described the Turkish dress which thou hast here, with the head-tire and jewels, and when she named thy maid Amy too, and several other circumstances concurring? I should certainly have believed it," said she, "if thou hadst not contradicted it; but as soon as I heard thee speak, I concluded it was otherwise." "That was very kind," said I, "and I am obliged to you for doing me so much justice; 'tis more, it seems, than that young talking creature does." "Nay," says the Quaker, "indeed she does not do thee justice; for she as certainly believes it still as ever she did." "Does she?" said I. "Ay," says the Quaker, "and I warrant thee she'll make thee another visit about it." "Will she?" said I. "Then I believe I shall downright affront her." "No, thou shalt not affront her," says she (full of her good-humour and temper). "I'll take that part off thy hands, for I'll affront her for thee, and not let her see thee." I thought that was a very kind offer, but was at a loss how she would be able to do it; and the thought of seeing her there again half distracted me, not knowing what temper she would come in, much less what manner to receive her in; but my fast friend and constant comforter, the Quaker, said she perceived the girl was impertinent, and that I had no inclination to converse with her, and she was resolved I should not be troubled with her. But I shall have occasion to say more of this presently, for this girl went farther yet than I thought she had.

It was now time, as I said before, to take measures with my husband, in order to put off my voyage; so I fell into talk with him one morning as he was dressing, and while I was in bed. I pretended I was very ill; and as I had but too easy a way to impose upon him, because he so absolutely believed everything I said, so I managed my discourse so as that he should understand by it I was a-breeding, though I did not tell him so.

However, I brought it about so handsomely that, before he went out of the room, he came and sat down by my bedside and began to talk very seriously to me upon the subject of my being so every day ill, and that, as he hoped I was with child, he would have me consider well of it, whether I had not best alter my thoughts of the voyage to Holland; for that being sea-sick, and which was worse, if a storm should happen, might be very dangerous to me. And after saying abundance of the kindest things that the kindest of husbands in the world could say, he concluded that it was his request to me that I would not think any-more of going till after all should be over; but that I would, on the contrary, prepare to lie-in where I was, and where I knew, as well as he, I could be very well provided and very well assisted.

This was just what I wanted, for I had, as you have heard, a thousand good reasons why I should put off the voyage, especially with that creature in company; but I had a mind the putting it off should be at his motion, not my own; and he came into it of himself, just as I would have had it. This gave me an opportunity to hang back a little, and to seem as if I was unwilling. I told him I could not abide to put him to dif-

ficulties and perplexities in his business; that now he had
hired the great cabin in the ship, and, perhaps, paid some of
the money, and, it may be, taken freight for goods; and to
make him break it all off again would be a needless charge to
him or, perhaps, a damage to the captain.

As to that, he said, it was not to be named, and he would
not allow it to be any consideration at all; that he could easily pacify the captain of the ship by telling him the reason of
it, and that if he did make him some satisfaction for the disappointment, it should not be much.

"But, my dear," says I, "you ha'n't heard me say I am with
child, neither can I say so; and if it should not be so at last,
then I shall have made a fine piece of work of it indeed;
besides," says I, "the two ladies, the captain's wife and her
sister, they depend upon our going over, and have made great
preparations, and all in compliment to me. What must I say
to them?"

"Well, my dear," says he, "if you should not be with child,
though I hope you are, yet there is no harm done; the staying
three or four months longer in England will be no damage to
me, and we can go when we please, when we are sure you
are not with child, or, when it appearing that you are with
child, you shall be down and up again; and as for the captain's wife and sister, leave that part to me; I'll answer for it
there shall be no quarrel raised upon that subject. I'll make
your excuse to them by the captain himself, so all will be
well enough there, I'll warrant you."

This was as much as I could desire, and thus it rested for
a-while. I had indeed some anxious thoughts about this impertinent girl, but believed that putting off the voyage would
have put an end to it all, so I began to be pretty easy; but I
found myself mistaken, for I was brought to the point of
destruction by her again, and that in the most unaccountable
manner imaginable.

My husband, as he and I had agreed, meeting the captain
of the ship, took the freedom to tell him that he was afraid
he must disappoint him, for that something had fallen out
which had obliged him to alter his measures, and that his
family could not be ready to go time enough for him.

"I know the occasion, sir," says the captain. "I hear your
lady has got a daughter more than she expected; I give you
joy of it." "What do you mean by that?" says my spouse.
"Nay, nothing," says the captain, "but what I hear the

women tattle over the tea-table. I know nothing, but that you don't go the voyage upon it, which I am sorry for; but you know your own affairs," added the captain; "that's no business of mine."

"Well, but," says my husband, "I must make you some satisfaction for the disappointment," and so pulls out his money. "No, no," says the captain; and so they fell to straining their compliments one upon another; but, in short, my spouse gave him three or four guineas, and made him take it. And so the first discourse went off again, and they had no more of it.

But it did not go so easily with me, for now, in a word, the clouds began to thicken about me, and I had alarms on every side. My husband told me what the captain had said, but very happily took it that the captain had brought a tale by halves, and having heard it one way, had told it another; and that neither could he understand the captain, neither did the captain understand himself, so he contented himself to tell me, he said, word for word, as the captain delivered it.

How I kept my husband from discovering my disorder you shall hear presently; but let it suffice to say just now that if my husband did not understand the captain, nor the captain understand himself, yet I understood them both very well; and, to tell the truth, it was a worse shock than ever I had yet. Invention supplied me, indeed, with a sudden motion to avoid showing my surprise; for as my spouse and I was sitting by a little table near the fire, I reached out my hand, as if I had intended to take a spoon which lay on the other side, and threw one of the candles off of the table; and then snatching it up, started up upon my feet, and stooped to the lap of my gown and took it in my hand. "Oh!" says I, "my gown's spoiled; the candle has greased it prodigiously." This furnished me with an excuse to my spouse to break off the discourse for the present, and call Amy down; and Amy not coming presently, I said to him, "My dear, I must run upstairs and put it off, and let Amy clean it a little." So my husband rose up too, and went into a closet where he kept his papers and books, and fetched a book out and sat down by himself to read.

Glad I was that I had got away, and up I run to Amy, who, as it happened, was alone. "Oh, Amy!" says I, "we are all utterly undone." And with that I burst out a-crying, and could not speak a word for a great while.

I cannot help saying that some very good reflections offered themselves upon this head. It presently occurred, what a glorious testimony it is to the justice of Providence, and to the concern Providence has in guiding all the affairs of men (even the least as well as the greatest), that the most secret crimes are, by the most unforeseen accidents, brought to light and discovered.

Another reflection was, how just it is that sin and shame follow one another so constantly at the heels; that they are not like attendants only, but, like cause and consequence, necessarily connected one with another; that the crime going before, the scandal is certain to follow; and that 'tis not in the power of human nature to conceal the first, or avoid the last.

"What shall I do, Amy?" said I, as soon as I could speak, "and what will become of me?" And then I cried again so vehemently that I could say no more a great while. Amy was frighted almost out of her wits, but knew nothing what the matter was; but she begged to know, and persuaded me to compose myself and not cry so. "Why, madam, if my master should come up now," says she, "he will see what a disorder you are in; he will know you have been crying, and then he will want to know the cause of it." With that I broke out again. "Oh, he knows it already, Amy," says I, "he knows all! 'Tis all discovered, and we are undone!" Amy was thunderstruck now indeed. "Nay," says Amy, "if that be true, we are undone indeed: but that can never be; that's impossible, I'm sure."

"No, no," says I, " 'tis far from impossible, for I tell you 'tis so." And by this time, being a little recovered, I told her what discourse my husband and the captain had had together, and what the captain had said. This put Amy into such a hurry that she cried, she raved, she swore and cursed like a mad thing; then she upbraided me that I would not let her kill the girl when she would have done it, and that it was all my own doing, and the like. Well, however, I was not for killing the girl yet. I could not bear the thoughts of that neither.

We spent half an hour in these extravagances, and brought nothing out of them neither; for indeed we could do nothing or say nothing that was to the purpose; for if anything was to come out-of-the-way, there was no hindering it, nor help for it; so after thus giving a vent to myself by crying, I began to reflect how I had left my spouse below, and what I had pretended to come up for; so I changed my gown that I pretended the candle fell upon, and put on another, and went down.

When I had been down a good while, and found my spouse did not fall into the story again, as I expected, I took heart and called for it. "My dear," said I, "the fall of the candle put you out of your history; won't you go on with it?" "What history?" says he. "Why," says I, "about the captain." "Oh," says he, "I had done with it. I know no more than that the captain told a broken piece of news that he had heard by halves, and told more by halves than he heard it—namely, of your being with child, and that you could not go the voyage."

I perceived my husband entered not into the thing at all, but took it for a story, which, being told two or three times over, was puzzled, and come to nothing, and that all that was meant by it was what he knew, or thought he knew already—viz., that I was with child, which he wished might be true.

His ignorance was a cordial to my soul, and I cursed them in my thoughts that should ever undeceive him; and as I saw him willing to have the story end there, as not worth being farther mentioned, I closed it too, and said I supposed the captain had it from his wife; she might have found somebody else to make her remarks upon; and so it passed off with my husband well enough, and I was still safe there, where I thought myself in most danger. But I had two uneasinesses still; the first was lest the captain and my spouse should meet again and enter into farther discourse about it; and the second was lest the busy impertinent girl should come again, and when she came, how to prevent her seeing Amy, which was an article as material as any of the rest; for seeing Amy would have been as fatal to me as her knowing all the rest.

As to the first of these, I knew the captain could not stay in town above a week, but that his ship being already full of goods, and fallen down the river, he must soon follow, so I contrived to carry my husband somewhere out of town for a few days, that they might be sure not to meet.

My greatest concern was where we should go. At last I fixed upon North Hall; not, I said, that I would drink the waters, but that I thought the air was good and might be for my advantage. He, who did everything upon the foundation of obliging me, readily came into it, and the coach was appointed to be ready the next morning; but as we were settling matters, he put in an ugly word that thwarted all my design, and that was that he had rather I would stay till afternoon, for that he should speak to the captain the next morning if he could, to give him some letters, which he could do and be back again about twelve o'clock.

I said, "Ay, by all means." But it was but a cheat on him, and my voice and my heart differed; for I resolved, if possible, he should not come near the captain, nor see him, whatever came of it.

In the evening, therefore, a little before we went to bed, I pretended to have altered my mind, and that I would not go to North Hall, but I had a mind to go another way, but I told him I was afraid his business would not permit him. He wanted to know where it was. I told him, smiling, I would not tell him, lest it should oblige him to hinder his business. He answered with the same temper, but with infinitely more sincerity, that he had no business of so much consequence as to hinder him going with me anywhere that I had a mind to go. "Yes," says I, "you want to speak with the captain before he goes away." "Why, that's true," says he, "so I do," and paused a-while and then added, "but I'll write a note to a man that does business for me to go to him; 'tis only to get some bills of loading signed, and he can do it." When I saw I had gained my point, I seemed to hang back a little. "My dear," says I, "don't hinder an hour's business for me; I can put it off for a week or two rather than you shall do yourself any prejudice." "No, no," says he, "you shall not put it off an hour for me, for I can do my business by proxy with anybody but my wife." And then he took me in his arms and kissed me. How did my blood flush up into my face when I reflected how sincerely, how affectionately, this good-humoured gentleman embraced the most cursed piece of hypocrisy that ever came into the arms of an honest man! His was all tenderness, all kindness, and the utmost sincerity; mine all grimace and deceit—a piece of mere manage and framed conduct to conceal a past life of wickedness, and prevent his discovering that he had in his arms a she-devil, whose whole conversation for twenty-five years had been black as hell, a complication of crime, and for which, had he been let into it, he must have abhorred me and the very mention of my name. But there was no help for me in it; all I had to satisfy myself was that it was my business to be what I was, and conceal what I had been; that all the satisfaction I could make him was to live virtuously for the time to come, not being able to retrieve what had been in time past; and this I resolved upon, though, had the great temptation offered, as it did afterwards, I had reason to question my stability. But of that hereafter.

After my husband had kindly thus given up his measures to mine, we resolved to set out in the morning early. I told him that my project, if he liked it, was to go to Tunbridge, and he, being entirely passive in the thing, agreed to it with the greatest willingness; but said if I had not named Tunbridge, he would have named Newmarket, there being a great court there, and abundance of fine things to be seen. I offered him another piece of hypocrisy here, for I pretended to be willing to go thither, as the place of his choice, but indeed I would not have gone for a thousand pounds; for the court being there at that time, I durst not run the hazard of being known at a place where there were so many eyes that had seen me before. So that, after some time, I told my husband that I thought Newmarket was so full of people at that time that we should get no accommodation; that seeing the court and the crowd was no entertainment at all to me, unless as it might be so to him, that if he thought fit, we would rather put it off to another time; and that if, when we went to Holland, we should go by Harwich, we might take a round by Newmarket and Bury, and so come down to Ipswich, and go from thence to the sea-side. He was easily put off from this, as he was from anything else that I did not approve; and so, with all imaginable facility, he appointed to be ready early in the morning to go with me for Tunbridge.

I had a double design in this, viz., first, to get away my spouse from seeing the captain any-more; and secondly, to be out of the way myself, in case this impertinent girl, who was now my plague, should offer to come again, as my friend the Quaker believed she would, and as indeed happened within two or three days afterwards.

Having thus secured my going away the next day, I had nothing to do but to furnish my faithful agent the Quaker with some instructions what to say to this tormentor (for such she proved afterwards), and how to manage her, if she made any more visits than ordinary.

I had a great mind to leave Amy behind too, as an assistant, because she understood so perfectly well what to advise upon any emergence; and Amy importuned me to do so. But I know not what secret impulse prevailed over my thoughts against it; I could not do it for fear the wicked jade should make her away, which my very soul abhorred the thoughts of; which, however, Amy found means to bring to pass afterwards, as I may in time relate more particularly.

It is true I wanted as much to be delivered from her as ever a sick man did from a third-day ague; and had she dropped into the grave by any fair way, as I may call it, I mean, had she died by any ordinary distemper, I should have shed but very few tears for her. But I was not arrived to such a pitch of obstinate wickedness as to commit murder, especially such as to murder my own child, or so much as to harbour a thought so barbarous in my mind. But, as I said, Amy effected all afterwards without my knowledge, for which I gave her my hearty curse, though I could do little more; for to have fallen upon Amy had been to have murdered myself. But this tragedy requires a longer story than I have room for here. I return to my journey.

My dear friend the Quaker was kind, and yet honest, and would do anything that was just and upright to serve me, but nothing wicked or dishonourable. That she might be able to say boldly to the creature, if she came, she did not know where I was gone, she desired I would not let her know; and to make her ignorance the more absolutely safe to herself, and likewise to me, I allowed her to say that she heard us talk of going to Newmarket, &c. She liked that part, and I left all the rest to her, to act as she thought fit; only charged her that if the girl entered into the story of the Pall-Mall, she should not entertain much talk about it, but let her understand that we all thought she spoke of it a little too particularly; and that the lady (meaning me) took it a little ill to be so likened to a public mistress, or a stage-player, and the like; and so to bring her, if possible, to say no more of it. However, though I did not tell my friend the Quaker how to write to me, or where I was, yet I left a sealed paper with her maid to give her, in which I gave her a direction how to write to Amy and so, in effect, to myself.

It was but a few days after I was gone, but the impatient girl came to my lodgings on pretence to see how I did, and to hear if I intended to go the voyage, and the like. My trusty agent was at home and received her coldly at the door; but told her that the lady, which she supposed she meant, was gone from her house.

This was a full stop to all she could say for a good while;

but as she stood musing some time at the door, considering what to begin a talk upon, she perceived my friend the Quaker looked a little uneasy, as if she wanted to go in and shut the door, which stung her to the quick; and the wary Quaker had not so much as asked her to come in; for seeing her alone, she expected she would be very impertinent and concluded that I did not care how coldly she received her.

But she was not to be put off so. She said if the Lady ———— was not to be spoke with, she desired to speak two or three words with her, meaning my friend the Quaker. Upon that, the Quaker civilly but coldly asked her to walk in, which was what she wanted. Note: She did not carry her into her best parlour, as formerly, but into a little outer room, where the servants usually waited.

By the first of her discourse she did not stick to insinuate as if she believed I was in the house, but was unwilling to be seen; and pressed earnestly that she might speak but two words with me; to which she added earnest entreaties, and at last tears.

"I am sorry," says my good creature the Quaker, "thou hast so ill an opinion of me as to think I would tell thee an untruth, and say that the Lady ———— was gone from my house if she was not! I assure thee I do not use any such method; nor does the Lady ———— desire any such kind of service from me, as I know of. If she had been in the house, I should have told thee so."

She said little to that, but said it was business of the utmost importance that she desired to speak with me about, and then cried again very much.

"Thou seem'st to be sorely afflicted," says the Quaker. "I wish I could give thee any relief; but if nothing will comfort thee but seeing the Lady ————, it is not in my power."

"I hope it is," says she again; "to be sure it is of great consequence to me, so much that I am undone without it."

"Thou troublest me very much to hear thee say so," says the Quaker, "but why, then, didst thou not speak to her apart when thou wast here before?"

"I had no opportunity," says she, "to speak to her alone, and I could not do it in company; if I could have spoken but two words to her alone, I would have thrown myself at her foot and asked her blessing."

"I am surprised at thee; I do not understand thee," says the Quaker.

"Oh!" says she, "stand my friend if you have any charity, or if you have any compassion for the miserable; for I am utterly undone!"

"Thou terrifiest me," says the Quaker, "with such passionate expressions, for verily I cannot comprehend thee."

"Oh!" says she, "she is my mother; she is my mother and she does not own me."

"Thy mother!" says the Quaker, and began to be greatly moved indeed. "I am astonished at that. What dost thou mean?"

"I mean nothing but what I say," says she. "I say again, she is my mother and will not own me." And with that she stopped with a flood of tears.

"Not own thee!" says the Quaker, and the tender good creature wept too. "Why," she says, "she does not know thee and never saw thee before."

"No," says the girl, "I believe she does not know me, but I know her; and I know that she is my mother."

"It's impossible, thou talk'st mystery!" says the Quaker. "Wilt thou explain thyself a little to me?"

"Yes, yes," says she, "I can explain it well enough. I am sure she is my mother, and I have broke my heart to search for her; and now to lose her again, when I was so sure I had found her, will break my heart more effectually."

"Well, but if she be thy mother," says the Quaker, "how can it be that she should not know thee?"

"Alas!" says she, "I have been lost to her ever since I was a child; she has never seen me."

"And hast thou never seen her?" says the Quaker.

"Yes," says she, "I have seen her; often enough I saw her; for when she was the Lady Roxana I was her house-maid, being a servant, but I did not know her then, nor she me; but it has all come out since. Has she not a maid named Amy?" (Note: The honest Quaker was nonplussed and greatly surprised at that question.)

"Truly," says she, "the Lady —— has several women servants, but I do not know all their names."

"But her woman, her favourite," adds the girl, "is not her name Amy?"

"Why, truly," says the Quaker, with a very happy turn of wit, "I do not like to be examined; but lest thou shouldst take up any mistakes by reason of my backwardness to speak, I will answer thee for once that what her woman's name is I know not, but they call her Cherry."

N.B. My husband gave her that name in jest on our wedding-day, and we had called her by it ever after; so that she spoke literally true at that time.

The girl replied very modestly that she was sorry if she gave her any offence in asking; that she did not design to be rude to her or pretend to examine her, but that she was in such an agony at this disaster that she knew not what she did or said; and that she should be very sorry to disoblige her, but begged of her again, as she was a Christian and a woman, and had been a mother of children, that she would take pity on her and, if possible, assist her, so that she might but come to me and speak a few words to me.

The tender-hearted Quaker told me the girl spoke this with such moving eloquence that it forced tears from her; but she was obliged to say that she neither knew where I was gone or how to write to me; but that if she did ever see me again, she would not fail to give me an account of all she had said to her, or that she should yet think fit to say, and to take my answer to it, if I thought fit to give any.

Then the Quaker took the freedom to ask a few particulars about this wonderful story, as she called it; at which the girl, beginning at the first distresses of my life, and indeed of her own, went through all the history of her miserable education, her service under the Lady Roxana, as she called me, and her relief by Mrs. Amy, with the reasons she had to believe that as Amy owned herself to be the same that lived with her mother, and especially that Amy was the Lady Roxana's maid too, and came out of France with her, she was by those circumstances, and several others in her conversation, as fully convinced that the Lady Roxana was her mother as she was that the Lady ———— at her house (the Quaker's) was the same Roxana that she had been servant to.

My good friend the Quaker, though terribly shocked at the story, and not well knowing what to say, yet was too much my friend to seem convinced in a thing which she did not know to be true, and which, if it was true, she could see plainly I had a mind should not be known; so she turned her discourse to argue the girl out of it. She insisted upon the slender evidence she had of the fact itself, and the rudeness of claiming so near a relation of one so much above her, and of whose concern in it she had no knowledge, at least no sufficient proof; that as the lady at her house was a person above any disguises, so she could not believe that she would deny her being her daughter, if she was really her mother; that she was able sufficiently to have provided for her if she had not a mind to have her known; and, therefore, seeing she had heard all she had said of the Lady Roxana, and was so far from owning herself to be the person, so she had censured that sham lady as a cheat and a common woman; and that 'twas certain she could never be brought to own a name and character she had so justly exposed.

Besides, she told her that her lodger, meaning me, was not a sham lady, but the real wife of a knight-baronet; and that she knew her to be honestly such, and far above such a person as she had described. She then added that she had another reason why it was not very possible to be true. "And that is," says she, "thy age is in the way; for thou acknowledgest that thou art four and twenty years old, and that thou wast the youngest of three of thy mother's children; so that, by thy account, thy mother must be extremely young, or this lady cannot be thy mother; for thou seest," says she, "and any one may see, she is but a young woman now, and cannot be supposed to be above forty years old, if she is so much; and is now big with child at her going into the country; so that I cannot give any credit to thy notion of her being *thy* mother; and if I might counsel thee, it should be to give over that thought, as an improbable story that does but serve to disorder thee, and disturb thy head. For," added she, "I perceive thou art much disturbed indeed."

But this was all nothing; she could be satisfied with nothing but seeing me; but the Quaker defended herself very well, and insisted on it that she could not give her any account of me; and finding her still importunate, she affected at last being a little disgusted that she should not believe her, and added, that indeed, if she had known where I was gone, she would not have given anyone an account of it, unless I had given her orders to do so. "But seeing she has not acquainted me," says she, "where she has gone, 'tis an intimation to me she was not desirous it should be publicly known." And with this she rose up, which was as plain a desiring her to rise up too and be gone as could be expressed, except the downright showing her the door.

Well, the girl rejected all this, and told her she could not indeed expect that she (the Quaker) should be affected with the story she had told her, however moving, or that she should take any pity on her. That it was her misfortune that when she was at the house before, and in the room with me, she did not beg to speak a word with me in private, or throw herself upon the floor at my feet and claim what the affection of a mother would have done for her; but since she had slipped her opportunity, she would wait for another; that she found by her (the Quaker's) talk that she had not quite left her lodgings, but was gone into the country, she supposed for the air; and she was resolved she would take so much knight-errantry upon her that she would visit all the airing-places in the nation, and even all the kingdom over, ay, and Holland too, but she would find me; for she was satisfied she could so convince me that she was my own child that I would not deny it; and she was sure I was so tender and compassionate, I would not let her perish after I was convinced that she was my own flesh and blood; and in saying she would visit all the airing-places in England, she reckoned them all up by name, and began with Tunbridge, the very place I was gone to; then reckoning up Epsom, North Hall, Barnet, Newmarket, Bury, and at last, the Bath; and with this she took her leave.

My faithful agent the Quaker failed not to write to me immediately; but as she was a cunning as well as an honest woman, it presently occurred to her that this was a story which, whether true or false, was not very fit to come to my husband's knowledge; that as she did not know what I might have been, or might have been called in former times, and how far there might have been something or nothing in it, so she thought if it was a secret, I ought to have the telling it myself; and if it was not, it might as well be public afterwards as now; and that, at least, she ought to leave it where she found it, and not hand it forwards to anybody without my consent. These prudent measures were inexpressibly kind, as well as seasonable; for it had been likely enough that her letter might have come publicly to me, and though my husband would not have opened it, yet it would have looked a little odd that I should conceal its contents from him, when I had pretended so much to communicate all my affairs.

In consequence of this wise caution, my good friend only wrote me in few words that the impertinent young woman had been with her, as she expected she would; and that she thought it would be very convenient that, if I could spare

Cherry, I would send her up (meaning Amy), because she found there might be some occasion for her.

As it happened, this letter was enclosed to Amy herself, and not sent by the way I had at first ordered; but it came safe to my hands; and though I was alarmed a little at it, yet I was not acquainted with the danger I was in of an immediate visit from this teasing creature till afterwards; and I run a greater risk, indeed, than ordinary, in that I did not send Amy up under thirteen or fourteen days, believing myself as much concealed at Tunbridge as if I had been at Vienna.

But the concern of my faithful spy (for such my Quaker was now, upon the mere foot of her own sagacity), I say, her concern for me, was my safety in this exigence, when I was, as it were, keeping no guard for myself; for, finding Amy not come up, and that she did not know how soon this wild thing might put her designed ramble in practice, she sent a messenger to the captain's wife's house, where she lodged, to tell her that she wanted to speak with her. She was at the heels of the messenger and came eager for some news; and hoped, she said, the lady (meaning me) had been come to town.

The Quaker, with as much caution as she was mistress of, not to tell a downright lie, made her believe she expected to hear of me very quickly; and frequently, by the by, speaking of being abroad to take the air, talked of the country about Bury, how pleasant it was, how wholesome, and how fine an air; how the downs about Newmarket were exceeding fine, and what a vast deal of company there was, now the court was there; till at at last the girl began to conclude that my ladyship was gone thither; for, she said, she knew I loved to see a great deal of company.

"Nay," says my friend, "thou takest me wrong. I did not suggest," says she, "that the person thou inquirest after is gone thither; neither do I believe she is, I assure thee." Well, the girl smiled and let her know that she believed it for all that. So, to clench it fast, "Verily," says she, with great seriousness, thou dost not do well, for thou suspectest everything and believest nothing. I speak solemnly to thee that I do not believe they are gone that way; so if thou givest thyself the trouble to go that way and art disappointed, do not say that I have deceived thee." She knew well enough that if this did abᵒᵗ her suspicion, it would not remove it, and that it would ᵉ more than amuse her; but by this she kept her in sus-ᵗ'll Amy came up, and that was enough.

When Amy came up, she was quite confounded to hear the relation which the Quaker gave her, and found means to acquaint me of it; only letting me know, to my great satisfaction, that she would not come to Tunbridge first, but that she would certainly go to Newmarket or Bury first.

However, it gave me very great uneasiness; for as she resolved to ramble in search after me over the whole country, I was safe nowhere, no, not in Holland itself. So indeed I did not know what to do with her; and thus I had a bitter in all my sweet, for I was continually perplexed with this hussy, and thought she haunted me like an evil spirit.

In the meantime Amy was next door to stark-mad about her; she durst not see her at my lodgings for her life; and she went days without number to Spitalfields, where she used to come, and to her former lodging, and could never meet with her. At length she took up a mad resolution that she would go directly to the captain's house in Redriff and speak with her. It was a mad step, that's true; but as Amy said she was mad, so nothing she could do could be otherwise. For if Amy had found her at Redriff, she (the girl) would have concluded presently that the Quaker had given her notice, and so that we were all of a knot; and that, in short, all she had said was right. But as it happened, things came to hit better than we expected; for that Amy going out of a coach to take water at Tower Wharf, meets the girl just come on-shore, having crossed the water from Redriff. Amy made as if she would have passed by her, though they met so full that she did not pretend she did not see her, for she looked fairly upon her first, but then turning her head away with a slight, offered to go from her; but the girl stopped, and spoke first, and made some manners to her.

Amy spoke coldly to her, and a little angry; and after some words, standing in the street or passage, the girl saying she seemed to be angry, and would not have spoken to her, "Why," says Amy, "how can you expect I should have anymore to say to you after I had done so much for you, and you have behaved so to me?" The girl seemed to take no notice of that now, but answered, "I was going to wait on you now." "Wait on me!" says Amy. "What do you mean by that?" "Why," says she again, with a kind of familiarity, "I was going to your lodgings."

Amy was provoked to the last degree at her, and yet she thought it was not her time to resent, because she had a more fatal and wicked design in her head against her; which, indeed, I never knew till after it was executed, nor durst Amy ever communicate it to me; for as I had always expressed myself vehemently against hurting a hair of her head, so she was resolved to take her own measures without consulting me any-more.

In order to this, Amy gave her good words, and concealed her resentment as much as she could; and when she talked of going to her lodging, Amy smiled and said nothing, but called for a pair of oars to go to Greenwich; and asked her, seeing she said she was going to her lodging, to go along with her, for she was going home and was all alone.

Amy did this with such a stock of assurance that the girl was confounded, and knew not what to say; but the more she hesitated, the more Amy pressed her to go; and talking very kindly to her, told her if she did not go to see her lodgings, she might go to keep her company, and she would pay a boat to bring her back again; so, in a word, Amy prevailed on her to go into the boat with her, and carried her down to Greenwich.

'Tis certain that Amy had no more business at Greenwich than I had, nor was she going thither; but we were all hampered to the last degree with the impertinence of this creature; and, in particular, I was horribly perplexed with it.

As they were in the boat, Amy began to reproach her with ingratitude in treating her so rudely who had done so much for her, and been so kind to her; and to ask her what she had got by it, or what she expected to get. Then came in my share, the Lady Roxana. Amy jested with that, and bantered her a little, and asked her if she had found her yet.

But Amy was both surprised and enraged when the girl told her roundly that she thanked her for what she had done for her, but that she would not have her think she was so ignorant as not to know that what she (Amy) had done was by her mother's order, and who she was beholden to for it. That she could never make instruments pass for principals, and pay the debt to the agent when the obligation was all to the original. That she knew well enough who she was, and who she was employed by. That she knew the Lady ———— very well (naming the name that I now went by), which was my husband's true name, and by which she might know whether she had found out her mother or no.

Amy wished her at the bottom of the Thames; and had

there been no watermen in the boat, and nobody in sight, she swore to me she would have thrown her into the river. I was horribly disturbed when she told me this story and began to think this would, at last, all end in my ruin; but when Amy spoke of throwing her into the river and drowning her, I was so provoked at her that all my rage turned against Amy, and I fell thoroughly out with her. I had now kept Amy almost thirty years, and found her on all occasions the faithfullest creature to me that ever woman had—I say, faithful to me; for, however wicked she was, still she was true to me; and even this rage of hers was all upon my account, and for fear any mischief should befall me.

But be that how it would, I could not bear the mention of her murdering the poor girl, and it put me so beside myself that I rose up in a rage, and bade her get out of my sight and out of my house; told her I had kept her too long, and that I would never see her face more. I had before told her that she was a murderer, and a bloody-minded creature; that she could not but know that I could not bear the thought of it, much less the mention of it; and that it was the impudentest thing that ever was known, to make such a proposal to me, when she knew that I was really the mother of this girl, and that she was my own child; that it was wicked enough in her, but that she must conclude I was ten times wickeder than herself if I could come into it; that the girl was in the right, and I had nothing to blame her for; but that it was owing to the wickedness of my life that made it necessary for me to keep her from a discovery; but that I would not murder my child, though I was otherwise to be ruined by it. Amy replied, somewhat rough and short, Would I not? But she would, she said, if she had an opportunity; and upon these words it was that I bade her get out of my sight and out of my house; and it went so far that Amy packed up her alls, and marched off, and was gone for almost good-and-all. But of that in its order; I must go back to her relation of the voyage which they made to Greenwich together.

They held on the wrangle all the way by water; the girl insisted upon her knowing that I was her mother, and told her all the history of my life in the Pall-Mall, as well after her being turned away as before, and of my marriage since; and, which was worse, not only who my present husband was, but where he had lived, viz., at Rouen in France. She knew nothing of Paris or of where we were going to live, namely, at Nimeguen; but told her in so many words that if she could not find me here, she would go to Holland after me.

They landed at Greenwich, and Amy carried her into the park with her, and they walked above two hours there in the farthest and remotest walks; which Amy did because, as they talked with great heat, it was apparent they were quarrelling, and the people took notice of it.

They walked till they came almost to the wilderness at the south side of the park; but the girl, perceiving Amy offered to go in there among the woods and trees, stopped short there and would go no further; but said she would not go in there.

Amy smiled, and asked her what was the matter. She replied short, she did not know where she was, nor where she was going to carry her, and she would go no farther; and without any-more ceremony, turns back and walks apace away from her. Amy owned she was surprised, and came back too, and called to her, upon which the girl stopped, and Amy coming up to her, asked her what she meant.

The girl boldly replied she did not know but she might murder her; and that, in short, she would not trust herself with her, and never would come into her company again alone.

It was very provoking, but, however, Amy kept her temper with much difficulty, and bore it, knowing that much might depend upon it; so she mocked her foolish jealousy, and told her she need not be uneasy for her, she would do her no harm, and would have done her good if she would have let her; but since she was of such a refractory humour, she should not trouble herself, for she should never come into her company again; and that neither she or her brother or sister should ever hear from her or see her any-more; and so she should have the satisfaction of being the ruin of her brother and sister as well as of herself.

The girl seemed a little mollified at that, and said that for herself, she knew the worst of it, she could seek her fortune; but 'twas hard her brother and sister should suffer on her score; and said something that was tender and well enough on that account. But Amy told her it was for her to take that into consideration; for she would let her see that it was all her own; that she would have done them all good, but that having been used thus, she would do no more for any of them; and that she should not need to be afraid to come into her company again, for she would never give her occasion for it any-more. By the way, this was false in the girl too; for she did venture into Amy's company again after that, once too much, as I shall relate by itself.

They grew cooler, however, afterwards, and Amy carried her into a house at Greenwich, where she was acquainted, and took an occasion to leave the girl in a room a-while, to speak to the people in the house, and so prepare them to own her as a lodger in the house; and then going in to her again told her there she lodged, if she had a mind to find her out, or if anybody else had anything to say to her. And so Amy dismissed her and got rid of her again; and finding an empty hackney-coach in the town, came away by land to London, and the girl, going down to the water-side, came by boat.

This conversation did not answer Amy's end at all, because it did not secure the girl from pursuing her design of hunting me out; and though my indefatigable friend the Quaker amused her three or four days, yet I had such notice of it at last that I thought fit to come away from Tunbridge upon it. And where to go I knew not; but, in short, I went to a little village upon Epping Forest, called Woodford, and took lodgings in a private house, where I lived retired about six weeks, till I thought she might be tired of her search and have given me over.

Here I received an account from my trusty Quaker that the wench had really been at Tunbridge, had found out my lodgings, and had told her tale there in a most dismal tone; that she had followed us, as she thought, to London; but the Quaker had answered her that she knew nothing of it, which was indeed true; and had admonished her to be easy, and not hunt after people of such fashion as we were, as if we were thieves; that she might be assured that since I was not willing to see her, I would not be forced to it; and treating me thus would effectually disoblige me. And with such discourses as these she quieted her; and she (the Quaker) added that she hoped I should not be troubled much more with her.

It was in this time that Amy gave me the history of her Greenwich voyage, when she spoke of drowning and killing the girl in so serious a manner, and with such an apparent resolution of doing it, that, as I said, put me in a rage with her, so that I effectually turned her away from me, as I have said above, and she was gone; nor did she so much as tell me whither or which way she was gone. On the other hand, when

I came to reflect on it that now I had neither assistant or confidant to speak to, or receive the least information from, my friend the Quaker excepted, it made me very uneasy.

I waited and expected and wondered from day to day, still thinking Amy would one time or other think a little and come again, or at least let me hear of her; but for ten days together I heard nothing of her. I was so impatient that I got neither rest by day or sleep by night, and what to do I knew not. I durst not go to town to the Quaker's for fear of meeting that vexatious creature, my girl, and I could get no intelligence where I was; so I got my spouse, upon pretence of wanting her company, to take the coach one day and fetch my good Quaker to me.

When I had her, I durst ask her no questions, nor hardly knew which end of the business to begin to talk of; but of her own accord she told me that the girl had been three or four times haunting her for news from me; and that she had been so troublesome that she had been obliged to show herself a little angry with her; and at last told her plainly that she need give herself no trouble in searching after me by her means, for she (the Quaker) would not tell her if she knew; upon which she refrained a-while. But, on the other hand, she told me it was not safe for me to send my own coach for her to come in, for she had some reason to believe that she (my daughter) watched her door night and day; nay, and watched her too every time she went in and out; for she was so bent upon a discovery that she spared no pains, and she believed she had taken a lodging very near their house for that purpose.

I could hardly give her a hearing of all this for my eagerness to ask for Amy; but I was confounded when she told me she had heard nothing of her. 'Tis impossible to express the anxious thoughts that rolled about in my mind and continually perplexed me about her; particularly I reproached myself with my rashness in turning away so faithful a creature that for so many years had not only been a servant but an agent; and not only an agent, but a friend, and a faithful friend too.

Then I considered too that Amy knew all the secret history of my life; had been in all the intrigues of it, and been a party in both evil and good; and at best there was no policy in it; that as it was very ungenerous and unkind to run things to such an extremity with her, and for an occasion, too, in which all the fault she was guilty of was owing to her excess of care for my safety, so it must be only her steady kindness to me, and an excess of generous friendship for me, that should keep her from ill-using me in return for it; which ill-using me was enough in her power, and might be my utter undoing.

These thoughts perplexed me exceedingly, and what course to take I really did not know. I began, indeed, to give Amy quite over, for she had now been gone above a fortnight, and as she had taken away all her clothes, and her money too, which was not a little, and so had no occasion of that kind to come any-more, so she had not left any word where she was gone, or to which part of the world I might send to hear of her.

And I was troubled on another account too, viz., that my spouse and I too had resolved to do very handsomely for Amy, without considering what she might have got another way at all; but we had said nothing of it to her, and so I thought, as she had not known what was likely to fall in her way, she had not the influence of that expectation to make her come back.

Upon the whole, the perplexity of this girl, who hunted me as if, like a hound, she had had a hot scent, but was now at a fault, I say, that perplexity, and this other part of Amy being gone, issued in this—I resolved to be gone, and go over to Holland; there, I believed, I should be at rest. So I took occasion one day to tell my spouse that I was afraid he might take it ill that I had amused him thus long, and that at last I doubted* I was not with child; and that since it was so, our things being packed up, and all in order for going to Holland, I would go away now when he pleased.

My spouse, who was perfectly easy whether in going or staying, left it all entirely to me; so I considered of it, and began to prepare again for my voyage. But, alas! I was irresolute to the last degree. I was, for want of Amy, destitute; I had lost my right hand; she was my steward, gathered in my rents (I mean my interest money) and kept my accounts, and, in a word, did all my business; and without her, indeed, I knew not how to go away nor how to stay. But an accident thrust itself in here, and that even in Amy's conduct too, which frighted me away, and without her too, in the utmost horror and confusion.

* "doubted." Feared.

I have related how my faithful friend the Quaker was come to me, and what account she gave me of her being continually haunted by my daughter; and that, as she said, she watched her very door night and day. The truth was, she had set a spy to watch so effectually that she (the Quaker) neither went in or out but she had notice of it.

This was too evident when, the next morning after she came to me (for I kept her all night), to my unspeakable surprise I saw a hackney-coach stop at the door where I lodged, and saw her (my daughter) in the coach all alone. It was a very good chance, in the middle of a bad one, that my husband had taken out the coach that very morning, and was gone to London. As for me, I had neither life or soul left in me; I was so confounded I knew not what to do or to say.

My happy visitor had more presence of mind than I, and asked me if I had made no acquaintance among the neighbours. I told her, yes, there was a lady lodged two doors off that I was very intimate with. "But hast thou no way out backward to go to her?" says she. Now it happened there was a back-door in the garden, by which we usually went and came to and from the house, so I told her of it. "Well, well," says she, "go out and make a visit then, and leave the rest to me." Away I run, told the lady (for I was very free there) that I was a widow to-day, my spouse being gone to London, so I came not to visit her, but to dwell with her that day, because also our landlady had got strangers come from London. So, having framed this orderly lie, I pulled some work out of my pocket and added I did not come to be idle.

As I went out one way, my friend the Quaker went the other to receive this unwelcome guest. The girl made but little ceremony, but having bid the coachman ring at the gate, gets down out of the coach and comes to the door, a country girl going to the door (belonging to the house), for the Quaker forbid any of my maids going. Madam asked for my Quaker by name, and the girl asked her to walk in.

Upon this, my Quaker, seeing there was no hanging back, goes to her immediately, but put all the gravity upon her countenance that she was mistress of, and that was not a little indeed.

When she (the Quaker) came into the room (for they had showed my daughter into a little parlour), she kept her grave countenance but said not a word, nor did my daughter speak a good while; but after some time my girl began and said, "I suppose you know me, madam?"

"Yes," says the Quaker, "I know thee." And so the dialogue went on.

Girl. Then you know my business too?

Quaker. No, verily, I do not know any business thou canst have here with me.

Girl. Indeed, my business is not chiefly with you.

Qu. Why, then, dost thou come after me thus far?

Girl. You know who I seek. [*And with that she cried.*]

Qu. But why shouldst thou follow me for her, since thou know'st that I assured thee more than once that I knew not where she was?

Girl. But I hoped you could.

Qu. Then thou must hope that I did not speak truth, which would be very wicked.

Girl. I doubt not but she is in this house.

Qu. If those be thy thoughts, thou may'st inquire in the house; so thou hast no more business with me. Farewell! (*Offers to go.*)

Girl. I would not be uncivil; I beg you to let me see her.

Qu. I am here to visit some of my friends, and I think thou art not very civil in following me hither.

Girl. I came in hopes of a discovery in my great affair, which you know of.

Qu. Thou cam'st wildly, indeed; I counsel thee to go back again, and be easy; I shall keep my word with thee, that I would not meddle in it, or give thee any account, if I knew it, unless I had her orders.

Girl. If you knew my distress, you could not be so cruel.

Qu. Thou hast told me all thy story, and I think it might be more cruelty to tell thee than not to tell thee; for I understand she is resolved not to see thee, and declares she is not thy mother. Will'st thou be owned where thou hast no relation?

Girl. Oh, if I could but speak to her, I would prove my relation to her so that she could not deny it any longer.

Qu. Well, but thou canst not come to speak with her, it seems.

Girl. I hope you will tell me if she is here. I had a good account that you were come out to see her, and that she sent for you.

Qu. I much wonder how thou couldst have such an ac-

count. If I had come out to see her, thou hast happened to
miss the house, for I assure thee she is not to be found in this
house.

Here the girl importuned her again with the utmost earnestness, and cried bitterly, insomuch that my poor Quaker
was softened with it, and began to persuade me to consider
of it, and, if it might consist with my affairs, to see her, and
hear what she had to say; but this was afterwards. I return to
the discourse.

The Quaker was perplexed with her a long time; she talked
of sending back the coach and lying in the town all night.
This, my friend knew, would be very uneasy to me, but she
durst not speak a word against it; but on a sudden thought,
she offered a bold stroke, which, though dangerous if it had
happened wrong, had its desired effect.

She told her that, as for dismissing her coach, that was as
she pleased, she believed she would not easily get a lodging in
the town; but that as she was in a strange place, she would so
much befriend her that she would speak to the people of the
house, that if they had room, she might have a lodging there
for one night, rather than be forced back to London before
she was free to go.

This was a cunning, though a dangerous step, and it
succeeded accordingly, for it amused the creature entirely,
and she presently concluded that really I could not be there
then, otherwise she would never have asked her to lie in the
house. So she grew cold again presently as to her lodging
there, and said, No, since it was so, she would go back that
afternoon, but she would come again in two or three days,
and search that and all the towns round in an effectual manner, if she stayed a week or two to do it; for, in short, if I
was in England or Holland she would find me.

"In truth," says the Quaker, "thou wilt make me very hurt-
ful to thee, then." "Why so?" says she. "Because wherever I
go, thou wilt put thyself to great expense, and the country to
a great deal of unnecessary trouble." "Not unnecessary," says
she. "Yes, truly," says the Quaker, "it must be unnecessary,
because 'twill be to no purpose. I think I must abide in my
own house to save thee that charge and trouble."

She said little to that, except that, she said, she would give
her as little trouble as possible; but she was afraid she should
sometimes be uneasy to her, which she hoped she would excuse. My Quaker told her she would much rather excuse her

if she would forbear; for that if she would believe her, she would assure her she should never get any intelligence of me by her.

That set her into tears again; but after a-while, recovering herself, she told her perhaps she might be mistaken; and she (the Quaker) should watch herself very narrowly, or she might one time or other get some intelligence from her, whether she would or no; and she was satisfied she had gained some of her by this journey, for that if I was not in the house, I was not far off; and if I did not remove very quickly, she would find me out. "Very well," says my Quaker, "then if the lady is not willing to see thee, thou givest me notice to tell her that she may get out of thy way."

She flew out in a rage at that, and told my friend that if she did, a curse would follow her, and her children after her, and denounced such horrid things upon her as frighted the poor tender-hearted Quaker strangely, and put her more out of temper than ever I saw her before; so that she resolved to go home the next morning, and I, that was ten times more uneasy than she, resolved to follow her and go to London too; which, however, upon second thoughts, I did not, but took effectual measures not to be seen or owned if she came any-more; but I heard no more of her for some time.

I stayed there about a fortnight, and in all that time I heard no more of her, or of my Quaker about her; but after about two days more, I had a letter from my Quaker, intimating that she had something of moment to say, that she could not communicate by letter, but wished I would give myself the trouble to come up, directing me to come with the coach into Goodman's Fields, and then walk to her back-door on foot, which being left open on purpose, the watchful lady, if she had any spies, could not well see me.

My thoughts had for so long time been kept, as it were, waking, that almost everything gave me the alarm, and this especially, so that I was very uneasy; but I could not bring matters to bear to make my coming to London so clear to my husband as I would have done; for he liked the place and had a mind, he said, to stay a little longer, if it was not against my inclination; so I wrote my friend the Quaker word that I could not come to town yet; and that, besides, I could not think of being there under spies, and afraid to look out-of-doors; and so, in short, I put off going for near a fortnight more.

At the end of that time she wrote again, in which she told me that she had not lately seen the impertinent visitor which had been so troublesome; but that she had seen my trusty agent, Amy, who told her she had cried for six weeks without intermission; that Amy had given her an account how troublesome the creature had been, and to what straits and perplexities I was driven by her hunting after and following me from place to place; upon which Amy had said, that notwithstanding I was angry with her, and had used her so hardly for saying something about her of the same kind, yet there was an absolute necessity of securing her, and removing her out of the way; and that, in short, without asking my leave, or anybody's leave, she would take care she should trouble her mistress (meaning me) no more; and that after Amy had said so, she had indeed never heard any-more of the girl; so that she supposed Amy had managed it so well as to put an end to it.

The innocent, well-meaning creature, my Quaker, who was all kindness and goodness in herself, and particularly to me, saw nothing in this; but she thought Amy had found some way to persuade her to be quiet and easy, and to give over teasing and following me, and rejoiced in it for my sake; as she thought nothing of any evil herself, so she suspected none in anybody else, and was exceeding glad of having such good news to write to me. But my thoughts of it run otherwise.

I was struck, as with a blast from heaven, at the reading her letter; I fell into a fit of trembling from head to foot, and I ran raving about the room like a mad-woman. I had nobody to speak a word to, to give vent to my passion; nor did I speak a word for a good while, till after it had almost overcome me. I threw myself on the bed and cried out, "Lord, be merciful to me, she has murdered my child!" and with that a flood of tears burst out, and I cried vehemently for above an hour.

My husband was very happily gone out a-hunting, so that I had the opportunity of being alone, and to give my passions some vent, by which I a little recovered myself. But after my crying was over, then I fell in a new rage at Amy. I called her a thousand devils and monsters and hard-hearted tigers; I reproached her with her knowing that I abhorred it, and had let her know it sufficiently, in that I had, as it were, kicked her out of doors, after so many years' friendship and service, only for naming it to me.

Well, after some time, my spouse came in from his sport, and I put on the best looks I could to deceive him; but he did not take so little notice of me as not to see I had been crying, and that something troubled me, and he pressed me to tell him. I seemed to bring it out with reluctance, but told him my backwardness was more because I was ashamed that such a trifle should have any effect upon me than for any weight that was in it; so I told him I had been vexing myself about my woman Amy's not coming again; that she might have known me better than not to believe I should have been friends with her again, and the like; and that, in short, I had lost the best servant by my rashness that ever woman had.

"Well, well," says he, "if that be all your grief, I hope you will soon shake it off; I'll warrant you in a little while we shall hear of Mrs. Amy again." And so it went off for that time. But it did not go off with me; for I was uneasy and terrified to the last degree, and wanted to get some farther account of the thing. So I went away to my sure and certain comforter, the Quaker, and there I had the whole story of it; and the good innocent Quaker gave me joy of my being rid of such an unsufferable tormentor.

"Rid of her! Ay," says I, "if I was rid of her fairly and honourably; but I don't know what Amy may have done. Sure, she ha'n't made her away?" "Oh fie!" says my Quaker. "How canst thou entertain such a notion! No, no. Made her away? Amy didn't talk like that; I dare say thou may'st be easy in that; Amy has nothing of that in her head, I dare say," says she; and so threw it, as it were, out of my thoughts.

But it would not do; it run in my head continually; night and day I could think of nothing else; and it fixed such a horror of the fact upon my spirits, and such a detestation of Amy, who I looked upon as the murderer, that, as for her, I believe if I could have seen her, I should certainly have sent her to Newgate, or to a worse place, upon suspicion; indeed, I think I could have killed her with my own hands.

As for the poor girl herself, she was ever before my eyes; I saw her by night and by day; she haunted my imagination, if she did not haunt the house; my fancy showed me her in a hundred shapes and postures; sleeping or waking, she was with me. Sometimes I thought I saw her with her throat cut; sometimes with her head cut, and her brains knocked out; other times hanged up upon a beam; another time drowned in the great pond at Camberwell. And all these appearances were terrifying to the last degree; and that which was still worse, I could really hear nothing of her; I sent to the captain's wife in Redriff, and she answered me, she was gone to her relations in Spitalfields. I sent thither, and they said she was there about three weeks ago, but that she went out in a coach with the gentlewoman that used to be so kind to her, but whither she was gone they knew not, for she had not been there since. I sent back the messenger for a description of the woman she went out with, and they described her so perfectly that I knew it to be Amy, and none but Amy.

I sent word again that Mrs. Amy, who she went out with, left her in two or three hours, and that they should search for her, for I had a reason to fear she was murdered. This frighted them all intolerably. They believed Amy had carried her to pay her a sum of money, and that somebody had watched her after her having received it, and had robbed and murdered her.

I believed nothing of that part; but I believed, as it was, that whatever was done, Amy had done it; and that, in short, Amy had made her away; and I believed it the more, because Amy came no more near me, but confirmed her guilt by her absence.

Upon the whole, I mourned thus for her for above a month; but finding Amy still come not near me, and that I must put my affairs in a posture that I might go to Holland, I opened all my affairs to my dear trusty friend the Quaker, and placed her, in matters of trust, in the room of Amy; and with a heavy, bleeding heart for my poor girl, I embarked with my spouse, and all our equipage and goods, on-board another Holland's trader, not a packet-boat, and went over to Holland, where I arrived, as I have said.

I must put in a caution, however, here, that you must not understand me as if I let my friend the Quaker into any part of the secret history of my former life; nor did I commit the grand reserved article of all to her, viz., that I was really the girl's mother, and the Lady Roxana; there was no need of that part being exposed; and it was always a maxim with me that secrets should never be opened without evident utility. It could be of no manner of use to me or her to communicate that part to her; besides, she was too honest herself to make it safe to me; for though she loved me very sincerely, and it was plain by many circumstances that she did so, yet she would not lie for me upon occasion, as Amy would, and therefore it was not advisable on any terms to communicate that part; for if the girl, or any one else, should have come to her afterwards, and put it home to her, whether she knew that I was the girl's mother or not, or was the same as the Lady Roxana or not, she either would not have denied it, or would have done it with so ill a grace, such blushing, such hesitations and falterings in her answers, as would have put the matter out of doubt, and betrayed herself and the secret too.

For this reason, I say, I did not discover anything of that kind to her; but I placed her, as I have said, in Amy's stead in the other affairs of receiving money, interests, rents, and the like, and she was as faithful as Amy could be, and as diligent.

But there fell out a great difficulty here, which I knew not how to get over; and this was how to convey the usual supply of provision and money to the uncle and the other sister, who depended, especially the sister, upon the said supply for her support; and indeed, though Amy had said rashly that she would not take any more notice of the sister, and would leave her to perish, as above, yet it was neither in my nature, or Amy's either, much less was it in my design; and therefore I resolved to leave the management of what I had reserved for that work with my faithful Quaker, but how to direct her to manage them was the great difficulty.

Amy had told them in so many words that she was not their mother, but that she was the maid Amy, that carried them to their aunt's; that she and their mother went over to the East Indies to seek their fortune, and that there good things had befallen them, and that their mother was very rich and happy; that she (Amy) had married in the Indies, but being now a widow, and resolving to come over to England, their mother had obliged her to inquire them out, and do for them as she had done; and that now she was resolved to go back to the Indies again; but that she had orders from their mother to do very handsomely by them; and, in a word, told them she had £2000 a-piece for them, upon condition that they proved sober, and married suitably to themselves, and did not throw themselves away upon scoundrels.

The good family in whose care they had been, I had resolved to take more than ordinary notice of; and Amy, by my order, had acquainted them with it, and obliged my daughters to promise to submit to their government, as formerly, and to be ruled by the honest man as by a father and counsellor; and engaged him to treat them as his children. And to oblige him effectually to take care of them, and to make his old age comfortable both to him and his wife, who had been so good to the orphans, I had ordered her to settle the other £2000, that is to say, the interest of it, which was £120 a year, upon them, to be theirs for both their lives, but to come to my two daughters after them. This was so just, and was so prudently managed by Amy, that nothing she ever did for me pleased me better. And in this posture, leaving my two daughters with their ancient friend, and so coming away to me (as they thought to the East Indies), she had prepared everything in order to her going over with me to Holland; and in this posture that matter stood when that unhappy girl, who I have said so much of, broke in upon all our measures, as you have heard, and, by an obstinacy never to be conquered or pacified, either with threats or persuasions, pursued her search after me (her mother) as I have said, till she brought me even to the brink of destruction; and would, in all probability, have traced me out at last, if Amy had not, by the violence of her passion, and by a way which I had no knowledge of, and indeed abhorred, put a stop to her, of which I cannot enter into the particulars here.

However, notwithstanding this, I could not think of going away and leaving this work so unfinished as Amy had threatened to do, and for the folly of one child to leave the other to starve, or to stop my determined bounty to the good family I have mentioned. So, in a word, I committed the finishing it all to my faithful friend the Quaker, to whom I communicated as much of the old story as was needful to empower her to perform what Amy had promised, and to make her talk so much to the purpose, as one employed more remotely than Amy had been needed to do.

To this purpose she had, first of all, a full possession of the money; and went first to the honest man and his wife and settled all the matter with them; when she talked of Mrs. Amy, she talked of her as one that had been empowered by the mother of the girls in the Indies, but was obliged to go back to the Indies, and had settled all sooner if she had not been hindered by the obstinate humour of the other daughter; that she had left instructions with her for the rest; but that the other had affronted her so much that she was gone away without doing anything for her; and that now, if anything was done, it must be by fresh orders from the East Indies.

I need not say how punctually my new agent acted; but, which was more, she brought the old man and his wife, and my other daughter, several times to her house, by which I had an opportunity, being there only as a lodger, and a stranger, to see my other girl, which I had never done before, since she was a little child.

The day I contrived to see them I was dressed up in a Quaker's habit, and looked so like a Quaker that it was impossible for them, who had never seen me before, to suppose I had ever been anything else; also my way of talking was suitable enough to it, for I had learned that long before.

I have not time here to take notice what a surprise it was to me to see my child; how it worked upon my affections; with what infinite struggle I mastered a strong inclination that I had to discover myself to her; how the girl was the very counterpart of myself, only much handsomer; and how sweetly and modestly she behaved; how, on that occasion, I resolved to do more for her than I had appointed by Amy, and the like.

'Tis enough to mention here that as the settling this affair made way for my going on-board, notwithstanding the absence of my old agent Amy, so, however, I left some hints for Amy too, for I did not yet despair of my hearing from her; and that if my good Quaker should ever see her again, she should let her see them; wherein, particularly, ordering her to leave the affair of Spitalfields just as I had done, in the hands of my friend, she should come away to me; upon this condition, nevertheless, that she gave full satisfaction to my friend the Quaker that she had not murdered my child; for if she had, I told her I would never see her face more. However, notwithstanding this, she came over afterwards, without giving my friend any of that satisfaction or any account that she intended to come over.

I can say no more now, but that, as above, being arrived in Holland, with my spouse and his son, formerly mentioned, I appeared there with all the splendour and equipage suitable to our new prospect, as I have already observed.

Here, after some few years of flourishing and outwardly happy circumstances, I fell into a dreadful course of calamities, and Amy also; the very reverse of our former good days. The blast of Heaven seemed to follow the injury done the poor girl by us both, and I was brought so low again that my repentance seemed to be only the consequence of my misery, as my misery was of my crime.

Afterword

❧❧❧

When Roxana refuses to marry the Dutch merchant who has made love to her, she challenges two basic assumptions of her time: that marriage is necessarily desirable for women and that a woman who has lost her chastity has lost everything. Though she immediately condemns herself for immorality, Daniel Defoe lets us see the force of her arguments. Traditional British law pronounced man and wife one person; in effect, this person was the husband. The law gave him total control of the family property, and the Church told him his wife was obliged to obey him in all secular matters. Roxana points out that a woman, born as free as a man, makes herself a servant by marrying, since she must promise to obey her husband; indeed, she is more like a slave, since marriage cannot be dissolved. The merchant answers that the woman still profits, since the man takes on the whole care and responsibility for the household, leaving her free to enjoy his earnings. Roxana of course knows better from her own marriage, and in any case does not want a life of passive ease. She thinks a woman can enjoy self-direction and independence quite as well as a man; she might even take a lover, as a man takes a mistress. He can only appeal to custom and claim that mutual love rules out the possibility of bondage. She trenchantly cuts through this sentimental argument: "the pretence of affection takes from a woman every thing that can be called *herself*"; her interests are submerged in her husband's, she becomes dependent on him, and is reduced to a "passive creature," who lives "by faith not in God, but in her husband."

Their discussion proceeds to expose the intrinsic flaw in an institution that gives disproportionate power to one party, however good his intentions may be. When the merchant offers to let her supervise the family finances, she suspects that she would be nominally supervising while he made the actual decisions; and, in any case, privileges are not worth much when they can be lawfully withdrawn at will. Even though he may be personally trustworthy, she shrewdly recognizes, marriage would give him power over her that would necessarily influence his attitude: Under a law which "commands you to command, and binds me . . . to obey," he could not continue to respect her as a self-governing person.

The merchant assumes that Roxana, having yielded to him sexually, will be eager to marry him in order to patch up her chastity. Her refusal, astoundingly unconventional in her time, shows the liberating effect of disregarding the chastity and reputation that women were trained to value above all else. Had Roxana still cared about these, she would have been in the merchant's power, waiting to seize an opportunity for marriage if he should be so kind as to offer one. As it is, she can plan her life as she sees fit. Moreover, through casting off the conventional sexual inhibitions, she has become free to think unconventionally about women's nature and position in general. She sees a new possibility of freedom and claims it.

Characteristically, Roxana immediately discredits her own motives, declaring that her theoretical objections to the subjection of women are mere rationalizations for her greedy desire to keep her money for herself. But Defoe has given her good arguments, and the merchant's counter-arguments are feeble. Throughout the book, Defoe sets up situations that belie Roxana's explicit comments as first-person narrator. One would like to trust the tale, not the teller, as D. H. Lawrence said, but one cannot be sure whether Defoe meant Roxana's declaration of freedom and equality to be a just claim, as it sounds, or a mere rationalization, as she says.

There is no question but that the book opens with an indictment of the oppression of women in eighteenth-century marriage. Roxana, married at fifteen to a fool her father picked out for her, can do nothing but watch him dissipate the family business and property. Nor is there any way for her to support herself and their five children after he abandons them. And yet, despite this enforced passivity, she is held responsible: Her sister-in-law speaks with the voice of society when she says, "Let her that brought them into the world, look after them if she will." Defoe realized that in a society in which a man controlled the fate of his family, a fool was the worst kind of husband a woman could have. The dependence of able, enterprising Roxana upon this witless wastrel is a devastating comment on patriarchal marriage.

Defoe sets up a situation in which Roxana must choose between starvation and prostitution, and it is hard to believe that he agrees with her that she should prefer the first to the second. Roxana does not acknowledge the extenuating circumstances that Defoe makes plain to the reader, and surely she unduly degrades her satisfying common-law marriage when she calls herself and the jeweler no more than a whore and a rogue. Surely, society is hypocritical in condemning a woman for choosing the only opportunity for survival open to her, and equally hypocritical in claiming that loss of chastity leads to ruin. As a wife, Roxana is helpless and despised; as a mistress, she wins wealth, independence, and power.

What Defoe loses in clarity of moral criticism, from the discrepancy between what his narrator says and what his book seems to mean, he gains in realism. Roxana's self-recriminations may seem disproportionate, but they are entirely in accord with her character. Since respectable women were brought up to believe that chastity was all-important, it is to be expected that she would feel more guilt for committing adultery with the jeweler than for abandoning her children. Her loss of chastity naturally leads to a disastrous loss of self-respect, as we see when she gratuitously forces Amy into bed with her common-law husband. Partly she wants to bring Amy down to her own level as punishment for Amy's having persuaded her to be a prostitute; but also she is debasing herself (and the man) by denying that there is a relationship between them that deserves to be respected. It would not be in character for Roxana to be an advanced feminist thinker. A pragmatist rather than a theorist, she never intellectually frees herself from the belief, relentlessly inculcated by moral authorities in her day, that a woman without chastity is without human worth.

Defoe deals as unsentimentally with prostitution as he does with marriage. Roxana does not live to have orgasms, like Fanny Hill, a typical projection of male fantasy whose adventures John Cleland gave the world in 1748. She is a cold woman, who, having been betrayed by one man, keeps herself from getting emotionally involved with any other. By never mentioning any motive but prudence, obligation, or ambition, she reveals her unawareness that love would be appropriate in a relationship with a man. She takes no pleasure in sexual activity, but wants to acquire property and gratify her pride through being courted by distinguished men. Roxana heaps up property partly as a compulsive reaction against the years of destitution that scarred her as a young woman, but also because it is normal in her materialistic capitalist society. Having accumulated capital in the only way a woman could, she enjoys investing it just like a man who has made money in business. Roxana shares her creator's fascination with commerce and his preference for successful merchants over the landed gentry.

Among eighteenth-century heroines, Roxana, and Defoe's earlier Moll Flanders, are uniquely independent. They make their own way with talent and resourcefulness, freeing themselves from sexual and economic control by men. Roxana, however, is developed with more complexity, for she shows the conflict still felt by "free" women as she is torn between self-fulfillment and obligation to her children. She wants freedom to run her own life, but also she wants the freedom of a clear conscience. She can resist neither the excitement and ego gratification of being a mistress nor the secure self-esteem of being a responsible mother respected by her children. It is not her sins but her attempt to do the right thing by her children that leads to the murder of her daughter, and thus her ruin.

Roxana's conflict is vividly symbolized by the two costumes that she so enjoys wearing: the Turkish harem outfit and the Quaker dress. The Turkish costume suggests freedom (sexual and otherwise), not only because it calls forth associations of Oriental licentiousness, but because, being loose-fitting, it would reveal the natural female form, which in Roxana's time was normally compressed into a tight corset. Quakers wore a distinctively plain dress, abstaining from the ribbons, lace, brocades, and elaborate hair styles customary among fashionable women. Although Roxana characteristically dismisses her wearing of the Quaker costume as a mere expedient, it seems clear that she is genuinely attracted to the innocence and respectability it symbolizes. At the same time, the fact that she keeps and even displays the Turkish costume, an obvious source of danger, shows her reluctance to give up her old life completely. It is significant that her virtuous Quaker friend is also attracted to this costume: A woman need not be abandoned to long for freedom and excitement.

Roxana, like all Defoe's novels, is shaped as an autobiography. Defoe undoubtedly chose this form to give his stories the semblance of factual accounts, to make the sensational events plausible by relating them in the authentic voice of the lifelike, prosaic character who is supposed to have experienced them. The novels actually sound very much like Defoe's journalism and developed naturally from it. An incredibly prolific writer, Defoe had produced newspapers and political pamphlets, economic proposals, lives of notorious criminals, and manuals on domestic relations, such as *The Family Instructor* (1715, 1718) and *Religious Courtship* (1722). He conducted and single-handedly wrote *The Review,* a newspaper that appeared from twice to five times per week from 1704 to 1713, and in a single year, 1722, published *Moll Flanders, Religious Courtship, A Journal of the Plague Year,* and *Colonel Jacque.* Many descriptions and illustrative anecdotes in his domestic journalism are as lively as anything in his fiction, such as a characterization of bad husbands in *The Review,* which culminates in a fool as the worst of all, or the story of a businessman's widow in *The Complete English Tradesman* (1726), who, although respectable, is as successfully enterprising as Moll or Roxana.

From this vivid journalism, Defoe moved almost imperceptibly into fiction presented as fact, as in his recreation of daily life during the bubonic plague epidemic that struck London in 1665, when he was only five years old. This *Journal of the Plague Year* was long accepted as what it purports to be, the eyewitness account of a middle-aged saddler. Through effective use of detail, Defoe gave the same appearance of actuality to the more extraordinary adventures of Robinson Crusoe (1719), Moll Flanders, Colonel Jacque, and Roxana. His skill is particularly apparent in the way he supplies unnecessary information, probable details that do not advance the central fiction but solidify the setting in which it takes place. For example, Defoe specifies that the coach Roxana kept when she was first married was a mock-coach because the horses pulled brewery wagons during the week, and that the pseudo-Oriental dance that won her the name of Roxana pleased better than a genuine Oriental dance performed at the same party.

Defoe's blurred differentiation among factual reports,

moral illustrations, and fiction was natural in his time, when the novel had not yet taken shape as a literary form. Prose fiction, disparaged as subliterary, consisted of romances, which made little pretense of realism, and picaresque tales, which presented a realistic but narrow view of life, sordid and lacking in feeling. Both types are deficient in construction and, more crucially, in character development. Their central characters are too sketchy either to hold the reader's interest or to give emotional force to their adventures.

Defoe's achievement was to create characters so convincing that their adventures seem believable and engage our interest. He did this not only by surrounding them with plausible detail, but by identifying with them to the point that he could imagine their thoughts and feelings in any situation. Unlike earlier protagonists in English fiction, they are interesting, individual human beings—not just vehicles for adventures, but characters shaped by their society and experiences and in turn shaping the course of their own lives.

While Defoe's works provide the solid realism essential to the novel, they lack the artistry of the fully developed form. The chronology of *Roxana* is vague and inconsistent, the impact of its narrative flattened by a tendency to give equal emphasis to crucial and to unimportant events, and its ending abrupt and inconclusive. One reason Defoe could not bring his story to a convincing conclusion was that he was torn between morality and realism: He felt he could not leave Roxana flourishing in spite of her sins, and yet a person of her competence could not realistically fall into destitution.

Yet he did find a powerful solution to the dilemma by punishing her psychologically through the murder of her daughter Susan. Her feelings for the girl are strong, as we see in the shipboard scene when she is stirred to deep pleasure by kissing her, despite her terror that this close contact will lead to discovery; and her guilty visions on realizing Susan has been murdered are genuinely haunting. Roxana's remorse is in every way a fitting punishment: It is sufficient to poison her outward prosperity, and it is morally just because she had wished the girl dead and had originally corrupted Amy, the murderer. Roxana escapes from the consequences of her voluntary crimes—whoring and avarice—but is caught by the effects of the involuntary one. This retribution realistically could strike someone like Roxana, and it is subtle enough to be morally convincing. However, the ending would be more effective if Defoe had focused more consistently on the murder of Susan and its consequences; one wishes for more consistent building of suspense, as in the two long scenes, on shipboard and at the Quaker's house, in which Roxana expects her daughter to expose her at any moment.

Defoe's choice of point of view does more serious damage to the book, since he had not worked out techniques for separating himself from his narrator, as, for example, Mark Twain did in *Huckleberry Finn.* By expressing himself through a woman like Roxana, he imposed her intellectual and moral limitations upon the picture of life he presented. In the fully developed novels of Samuel Richardson and Henry Fielding in the 1740s, action is more satisfactorily concluded, chronology is carefully worked out, and a clearly maintained distinction between the author's view and that of his characters communicates a better developed criticism of life.

Defoe's inadequate presentation of relationships also marks *Roxana* as a primitive novel. Although Roxana herself seems very real, the other characters are shadowy. Few even have names. It is true that Roxana is more convincingly involved with her children than was her predecessor, Moll Flanders, as we see in her painfully mixed feelings toward the daughter who is determined to unearth her past. Susan herself is both sinister and pathetic. She persistently hounds her mother, driven by a compulsion to establish the truth or possibly an intent to blackmail, but at the same time pitifully eager to find the mother she missed as a child. (Her urgent quest suggests the need adopted children have to find their biological parents.) Amy functions effectively as a foil to Roxana, following the same harlot's progress but unhampered by her ladylike inhibitions—her delicacy and her hypocrisy alike. But all the male characters seem to exist simply to fill their allotted functions in Roxana's life.

Defoe's identification with Roxana enabled him to realize her as a character and make her the protagonist of a major novel. In addition, it caused him to look at moral and social issues from a woman's point of view. He recognized the desperate disadvantages under which women had to struggle for survival, and yet he demonstrated that a woman could have sufficient ability and strength to make a satisfying life for herself. He understood that women shared with men a need for excitement, independence, worldly success. His heroine is unmistakably feminine—being both sexually attractive and emotionally enmeshed with her children—but she is motivated by the basic drives of all human beings, male or female. While Roxana's anxiety and remorse show the perils a woman confronts when she breaks out of traditional restrictions, her assertion of a single standard for women and men, however weakened by her own disclaimers, raises exhilarating possibilities of emancipation.

Selected Bibliography

Works by Daniel Defoe

There is no complete edition of Defoe's voluminous writings. The most significant are to be found in:

Defoe, Daniel. *The Best of Defoe's Review*, ed. William L. Payne. New York: Columbia University Press, 1951.

———. *Conjugal Lewdness, or Matrimonial Whoredom* Gainesville, Florida: Scholars' Facsimiles & Reprints, 1967.

———. *An Essay upon Projects*. Menston, England: The Scolar Press, 1969.

———. *The Novels and Selected Writings*. Oxford: Basil Blackwell, 1927-28, 14 vols. (The Shakespeare Head Edition).

Lee, William. *Daniel Defoe; His Life, and Recently Discovered Writings*. London: J. C. Hotten, 1869, 3 vols.

A Journal of the Plague Year (CW 927), *Moll Flanders* (CW 1170), and *Robinson Crusoe* (CW1052) are available in Signet Classic editions.

Works About Daniel Defoe

Dobrée, Bonamy. *English Literature in the Early Eighteenth Century, 1700-1740.* (Vol. VII, *Oxford History of English Literature*). Oxford: Clarendon Press, 1959.

McKillop, Alan Dugald. *The Early Masters of English Fiction.* Lawrence: University of Kansas Press, 1956.

Moore, John Robert. *Daniel Defoe: Citizen of the Modern World.* Chicago: University of Chicago Press, 1958.

Novak, Maximilian E. *Defoe and the Nature of Man.* London: Oxford University Press, 1963.

Richetti, John J. *Defoe's Narratives: Situations and Structures.* London: Oxford University Press, 1975.

Rogers, Katharine M. "The Feminism of Daniel Defoe," *Woman in the 18th Century and Other Essays,* ed. Paul Fritz and Richard Morton. Toronto: Hakkert, 1976.

Sutherland, James. *Defoe.* London: Methuen, 1950.

Watt, Ian. *The Rise of the Novel: Studies in Defoe, Richardson, and Fielding.* Berkeley: University of California Press, 1957.

Woolf, Virginia. "Defoe," *The Common Reader, First Series.* New York: Harcourt, Brace & Co., 1925.

SIGNET CLASSICS by American Authors

☐ **BABBITT by Sinclair Lewis.** Afterword by Mark Schorer.
(#CW1097—$1.50)

☐ **THE SEA-WOLF and Selected Stories by Jack London.**
Afterword by Franklin Walker. (#CW1144—$1.50)

☐ **BILLY BUDD and Other Tales by Herman Melville.** Afterword by Willard Thorp. (#CE1168—$1.75)

☐ **THE CALL OF THE WILD and Selected Stories by Jack London.** Foreword by Franklin Walker. (#CY1074—$1.25)

☐ **MAIN STREET by Sinclair Lewis.** Afterword by Mark Schorer. (#CE1140—$2.25)

☐ **EVANGELINE and Selected Tales and Poems by Henry Wadsworth Longfellow.** Afterword by Horace Gregory.
(#CY1093—$1.25)

☐ **THE FALL OF THE HOUSE OF USHER and Other Tales by Edgar Allen Poe.** Foreword by R. P. Blackmur.
(#CE1164—$1.75)

☐ **THE FINANCIER by Theodore Dreiser.** Afterword by Larzer Ziff. (#CE962—$2.25)

☐ **THE HOUSE OF SEVEN GABLES by Nathaniel Hawthorne.**
Afterword by Edward C. Sampson. (#CY1043—$1.25)

☐ **McTEAGUE by Frank Norris.** Afterword by Kenneth Rexroth. (#CE1119—$1.75)

☐ **THE PIONEERS by James Fenimore Cooper.** Afterword by Robert E. Spiller. (#CJ1156—$1.95)

☐ **THE PORTRAIT OF A LADY by Henry James.** Afterword by Oscar Cargill. (#CE1174—$2.25)

☐ **THE TURN OF THE SCREW and Other Short Novels by Henry James.** Afterword by Willard Thorp.
(#CW1112—$1.50)

☐ **THE RISE OF SILAS LAPHAM by William Dean Howells.**
Afterword by Harry T. Moore. (#CW1121—$1.50)

☐ **SISTER CARRIE by Theodore Dreiser.** Afterword by Willard Thorp. (#CW904—$1.50)

The Complete Plays of SHAKESPEARE from SIGNET CLASSIC

Superlatively edited paperbound volumes of Shakespeare's complete plays are now being offered in Signet Classic editions. Under the general editorship of Sylvan Barnet, of the English Department of Tufts University, each volume features a general Introduction by Dr. Barnet, a special Introduction and notes by an eminent Shakespearean scholar, critical commentary from past and contemporary authorities, and when possible, the actual source, in its entirety or in excerpt, from which Shakespeare derived his play.

☐ **AS YOU LIKE IT.** Edited by Albert Gilman.
(#CW1186—$1.50)
☐ **HAMLET.** Edited by Edward Hubler. (#CW1147—$1.50)
☐ **HENRY IV, PART I.** Edited by Maynard Mack.
(#CY1122—$1.50)
☐ **HENRY IV, PART II.** Edited by Norman N. Holland.
(#CY995—$1.25)
☐ **JULIUS CAESAR.** Edited by William and Barbara Rosen.
(#CW1166—$1.50)
☐ **KING LEAR.** Edited by Russell Fraser. (#CY967—$1.25)
☐ **MACBETH.** Edited by Sylvan Barnet. (#CY974—$1.25)
☐ **MEASURE FOR MEASURE.** Edited by S. Nagarajan.
(#CY1085—$1.25)
☐ **OTHELLO.** Edited by Alvin Kernan. (#CY958—$1.25)
☐ **RICHARD II.** Edited by Kenneth Muir. (#CY1072—$1.25)
☐ **RICHARD III.** Edited by Mark Eccles. (#CY1082—$1.25)
☐ **ROMEO AND JULIET.** Edited by Joseph Bryant.
(#CY968—$1.25)
